SUCCUBUS UNDONE

THE (UN)LUCKY SUCCUBUS

SUCCUBUS HAREM SERIALS 38-43

L.L. FROST

SUCCUBUS UNDONE

THE (UN)LUCKY SUCCUBUS BOOK 7

Cover design by L.L. Frost

Book design by L.L. Frost

Printed in the United States of America.

First Printing, 2021

ALSO BY L. L. FROST

THE VEIL UNIVERSE

The (un)Lucky Succubus

First Serialized in Succubus Harem

Succubus Bargain

Succubus Studies

Succubus Mission

Succubus Hunted

Succubus Dreams

Succubus Trials

Succubus Undone

Succubus Reborn

Succubus Ascended

Demonic Messes (And Other Annoyances)

Drunk Girl *(novella)*

Doom Dog *(novella)*

The Cleaners

The Witchblood

The Fox God

Tally & Her Witches

MONSTERS AMONG US

Monsters Among Us: Hartford Cove

First Serialized in Hartford Cove

A Curse of Blood

Bathe Me In Red

A Feud to Bury

For the Babies

Metal clunks in my oversized shopping bag as I stealthily open the front door, my eyes and ears on high alert for the sounds of anyone else awake in the house. I left the closing of the bakery to Tally tonight so I could sneak in before Kellen arrived home from the club but after Tobias and Emil had gone to bed.

From the silence of the house, I nailed my entry.

Kicking off my shoes under the entryway bench, I close the front door with a quiet click and tiptoe into the living room.

"Just what do you think you're doing?" a chilly voice demands from the shadows.

With a squeak of surprise, I hide the shopping bag behind me as I turn to face the chair where Tobias usually sits. My sneaky ice demon sits curled up in the leather upholstery, a magazine balanced on his knees and a square of sticky notes on the arm, ready to tag anything that catches his interest.

One white brow lifts, and his eyes drop to the space behind me. "What did you bring home this time?"

"Absolutely nothing you need to worry your pretty little head about," I reassure him as I inch toward the stairs to the left of the large fireplace that leads up to our rooms.

With precise movements, he sets his magazine aside and rises to his feet. "Tobias said you were acting suspiciously. I see he had cause for concern."

"No concern here." I shake my head, my braid slipping over my shoulder, the blue tips dancing against my breast. "Absolutely nothing to be concerned about."

My heel knocks against the first of the steps, and the contents in the bag clunk together. I cringe, then plaster a smile on my lips and inch my way up the first two steps.

Emil follows, shutting off the lamp left on in the living room as he passes. "If it's nothing to be concerned about, then why don't you show me?"

"It's a surprise!" I back up a couple more steps.

His foot lands on the first of the steps, his arms

spread wide to press on the wall on either side, blocking me from going back downstairs. "A surprise for *me?*"

"No," I drag the word out as I scurry up a couple more stairs.

He prowls closer. "Then, let me see it."

"But you'll ruin the surprise," I protest, my eyes fixed on his every move.

"I don't *need* to be surprised if it's not for me," he says with icy calm.

I back my foot onto the landing, my eyes darting down the short hall that leads to Emil's bedroom, where soft light flickers from beneath the door. He has the fire on tonight, the same as he has for the last two weeks. With the end of the year looming ever nearer, winter is setting in fast, with frost on the grass every morning and the news cautioning against early snow. He'll have his heated blanket on full blast, too, and an extra fur blanket on his bed.

My attention returns to him. "How come you're up so late? Shouldn't you be snuggled in for the night?"

His eyes move over me, and pink tints his high cheekbones. "Maybe I wanted to see you."

My spine straightens with happiness, and the

wings that hide along my spine rustle to attention. "You did?"

"No." Hot hands land on my shoulders, and the smell of avalanches curls around me. "What's in the bag, little succubus?"

I tip my head back to glare up at Tobias. It's been harder to pick out his scent from Emil's since the weather's grown colder and the chance of fires is at an all-time low. "You tricked me!"

Tobias massages my shoulders as he advises, "Be less easy to trick."

A tug comes from the bag in my hand, and I jerk upright, the handle escaping my grip as Emil steals it. "Hey! That's not for you!"

Unrepentant, he snaps the bag open and studies the contents. "It's as we feared."

Tobias's hands slip down to cage my biceps. "We've talked about this, Adie."

My lower lip juts out. "You don't own my bank account."

"Maybe I *should*." He turns me around to face the stairs that lead up to my bedroom in the attic. "Go to your room. You're grounded."

Eyes wide, I twist to stare back at them. "But—"

"No buts." Emil closes the bag and tucks it

under his arm. "You were warned about continuing this bad habit."

My shoulders slump, and I trudge up the stairs, their gazes heavy on my back as they watch until I dutifully close my bedroom door.

As soon as I'm out of their sights, though, I dash across the room and throw open the shutters on my window, poking my head and shoulders out.

Tac crouches on the slope of the rooftop that faces the backyard, three large shopping bags clamped in his jaw. At my appearance, his tail thumps against the shingles, and I lift a finger to my lips. "Quiet, or they'll get suspicious. Hurry up and climb inside."

I back away from the window to make room for the large cat monster to squeeze through. He shakes his large wings, the feathers flexing before he folds them against his back.

I take the bags from his mouth and hurry to the bed, dumping the contents out.

Tac nudges up against me, his large, wedge-shaped head butting against my arm, and a loud, chainsaw purr vibrates out of him.

"I know," I agree. "They're perfect."

We take a moment to stare in awe at the dolls,

their armor practically glowing beneath the light cast by my lamps. Six knights in total, though I wish we had the full eight. It doesn't matter, though. One of my imps can find them wherever Emil and Tobias try to hide them away.

"Be sneakier," I tell Tac in a deep-voiced imitation of Tobias. "Ha! Look who got tricked."

"And who would that be?" Tobias purrs from behind us.

Tac and I look at each other, and I narrow my eyes at him. "You made too much noise."

His lip curls back to display his dagger-long fangs.

I glare harder. "No, this is *not* my fault."

"It's both of your faults," Emil snaps, ice cracking through the words.

Reluctant, Tac and I turn to find my bedroom door open, Emil and Tobias filling the doorway.

Past them, I catch the glow of Kellen's fiery hair as he adds, "Told you she wouldn't go down that easily."

I point a finger at them. "You can't stop the love! Our babies *need* these!"

Tac snorts loudly in agreement, and he spreads his wings, blocking the bed and its prizes from view.

Emil shakes the bag in his hand. "They chew through them in under a day and leave shards of plastic knight suits all over the house. They do *not* need replacements to demolish."

"They're *teething*. This is helping them."

"Then, get them a chew toy like a normal person."

Reaching back, I grab one of the toy knights and hold it in front of myself like a shield. "This is their heritage. They need to learn about their dad's side of things."

Tac's tail thumps hard enough to rattle my side table.

I nod. "See? He's worried they're learning too much from their mom. They need to know about their dad's interests, too!"

Tobias lifts a skeptical brow. "By hunting toy knights?"

Tossing the knight back on the bed, my hands move to my hips. "Well, it's not like we have *real* knights to practice on."

Tac's wing whacks me in the back of the head.

I turn another glare on him. "No. We already talked about this. We are *not* dressing one of my imps up as a knight for your whelps to hunt."

"I like that idea," Emil counters. "Let's dress them *all* up as knights and let the kids eat them."

I swing back around, my braid smacking Tac in the face. "How dare you!"

"I want them out of my house!" he yells, red now flushing his cheeks. "It's been over a *month*."

"It's been less than four weeks!" I protest.

"Eh." Kellen waves his hand back and forth in an iffy gesture.

"Okay, maybe four and a half weeks," I grumble. "But they're being helpful."

"They're hiding all our stuff." Tobias's arms fold over his chest. "I'm with Emil. They need to go."

Eyes wide, I clutch the space over my heart. "You want to let the babies eat my imps?"

"Aww, look at that face." Kellen pushes past the other two men, his arms spread wide. "Come here, honey. No one's going to eat your imps."

"Says you." Emil shakes the bag still in his hand and metal clanks around inside. "I say we stuff the smallest one into the doll suit and see what happens."

Halfway to Kellen's embrace, I lean to the side so Emil has a full view of my displeasure. "Why do you have it out for Jesse?"

"She hit me," he seethes from between clenched teeth. "With a *spoon*."

I cringe at the reminder. Yeah, I fully agree that the imps need to go, but at the same time, it's been so convenient to have them here, especially since we haven't resolved the whole car issue yet. Which I blame on the guys. *I* have a van, however much Kellen grumbles about it. The baby blue and orange beast on wheels suits me and my imps just fine for going back and forth from the bakery.

But having to take Tobias and Emil to work is a bit of a hassle since they go in so much earlier than we do. Tobias refuses to ride his motorcycle in the sleet and rain, not that Emil would ever get on the thing, anyway. At least Kellen still has a car, though even his patience is fraying.

The issue comes in who holds responsibility for replacing the cars. I hold myself unaccountable since Victor Hesse would have blown Emil and Tobias's car up regardless of who parked it at the bank. But they're being stick-in-the-muds about how they'd 'owned' *my* car at the time that I ripped the door off the hinges in my desperation to get Emil out of it. Since I totaled one vehicle and technically 'owned' the other, they think I should be buying everyone new cars.

Which so isn't fair.

So, I continue to dig my heels in about it. I can't afford to buy everyone new cars. At least, not yet. I have ways, but I'm not yet committed to using them if there's a chance the guys will give in. It's a war of stubbornness right now, and I'm hoping my annoying imps will tip them over the edge.

Rising onto my toes, I puff my chest out. "I'll move the imps out tomorrow if you drop the car issue."

"I'll move the imps out right now, and you'll still replace the cars," Emil counters.

Okay, yeah, I didn't expect that one to work.

Kellen edges closer, his arms still outstretched. "Someone looks like they need a hug." He wiggles his fingers. "Come on. You know you want the Kellen magic."

Eyeing him, I bounce on my toes. I *do* want the Kellen magic. He gives the best hugs.

As if he reads my mind, he shuffles even closer, filling the air with his static charge.

Unable to resist, I step into his arms, sighing with contentment as little sparks of electricity wash over me. I snuggle my head against his chest. "You are so my favorite right now."

His arms tighten around me. "You're not making this easy."

I tip my head back to stare up at him. "Making what easy?"

In answer, he swings me in a circle, taking me away from the bed. "Get them!"

"Traitor!" I howl as Tobias and Emil rush into the room.

Tac crouches, then pounces, taking Emil down, but it leaves the bed with its precious cargo wide open for Tobias to swoop in and grab the remaining toy knights.

"No! I resend your invitation!" I shout, and an invisible weight shoves Tobias toward the door. But he already has the toys and takes them with him out to the landing. "All of you out! Except for Tac! He's the only one I love, now!"

Kellen's laugh fills my ear as he drags me with him toward the door, and I break free just in time to avoid a collision as Emil skids across the floor on his back, his frosty gaze shooting daggers at me.

The door slams shut on the disgruntled demons, and Tac and I look at each other then back at the door. Silent, we wait to hear their footsteps as they pick themselves up and walk downstairs, congratulating each other on their ill-gotten victory.

I lift a finger to my lips, my head tilted, listening for the sound of Emil's bedroom door closing before I tiptoe back to the window.

Tac gently grabs the back of my shirt in his teeth as I lean my body out over the sill and grab the toy bags he stashed on the roof just outside. Inside, the shine of toy armor winks back at me.

Ha! And they said I couldn't be sneaky.

KNIGHT

Something sharp nips at my toes, and I kick my foot out, knocking against a soft, furry body.

A small *cheep* sounds, muffled by my pile of pillows, followed by a harder chomp.

"Shit, that *hurts*!" I yell as I reach down and grab the small invader by the scruff.

Twin tails bat at my arm as I drag Tac's wingless whelp up and shove her beneath my chin. "Shut up and let me sleep, Merp."

Fuyumi had started letting them stay the night a week ago, and so far, I'm not a fan.

Little Merp thrashes and hisses, her needle-filled paws shoving against my arm for freedom.

I squash her flatter, half laying on top of her. "Don't tell me Emil didn't feed you. I know you're lying."

Her cheeps grow in volume, and a moment later,

a light weight on my calf announces Prem's arrival as he comes in search of his sister. His little, needle-like claws dig into my skin for balance as he crawls up my body, and I wince at each four-pointed stab wound.

When he reaches my head, he flops down on the side of my face, the better to bap my head with his small wings.

If that weren't bad enough, the bed shifts with a heavier weight, and the faint scent of baby powder fills my pillow cave. "Master."

"Not now, Jesse," I mumble through Prem's wings. "I'm sleeping."

"Master is awake," Jesse points out.

"Master is *trying* to sleep," I revise. "What do you want?"

"The freezer is locked."

"Of course, the freezer's locked." Reaching up, I grab Prem and shove him down next to his thrashing sister. "Whose fault is that?"

"Master's fault. Master put the lock on the freezer."

I crack an eye open to glare at her through the hole in my pillows. "But *why* did Master put the lock on the freezer?"

Jesse scowls at me, her expression full of

judgment. "Because Master is cruel and wants to starve the babies."

"*Or*," I growl, "it's because *you* kept feeding them whenever they opened their little mouths."

"Babies need food to grow."

"Not the amount you were giving them."

Sensing an ally, Merp escapes my hold and scampers out of the pillow cave.

Jesse scoops her up, cradling the little monster against her small chest. Her expression turns crafty as she eyes me. "Keys are easy to find."

"You stay away from my keys, Jesse," I warn as I stuff Prem under my arm and crawl out of my cave, now fully awake. "You touch my keys, and you know what happens."

Her large brown eyes narrow. "Master is soft. Master will not take away my frosting."

"Oh?" I lift my brows. "You want to go there, huh?"

Her little mouth puckers mutinously, but she stays silent.

"That's what I *thought*." Triumphant, I move toward the edge of the bed.

"Master brought knights into the house," Jesse whispers. "Emil will want to know."

I freeze, one foot on the floor and the other still

on my bed. Tricky, tricky imp. It's definitely time for them to go home.

"Fine, I'll take the lock off the freezer," I say sweetly as I head out of the room.

"Master is kind," Jesse gloats.

My wings twitch against my spine. "Yes, Master is very kind."

"We will give the whelps the fillet," she pushes.

I nod in agreement. "Sure, if that's what you think is best for them."

"Good meat for good babies," she coos.

We reach the bottom of the stairs, and I pull the key from the pocket of my pajama pants. "Here, why don't you go fetch that for them."

The key vanishes from my hand before I can blink, and Jesse races for the kitchen.

I walk more slowly, my fingers running through Prem's small feathers until he starts to rumble with a miniature version of Tac's chainsaw purr.

When I enter the kitchen, Jesse already has the freezer open, Merp balanced on her shoulder as she rummages inside for the expensive cuts of meat I bought for a special night I was planning to have with Tobias.

From under the kitchen table on the right, Tac lifts his head, blinking with sleepy interest. Even though he would have already eaten with the babies this morning, and probably let them gnaw on his roast, he slowly crawls out from under the table and lumbers to his feet, resettling his wings.

I walk over and deposit Prem on Tac's head, right between his ears, where his miniature calico version kneads and turns in a circle before plopping down, eyes closing. Now that I have a good look at him, his little belly still looks round and tight from his breakfast. Feeding him more will just make him sick, but Jesse's all about spoiling them, the same way she spoils Torch when she gets her greedy little hands on the expensive wood pellets.

While I adore her for her generosity, she needs to learn some moderation.

I lean against Tac's side, my gaze on the smallest of my imps. "Emil had an idea about our hunting sessions with the whelps."

She perks up. "The knights will be good practice."

Which is why I keep buying them, despite Emil's fussy protests. "They are, but they're a little...easy."

"Make witches enchant them," Jesse advises as she pulls out the good plates and sets one eight-ounce fillet mignon in the center of each.

Not a bad idea, but I'm pretty sure Tally's

witches don't have a spell for enchanted dolls, and images of how that could get out of hand quickly dance through my head. I've seen enough animated movies to foresee a hostile takeover from enchanted objects in the future.

My eyes narrow as she scoops Merp off her shoulder and sets her on the counter, where she *knows* the whelps aren't allowed to be. "Emil had a different idea. One that would really challenge them."

"You should listen to Emil." Jesse strokes Merp's twin tails. "He will make the babies strong."

"I thought you might say that." Energy floods my limbs, and I hyper-speed across the kitchen and catch my little imp, tucking her under my arm. "Let's go see how you look in a knight's armor."

For a moment, Jesse hangs limp in my hold before my words register, and she begins to flail. "No! Do not feed me to the babies!"

"You should have thought about that before you challenged me!" I walk toward the basement door. "Now, you'll be their target for practice."

"But Master is kind!" She kicks her legs, trying to wiggle from my grasp. "Master will not harm Jesse!"

"Master has faith that Jesse can dodge the

babies," I tell her as I throw open the door and march down to the imps' makeshift bedroom, where the others still sleep. "Wakey-wakey, everyone! Jesse has volunteered everyone for hunting practice! Grab your shinies, because you're all expected on the lawn in ten minutes!"

"I didn't think you'd really do it," Emil murmurs as he sips hot chocolate from his bewitched mug.

"I had a change of heart," I growl.

Jesse clanks back and forth across the lawn, the stiff armor pieces making it hard for her to stay ahead of the small beasts who chase after her. The other imps carry various reflective objects and try to distract Merp and Prem, but like their daddy, they're quite fixated on the 'knight' in their presence.

"This is entertaining." Fuyumi nibbles on her muffin. "We should do this every morning."

"Kellen will be sad he missed it," Tobias agrees.

"Don't worry, I'll show him the video." I track Jesse's progress with my phone, the recorder clocking in at fifteen minutes now.

Since we'd started sharing the care of Tac's whelps, our neighbor, Fuyumi, has been coming over more and more often, even joining us for dinner some nights, though she never leaves her nekomata alone for long. She's a cautious caretaker, but she's thawing a little; not an easy task for an ice demon.

When we started letting the whelps learn to hunt, Emil had begrudgingly allowed us to install a door to the backyard, and Tobias and Jax built a covered deck. Considering how quickly the project went, it made me wonder why it took them so long to finish repairing the imps' house, but I'm not complaining. And even Emil begrudgingly admitted it was a good idea, especially when it meant he got to pick out furniture for the deck and buy a heat lamp, which currently sizzles away, settling a warm cloud around where he sits on the padded outdoor couch.

I sit between him and Tobias, cold on one side and hot on the other. Fuyumi sits in one of the side chairs, a basket of muffins on her lap that she refuses to share with anyone, claiming she plans to take some home for her nekomata. By the wrappers that scatter the table in front of her, I doubt they'll make it that far.

"The small one is quite good with the babies," Fuyumi observes as Jesse barely dodges Prem's awkward attempt at an air attack. "She is quite adept at looking like they might catch her. It is a good method of encouraging them."

"Yeah, she's one smart imp," I lie.

There's no way Jesse's purposefully almost getting caught, not after the fit she threw while I stuffed her into that outfit. I was actually shocked she fit, but I *did* buy the extra-large knights, and imps are malleable.

A loud slurp fills the air as Emil sucks the last of his hot chocolate up before he releases the straw. "This does not change my opinion about them leaving."

"No, I didn't think it would." I snuggle against Tobias's side. "We'll get them moved back to their house on Sunday."

Tobias shifts, his arm lifting to invite me closer to his warmth. "By *we*, I hope you mean you and the imps."

"But you guys are such *amazing* movers," I argue as I snuggle against him. "You had my old apartment packed and moved in no time."

"We paid professionals to do that." Emil, seeing me giving Tobias too much attention, shifts closer, wedging his icicle body against my other side. "Are you going to *pay* us?"

I let out a deep sigh. "Isn't getting the imps out payment enough?"

"No," the two men respond at the same time.

I sigh again. These demons. They just won't give an inch. "I'll get Landon and Julian to help, then."

"You'll have to rescue Landon from the Librarian, first," Tobias reminds me.

I twitch at that. Honestly, I thought when I delivered him after the Thanksgiving party that he would escape the Library in a matter of days. But despite the lack of internet, he seems to have shacked up with the hag, and it may mean having to knock him out again to pull him away. I shudder at the thought of what they've been up to over the last month.

"Oh, Merp has caught the knight!" Fuyumi announces with delight and claps. "I *knew* she was the more skilled of the two."

Another sigh slips from me. She just likes Merp better because she more closely resembles her nekomata. Prem is equally as skilled as his sister, he just has wings he's still struggling to figure out. Not that I *want* him figuring them out. I'll need to buy a leash once he starts flying. Yet another item to add to my list of to-dos.

"Fuyumi." I shift to look at her. "Have you decided about this Saturday?"

"I'm just not sure it's a good idea," she demurs as she plucks out a fresh muffin. "Downtown is so far away, and my precious gets lonely so quickly."

"There will be free cupcakes in various flavors," I offer as temptation.

I had invited Fuyumi to Martha and Tally's promotion party a few weeks ago in the hope of getting on her good side, but so far, she refuses to commit.

"I'll see how my precious is feeling." Her icy gaze shifts back to the frost-covered backyard. "With the imps gone, there will be fewer people to look after the whelps."

Look at her now worrying about not being able to share the kittens with *more* people. She's done a complete one-eighty from not even wanting Tac to meet his whelps.

"Jesse's been begging for a kitten," Emil murmurs. "Pack one of them up and send it with them when they leave."

"Shh!" I throw a palm over his icy lips. "Not where she can *hear* you!"

His pale blue eyes meet mine over my hand before he tugs it down. "Was your agreement not that she prove she can take on the responsibility of caring for a cat? She has proven it and then some. I've even reviewed the contents of her piggy bank. She's saved enough to cover purchasing meat."

I glare at him. "How do you know the details of our agreement?"

"She came to the bank to make a deposit," he says coolly.

I twist in my seat, rising onto one knee to glare down at my ice demon. "And you didn't tell me?"

Snow flurries across his pupils, blotting out the color as the temperature drops around us. "What other demons come to the bank for is none of your business, Ms. Pond."

"Why you stuffed shirt popsicle," I hiss, my breath fogging in the air despite the heater right above us. "If you put *my* imp under contract—"

"Then that is between Jesse and me," he cuts in with a snap of icy anger.

Behind me, Tobias stays suspiciously quiet, and I turn to glare down at him, too. "What kind of contract did you lock my imp in?"

Unconcerned by my ire, Tobias stares up at me, his thick eyebrows raised to taunt me. "Are you challenging my dominance right now?"

I stare down at him from my superior position. "Obviously."

"I was hoping you'd say that," he purrs, his pupils expanding to block out the whites of his eyes until only an abyss stares back. "It's been too long since I showed you—"

"We are no longer alone," Fuyumi cuts in.

The Guard

"Northern border," Fuyumi says under her breath, her focus on the muffin basket in her lap.

Only Tobias's gaze shifts as he looks past me, and he gives an imperceptible nod of acknowledgment.

"You guys *suck*," I whine loudly and flop back to half sprawl across Emil's lap. "As Jesse's contract holder, I have first claim on her."

Emil's cold hand cups my chin, turning my head so he can rub the spot behind my right ear. "Then be smart enough to know there's no contract, Ms. Pond. She simply made a deposit. We *are* a bank."

Despite his words, the bite he'd usually deliver them with is missing, which is good because, in my new position, I'm no longer paying attention to him.

Instead, I focus on the Northern border of the backyard, on the stone wall adjacent to the one that separates our property from Fuyumi's. The demon hides in the shadows of morning, counting on the angle of the sun to provide enough darkness for him to hide.

I pretend to yawn, using the move to hide my mouth. "They're getting more ballsy."

Tobias bends over me, his hands pushing beneath my shirt. "They're getting desperate the longer Lord Marius's judgment remains unfulfilled."

Victor Hesse, with his warped demon-witch magic, continues to evade the high council's guard, much to their frustration. About once a week, one of these guards pops up either here or outside of our places of business, hoping the crazed mortifier demon will return and claim his unsanctioned vengeance against us. We'd destroyed his plans to claim Domnall's territories and bring down the most powerful demons in our city, and he had not taken the loss lightly.

He'd risked exposing demons to humankind, and in return, was sentenced to imprisonment until he could face trial. But he'd escaped from a room filled with demons more powerful than my demons of destruction, a feat that should have been impossible for someone of his power level. Which made Lord Marius and the other judges the ridicule of our kind. One does not simply walk away from a demon of

Lord Marius's caliber, and yet Victor Hesse had and still continues to elude his punishment.

"It's time I take my leave." Fuyumi stands and whistles sharply.

Merp and Prem immediately release Jesse and bound toward us, Jesse following at an awkward gallop behind them.

The kittens disappear beneath the wide bell of Fuyumi's white robe, hidden from view, and she lifts her muffin basket into her arms. "I will inform you of my decision before Saturday."

"Safe travel, Fuyumi," I call with a wave of my hand.

Tobias's hands move unnecessarily higher to brush the undersides of my breasts, bringing my nipples to attention. "Perhaps we should move this discussion to a less public venue?"

"I concur." Emil stands, and only fast reflexes keep me from landing face-first on our new deck.

Whoa, way to ruin the mood. Not that I want Tobias groping my boobs in front of the council guard. Much...

No, no boob groping.

I spring to my feet, shaking my hair from my face. My blue tips are growing longer, the color deepening as the power inside me continues to grow from regular feedings from the guys.

My relationship with them has gone a long way toward fixing everything I broke with my impulsiveness. But the new power that rolls in my core, the power of ice ages, tsunamis, and choice, doesn't make it any easier to turn my back on the interloper in our yard. They invaded our private territory, a space no demon should enter without invitation, and ruined an otherwise pleasant morning on our deck.

Hot hands land on my shoulders, pushing me toward the newly installed backdoor. "Do not engage."

My wings shift against my spine, restless to do the exact opposite of Tobias's command, and only partly because I like to challenge my catalyst demons. As a demon, I need to defend my territory from other demons, and to walk away now just feels *wrong*.

But walk away I do, as I have every other time I've caught one of the guards lurking nearby. To challenge a guard is to challenge the council, and no one here wants that. Not when we so narrowly escaped our last encounter.

The imps file in after us, Jesse coming in last despite having a head start.

Jesse sheds the toy armor in the kitchen. "Time to go to work?"

"Yeah, time to go to work," I agree. "Everyone, get ready."

They vanish into the depths of the basement while Tobias heads for his room to change, completely forgetting about the boob groping. *Or*, he's playing some kind of game where he sees how long he can tease me before I jump him.

Boy is he in for a surprise. I'm the champ of self-restraint. We'll just see how blue his balls get before he comes crawling to me.

Before I can stomp off and implement my Blue-Balls-For-Tobias plan, Emil catches my hand. "Ms. Pond."

I turn back to find concern and worry on his face, and my heart melts. Damn, this ice demon makes me so soft and squishy.

"Oh, shut it, fussy pants." I rise onto my tiptoes to press a kiss against his frosty lips. "I hear what you're saying. Jesse's acclimated to the human plane and more than capable of caring for a pet. Doesn't mean I have to like seeing another of my imps cut free of the apron strings."

"They are not your children," he says gently. "Not the imps and not the whelps."

The reminder opens a hollow ache in my chest, and I look away. "Yeah, I know.

Most demons can't have children, and certainly not the way humans do, by carrying the life inside of themselves and nurturing it from nothing to adulthood. Human belief and magic created Tac—and other beasts like him. We claim the monsters as our own and protect them from the humans who would destroy them, but they're not really demon children. Baku sunder themselves, giving up one of their hearts and their power to create new baku. Only the imps with their spawning can really claim the right of procreation, and most imps never make it past their wobbly, gelatinous form.

I take pride in the lives my imps have chosen for themselves. But, had I known how attached I'd become to them, would I have taken them on? Many demons would call what I have an unhealthy attachment, especially to Jesse, the smallest and most reluctant of my imps to integrate. But once our contract is fulfilled, none of them will be mine anymore, and the realization hits me hard.

Cold fingers brush my cheek, and I look up to meet Emil's knowing gaze. "It never gets easier."

My lips part in surprise before I snap my mouth closed. "I don't know what you're talking about."

He steps closer, the chill of his body pushing away my heat. "Do you know why demons frown upon softer emotions, like love? Why it makes us weak?"

A frown pinches my brows together. I never considered the why behind how my people are, just struggled to live under the pretense of not feeling the softer emotions.

Emil cups my cheek, and frost slowly crawls along my skin. "We crave what we can't have, and loving another being makes that craving nearly impossible to bear."

"But..." I lick my lips, tasting the metallic hint of snow. "You..."

I don't know how to speak my thoughts without making it sound like I think he's weak. There's no room in the way demons communicate with each other that can't leave him offended. And I very much don't want to offend Emil over matters of the heart.

"I fell hard and fast," he says simply, as if it doesn't kill him to admit it so freely. "I didn't like you; I didn't want you in my home." His thumb rubs away my instant frown. "You're summer heat and roaring fire, blazing paths wherever you tread.

And I was a frozen statue, growing colder by the day."

My mouth opens, just his fingers stop me from speaking, as if he needs to get his words out without my interruption.

"The ice called to me every day, and Tobias and Kellen's friendships were no longer enough. I wanted to join the winter, to just let go and damn the consequences." His head dips, his lips briefly replacing his fingers. "And then, there you were, blazing like a supernova, offering to thaw my icy heart, and it made me *want* again, made me crave what I had given up on a millennium ago. And I liked you even less for it, because I know what that pain feels like, I know what I will do to stop from feeling it again."

He traces the curve of my cheek, his touch light as if he touches something fragile. "I see you putting yourself in danger constantly, and it *terrifies* me. If I didn't love you, I wouldn't consider ripping the world apart to keep you safe. And that is a very dangerous thing to feel. It's why we're told love is a weakness. We're not human. We aren't bound by short lives, locked into bodies with barely enough energy to sustain themselves for a century. We're timeless, and we pay a steep price for that."

I close the inches between us to brush his lips with kisses. "Loving you doesn't make me weak. It makes me strong."

"You say that now..."

"I'll say it again at the end of our year, and every year after that." I kiss him again. "I don't need children of my body, however much I may envy humans for that power. I just need you, Kellen, and Tobias, and your endless patience when I bring home strays."

His eyes narrow on me, though there's no heat in the glare. "I wouldn't say we have *endless* patience."

"Don't worry, we'll keep working on it. We have time, and there will always be more strays to bring home." Then the teasing drops from my voice as I bring up something that's been on my mind for quite a while. "About our contract..."

"You still have to pay it back," he responds instantly. "Love doesn't cancel that."

I blow a raspberry in his face for the reminder before I step back. "That's not what I was going to ask."

His hands remain on me, not letting me go far as he gives me a regal nod. "Go on."

"What happens at the end of the year?" I blurt.

His white brows sweep together. "Your contract expires."

"But..." I wiggle in place. "Doesn't part of you guys being allowed to be here stipulate you always have a succubus under contract to siphon off your power?"

"Ah." His expression clears. "We'll just sign you for another year."

Now, it's my turn to frown. "I don't want to remain your contractee."

His grip on me tightens. "You want to leave?"

I reach up to pinch his icy cheek. "Don't get your panties in a bunch. You couldn't kick me out of this house if you tried." Beneath our feet, the house groans in agreement, and I let a thread of power trickle into the floor joists as a reward. "But I want to be equal. So, if I sign another contract, you will sign one, too. And not the half-assed, I-promise-not-to-murder-my-succubus contract currently in place. A real one, where the cost of breaking it is equal on all sides."

His lips thin, stillness settling over him.

Something in my chest cracks. "No?"

"It's... not that easy." His hands fall away, and he strides past me. "We need to get to work."

"Emil?" I call after him, my feet frozen to the spot where he left me. "What...?"

He pauses in the kitchen archway without looking back. "There are... issues that must be resolved before anything like what you propose can happen."

Bewildered, I stare at the hard lines of his back until he disappears from view.

How did we just go from earth-destroying declarations of love to him walking away from me?

Out of all my men, I thought Tobias would be the most resistant because he's *horrible* with verbal expressions of love.

I never thought *Emil* would be the one to crush my hope of our future together.

Treasure Box

Martha pulls the van up in front of K&B Financial, and Tobias and Emil hop out.

Emil had been quiet for the entire ride, with none of his usual fussing about when they were going to be able to drive themselves to work again. Tobias had noticed his friend's distraction, which had, in turn, distracted him, and we'd taken the brunt of that as every car we passed suddenly decided they wanted to be in our lane.

Usually, Tobias's presence means cars move *out* of our way, clearing the lanes ahead of us. But when he's not paying attention, it seems the scales tip in the opposite direction, and we narrowly avoided three accidents between home and here.

We all breathe a sigh of relief as Tobias slides the side door closed behind them.

"So," Kellen says as he props his arms on the back of my seat. "That was fun."

"Shouldn't you be napping?" I grumble as I watch the two men walk into the bank they co-own.

"How could I *possibly* have napped through that?" Kellen demands. He tickles my cheek with a snap of static electricity. "Now, why'd you *really* haul me out of bed so early? I have my own ride to work, you know."

"It's going to rain today." The two men disappear, and I motion for Martha to pull back onto the road. "The roads will be dangerous."

"I know how to drive in the rain." Another static snap on my cheek pulls my attention around to meet his lightning-kissed eyes. "Now, spill."

"We're going car shopping," I whisper, but I don't know why I bother.

By the squeal that goes up from the imps, they heard every word.

I glare at Kelly and Jesse, who sit at the back of the van. "Not for *you*."

Kellen purses his lips for a moment, before he says, "You're never going to be able to afford a car they're satisfied with."

After a lot of thought, I'd decided Tobias and Emil would kill my imps before giving in to replacing our cars and had resigned myself to dipping into my emergency reserves.

I pat the large purse in my lap. "I have resources."

Kellen immediately lunges forward to grab the bag, but I curl my body over it, keeping it from him.

"You're broke, so what have you been withholding?" he demands as he snags the strap and tugs.

I yank it back, almost snapping it in the process. "I'll show you once we get to the bakery."

"Master has *feathers*," Jesse announces.

"Shiny feathers," Kelly adds.

"Baby feathers," Martha whispers.

"The softest," all three sigh together, their voices full of appreciation.

"You snoops!" My shout echoes around the van. "That's it, you're all moving out!"

"Let me see." Kellen makes grabby hands. "I want to touch."

I clutch the purse tighter. "No."

Selling pieces of myself is hard enough without Kellen pawing through them.

"How are you planning to monetize them?" He grabs the back of my seat and shakes it. "That's why

I'm here, right? You don't know where to find the black market."

"I was going to ask Julian," I mumble. "We're going there after we drop Jesse, Iris, and Kelly off."

"Julian," Kellen scoffs. "I'm *way* better at backroom bartering."

Reluctantly, I pass my purse over the seat to him, and Kellen snatches it up with more excitement than a handful of feathers warrant. Mature succubi and incubi feathers go for a lot on the black market, tears bringing in even more. I'd actually used one of my tears as a bargaining chip to resolve my debt to Kellen before I signed my contract with the guys. But my washed-out feathers won't bring in as much, since they're not nearly as rare or powerful.

Tossing my purse back in my face, Kellen settles the wooden box on his lap, tracing the rounded edges with his fingers before he cracks it open. Tiny white feathers from when I first arrived on the human plane mix with a few slightly larger feathers from after I'd moved out of Landon's house, but before I joined the demons of destruction. Sitting on top are two of the biggest, collected from my last shower when I let my wings out.

Kellen lifts one of the smallest, a pure white

feather the size of his pinky nail. "Oh, will you look at that?"

"Softest," the imps sigh again.

Embarrassed heat flushes my cheeks. "Do you really need to fondle them that much?"

Kellen makes puppy dog eyes at me. "Can't I?"

Despite my best effort to resist, I melt. "Just don't get them dirty."

"I would *never.*" Then he plucks out one of my newer feathers and strokes it against his cheek. "Well, maybe *this* one."

My hand lifts to cover my face. "Ugh. Not in front of the children."

"They have to learn about the birds and the bees sometime." But he sets the feather back in the box and closes the lid. "I have the perfect buyer. He'll pay top dollar."

I perk up at that. "Yeah?"

"Trust me." With a wink, he pulls his cell phone from his pocket and dials a number before he lifts it to his ear. "Tobias, Adie's finally selling those feathers you've been after."

"No!" Frantic, I lunge across the seat, but the seat belt snaps me back into place.

"Yeah, even the baby ones." Kellen grins and blows me a kiss.

I slap at the lock on my seatbelt, but the damn thing sticks.

"The whole box?" Kellen's eyebrows lift, and he opens the box in question again, sifting through the contents. "Yeah, only feathers."

The lock finally snaps free, and I whip the seatbelt off.

"Done." Kellen hangs up the phone and grins. "You just became a very rich woman."

"I'll kill you!" I dive across the back of my seat, hands outstretched and claws extended.

"Whoa!" Kellen snaps the box closed once more. "Careful of the merchandise! This is someone else's property now!"

"How could you sell them to that feather obsessed asshole?" I yell. "Do you know what he's going to do with them?"

Kellen's fiery brows arch. "Probably less than someone on the black market would have?" He leans a little closer, but still out of swiping range. "Feather obsessed?"

"He's always up in my feathers! *Adie, let out your wings. Adie, glow for me,*" I mock in a deep voice.

"*Adie, let me play with your wings,*" Jesse mocks in a perfect imitation of Tobias.

"Yes! That!" I point at her. "And stop spying on sexy time!"

Kellen settles back. "Fascinating."

"What? Why?" I slump back into my seat. "He's been like that since day one. Even at the coffee shop when he was pretending to be a gigolo, he wanted to see my wings."

The eyebrows make another climb up his forehead. "Gigolo?"

I tilt my head. "What? You didn't know?"

"Jog my memory," Kellen breathes with excitement.

I grin. "He pretended to be one of Julian's meal delivery demons to lure me into the bathroom where he *begged* me to take all his power."

"I love this so much." Kellen throws his head back to rest against the bench seat and stares up at the ceiling. "He will *never* live this down."

"Why are you acting like this isn't Tobias's personality? He's a possessive freak."

"Well, yeah, which is why I knew he wouldn't like it if he found out I helped you sell this box of treasures to some random demon." Kellen lifts his head. "People would be smoking these to get it on. You know that, right?"

"Yeah, I'm better than Viagra. *Duh*." I twist to

glare at him once more. "How did you guys know about the box?"

"Why do you think only you can be sneaky?" He shakes his head with a sympathetic pout. "We knew the second you brought it home from Landon's."

"But *how?*" I throw up my hands in frustration. "It's like you have cameras everywhere!"

"You won't get our secrets that easily." He strokes the box in his lap. "So, car shopping? You're finally giving in and taking full responsibility?"

"Hell, no!" I frown at him for even thinking it. "If the imps are moving back to their house, then they'll need the van, which means *I* need a new car. For *me*."

"Oh, I can't wait to hear how *that* goes down when Tobias and Emil find out." He rubs his hands together. "So, do you want to start out at the Sports Imports dealership? It's a bit of a drive, but we can get there and back before dinner time. Are we talking Lamborghini? Porsche? Oh, say you want a Mercedes. You'd look so hot in a Mercedes."

I mask my surprise at his suggestion. I knew I'd get some decent money for the feathers, but Tobias must have offered three times their value for Kellen to be suggesting an out of town shopping trip for my new car.

Stealthily, I take my phone from my pocket and pull up the K&B Financial bank app, logging into my account. My eyes widen as I stare at all the zeroes. Where I used to have a couple hundred, I now have over half a million.

"How does it feel to be rich?" Kellen asks as he peers over my shoulder.

My heart races, and I shove my phone back into my pocket before I drop it. I can do a lot with over half a million, and Kellen wants me to blow it on a *car*.

No way in hell.

Glancing at Martha, who looks like a grandma taking her kids to soccer practice, a smile twitches at my lips. "I have just the car in mind."

Wooing With Style

"You're just *trying* to piss them off, right?" Kellen shakes his head as he stares at the cars now parked in the garage back at our house. "I mean, you *want* to die? Because I can think of better methods than what you're instigating with this stunt."

"What are you talking about?" I smooth a hand up the long nose of the sports car and caress the air intake that bumps up the hood. "This is amazing."

"Amazingly *horrible*. You could have had a Mercedes! You could have had *two* Mercedes!" He throws his hands up in the air. "Why?"

I hug the low roof and glare at him. "You didn't kick up this much of a fuss at the dealership."

"I was still in denial at the dealership." He stares at the two cars. "I'm *still* in denial." He sticks out his arm. "Pinch me and wake me up from this nightmare."

Reaching out, I punch him hard, adding a twist at the end.

He jerks his arm back to cradle it against his chest. "Ow! What did you do that for?"

I arch my brows at him. "Are you awake now?"

He shakes his head. "I don't want to be. I'm going to work before they get home."

"Chicken." I *bok, bok* at his back. "They'll know you helped, even if you're hiding."

He spins back, his finger jabbing toward me. "I did *not* help. I had no part in this monstrosity."

"You literally drove one home." I straighten from the sports car and wipe the dust from my hands.

"I thought I was dreaming," he protests. "I thought I'd gone mad and never woken up this morning."

"You thought you'd go ninety on the freeway," I say drily.

"To escape my nightmare!" he yells. "They're never going to accept this as a replacement."

"Well, it's not like I'm just going to *give* them this beauty for *free*." I turn back to the car, petting its nose once more. "You are going to be *so* pretty when we're done with you."

"Is this like the imps?" Kellen demands. "This is your next stray project?"

"This is me wooing Tobias." Leaning forward, I sprawl across the wide hood. "He's going to be enthralled."

"He's going to throttle you," Kellen mutters. "You've disappointed me so much today."

I frown after him as he stomps out of the garage. He's being *way* too dramatic about this whole thing.

Instead of going to one of the expensive dealerships a couple cities away, I'd directed Martha to drop us off at the local used car lot and return to work, which meant there was no way for Kellen to escape what looked like a junkyard without walking his fine ass back home.

We'd spent hours digging through the options and test driving my top choices to make sure they ran. I'd lucked out with the sports car. It was a sleek two-door with an aggressive hood that Tobias will love, just as soon as he fixes it up.

I roll off the car, taking a couple years of dirt with me to reveal the dull, matte blue paint beneath. The driver's door is gray primer. The previous owner had wrecked the car and replaced the parts without paying the extra money for a new paint job. And why would they with the other patches that dot the exterior? But the inside still looks great. I poke my head through the driver's side window. Kellen had rolled it down on the drive back to air it out, and now it won't go back up.

The leather interior holds a layer of dust, too, except for a Kellen shaped smear of clean material from his drive home. Beneath all the dirt, though, the leather is worn but scratch-free. With a little elbow grease, it will be supple and so cozy to sit in. And, as Kellen the speed demon proved, it's fast enough to satisfy Tobias's desire for luxury. The heated seats and cup holder I ordered from the dealer before we left will warm up my ice demon to the idea of a fixer-upper, too.

I glance through the sports car to my more modest four-door sedan. It's basically the same car I had before, just a couple years newer. It, too, needs some work, but not a lot. Maybe just some cleaning and a tune-up, though I won't know until Tobias looks under the hood. My catalyst demon will have to work for the reward of his sports car.

Happiness bubbles through me, and my wings rustle for release. I can practically feel the glow shimmering under my skin, but I restrain the need to preen. I'll keep that for when Tobias sees my offer of love.

The growl of an engine in the driveway pulls me out of the car, and I straighten with excitement.

Just in time.

The shopping, and the haggling that followed, had eaten up the entire day. But making the slimy salesman sweat had been worth five hours of negotiation. The free floor mats in the trunk will be my first bribe for Emil to give this a chance.

Steps bouncy, I run for the door and poke my head out. The van idles at the curb, Martha waiting to take me back to the bakery with her after dropping off the guys. She's such a good imp.

But first, my surprise.

I wave my arm for my demons' attention. "Over here!"

Tobias and Emil pause in front of the porch to glance over, and their course shifts.

Tobias's thick brows arch. "Have you finally admitted responsibility?"

Emil's suspicious eyes sweep over my dusty appearance, then shift to the garage. "Ms. Pond. You're quite...messy."

I ignore them both and beckon for them to follow before I duck into the garage once more.

Spinning, I spread my arms wide as they enter. "Surprise!"

Emil takes one look, turns on his heel, and leaves.

"Oh, come on!" I call after him, then shift my attention to Tobias. "It's okay, he'll come around."

"I highly doubt that." Tobias bends to set his briefcase by the door before he prowls around the sports car. "Is this supposed to be an equivalent replacement? Please say you didn't dump your entire fortune into this heap?"

Chin jutting out, I cross my arms under my breasts. "No, I'm investing that elsewhere. And this isn't a replacement for the car you happened to lose while parked in *your* parking lot."

His brows make another climb up toward his hairline. "No?"

"These are *my* cars." I use the edge of my shirt to wipe the dirt away from one tail light. "That I may consider selling to you, for a price."

He looks through the driver's side window. "If I wanted something like this, I could have simply gone to the dump."

"And wasted hours of your time doing so." I skip around to peek through the window opposite him. "This one runs."

He rests his elbows on the door. "And, what, exactly, did you think I would give you for finding this thing?"

I hook a thumb over my shoulder toward the car

I plan to keep for myself. "Keep my other one in good condition so I have a reliable way to go to and from work."

Interest shimmers in his dark eyes, and he straightens to circle around to my side. "That's it?"

I nod. "I'll even pay for all the parts."

He opens the sedan's door and pops the hood. "So, all I have to do is get this one running, and you *give* me the other one as payment?"

"*No*," I stress the word. "It already runs. You *keep* it running."

"A lifetime of car maintenance for a trashed sports car?" He fiddles with the exposed engine. "Doesn't seem like a good bargain to me."

Joining him, I snuggle up to his side. "You get the pleasure of turning that sports car into anything you desire." A low purr vibrates from him, and my wings push for release once more. "You're interested."

His head turns, and he stares down at me. "I haven't agreed."

I rise onto my tiptoes. "In case I'm not being clear, this is me wooing you."

"You're being clear." He bends, his lips a fiery brush against mine.

My mouth opens under the first sweep of his

tongue, and I groan as he pushes his way in, making a home in my mouth as if it belongs to him. And, in a way, it does. I crave this demon like I crave my next breath, like I crave the shiver of earthquakes that roll down my throat. Tobias is more than just his power to me, though. I love the way he challenges and pushes, the way he bends and pulls. He's a constant balance of give and take, of hardness and the rare glimpse of mushy center.

He cups the back of my head, his fingers pushing through the bound hair of my braid to scrape blunt nails against my scalp. Sighing, I melt against his hard body, giving myself wholly to him.

A honk from outside disrupts our moment, and I pull back to glare toward the waiting van.

"Ignore it," he growls, nipping sharp kisses along my jaw that come with the promise of pain and pleasure.

I shiver, my eyes drifting shut, more than willing to let him christen his new car in any way he pleases.

The honk comes again, and I groan, my lashes fluttering up once more. "I can't. I promised Tally I'd close the bakery tonight."

He growls but doesn't tell me to break my promise, which makes me love him all the more. Promises among demons aren't given lightly, and my contract writer is even more aware of that than most.

Tobias releases me and glances around the garage. "Where are my feathers?"

"Kellen has them safe and secure." I back toward the door. "Whether he just hands them over..."

Tobias's brows sweep together. "I already paid for those."

"Well, that's entirely *your* problem." The smell of scorched leaves fills the air between us, a precursor to Tobias's anger, and I laugh as I dart out of the garage, yelling back, "I expect my car to be usable by tomorrow!"

I run for the van, sliding into the passenger seat and locking the door as Tobias storms out of the garage.

"Go, go, go!" I motion toward the open road.

Martha, ever the safe driver, turns on her blinker and checks all her mirrors before pulling onto the empty street.

It's a good thing Tobias wasn't chasing me, or we'd have been caught for sure.

Note to self: Avoid Martha as a getaway driver.

She makes a three-point turn, rolling back in front of the house, and I lean over to honk the horn and wave out the window as we pass Tobias on the porch. Kellen better cough up those feathers right away, if the black cloud that hangs around Tobias is any indication of his mood.

Honestly, I'd been shocked when I received the funds so quickly. Tobias showed a huge level of trust in sending the payment before he received his product.

It makes warmth swell in my chest to be included in the limited number of people he trusts without question.

And it also shows how much he wanted those feathers. I better not catch him sniffing them.

The drive back to the bakery passes quickly, and I arrive well before I promised Tally I would, which gives me plenty of time to use a box of wet wipes to clean myself off in my new office.

Jax did a good job on the space. It's not large, but it holds my desk with a computer, printer, and filing cabinet. Next to me is the office Tally and Martha use as the unofficial managers. I can't wait for the party on Saturday, when I can drop the unofficial part. Without them, my bakery would have failed within a month.

Too much has happened to pull me away from running a business, first with the Hunters, then the Dreamer, and then the trial over Domnall's death.

As I throw the used wipes into the trash, I glance out the window and catch sight of the hulking figure across the street. The humans walk past him without notice, their steps turning aside as if of their own accord, to create a small pocket of emptiness for him to exist in. He wears a muscle shirt and tight pants, his biceps bulging so thickly his arms can't rest at his side.

A slag demon wearing an illusion. And not a very good one. The humans who pass by huddle in their winter coats, but he looks ready for summertime fun. He might fit in if he were at a gym. But standing rock still in the middle of a freezing drizzle looks suspicious on every level.

Even if Victor Hesse thought to come here, the obvious council guard would scare him away. It's a bittersweet show of protection. Bitter because it means the mortifier demon is still on the loose. More bitter still because it keeps my friends, Tally's witches, wary of visiting. Sweet because, at least for now, Victor Hesse won't risk capture to come to my place of business.

I never knew living my dreams would come with so many bumps in the road.

Fall Forever

At one-thirty in the morning, the rush of midnight snackers from the bars and clubs trickle away, and the bell rings, alerting me to a new customer.

I glance up from the register, and a smile escapes when I spot Emil at the door. He should be asleep right now, not here, but I welcome the visit and hurry to the espresso machine to make him a hot chocolate.

He walks up to the counter, his eyes sweeping the pastry case.

"We have some of the spiced chocolate left, if you'd like a treat," I call over the hiss of steaming milk.

He gives me a suspicious look. "The weird kind?"

My smile widens. "What's so weird about thinking happy thoughts while baking?"

Granted, the recipe had come from the

Librarian's demon baking book, but with how much Fuyumi liked it, and with how normal the ingredients are, I'd added it to our menu, much to my customers' delight. Chocolate and cayenne pepper. Who knew?

Emil gives me a regal nod, and I quickly mix the piping hot milk into the flakes of real chocolate then grab a small plate and fetch his treat.

"To what do I owe the pleasure of your visit?" I ask as I slide the items to him over the top of the display case.

He takes them eagerly. "I thought you might like a ride home tonight."

My brows arch. "Does that mean my car passed inspection?"

"It didn't melt under a good washing, if that's what concerns you." He sniffs the cake, still suspicious of its magical properties. But, really, only good thoughts and normal ingredients went into this batch.

"I wasn't worried it would melt." I walk back toward the cash register. "I made sure it didn't have any rust spots before I bought it."

"No, just a dozen patch jobs." Emil nibbles at the frosting, leaving a dot of chocolate on the tip of his nose.

I lick my lips, wanting to clean it off but also delighted to see my fussy demon less than pristine. "Martha could have driven me home."

As if she heard her name, Martha comes bustling from the kitchen, carrying a clean stack of plates, which she stores under the display case. She frowns when she catches sight of Emil's cup of cocoa, and I give her a frown of my own for doubting my skills.

Just because she's become a master of the espresso machine doesn't mean I can't make a delicious cup of hot chocolate. She's forgetting who trained her in the art of steaming milk and pulling shots. Not that I'd had a ton of experience before I opened the bakery. Just hundreds and hundreds of practice pulls, which she surpassed in her first week here.

Which changes *nothing*. I lift my chin, and she busies herself with counting to-go cups.

When I turn back to Emil, I find him with an empty cupcake wrapper on his plate as he eyes the display case once more.

Did he inhale the damn thing?

My eyes narrow on him. "Did you come here to pick me up or raid my pastries?"

"Yes." He nods and, with one long finger, nudges

his empty plate toward me in an unsubtle hint for a refill.

Taking the plate, I add it to the dirty dish bucket under the counter and pull a new one from the fresh stack Martha just brought out. With tongs, I add two new cupcakes to Emil's plate. It's doubtful we'll sell what's left tonight, and the old cupcakes usually go home with the imps. They can spare a few for Emil's late-night sweet tooth.

When I straighten, Emil sits at the front of the shop, framed by the large picture window, and I walk out from behind the counter to deliver his treat.

As I set it on the table in front of him, I follow his gaze out to the darkened street. At this time of night, most of the cars are gone from the curb, so it's easy to pick out my new, old sedan. I'm surprised Emil put aside his fussiness long enough to sit inside it, and I take his empty cup of cocoa, ready to give him another reward.

"How long has he been out there?" Emil murmurs, and I look past the mottled paint of my car to the other side of the street.

The bodybuilder still stands on the sidewalk, his attention clearly on my bakery. "He was here when I arrived earlier."

Emil continues to stare at the slag demon. "There are more of them than there were last week."

I'd noticed that, too, but hoped I was just miscounting. They change their glamour daily, but they have a certain look about them that makes them easy to distinguish. This one favors platinum hair and a mustache that would have fit in perfectly in the seventies.

Emil finally turns away to pick up his new cupcake, though he doesn't unwrap it as quickly as he did the first. "They must have tracked Victor Hesse back to town."

"Or they've lost any leads so they're just hanging around, hoping he'll show up." I sift my fingers through the fine white hairs on the back of Emil's neck. "Is that the real reason you came to bring me home?"

Finally, he picks at his wrapper. "Your wards are lacking."

"Are you worried about me?" I drag my fingernails against his scalp. "It's okay to admit it."

He stares down at the cupcake in his hand. "I don't want to have a reason to worry."

"Without locking me in the house, there will always be the risk of danger," I tease.

When he glances up at me, snow fills his pupils.

I fist the short hairs on the back of his head and tug sharply. "You are not allowed to lock me in the house."

"It has better wards," he hisses. "The bakery runs fine without you. Martha and Tally have things cover—"

I yank harder, tipping his head back until his lips part on a sharp breath. "I will repeat. You are not locking me in the house."

His eyes narrow, the snow growing into a blizzard. "You need to be protected."

I glare right back. I'm not the only one Victor Hesse wants revenge against. "And what about you?"

"I'm happy to lock myself in with you," he says.

Surprised, I release my hold. "What?"

He catches my hand to press it against his cold cheek. "I don't need the bank. I'm happy to go on vacation until this matter is dealt with permanently."

"That could take *years*," I protest. "Even decades."

His head turns, and he kisses my palm. "A decade or two spent with you is a pleasure."

"Of course, it's a pleasure. I'm a succubus." I pull my hand away, my fingers curling around the snowflakes he left before they melt. "But we'd murder each other within a month."

The corners of his lips twitch. "Not if I kept your mouth busy."

"Within a week," I revise. "It's not happening."

Taking his empty cup, I walk it back to the counter, where I find Martha ready with a new one. I swap them without comment as Iris and Kelly bustle through the two-way door carrying cleaning supplies.

They fall into an easy rhythm of cleaning the front of the store, Iris wiping down tables with Kelly following behind, stacking the chairs up onto them. They don't even need directions anymore, and I'm sure, if I ducked into the kitchen, I'd find Jesse storing away the frosting and scrubbing down the pans.

Emil's right, they run the place just fine without me. If I wanted to, I could sit at home and just take the income of their labor. I don't even need the passive emotions that linger in the air from humans happy with their indulgences.

I'd originally opened the bakery as a way to feed without having to suck away human's energy through sex, a dangerous pastime for a succubus on the human plane. It's easier, when out of Dreamland, to take too much and wind up killing them, and I hadn't wanted to risk it after someone I touched died.

But with Emil, Tobias, and Kellen, I don't have to worry about starving anymore.

I take a sip of the rich hot chocolate and sigh. Martha really is better at making these than I am. She even added a hint of cinnamon to complement the spiced chocolate cupcakes.

I settle into the seat opposite Emil and gaze around my shop. So many dreams went into its creation. I don't *want* to give it up, but my reason for having it has evolved. Now, it's a place for wayward demons to learn humanity.

The imps had resisted Julian's method of training, and while I'm sure they would have eventually complied, coming here gave them options other than becoming strippers for hire. And cousin Sophia, while not fantastic, is growing by the day, learning to spread her wings, metaphorically, of course. No actual wing spreading happens in my bakery. Can't risk feathers getting into the cupcakes and turning our customers into a horny mass of sex-crazed zombies.

Though, aphrodisiac cupcakes would probably sell well in the circles Julian moves in. I file that thought away to bring up the next time I see him.

Might be a good side business, as long as all parties are consenting adults.

Emil interrupts my thoughts as Martha delivers a new hot chocolate for him, since I kept the original. "Are you reconsidering your stance?"

"I'm thinking of expanding, actually." I take another sip from my mug, letting the chocolate roll over my tongue. "I have quite a bit of money now."

"Yes, I'm aware." Emil's frosty brows lift. "Why didn't you just use those feathers in the beginning? You never would have had to take a loan from the bank."

I'd considered it, at the time, but Julian hadn't been willing to help me back then. Though I know the reason why, now. "I didn't have as many collected, and Julian and Landon wouldn't help. They said my baby feathers would draw the wrong kind of interest."

"Well, they *did* attract Tobias, so..."

We share a smile.

"So, expansion?" Emil prods.

"Just a thought." I give Kelly a wistful glance as he passes with the mop. "I was also considering taking on a new set of imps."

Emil frowns at that. "Surely your contract isn't near expiration."

"Nowhere close." I shake my head. "But...contracts can be fulfilled in other ways, as you'd shown with mine. There's nothing that says they have to work *here* to earn their way out. The point of the sponsorship is to learn to integrate. They only stay after they learn that in order to pay back the cost of sponsoring them here. But if they can pay back the sponsor fee in a different way, why not let them? Holding them here if they no longer wish to stay feels too much like slavery, don't you think?"

"I think few demons are troubled by the idea of slavery," Emil murmurs into his hot chocolate. "It's standard practice."

"But it shouldn't be, and it's not something I want to be a part of." I lower my voice. "Kelly stays because he's grateful, but given the option? He's found a passion. He should have the freedom to pursue that."

Emil's expression softens before he looks down at the mug in his hand. "You're a horrible demon."

"I'm beginning to take that as a compliment." I reach across the table and nudge his chin up so he meets my eyes. "Be a horrible demon with me."

He searches my face. "I already am. How far do you want me to fall?"

"All the way." I trace the hard line of his jaw. "Fall forever with me."

His breath catches, and his hand curls around mine, frost sweeping over my skin. "You don't ask for much, do you, Ms. Pond?"

"Of course, I do." I smile. "I'm a horrible demon who doesn't know when to stop."

"You're going to be the death of me," he mutters.

I lean across the table. "I was hoping to be the opposite."

He holds my eyes, and desires sweep through me. His need for warmth, for someone to cherish, the desire to be loved.

I blink, breaking the connection, and pull his hand toward me to kiss his frozen knuckles. "You already have all that, you silly man."

He swallows hard, his lips parting before he looks away and tugs his hand from mine. "Close up shop so I can take you home."

My chest tightens, but I don't take this as a rejection. Emil said he had to do something before he could commit wholly to me, and I just need to trust that, when he finishes, he'll come to me.

Preferably on his knees.

Storming the Library

The next few days pass with more frequent sightings of the council's guard, their hulking figures appearing at every turn. Whether it's at my bakery or when I go to visit Kellen at Club Fulcrum, they're always there, just watching, guarding and threatening in equal measure.

The creepy fuckers.

I keep my senses open for any sign of the mortifier demon, but either he's not here, or he's gotten better at hiding. While the city is rife with many an unpleasant odor, none of them are the telltale stench of rotting meat and grave dirt.

As Saturday nears, I bite the bullet and take the afternoon to drive out to the local high school after it closes. I need to beard the lion in its den, so to speak, if I want Landon or the hag to come to my party. I've tried talking to the doorways, but it looks like the Librarian is too caught up in whatever games she's playing to pay any attention. The old girl deserves her fun, but she's had Landon locked up long enough.

Checking for any humans nearby, I approach the shed next to the sports field and slip through the door. The power of a portal shivers over my skin, then warmth replaces the chill December air. The crowd I run into in front of the Demon Clerk's office takes me by surprise, the chairs inside overflowing and leaving demons clutching call numbers out in the hall.

I give them a wide berth, carefully looking in the opposite direction to avoid catching anyone's eye and being pulled into conversation. I've dodged more than one call from John Smith, the imp who wants me to take on his precious Imperial Rex. While I'm possibly in the market for more imps, I'm not ready to commit, and he has dozens of spawn. If I take one, he'll try to get me to take them all. I'm trying to run a business, not a way station.

Once I make it past the masses, ducking under the reaching tendrils of an inquisitive siren, the hall clears, and I turn toward the Library.

At the end of the hall, the tall, double-doors reach up to the ceiling, thick and locked tight to discourage casual passersby from entering. I pull my Library card from my pocket and stop next to the reader, flipping it over and holding it under the device. A red scanner comes to life, reading the barcode, before it buzzes a denial.

Frowning, I rub the card against my pant leg and try again. And again, it buzzes a denial.

Tucking the card away, I stomp up to the intimidating doors and pound my fist against one. "Hey, hag! Get off my mentor and open up!"

"Is there a problem, here?" a low voice rumbles, and power washes down the hall, pushing at me to kneel.

I stiffen my spine and slowly turn to give Lord Marius a short bow. "No trouble, Lord Marius."

His heavy gaze sweeps over me, making my knees tremble before it moves past me to the doors. "The Library is closed?"

"So it would appear." My knees begin to fold, and I force them to stay firm.

"I can't remember the last time the Library closed." He steps forward, and the wall of his power pushes me flat against the door.

He reaches past me to test the handle, and I wait for it to turn. Surely it can't stand against his might.

But the door stays firmly shut.

He steps back, and I drag in a shaky breath, my ribs struggling to expand enough to let in oxygen.

His head tilts to the side. "The last time the Library was locked was when the previous Librarian met a gruesome end. It remained barred against entry until it claimed the next Librarian."

Panic lends me strength, and I turn once more to hammer on the door. "Don't make me regret that ball gag, you saucy wench! Give Landon a break and open up!"

Deafening silence answers, and even the air stills.

"Well, I suppose that is answer enough," Lord Marius says into the quiet. "Landregath is in there?"

"He's supposed to be." Spindling energy through my limbs, I kick the door, and my toes bounce off, pain shooting up my leg.

Hopping on one foot, I glare at the stupid doors.

"Did you really think that would work?" Curiosity fills Lord Marius's voice, and when I glance up, I find him staring down at me, his brows pinched with the same kind of look a scientist might give a frog he's about to dissect.

"She's cranky, so it might have." I lower my foot to the ground. "Can't you *umph* your way in?"

"And why would I risk the wrath of the Library to do that?" he asks, his head tilting the other way.

Yeah, I'm definitely a frog to him.

I hobble a couple steps away, breathing easier for the distance I put between us. "Didn't you want something from the Library?"

"No." He straightens and turns the weight of his attention down the hall. "I came to see what the commotion was about at the Clerk's Office."

I follow his gaze as I wiggle my toes inside my shoe to make sure they're not broken. "Lots of people filing claims."

"Yes." His eyes swing back to me, and I begin to crouch before forcing myself upright again.

Damn, being around a higher-up is a pain in the ass.

"Try not to abuse the Library too much in your efforts to get inside." With an amused final glance, he strides toward the Demon Clerk's Office.

People scurry out of his way before they notice his actual presence, his power acting as a wedge to move them aside.

With a last look at the locked doors behind me, I make my escape.

No way am I waiting around to see the fallout here.

On the way back to the bakery, I call Julian on his cell phone, but it dumps me to voicemail.

Annoyed, I try the office line and get the message that they're with another client and to leave a message.

I scowl as the cars in front of me grind to a halt, and the first splat of rain hits my windshield before the skies open up in a downpour.

Well, today's turning out to be just awesome.

By the time I park and run inside, the rain has turned to sleet that soaks through my clothes. I squeak down the hallway in soggy tennis shoes, leaving footprints behind.

Upstairs, I run into Tally coming out of the manager's office, and she frowns at my drenched state. "Adie, what...?"

"Sudden downpour," I say as I grab a towel and wring the water from my hair.

"Yes, I can see that." Her pink eyebrows sweep up. "Do you have a change of clothes? A large delivery order came in that I was hoping you could take. But I can go instead."

"Yeah, that won't be a problem. Just give me a minute." I walk into my office and open the tall cabinet next to the door.

I ordered uniforms that I plan to present to the

staff before the party on Saturday, and I grab a set in my size.

Shimmying out of my wet clothes, I use another towel to dry off before tugging the new outfit over my slightly damp skin. The black pants fit nicely, and the pink t-shirt with my Boo's Boutique Bakery logo on the front only pulls a little over my breasts.

I slip into the clogs I keep here to work in the kitchen and pop back out, my arms spread. "Ta-da!"

Tally takes in my new outfit and claps her hands in delight. "Do we all get those?"

I spin in a circle. "Yep! There are different colors, but the theme is the same. Think it will pass with the others' approval?"

She nods vigorously. "It looks so official!"

"That's the goal!" I duck back into the office and grab my raincoat, which I should have brought with me the first time I left. "Okay, lead me to this order."

Not wanting to ruin the surprise for everyone, I zip up the jacket as I follow Tally down the stairs and into the walk-in refrigerator, where baker's racks hold pre-packaged cakes for today's orders.

Tally points to a stack of four dozen boxes, and my brows shoot up. "Whoa, that's a lot for a midweek order."

"Office birthday party." Tally lifts down the top

two boxes and passes them to me. "We might want to add a delivery van and driver to future growth plans. We're getting a lot more requests since we added that to the website."

I nod in agreement, and happiness trickles through me.

With what Tobias paid, and the savings I made on the two cars, that might be nearer in our future than Tally thinks. I'll have to sit down and look through my goals, though.

While Tobias paid a substantial amount, I didn't purchase beater-up cars without reason. I want to buy the imps' home and turn it into an investment property. If I can convince Kellen to sell it to me outright, then what I put toward rental can go toward something else, like a delivery van and driver. And a few more imps so people have more free time.

I should talk to Tobias about my options, since Emil will just tell me to put it into savings. But first, I need to haggle the price of the house from Kellen. He might not be too keen to lose one of his properties.

Tally stacks the second layer of boxes into my arms and throws a plastic garbage bag over it. "I'll help you out to the car."

"Grab a jacket," I tell her as I pull my hood up over my damp hair.

Tally runs down the hall and returns a moment later swaddled head to knee in a pink rain jacket that matches her cotton-candy pink hair. When she zips it up, the collar comes up to under her nose, leaving only her large, mahogany eyes visible.

I laugh at the image she presents. "Did one of the guys give you that?"

"They think I will melt," she says, her voice muffled by the fabric over her mouth. She reaches into one of the pockets and pulls out a pink polka dot folded umbrella. "It came with this."

"That's a bit excessive." I snicker. "I'm surprised there are no matching rain boots."

"Oh, there are." Her eyes widen for emphasis. "They come up over my knees."

I laugh harder. "You're cherished."

"I am." Though I can't see her lips, I hear the happiness in her voice. "Come on."

She motions toward the side door with her umbrella, then walks ahead to open it, snapping her umbrella open as I step past her.

Cold sleet splatters down and bounces off to the sides, and I make a mental note to thank the witches for giving her all the rain gear.

Side-by-side, we walk to my car, and I settle the cake boxes into my passenger side where I can keep a hand on them while I drive.

"The address is on the order slip," Tally says as she walks me around to the driver's side and holds the umbrella over the door as I open it.

"Thank you." I slip my phone from my pocket and attach it to the new holder clipped to the vent. "Get a dinner order from everyone. I'll stop on my way back."

She nods, the motion almost imperceptible from beneath the hood, and I close the car door.

Starting the engine, I watch until she disappears back into the bakery before I plug the address into GPS. Putting the car in gear, I drive toward the exit.

A hulking figure stands under the overhang next to the alley, and I honk my horn, giving the slag demon a happy wave before I drive off.

Really, the higher-ups need to give their guards more training on how to blend in. It's icy cold outside, and the dude is wearing a mesh tank top and shorts.

GPS directs me out of the historic district and deeper into the business part of town. It's not an area I spend a lot of time in, and I find myself circling the block, squinting through the rain to read the numbers on the buildings. At last, I pull up to the curb of an older, three-story building. A sign in the downstairs window announces available office space for rent, but light shines from the second floor.

I pull my hood back up and run around to the passenger side of the car, grabbing the cupcakes and making sure the trash bag covers the boxes before I dash to the front door.

Lamps in the lobby light the way to the elevator, and I check the ticket taped to the top box before stepping into the elevator and pressing the button for the second-floor suites.

It makes me happy, and a little amazed, that my bakery has grown enough that I can be making a delivery like this. In the quieter moments of my night, I dream of opening a chain of boutique bakeries, building the business up slowly. It would provide a comfortable place for other demons to work, making it easier for those of us who prefer the human plane to find a place to settle that doesn't require lying to everyone around them.

Maybe I can even lure more succubi and incubi away from leeching off humans. Sophia seems happy to be working for a living instead of living as someone's sex kitten, and she can't be the only one out there who'd like more from life.

But those are long-term plans, and ones that will need more capital than even Tobias provided through his purchase of my feathers. Which is totally fine. As a demon, I have the luxury of setting goals that span decades. There's no rush, so long as I love what I'm doing and the people I'm doing it with.

The elevator shivers to a stop, the door sliding open, and I step out, glancing left and right. The place looks similar to the building Julian rents his office from, with multiple spaces for businesses. But only one glows with the lights of being open, and I head right, deeper into the building.

The frosted glass on the door announces the business as Antonio's, and I check the number on a dark-brown, plastic plaque attached to the wall next to it before balancing the boxes on one hand and reaching for the handle.

With four boxes, it's hard to see where I'm going, and I call out, "Delivery from Boo's Boutique Bakery," as I hesitantly shuffle inside, afraid I'll run right into someone.

The door swings shut behind me with a slam as the cold air of the hallway vacuums out the warmer air of the office.

I shift the boxes to the side, looking for a receptionist, or someone to help.

"Here, allow me," a voice crackles behind me, like bones rattling in a grinder.

Alarm shoots through me, and I drop the boxes, but a boney arm loops around me from behind, and a sweet-smelling cloth covers my nose and mouth.

"Deep breath, Ms. Pond," Victor Hesse breathes into my ear.

I struggle against him, my limbs flooding with power, but he holds on, the chloroform-saturated cloth burning my nostrils. My legs weaken, the world fading around me.

"It was so nice of you to tell me about this weakness," he says as he eases me to the floor. "Now, be a good girl, and go to sleep."

The Pain of Transformation

The world slowly fades back in around me, and I stare at the room in blurry confusion, my mind slow to remember what happened. A headache pounds in my skull, driving daggers through my eyes as I squint at the fluorescent lights that hang above me. When I struggle to sit up, something holds me down.

I turn my head to see the laminate dark wood of a table beneath me. Black rubber softens the edges, like one of those cheap tables they sell at warehouse stores that can stand up to any abuse. Frowning, I crane my neck to see farther down and spy the wide, black straps that lock me in place. The fabric holds a subtle shimmer, similar to seatbelt material. When I try to move my legs, I find them restricted as well, and panic shoots through me, pushing away the fog in my brain.

Victor Hesse. He tricked me.

Straining against the bindings, I reach for the energy in my core, but I can't find it, and the panic grows. This feels like being trapped with the possessed dogs all over again, knowing I have power but unable to access it.

A door opens behind me, and I crane my neck, catching the shift of movement as someone joins me.

Victor Hesse steps into view, his milky blue eyes meeting mine. "Ah, I see the effects were shorter than expected."

He strides past me, and I lift my head to track his progress. "What the hell are you doing?"

"You want spoilers?" He grabs something and walks backward toward my head, revealing a metal cart on wheels that holds a scalpel and other items I can't identify. "Do you read the end of books first?"

Terror rushes through me, and I flex my muscles again. "Let me go!"

"In due time." He reaches beneath the table and yanks on something.

The straps around my body tighten, and I struggle to draw in air.

"Don't worry. I'm not going to kill you." He stands and returns to his cart. "I want to show you something. I think it will change your world view. It certainly changed mine."

He opens the dark glass jar on the cart, and black tendrils of slime crawl from the opening. Flicking them back inside, he lifts the scalpel and leans over me.

His tone sounds almost thoughtful as he positions the blade over my chest. "Domnall taught me much while he lived. The beauty of darkness, the vileness of humanity. They have so much, but they ruin it with their greed. If they knew how we live, the horrors we face on the demon plane, do you think they would change? I think they would continue as they are, hating for the sake of hating, destroying in the name of entitlement."

He presses the razorblade into my skin in a smooth arc that parts my flesh with ease. Pain registers a heartbeat later, and I scream, fire racing through my body.

Victor Hesse releases a sigh of contentment as he makes another cut. "Transformation is a painful process, but you'll be stronger in the end."

I can't see what he's doing from this angle, but I feel the fire of my flesh parting and thrash to escape the press of the blade.

After a moment, he steps back to study his handiwork before he reaches for the black jar. He brings it toward my wound, and I thrash harder, desperate to escape, but the straps secure me to the table, and my power refuses to come.

Black slime crawls from the jar, tendrils waving over my bleeding wound as if it senses the fresh blood. It slithers down, cold on my hot skin, and oozes over my wound to sink through the opening into my body.

Fire ignites inside me, a furnace of death that wants to burn me from the inside. The taste of ashes fills my throat, and I throw back my head, screaming. Smoke billows from my mouth, noxious and suffocating.

Then light floods my body, iridescent and filled with the power of life and death, of creation and destruction. It burns away the pain, destroying the black slime, and the pain fades to an angry throb.

I slump, panting for oxygen with lungs that can't be filled.

"Fascinating," Victor Hesse murmurs. "I thought the bindings would block you from your succubus powers, and since you haven't escaped, I assume I was partly correct." He moves to stand by my head and stares down at me. "You're like me, aren't you?"

"What are you talking about?" I pant, my muscles still spasming from the pain.

He tilts his head to the side with a click of bones.

"Domnall taught me so much while he was alive, but he taught me more once you took his head. Did you know he wasn't really a demon? Not to begin with?"

I turn my head to stare up at him. "What?"

"Well, he wasn't a *complete* demon." Victor Hesse recaps the jar and sets it back on the cart before he drags a stool over and sits next to me. As he bends forward, the overhead lights cast deep shadows into the hollows of his sunken face, turning his head into a skull. "Domnall was something the higher-ups don't want to be discussed." He lifts a long, bony finger to his lips as if hushing a secret from being told. "Domnall was a demon born of a witch."

My mouth drops open in shock.

Victor Hesse nods. "The higher-ups learned of his existence and planned to kill him. Such abominations could not be condoned. But when they went to capture him, they discovered him surrounded by the dead bodies of his supposed coven. Even as a baby, he hungered for their power, and he drained every single one of them in his need to feed. Of course, the higher-ups could not let such a valuable weapon escape. We were in the middle of a war, and our kind was being slaughtered by the witches. And so, a weapon was born."

I shake my head, unable to process this information or understand why Victor Hesse was sharing it now.

He reaches out and strokes the hair back from my sweaty forehead. "They lie to us. They limit us. But Domnall's death showed me how we can be free. And I want to share that with you."

Shaking my head, I try to dislodge his hand. "I don't want you to share with me."

"You will, once you understand." He sweeps a finger through the blood that drips down from my chest and brings it to his cracked, blackened lips. He licks it and hunger flickers across his face. "As I said, you're like me. Dabbling in the forbidden. But you haven't fully realized your potential. You're still focused too much on being a demon when you can be *more*. Like me."

As he stands, pushing the stool back, I stare up at him with wide eyes. "What are you doing?"

"I'm going to show you the beauty of darkness so you can better appreciate the light." He turns back to me, a cloth in his hand. "I had hoped you would be awake during your metamorphosis, but your magic is fighting me."

As he steps forward, panic shoots through me once more, and I turn my head away. But there's no escape, and the cloth covers my nose and mouth. I try to hold my breath, to stop from inhaling the sickening stench of chloroform, but I need to breathe, and my body's desperation to live forces me to gasp in a breath.

"That's it." Victor Hesse strokes my hair. "Soon, you'll be free." His voice begins to fade, the lights in the room dimming.

I blink, struggling to keep my eyes open, but weakness fills my body, and darkness takes me.

I fade in and out of consciousness, waking long enough to feel the pain as Victor Hesse carves into me, filling my wounds with the black slime, before he chloroforms me back into unconsciousness.

When I wake the final time, the overhead lights are off. I stare around the room in confusion, searching for my tormentor, but Victor Hesse and his torture cart are nowhere in sight.

Body sluggish, I lift an arm to scrub the crust of tears from my eyes, then stare at my hand in confusion. I shift my legs, and they move without restraint.

Victor Hesse freed me.

I struggle up onto my elbows and look down the length of my bare body. Only my underwear covers me, a courtesy I didn't expect from Victor Hesse, but he had no interest in me as a sex demon. No, his interest had lain elsewhere, as shown by the crust of blood that covers every inch of exposed skin.

My hand shakes as I touch my stomach, where I remember the slice of the knife cutting deep. But only firm skin remains. I scratch at the dried blood, searching for some proof of my torment, but only the echoing memory of pain reminds me of what I endured.

Something flutters off to my right, and I flinch, rolling off the table in the opposite direction. I land hard on the floor, my arms and legs too slow to catch me.

Slowly, I wobble to my knees and peer over the bloody table to the stool Victor Hesse sat on for his little story time. My clothes now rest on top of it, neatly folded, with a box of wet wipes on top.

Hesitant, my eyes bouncing around the room, I crawl around the table and to the stool. I grab the box of wet wipes, but my hands shake so hard I drop them. I stare at the door, waiting for Victor Hesse to stroll back inside, but it remains shut.

Did he lock me in here? Am I now his prisoner?

Fine tremors run over my body as I clean myself up and get dressed. Victor Hesse didn't take anything from me. Even my cell phone and the Dreamland amulet Reese gave me are tucked into my shoes.

I use the stool to help me stand and walk on shaky legs to the door. The knob turns easily beneath my hand, and I step through, a wash of tingles coating my skin. I freeze for a moment at the brush of magic, but when nothing happens, I continue into the shadow-filled office.

The boxes of cupcakes still lay on the floor, and I step around them, my eyes on the exit.

This door, too, opens without hesitation, and I walk out into the hall.

My body feels light and floaty, as if walking through a dream, and I make it to the elevator and back down to the lobby without anyone trying to stop me.

It's still raining when I step out onto the sidewalk, and humans rush past me, some with their hoods pulled up and others huddled under umbrellas. No one stops to ask if I'm okay as I stand in front of the building, rain drenching my hair and the front of my shirt where my coat doesn't cover me. Cold water gathers in my collar and trickles down my back, adding shivers to my trembling.

My car still sits at the curb, and when I finally reach into my coat pocket, I find my keys exactly where I left them.

Dazed, I walk to the car, slide behind the steering wheel, and start the engine. Then, I just stare out the windshield, watching the rain pelt the glass as my mind struggles to wrap around what happened.

The glow in the dashboard draws my attention. When I glance at the clock, I discover three hours have passed since I came here to make my delivery.

Tally and the imps must be so worried. I should have been back with food forever ago.

As if my thoughts triggered it, the phone in my pocket buzzes, but I can't find the will to check who's calling me.

The numbers on the clock hold my attention, clicking forward a minute at a time.

I drag in a shaky breath, feeling the sting around my nose and mouth left by the burn of the chloroform. That must be why my mind feels so foggy, why a headache pounds at my temples.

I force my attention to the steering wheel, to where my hands grip it so hard my knuckles turn white, but I don't feel the ache of tense muscles. Everything feels distant, one step removed from reality.

Phantom pain ripples over me, my body reminding me over and over again of the feel of flesh parting, followed by the burn of black slime crawling into my body.

He'd said he would transform me, that whatever he was doing would force me to evolve, and I need to know what that means.

Victor Hesse's crackling voice fills my ears, coming and going in spurts of consciousness. He'd talked a lot, not caring if I was awake to hear his words. But one sentence keeps looping back, as if he repeated it over and over again.

"When you're finally free of all these constraints, you'll come to me, and we will change the world."

Nasty Brew

I drive to the witches' house in a daze. Driving was probably not my smartest decision, but luckily, traffic was light and the one red light I drove through didn't cause an accident.

My phone vibrates in my pocket nonstop, and I continue to ignore it. I know people are worried, that soon someone will track me down, but I can't focus on that now.

I shut off my car then just sit, as if in a trance, until the interior heat dissipates and goose bumps rise on my skin. Finally, I force my limbs to move, to go through the simple motions of opening the door and climbing out.

At first, my legs don't want to work, my muscles too shaky to make walking easy. But then anger at my own weakness stiffens my knees and propels me up the short walk, across the porch, and to the front door.

Leaning against the solid wooden barrier, my hand shakes as I grasp the lion-head knocker and let it drop heavily against the plate. The ugly thing glares at me, its ruby eyes glowing with a malevolent light that sends prickles of irritation over my skin. It gives my anger a place to focus outside of myself, and I glare back, my lips peeling from my teeth in a snarl.

The door jerks open, and I stumble half a step before I catch myself.

Reese stares out at me in shock and confusion before he grasps my arms. "Adie?" His gaze moves over me, and his confusion deepens, uncertainty filling his voice. "Adie?" he asks again with far more hesitation.

"I need help," I say, and my voice cracks, my throat torn raw from screaming. "Help me."

Reese's hold on me shifts, and he slips an arm around my waist, helping me across the threshold. It shivers with resistance, the protections on their house not wanting me to enter, but Reese's presence allows me to pass. The tremble in my body that I held off since leaving the car returns, followed by a flutter of panic.

What did Victor Hesse do, that a house that

always welcomed me would now mark me as a danger to its residents?

"Xander!" Reese yells as he helps me through the foyer. "I have Adie!"

Xander appears in the hall that leads to the kitchen, relief filling his face when he sees me. "Thank goodness. I'll call the others."

"No!" I shout, the protest leaving the taste of copper in my mouth. "Not yet."

He frowns, and Reese's hold on me shifts as he looks down at me. "Adie, you've been missing for hours. Everyone's looking for you."

"Take me to the kitchen, please," I beg. "I'll explain."

Silent, he walks me past the curved staircase and down the hall. Xander steps back into the kitchen and pulls out a chair for me, but I ignore it as I release my hold on Reese. I sway for a moment, then struggle out of my jacket.

When I reach for the hem of my shirt, Reese's eyes widen. "What are you—"

Xander's hand on his arm stops him. "Get the grimoire."

Reese's troubled gaze sweeps over me as if he already sees what hides beneath my clothes before he nods and walks to the pantry. Xander steps forward, helping me out of my clothes when I falter. Then the two men walk to the kitchen island, the base of where they practice magic most often.

In only my bra and underwear, I stumble forward until my feet touch the circle of gold carved into their floor. It flares to life in fits and starts that shoot pain up my legs, but I stand firm, opening myself to the ley line, waiting for the power that lingers inside me to connect with the original power source.

Pops and cracks shoot up my nerves, making my muscles jump. It hurts, but I grit my teeth, refusing to move.

I've borne worse before.

The lights in the kitchen flicker and dim as magic interferes with the electricity. Then, with a sizzle that burns like lightning, iridescent light floods my body, and the circle in the floor solidifies.

The light in my body flickers, though, not as bright as it's been in the past. I stare down at my skin, seeing the patches of darkness where the light doesn't penetrate. From this angle, though, I can't make out the markings. I just know there are dozens of them, all over my body. The invisible markings Victor Hesse carved into my flesh, where even the magic of death and creation can't touch.

I look at Reese and Xander, who stare at me with wide eyes, and my lip trembles with fear. “What did he do to me?”

Xander shakes himself out of his shock to take the grimoire from his brother. He moves a large vase of flowers off to the side to make room and opens the book. “Get the sketchpad. Start drawing.”

Reese nods and crouches, digging beneath the counter before he stands with a thick notebook in his hands. He flips to a clean page as he walks around the island to stand in front of me.

“Do not infuse the drawings with power,” Xander warns as Reese’s pencil touches paper. “We don’t know what will happen.”

Which is why Reese is doing the drawing and not his brother. Xander puts magic in everything he does, consciously or not. I’ve seen the way a simple sigil comes to life on paper for him. It’s like, once he learned witchcraft, the magic now oozes from him like a sieve that can’t hold water.

I stand still as Reese walks around me, his pencil moving over his paper, filling pages as he draws the markings to scale. He draws other things, too, like the sweep of my shoulder and the curve of my waist, marking the location of each symbol.

As he works, Xander flips through the grimoire,

then strides to the pantry and comes back with the copy of the book on Hunters, flipping through that one as well.

At last, Reese steps back, and he begins to rip the pages from his notebook, laying them on the large island.

Xander glances at them and nods, then looks at me. "You can get dressed. We have them all."

I hesitate to leave the circle of magic. It tingles on my skin, bringing to life those places left numb by Victor Hesse's torture. But I can't stay here forever, so I force myself to step back.

The snap of separation makes me stumble, and I catch myself before I crash to the floor. Without the ley line, the weakness I felt before feels worse, more pervasive, my body shaking so hard my teeth rattle.

Reese runs past me, disappearing down the hall, before he returns, and a warm blanket surrounds me. "Sit. You need sustenance. You're crashing."

I eye the chair and decide I can't make it that far before I sink to the floor, pulling the blanket tighter around me. It doesn't feel warm, maybe because my skin is so cold, but at least it blocks the drafts of the old house from reaching me.

Pulling the edge of the blanket up over my

mouth and nose, I close my eyes, huddling in on myself.

A clatter sounds, followed by the click of a gas burner igniting, but I can't find the energy to lift my head.

"Adie," Reese's gentle voice rouses me, and I force my eyelids open. He holds a jar of peanut butter out to me. "Eat this."

My stomach tightens in protest, and I shake my head. "I don't want to."

"It will help." He scoops some up on a spoon and holds it out to me. "Just a bite."

Fighting him would take too much effort, so I open my mouth and let him feed me like a child.

The savory paste sticks to my tongue and the roof of my mouth, and I suck on it until it melts. I swallow, the peanut butter sticking in my throat before it lands in my stomach. After a moment, energy flickers through me, like the peanut butter fueled the dying fires inside me, and I open my mouth for another spoonful before I take the jar from Reese, shoveling the thick paste in faster than I can swallow.

Reese stands and comes back a second later with a steaming mug in his hands. He pries the half-eaten jar of peanut butter from my hands and replaces it with the mug. “Drink this, then you can eat more.”

I lift the mug to my lips, my nose wrinkling at the herb stench that rises from it, and swallow the contents in three burning hot gulps before thrusting it back at him.

As promised, he returns the peanut butter and stands, walking back to the stove where I now notice a saucepan steaming on the burner. He ladles out more of the nasty brew, and I cram more peanut butter into my mouth as I wearily watch him walk back toward me.

He smiles and settles on the floor in front of me. “I know. It’s not great. Had more than my fair share of this stuff. But it really does help.”

The last cup sits in a warm ball in my stomach, pushing warmth outward to my cold limbs, so I reluctantly drop my spoon into my peanut butter and reach out for the mug. “What is this?”

He shrugs. “Just some herbs that help replenish magic.”

Mug halfway to my lips, I pause to frown at him. “I don’t use magic. That’s for humans.”

His brows lift, and he glances pointedly at the gold circle around the kitchen island.

Scowling, I mutter, "That's different," before I guzzle down the nasty tea.

He takes the empty mug and settles it in his lap. "What was done..." His fae-touched eyes sweep over me, and he frowns before he shakes his head. "When witches use magic, without the aid of a ley line, it pulls from the energy we hold in our bodies. We can..."

His brows pinch, as if unsure how to explain. "Some of us can wind the magic up like a spool, storing it to pull from later. How big that spool is depends on the witch. But once it's empty, the magic pulls from other energy in the body until it runs out, and the witch either loses consciousness or dies."

I nod, totally understanding this concept. "That's what succubi do, too. Only we take the power from other living beings. I think of it as a ball of yarn that I wind up."

His brow clears, and he gives me a relieved look. "Good, that makes it easier. So, when the magic was done to you, it used your own resources, draining them in the process. You bottomed out, so it most likely moved to the next best thing, which is the core of what makes you a succubus."

I nibble my lip at that, wanting to protest that my energy core isn't magic, but not knowing what else to call it. What makes each demon is different for every species. Mine comes from storms and a buildup of suppressed emotions. Human energy and elemental power crashing together with enough force to create me. Which sounds pretty magical when I think about it hard enough.

Lifting the spoon, I gather up more peanut butter, focusing on that as I ask, "Is that why Victor Hesse can warp human magic?"

"I think, and it's only a guess, that any demon who has a foot in the human plane can probably do it." When I look up, Reese is staring at the empty mug in his hands. "Magic is mostly about desire, the will to manifest that desire, and the belief that it will happen. Demons already know magic is real, so it's more of a… setting aside the belief it's restricted to humans. But without the ability to connect to a ley line"—his eyes flick up to meet mine—"doing magic will kill demons."

"That's why he needs Domnall's slime," I mutter as realization dawns, followed by an immediate need to puke.

Eww, Domnall's slime is in me.

Reese's brows pinch together. "Domnall's slime?"

I choke down my revulsion to stare at him in

equal confusion. "Yeah, that black sludge that tried to murder Julian."

He tilts his head to the side. "That wasn't just Domnall being especially evil, even without his head?"

"Well, yeah, there's that, too." Then my confusion clears. "Oh, you guys were on the outskirts for all the nasty. We had that guy, Flint, helping us."

Reese pulls his knees up, the empty mug balanced on them. "The spirit guy."

I nod and glance at the peanut butter jar, but the sour knot in my stomach won't let me eat more, no matter how much my body may need it. Now that the initial surge of returned energy has passed, my limbs feel heavy, the need to sleep and heal setting in fast. The jar grows fuzzy around the rim, and my fingers slacken around it.

"So, what does the black slime, and this Flint, have to do with what's going on right now?" Reese prods when the silence continues to stretch.

I drag my gaze back up and blink at Reese as he blurs in and out of focus. "Magic."

Ever inquisitive, Reese's lips part, ready to pepper me with more questions, but the sound of the front door crashing open snaps his attention to the hall.

Scrambling, he wraps his arms around my blanket-swaddled body and drags us both across the circle before slamming a hand down on it.

Unlike when I tried to activate it, the gold flares to life without hesitation, and a shimmering bubble rises around the kitchen island. The fine hairs around my face lift with the surge of energy, then another surge sweeps through me as Xander adds his own power to reinforce the shield.

Just in time, too, as the house shakes with a demonic roll of rage, followed by the rumble of an avalanche. A wave of ice sweeps through the kitchen, crashing against the barrier the witches erected and rolling back in on itself.

My breath fogs on the air, and I huddle lower in my blanket as the numbing rush of winter sweeps over us.

Emil has arrived, and he is *not* happy.

An Ice God's Temper

Next to me, Reese shivers, his lips turning blue from the cold.

Behind us, Xander curses under his breath, and a moment later, the sweet kiss of spring chases out the burn of frost.

My next breath comes easier, and I stare with wide eyes at the globe of ice that surrounds us before I glare out toward the hall and yell, "Are you trying to kill us, you hyperactive popsicle?"

My voice gives out at the end, and I settle for a fierce frown Emil won't be able to see through all the damn ice.

The ice around us creaks and groans, and my ears pick up the soft crunch of footsteps on snow as Emil draws nearer.

Reese shivers and scoots farther back to put me in front of him, and I twist to stare over my shoulder. "What are you doing?"

His eyes jump from the ice wall to me. "Pretty sure he likes you more than he likes me."

"So, you're just going to use me as a shield?" I demand.

"Uh, yeah?" His brows lift as if the answer is obvious. "You have super-healing powers. If he breaks my arm, I'm out of commission for a month."

Well, when he puts it like that... I scoot a little farther in front of him. "Xander, you might want to duck."

"Already on it," he calls from somewhere on the other side of the island. "Can you make up fast, though? The warming spell will run out soon, and I really don't want frostbite."

The ice in front of me shifts, melting away to reveal the angry white stare of a god lost to winter.

I poke a hand out of my blanket and wave. "Hey, there, you delicious scoop of vanilla ice cream."

His head tilts as he studies me. "Are you naked, Ms. Pond?"

"No." I yank my blanket up to my neck. "Definitely not naked. So totally *not* naked."

His eyes sweep over the bubble before his frozen gaze looks past me. "Do you really think your childish tricks will keep me from what's mine?"

My toes curl at the possessiveness even as I shift to more fully block Reese from view. "What's with the temper tantrum, Frostypants?"

His focus shifts back to me, pressing on me with the weight of an iceberg. "You've been missing for over three hours, Ms. Pond. And when you finally reappear, you run, not to one of us, but to these *humans*. And you ask them to *hide* you. Did you really think you could escape us?"

My lips part. "How…?" Then my eyes narrow, and I search the shadows. "Aren, you interfering asshole!"

"He left as soon as you arrived," Reese whispers. "Sorry."

I twist to stare at him. "And you didn't think to mention that?"

He winces. "I didn't know Tally would call them."

"Tally didn't *need* to call," Emil growls, and the ice wall around us shivers. "I was *there* when he arrived. Your baku is horrible at subterfuge."

Worried for my friends now, I push to my feet, my legs unsteady beneath me. "I wasn't hiding from you. You were next on my—"

"First, Ms. Pond," he interrupts with frigid calm. "We should be *first* on your list."

"Maybe not," Xander breaks in, and a rustle of paper comes from the island. "What was done—"

"Done?" The ice groans as Emil's anger shifts to the witch. "What, precisely, was *done*?"

"That's what we're trying to figure out," Xander responds calmly, despite the way the temperature rapidly drops in our little bubble of safety.

My next breath fogs in front of me, and I glare at Emil. "Pull the ice back."

He steps closer to the barrier. "Why, so you can run again?"

"I'm not running, you Ice Princess!" I throw the jar of peanut butter at him.

He doesn't even duck as the jar bounces off the barrier and flies back at me. Reese's arm shoots out, and he catches it before it smacks me in the face. I stare at it in confusion. Why didn't *I* catch that? I stare at my hand, opening and closing my fingers. Where are my super reflexes? For that matter, where is my super healing?

The cuts Victor made had healed, and I assumed that was my succubus nature protecting me. But why hasn't my voice returned to normal? Did Victor Hesse's warped magic really drain so much of my energy that I'm basically *human* right now?

I snatch the peanut butter from Reese and, not

finding the spoon, stick my whole hand inside to scoop out the thick paste. “Get me more of that tea.”

He gestures to the ice bubble. “The stove’s not in here with us.”

Licking peanut butter from my fingers, I glare at Emil. “Ice. Down. Now.”

“Barrier. Down. Now,” he responds.

I turn toward Xander and find him shaking his head. “I’m not sure that’s a good idea. And not just because the barrier is supporting all this ice.”

“What’s the issue?” My lips tighten in worry as I study all the drawings laid out on the island. “Am I dangerous to Emil?”

“I don’t know.” Xander scrubs a hand through his hair in frustration. “These markings aren’t right, and I can *guess* at what some of them are *supposed* to be, but...”

“Intent means more than the marks do?” I guess as my chest tightens with panic.

Expression troubled, he nods, then shivers and rubs his hands together to keep circulation going. His voice lowers, and he speaks to the countertop so Emil can’t overhear. “It’s possible this is a setup to drain Emil and the others through you.”

“Adie drains us all the time,” Emil responds, proving Xander’s efforts useless.

Damn him and his super hearing. Though he's not wrong. "It's kind of my job to drain them."

"True." Xander glares at the drawings. "So why would he...?"

"If you pull the ice back, we'll drop the barrier," Reese calls out.

Xander and I both look at him in disbelief.

He shrugs. "What? I'd rather not freeze to death. And if Jax or Slater get home and see this, they'll come in cannons firing. We can't go to war with Kellen's people."

"As if you could even cross the firing line," Emil scoffs. "The only reason your barrier is still intact is through my kindness."

Xander's fist clenches on the countertop. "You know, you're being a real asshole right now while Adie's hurt. Instead of thinking about yourself, you should consider what she just went through."

My mouth drops open in shock as I stare at the witch. Did he just lose his everloving mind?

I pull the blanket up over my head, waiting for the ice to slam through the magical barrier and squash him flat.

Instead, the ice groans and slowly crawls away, dragging pieces of the kitchen with it. As soon as it pulls back far enough to not pose a danger of crushing us, the barrier drops, releasing the last of the heat trapped within.

The ice continues to crawl back, releasing the chairs and kitchen cart as it sinks into Emil, turning his already pale skin icy blue. Frost creeps up his cheeks and glitters in his hair, turning him into an ice sculpture before, with a shaky breath, he drags it deeper within himself. The frozen white of his eyes melts, revealing the pale blue beneath.

I glance around the kitchen. Aside from the shifted furniture, nothing remains of the ice storm except for a few glittering drops of water and the chill that still clings to the air.

My legs shake from the effort of all this standing, and I reach for one of the stools that had stayed on this side of the barrier, drawing it close enough to sit on. I keep a wary eye on Emil, waiting to see if he'll exact retribution for Xander's words. But he remains stiffly frozen just on the other side of the gold circle in the floor, as if waiting for an invitation to enter.

Reese returns the jar of peanut butter to me before he slowly backs around the kitchen island to the stove. There, he struggles to reignite the burner under the saucepan. The brew he made is probably frozen solid. I just hope all that ice didn't ruin the appliance. A shiver wracks through me, and I scoop out more peanut butter, my fingers scraping the bottom of the jar. I'm cold, and not in the pleasantly numb way Emil's chilly embrace usually leaves me.

Everyone stays silent for a long time, unsure what to do, before Xander slowly lifts the flowers off the kitchen island. They're now wilted and dead, all the life leeched out of them. As Xander turns to dump them into the sink, I stare at them in confusion.

They'd looked fresh when I arrived, the buds not even fully bloomed. But now their petals lay scattered on the countertop, their stems wilted and limp. Did the ice kill them?

Xander sweeps the petals into his hand and drops them in the trash without comment.

At last, Reese gets the burner lit, and the warm smell of gas fills the air.

I shiver again and look at my clothes, which lay on the floor near Emil's feet. "Any chance those are dry?"

Emil's head dips, the motion jerky as if his muscles are frozen, and he stares at the pink t-shirt and black pants for a long moment. "They smell like blood."

"Really?" I ask, voice innocent. "That's strange."

He crouches and lifts my t-shirt, sniffing it, and

his head jerks back. “What is this?”

“The new uniform for Boo’s Boutique Bakery,” I say, my tone carefully cheerful. “Do you like it?”

The shirt drops from his hand as ice begins to creep back out from under his skin. “It’s not good to hide things from your lover, Ms. Pond. Tobias returned to the location of your delivery. Will he find more blood there?”

So much blood. The bigger question, though, is what else he’ll find. I hadn’t been coherent enough to search the place. I’d been more worried about escaping before Victor Hesse returned.

What if Victor Hesse comes back while Tobias is searching the office? He’d overwhelmed me so quickly. What if he does the same to Tobias?

Alarm shoots through me, and I lurch off the stool, then grab the counter when I almost fall. “Did Kellen go with him?”

Emil’s frosty brows sweep together. “Kellen is on his way here. He was searching other areas of the city when I called to tell him that you’d been located.”

Panic at the idea of Tobias being alone, at Victor Hesse’s mercy, makes me light-headed, and dots of gray fill my vision.

No, Victor Hesse let me go, I reason with myself. He’s long gone from that torture room. Even so…

I meet Emil's eyes. "I'm safe. Send Kellen to Tobias's location."

"Tobias can take care of—"

"Send him!" My shout burns my throat, my mouth filling with the taste of pennies.

Emil stares at me in shock for only a moment before he nods and pulls his phone from his pocket, dialing quickly. Eyes on me, he speaks into the phone. "Verify Tobias is safe before coming to the witches' house."

Relief rushes through me, and I slump back onto the stool as all the energy drains from my body. I'm so tired, I think I pass out for a second, because when I blink my eyes open once more, Emil stands in front of me.

I flinch and almost fall backward off the stool, but his grip on my blanket saves me.

"You should be careful—" Xander begins, but Emil cuts him off.

"No danger will keep me from Adie." His arms carefully slip around me, his touch light with the uncertainty of his welcome.

Worry over Xander's words fills me, but I can't believe Victor Hesse would do something to *help* me drain the guys. What would be the point of that when it's something I do every day?

Motions equally hesitant, I lean forward to rest my head on Emil's chest. I hold my breath, my muscles tense as I wait for a sudden influx of power. When nothing happens, I slump forward, giving him my full weight.

His arms tighten around me, his head dropping to rest on my shoulder. "We couldn't find you. We went to the office where you were last seen, but we couldn't sense you."

"I know," I whisper into the curve of his neck. "There was a barrier."

"I hate barriers." He inhales deeply. "You smell horrible."

"Gee, thanks."

He snuffles around my ear. "And weak."

"You're such a smooth talker," I say drily.

He straightens, his hold firm to keep me on the stool. "What happened?"

"I only know pieces." Unable to meet his worried gaze, I focus on the buttons on his shirt. "I'll tell you guys what I know after the others arrive. I don't want to go through it more than once."

He shifts, and when I peek up through my lashes, I find him staring at the witches. "Do *they* know?"

"No." I reach out to tug on his shirt. "I only just got here when you stormed in."

When his focus shifts back to me, snowflakes swirl in his pupils as winter surges through him once more. "You were here long enough to strip. And long enough for these drawings to be made. More than long enough to call us."

"I wasn't thinking clearly." I tug on him harder, wanting to shake the snowflakes right out of him. "I wasn't choosing them over you. And I wasn't running away. I just wanted to know what was done to me. And they're *witches*. Are *you* a witch?"

His eyes narrow, refusing to provide the obvious answer.

"No, you're *not* a witch." I give him another tug. "So, we would have ended up here, regardless."

"No, they would have come to us." He pulls my fist free from his shirt. "You'd be safe in the protection of our house. You'd be warm in front of a fire. Clean and clothed, instead of shivering in this freezing kitchen."

My brows arch. "And who's fault is *that*?"

He leans down to put his nose against mine. "Yours, Ms. Pond. Entirely."

I blow a raspberry in his face, and he backs off instantly, the fussy demon. He's wrong. Our house is missing a key element that the witches' house possesses, which is the golden ring that surrounds the kitchen island. I don't know how to turn on my superpower at will, and I had hoped that coming here and connecting with the ley line would burn away the filth that Victor Hesse carved into my body.

But that reasoning requires more explanation than I have the energy to give. I haven't told the guys I can connect to the ley lines. That I can act as a conduit. I hadn't found out myself until I accidentally stepped on their protection circle, and we'd been in the middle of dealing with the trial at the time. Then, it had slipped my mind.

I'm a succubus. What do I need to access a ley line for, anyway? But now, I wish I'd thought to tell them. It might have spared us Emil's anger.

"We have a fireplace," Reese volunteers as he uses the ladle to fill my mug with the reheated brew. "It's in the living room."

"It will have to suffice." Emil bends and scoops me from the stool, lifting me into his arms. "Lead the way."

Nodding, Reese heads out of the kitchen, and I rest my head on Emil's shoulder as he strides after him.

Hot & Cold

I must have dozed off because, when I open my eyes again, a crackling fire fills my view from way too near. The warmth of the flames heat my face and suffuses the layers of blankets that swaddle me to near imprisonment.

I lift my head to glance around and find myself in an unfamiliar living room, the couch I lay on pulled up to within a foot of the fire.

Is Emil trying to roast me alive? Is this my punishment for not calling him first? Death by cozy fire?

Flailing, I free my arm, and a cold hand catches my wrist. "Adie, it's okay, you're safe."

"Safe?" I squeak out. "You're trying to burn me alive!"

"I am not." He tucks my arm firmly back under the blanket. "Stay still. You only just stopped shivering."

"I'm burning up!" I protest as he tugs the blanket tighter around my neck.

His hand moves to my forehead, stealing some of the heat. "You still feel cold."

I glare up at him. "That's *you*, Ice Princess."

A shiver shakes through me, though, belying my words. Beneath the blanket, sweat coats my body, leaving me sticky and uncomfortable.

Emil frowns and steps away from the couch only to return a moment later with a steaming mug in his hands. "Here, drink this."

My stomach revolts, though I vaguely remember asking Reese to make me more of the nasty tea. Emil helps me sit up, careful not to let the blanket fall into the fire, and lifts the mug to my lips.

I glare at him. "You know, I can do this by myself."

"Why risk exposing yourself when I'm here?" He tips the mug before I can protest again, and the nasty concoction floods into my mouth, burning my tongue.

Trying not to choke, I swallow convulsively until the mug runs dry.

Emil lowers it, and I gasp in air. "You're a horrible nursemaid."

He sets the mug on the arm of the couch. "I've never had to nurse someone before. Demons don't usually get sick."

"I'm not sick," I say, then sneeze.

Another sneeze follows, then another, leaving me light-headed and dizzy.

The heat in my body suddenly vanishes, like someone flipped a light switch, and chills run through me.

What the hell?

I shiver, my teeth chattering together as sweat breaks out on my forehead. Emil frowns and smooths my hair back, then eyes the fire as if contemplating putting me right into it.

"Don't you dare," I chatter out, my voice shaking. "I'm not a piece of firewood."

His gaze shifts back to me. "If we were *home*, I could put you in my bed, where you'd be surrounded by heated blankets."

That does sound nice, but I refuse to apologize for not going home as soon as I woke up on Victor Hesse's table. I had my reasons for my actions, and I stand by them.

Another shiver wracks through me, and I eye the mug, wishing it were full again.

As if he senses my thoughts, Emil grabs it then pins me with a stern look. "Don't move."

"I won't." I shiver harder, my nose tickling with another sneeze, and I poke my hand out to rub it.

The action hurts, and I pause before carefully feeling around my nose and mouth. My skin feels rough and dry, like a sunburn left unattended. I prod at the area, then wince at the discomfort. The chloroform the Hunters used on me didn't hurt this much or leave such a lasting effect. Of course, they hadn't used it in the same quantities Victor Hesse did, either.

I'm more troubled by the fact I still haven't healed, though. Even this surface wound, something that shouldn't take any energy, still lingers.

Emil returns with a fresh mug, and I take it, chugging it down in the hope of feeling that surge of energy once more. But while it warms my stomach, it leaves the rest of me still cold and sweating.

Maybe I just need to sleep. It's when succubi do most of their regeneration. Especially after a huge energy shift. I eye Emil, where frost still clings to his skin. Maybe I should feed, then sleep. But the idea of sex, or even just kissing, leaves me numb with disinterest.

Sleep sounds better.

I hand him back the mug and peer over the top of the couch toward the opening to the entryway. "Have they figured anything out? Where are Tobias and Kellen? Why aren't they here yet?"

Emil's brows sweep together. "I only just called them. You were out for less than five minutes."

"Oh." I scrub a hand over my face, then wince with pain. "I can dress now."

"I think you should just stay under the blanket next to the fire a little longer." Emil glances down at the empty mug he holds. "I'll get you more medicine."

"No, that's okay." I pull the blanket up to my chin. "My stomach's sloshy. I've had too much already. I just need to digest."

He nods and sets the mug off to the side before climbing over the couch. Settling himself with his back against the armrest, he opens his arms. "Come here."

Moving while swaddled in the blanket proves difficult as I inchworm my way over to him. When I'm within arm's reach, he pulls me across the cushions, settling me between his legs so I rest against him. My head lands on his chest, and I shiver from the cold. He smooths back my hair, then cups the back of my neck, adding to the chill of my skin.

The sweat on my forehead slowly freezes, turning into icy pebbles, and I blink sluggishly as frost creeps over my lashes. My shivers worsen, and I huddle lower in the blanket.

"Should I build the fire higher?" Emil murmurs as his hand moves from my neck to settle over the top of the blanket, holding me close.

I crack my eyes open, ice breaking away to dust my lashes, and stare at the dancing flames. "Any higher and you'll burn down the house."

His arms tighten around me. "If that's what it takes to warm you, I'll burn down the whole damn city."

That brings a smile to my lips, and the frost cracks on my cheeks.

Footsteps shuffle into the room, and Reese leans over the back of the couch, holding a stuffed sock in one hand. "Here, this will help."

Emil takes it and lifts my head to settle it around my neck. Warmth suffuses me as the fine grains of rice Reese filled it with contour around me.

I release an appreciative sigh which Emil echoes, and I smile up at him. "How come you don't have one of these at home?"

He shrugs. “They’re more troublesome than just having a heated blanket.”

“But you could have one around your shoulders when you’re on the couch,” I point out. “It would help keep you cozy warm.”

“True.” He gazes down at me. “Will you gift me one?”

I purse my lips at him. “Is it really a gift if you ask for it?”

His cold fingers brush the underside of my chin in a tickling motion. “It would warm me more, coming from you.”

Inside the blanket, my toes flex at the idea I could be warming Emil even when I’m not home with him. “We’ll see.”

He bends to kiss my forehead. “I like the ones that smell like peppermint.”

“Now you’re just getting greedy.” Desire stirs within me, and I tip my head back, my eyes dropping to his lips. “What will you offer me in return?”

“You’re asking for payment for your gift?” he teases as he tips my head back farther, his head dipping.

A loud bang comes from the front door, and Reese swears. “Doesn’t anyone knock anymore?”

Flinching, I pull back. I completely forgot Reese was standing there.

A cold breeze from the open door brings with it the burn of forest fires and the metallic ozone of lightning, and I sit up to stare toward the entryway. Tobias and Kellen have arrived, and while they don't smell happy, at least they didn't enter the house with the rush of power Emil had arrived with.

"We're in here," I call, voice cracking, and wiggle an arm out from the blanket to wave for their attention.

Tobias sweeps into the room, his black suit jacket open and billowing behind him. His blacked-out eyes fix on me. "I do *not* need a babysitter, little succubus."

"Hey, she was just worried," Kellen soothes from right behind him. "Appreciate her display of concern."

"I am not the one in the room who needs to be shown concern." Tobias strides to the couch and unceremoniously grabs one side to shove it away from the fire.

I yelp and grab the back of the couch for balance as it slides sideways, knocking over the coffee table and end tables that were behind it.

As soon as the path is clear, Tobias yanks me out of Emil's arms, stripping the blanket away.

"Tobias," Kellen protests. "You're being too rough."

"You didn't see what was in that room," Tobias growls as his eyes sweep over my exposed body.

When he doesn't find any obvious wounds, he leans over me, inhaling deeply. I stand still for his inspection, knowing it's every bit as necessary to him as Emil's need to ensure I wasn't running away and his desire to hold me despite my shivers.

Tobias's warm breath fans against my neck before he drops to his knees, pressing his face against my stomach. A tremor rolls through him, and his hold on me turns almost painful before he stands once more. Expression hard, he snatches the blanket off the ground and wraps it around me before thrusting me into Kellen's arms.

He catches me, his eyes wide with surprise, as Tobias storms out of the room and heads toward the kitchen.

Panic shoots through me, and I tap Kellen's shoulder. "Don't let him hurt Xander."

"He's not going to hurt Xander," Kellen reassures me, though uncertainty underscores his words.

Reese, who had stood silently through the

exchange, bends and retrieves the sock of rice from the floor before he follows after Tobias.

I urge Kellen to follow with a tug on his arm. "Come on. It's where my clothes are, anyway."

Emil rises from the couch. "You're not putting those back on. They stink."

"Hate to say it, but *Adie* stinks," Kellen says. "I doubt clothes will make a difference."

I duck my head to surreptitiously sniff my armpit. I still don't smell what they're smelling, but with the burn in my nostrils, maybe my senses are blunted. Everything around me feels dull except for the pound of a headache in my temples and the chill that fills my body.

Kellen helps me walk down the hall, returning to the kitchen just in time to see Tobias toss my clothes into a black trash bag. Well, I guess that answers that question.

I glance at Reese as he stuffs the sock into the microwave. "Can I borrow some of Tally's clothes?"

"Sure." He sets the timer, then skirts the long way around the island to avoid Tobias, and disappears down the hall.

I point to the chair Reese had offered me earlier, and Kellen helps me sit down, then I beckon to Tobias. "Come here."

Tobias pauses to stare at me for a moment before dropping the trash bag and stomping over.

I pat my lap.

His brows lift. "You can't be serious."

I pat my lap again. "I'm cold. Be angry while sitting on me."

"She has a fever," Emil cautions.

"I'm aware of her fever." Tobias circles around me, sniffing loudly. "She's sick. Succubi don't get sick. And she stinks of witch magic."

"For the love of—" I throw my hands into the air. "Will you guys stop telling me I stink?"

"Then stop stinking," Tobias hisses. "And I will *not* sit on you. That's ridiculous."

Before I can protest, he lifts me and takes my seat before setting me on his lap. His body heat filters through the blanket, heating my backside while leaving my front cold.

I open my arms toward Kellen. "Sparkypants, sit on me."

Kellen's eyes move from me to Tobias, and whatever he sees in the other man's eyes has him lifting his hands in refusal. "Yeah, that's so not happening."

The microwave dings, and Emil walks over to it, pulling the sock out. Steam instantly rises from it before it ices over, and he curses under his breath before tossing it back into the microwave and resetting the timer.

If I didn't feel so horrible, I'd totally be living it up with all this attention from the guys. But as it is, my nose tickles, snot dripping from the tip, and I sneeze hard enough to pop my eardrums. Another sneeze follows, then another, and only Tobias's arms around my waist stop me from toppling off his lap.

When the sneezes finally stop, I sag against him, light-headed as the world tips around me. Sweat breaks out over my body, the cold vanishing in an instant as my skin flushes. Panting, I shake off the blanket to expose my torso to the cool air of the kitchen.

"Witch," Tobias snaps, and Xander looks up from his books. "What's wrong with Adie? That's why she came here instead of coming to us, right?"

"I'm still trying to figure it out." Xander gestures to his notebook, then the drawings laid out on the island. "I can only guess at some of the meanings behind these. I need more time to research the various combinations."

Tobias's growl of displeasure rumbles through me. He's obviously not impressed by all of Xander's efforts.

Kellen crouches in front of me to take my hands, sparks snapping against my fingers. "Adie, honey, what happened?"

I swallow, the sound clicking in my throat. "Can I have some water?"

"I'll get it." Reese rushes back into the room, depositing a pile of clothes on my lap before he zooms over to the refrigerator.

Tobias helps me struggle into the shirt and pants. They sag around my waist and hang over my feet while my breasts and hips strain at the seams. Tally and I are *not* the same body type, which I've never felt so clearly. She's taller and less hourglass-shaped. While definitely female, her curves are more subtle than mine, less designed to induce lust.

When Tobias tries to wrap the blanket back around me, I refuse and stumble to my feet, wobbling over to lean against Emil's icy body. I sigh with appreciation as he steals my body heat and murmur a thanks to Reese as he passes me a cold bottle of water.

I take a large gulp, trying to wash away the desert in my throat, and almost choke.

Emil pats my back. "Slower."

I glare at him and take a smaller sip, the liquid trickling down my tight throat. After a few more sips, I turn to face the room. I don't want to talk about what happened, but they need to know, and hopefully, it will help Xander to decipher the markings.

With an unsteady breath, I begin. "I was delivering an order of cupcakes..."

In Sickness

By the time I get to the part about driving over here, tension and anger fill the room.

Xander and Reese stay on the ambiguously safety of the island, while Tobias paces back and forth, and Kellen's hair lifts from his shoulders, crackling with lightning. Emil stands behind me, once more as rigid as an ice sculpture, while power hangs heavy in the air, a physical weight that makes my knees shake with the effort to stay upright. Or maybe that's the exhaustion that fills my body.

Reese slowly raises his hand. "And you're sure this black slime that he was using came from Domnall?"

I nod, then frown. "Well, no, but I've never seen anything else like it before." My frown deepens as another memory surfaces. The shock of the torture had fuzzed it out, but now I remember. "Victor Hesse said Domnall was half witch."

Xander's and Reese's eyes widen, but my men don't look surprised, and I frown at them. "Did you know?"

Tobias shrugs. "It doesn't matter."

"Actually, it does." Xander flips through his grimoire. "I was wondering why his slime would be able to activate these spells. I assumed it was because of all the dark witches he drained, but if he was part witch himself..."

His voice fades as something in his book catches his attention.

Reese gives him a concerned look before he turns to us. "I don't know if we'll be able to resolve anything tonight, and Adie looks like she needs to rest. Why don't you take her home and..." A blush stains his cheeks. "Feed her? We'll call as soon as we learn something of value."

"Right." Tobias strides over to me and scoops me up into his arms, then jerks his chin toward the front of the house.

Emil strides ahead of us, with Kellen trailing behind.

I want to protest all the manhandling and tell him I'm capable of walking, but I'm not sure I actually am, especially when he steps out into the chilly December air and it slices through my borrowed clothes. It seems to flip a switch inside me, the cold chills returning, and I huddle against Tobias's warm chest.

His new sports car sits at the curb, parked behind my battered sedan, and Kellen's car waits behind it, the only car that looks like it can run.

Tobias stuffs me into the passenger seat of his car and tosses a set of keys to Emil. Did he pull those from my clothes before throwing everything else away? I try to feel bitter at the loss of my new uniform, but I can't pull the emotion to the surface. I'm tired and cold. All I want is to be home and forget today ever happened.

I must pass out, because the next time I focus on my surroundings, we're parked inside the shadowed garage back at our house, with the engine still idling. Heat blasts from the vents, but the driver's seat is empty. When I peer out the window in search of Tobias, I spot the other cars empty and dark beside us.

Did Tobias abandon me here? But, no, he wouldn't have left the heater on if he planned to just leave me out here.

I straighten in my seat, and his black suit jacket

slips off my shoulders to puddle in my lap.

A chill instantly rolls through me, and I pull it back up, my hands shaking as I struggle to hook it over my trembling shoulders. Is this what humans feel like when they have the flu? It's a horrible sensation. Not even being energy-starved felt like this.

The side door to the garage opens, and Tobias reappears. He strides quickly to my side of the car and opens the door, lifting me out. My head flops onto his chest, and I let my eyes drift closed one more, happy to let Tobias put forth all the effort of getting me inside the house.

When he passes me to a new pair of arms, I drag my eyelids open. Kellen's concerned face comes into focus, the room blurring around us as he strides quickly through the living room and up the stairs to the bathroom I share with Emil.

A steaming bath waits, and Kellen drops me into it, clothes and all. Water splashes over the sides, and I go under, the water hot on my chilled face, before he pulls me back up. I sputter the water from my mouth and glare when he scrapes my wet hair from my eyes.

Emil and Tobias crowd into the bathroom behind him, and even Tac peers in through the door.

I stare at them in bemusement. The bathroom is barely big enough for one person, let alone all of us.

Sleeves rolled up to his elbows, Kellen grabs the bottle of shampoo from the basket on the wall and squirts a generous dollop into his open palm.

"Do I seriously smell that bad?" I demand as he plops it on top of my head.

"Yes," they all say in unison.

Once he has my hair filled with suds, Kellen scoops warm water over my head to rinse it away, then drags my wet shirt off, nearly choking me.

I flail, my arms stuck over my head as the collar refuses to unhook from around my throat. "Wouldn't it have been easier to do this *before* dropping me in the bath?"

"You were cold as ice." With another yank, he gets the shirt off and tosses it aside before chafing my arms to get my circulation moving.

The shivers fade slowly, the fog of exhaustion clearing from my mind.

The persistent pounding at my temples goes with it, and I peer up at Kellen. "Wash my hair again."

He complies without question, making me wonder if he planned to do it, anyway. Just how bad do I smell right now? Is it all blood and human magic, or does the stench of Domnall's slime permeate my body? I shudder at the thought, and Kellen turns the hot water on to warm the bath.

"Should we call a doctor?" Emil's worried eyes fix on me. "Humans go to the doctor when they're sick, right?"

"What could a doctor do?" Tobias growls.

"I don't know." Frustration fills Emil's voice. "We've never had to care for someone who's *sick*."

Tobias pulls his phone from his pocket, tapping away at the screen. "We should give her Tylenol. And check for fever."

"We already know she has a fever." Kellen strips my bra off, then rubs soap over my torso, his motions unexpectedly brisk. "And we don't have Tylenol."

Usually, he'd use the opportunity to cop a feel, and that he doesn't worries me more than the pervasive weakness that fills me.

"She was with Victor Hesse for hours." Emil scrubs a hand through his usually pristine hair, standing it on end. "We have no way of knowing what he did during the times she was knocked out."

I know what he did. The phantom knife still cuts through me, marking all the places he cut me open. But I keep my thoughts to myself. They're already frustrated enough.

"Why couldn't Aren find her? That's what I want to know." Kellen lifts the necklace I wear from between my breasts. "She's still wearing the amulet. Isn't this supposed to give her a magical link to Dreamland?"

Emil shakes his head. "Aren said she was hidden from his view. Like what happened with the drones the Dreamer sent out."

"It's not a tracker for Aren." I swat his hand away. "It only works if *I'm* the one using it."

"He was doing something to block all of us out." Tobias shakes his head. "I couldn't track her through our contract, either. And we didn't sense her even when we stood in the office where he held her." His anger perfumes the air with the scent of burning leaves. "We couldn't even see the *door* she was behind."

"How is a mortifier demon this powerful?" Emil demands. "Why haven't the council guards caught him yet?" The temperature in the room drops as snow dances across his eyes. "He was in our city, right under our noses!"

Kellen twists to glare up at Emil as he turns the hot tap higher. "Stop it. Are you trying to put her back in shock?"

Emil shakes his head, ice cracking on his skin,

and the sudden chill eases. "We should get her into my bed. The fire's on, and the heated blankets will help more than the water."

Tobias turns abruptly toward the door. "I'll make some tea."

"I'll get more blankets," Emil adds, and the two men stride from the room.

Kellen turns back to me. "Come on, let's get the rest of you clean.

Together, we get my pants and underwear off, and Kellen soaps me down, then pulls the plug to drain the bathwater. "Do you think you can stand? I'll give you a final rinse."

"I..." I drag in a shaky breath. "Help me?"

"Anything you need." He cups his hands under my arms and hoists me to my feet.

I gasp in surprise. "I said help, not do it all for me."

"Hush. Let me manhandle you a little." He gives me a strained smile. "Tobias doesn't get to be the only one."

I put a hand on the wall for support as Kellen quickly rinses me off, then lifts me out of the tub.

He sets me down slowly on the bathmat, his hold staying in place while he waits patiently for my legs to hold my weight. When I stand firm, he releases me to grab a towel, drying me off before he wraps my hair up like a turban.

Emil reappears in the doorway, a soft, pink bathrobe in his hands. He passes it to Kellen, who wraps it around me.

The hem drags on the floor, and Kellen lifts me before it gets wet. He turns with me in his arms and strides out into the hall.

Emil walks ahead of us down the short hall to his room, where the fire casts golden light over his white comforter. He added a fur blanket, too, and brought pillows down from my room to form a makeshift nest. Warmth fills my heart at the care they're showing for me, and it chases away more of the horror of the last few hours.

I want to protest that I don't need to be coddled. But I also want to burrow into the warm nest Emil created and pull the blanket over my head. I want to pretend what happened was a nightmare and wake up again to the normalcy of watching Tac's whelps chase Jesse around the yard.

Kellen sets me in the center of Emil's bed, then follows me in. I expect Emil to protest the invasion, but instead, he climbs in from the other side, creating a crackling barrier on one side and a frozen wall on the other.

Then Tobias strides into the room, carrying a steaming mug of tea. He presses it into my hands, then shoves his way in behind Emil, crowding the already full mattress.

I search the room for Tac, expecting him to join us.

Movement by the open door draws my attention to the hall where Tac sits with his back to us, his feathered wings spread wide to block anyone else from entering.

My heart swells at the sight, at the obvious concern from my men, and I quickly drink Tobias's offering. Chamomile to soothe my nerves and help me rest. So much better than the disgusting brew Reese gave me.

Once I empty the cup, Kellen takes it and sets it off to the side on the floor, then tugs the towel from my hair, tossing it aside. His hand on my shoulder encourages me back until I lay down, my head tucked just below the pillows.

Kellen stretches out on my left, his body smashed against mine wherever possible. Emil lays down on my other side, adding his snap of ice, and Tobias spoons the ice demon, his hand reaching across him to settle over my stomach, adding his heat.

I stare at my three men with wide eyes. We haven't all snuggled in the same bed since we survived the Dreamer, and while I appreciate the snuggles, it also sets off my alarm bells.

Kellen and Emil reach down in unison and pull the blankets up over our heads, smothering us in heated darkness, and I lay there, listening to their quiet breaths as my heart pounds.

"Guys?" I say, my voice quivering. "What's going on?"

A static-filled hand strokes back my damp hair. "Do you feel safe?"

It's impossible not to with the demons of destruction huddled around me. "Yes?"

Emil's breath paints frost on my cheek. "Are you warm now? No more chills?"

"Yes?" For the most part, anyway. I won't mention the ice creeps along my body where I come in contact with Emil.

Tobias strokes my stomach through the thick cloth of the bathrobe. "Are you in any pain?"

Taking his question to heart, I flex my toes and take an inventory of my body. While my brain tells me I was cut open multiple times, none of the wounds remain aside from the chemical burn around my lips and nose.

"No," I say at least. "I'm not hurt."

A sigh of relief drifts from three throats, and silence descends. They don't demand further explanations or make any demands.

After a moment, Kellen slips something prickly and soft against my chest, and my arms lift automatically to wrap around my purple, sequined pillow.

Bewilderment fills me at their patience. Usually, if I was hurt, they would rage and go on a warpath for revenge. What's with all this gentleness? It confuses and unsettles me. I reach up and pinch my cheek hard, then wince at the pain.

Emil catches my hand, pulling it away from my face. "What are you doing?"

"Making sure I'm really not asleep." I shift, and Emil and Kellen press closer as Tobias's hand grows heavier on my stomach.

They're not letting me out of this refuge. But that's okay; I don't want out.

I wiggle until I sink as far between them as possible and practically disappear beneath them.

Covered by their weight, I relax, finally at peace, if only for the time that exists now, with the four of us hidden beneath the blanket, blocking out the rest of the world.

Prove It's Real

Surrounded by their bodies, exhaustion finally takes hold and I pass out.

Darkness and a sense of helplessness fill my dreams. Victor Hesse's voice crackles in and out, the monolog of a man driven insane and firm in his righteous beliefs.

Pain knifes through me, ripping through my body. Words I can't decipher cut into my flesh, writing instructions with acid on my bones. I try to escape the pain, but something holds me down, locking my body in place.

My mouth opens, a scream bubbling up my throat, and acrid smoke and ash floods in to choke me.

I jolt back to consciousness, my mouth still open in a silent scream.

Panic rips through me. I can't move. I can't see.

Reaching for the power in my core, I find only a burned-out husk.

I thrash, and the bonds that hold me down loosen a moment before the darkness vanishes.

Golden light fills my vision, dancing off a familiar white ceiling. Then, Kellen's concerned face fills my view, followed by Emil and Tobias as they lean over me.

I gasp for breath as my racing heart slows.

I'm home.

I'm safe.

But my mind doesn't want to accept this as ghost pain ignites across my body.

Kellen brushes my hair back from my forehead, sparks dancing across my skin. "Hey, it's okay. You're just having a bad dream."

"Am I?" My voice crackles like grating bones, and the phantom sensation of skeletal fingers on my skin shiver through me. I reach up to catch Kellen's hand and pull it down to my throat, more sparks snapping against my skin to chase away the memory of Victor Hesse's touch. "Make me believe it."

Kellen bends, his mouth covering mine, his tongue a teasing trace along my lower lip, coaxing me to open. More sparks snap against my mouth and tickle my tongue. I push against him, our tongues tangling together, and life surges through my limbs, fighting back the pain.

I should have done this at the beginning instead of letting Reese ply me with his witch's brew. I'm a succubus, and my demons' passions are all I need.

When Kellen drops to trail sparkling kiss down my throat, I turn my head, reaching for Emil.

His cold lips cover mine, frost soothing the sting of Kellen's desire. I lick my way into his mouth, lapping at the frozen lakes that live in his depths.

Kellen moves lower, parting my bathrobe to find my breasts, and his lips close around one nipple, lightning skating from my aching peak to my center. My moan melts the snowflakes on my tongue, my lips growing numb with the taste of winter.

Emil drifts away, shifting lower to lay claim to my other breast, and lava-hot lips seal over mine, Tobias surging into my mouth before I can even reach for him. Where the others gave, he takes, his lips and teeth chasing away the cold with burning demand.

The belt around my waist loosens, the robe spreading open to lay me bare, and Kellen shifts, his static-filled hands cupping my knees to pull my legs apart, making room for his body.

The mattress dips with his weight as he settles

between my legs. His hands skim along my inner thighs, pushing my legs wider, and warm breath heats my center before his mouth covers me, his tongue pushing inside my tight heat.

Emil cups my abandoned breast, plucking my nipple into a stiff peak as he paints fractals of ice over my other breast.

Tobias growls, the sound rumbling down my throat, and bites sharply at my lips, demanding attention. I lift one arm to curl around his neck, scraping my nails against his scalp, while I cup the back of Emil's head, urging him to give my other breast his sweet mouth.

All the seasons of earth hum through me, their elemental passions dispelling the last of my nightmares, and hunger rolls through me, demanding to be fed.

My hand clenches in Tobias's hair, holding him in place as I drive hooks into the power that waits at the back of his throat, catching it and reeling it into me. He groans, his lips becoming harder on mine, more forceful, taking even as he gives.

Kellen's lips and tongue work between my legs, heightening my pleasure, and Emil's hand joins him, his fingers slipping between my swollen folds to find the nub at the height of my sex. His cold finger circles it, adding to the desire burning through me, but I want more than fingers, and I shove his head down my body.

He goes willingly, his fingers spreading me open, and his cold tongue finds my clit, swiping against me in broad upward strokes.

Tobias's large hand covers my breast, steam rising from my body in a hiss as he melts away the ice Emil left. He squeezes and pinches, then catches my nipple between his fingers and rolls it. My back arches, pleasure rolling through me like waves.

My inner muscles clench around Kellen's skillful tongue, and he hums in appreciation as he pushes deeper inside of me. Sparks dance up my aching center to spark against my womb.

Emil's icy fingers stroke over my sensitive folds as his lips close around my clit, sucking on me like his favorite dessert.

A tremble starts in my toes, shivering up my body. Tobias plucks harder at my nipple, his tongue thrusting in to fill my mouth with his desire. It tastes like heat, like fire, all-consuming, destructive and unstoppable. And I swallow it down and demand more, demand he give me everything. To burn me alive so I can rise from the ashes new and ready to be consumed again.

My hands tighten on my men, my muscles tensing as their touches drive me over the precipice. I moan, Tobias drinking down my cries of release, as my inner muscles ripple and pulse around Kellen. He sucks and licks at my folds, greedily taking in my desire. Emil's tongue flicks and circles around my clit, drawing out my orgasm

Tobias releases my lips, and, with a last sweep of his tongue, Emil straightens.

Kellen pulls back to press a sloppy kiss against my inner thigh. "Real enough for you, honey?"

In answer, I lift my leg to drape it over his shoulder. "Not nearly enough."

Despite what Tobias gave me, and the lust that permeates the air, the hunger inside grows stronger, demanding to be filled.

Lightning skitters across Kellen's pupils, but he holds back, worry in his eyes as he glances at the other men.

Angry, I drop my leg from his shoulder and wrap both around Kellen's waist to yank him closer. How dare he look to them when I'm the one making the demand?

When his gaze shifts back to me, where it should never have left, I growl, "Why are your pants still on?"

He doesn't look away from me again as he grips my legs. "We're just a little worried—"

"Worry less. Fuck more." Reaching out, I grab his waistband at the zipper and yank his pants open.

His cock springs free, hard and glorious. I coo with appreciation, my inner muscles already flexing with anticipation as a hungry beast within me roars to life. I want him inside me, want to feel the storms he holds rolling through me, into my core. My talons lengthen with the need to sink into his flesh, to pin him in place until he slakes my hunger.

He eyes me warily as he tugs his shirt over his head, baring more beautiful, golden skin.

When I reach for him greedily, he sways back as far as the cage of my legs allows, staying just out of reach.

Hands catch mine, pinning them to the bed. My head whips to the side, and I hiss at Tobias. Black voids stare back at me, unconcerned with my desires as he holds me hostage. I snap my teeth at him, but his grip on me only tightens.

"Hey, now. Shouldn't you be focusing on me?" Kellen bends over me, cock nudging against my entrance, and my eyes snap back to him. "Isn't this what you want?"

My fingers flex, the need to sink into his flesh

warring with the hunger to feel him inside me. As skillful as his tongue was, I need more, need his cum filling me with power.

He reaches between us to fist his cock, rubbing his pre-cum against me. It crackles with power, feeding the hunger inside me, and my legs tighten around his waist to pull him to me.

His cock stretches me open, filling me, and my head falls back as I moan. Emil bends back over me, covering my open mouth with his, his tongue an icy treat. I suckle on it, drinking down the snowdrifts, licking away the vanilla ice cream sweetness as Kellen fills me with sparks of lightning. His slow pace quickly picks up speed, his hands on my hips pulling me into each thrust.

Emil's fingers return to my clit, circling and flicking to drive my pleasure faster toward release. But it's not my release I need, and I clench around Kellen, tightening around his cock until he groans and loses his steady pace. His gasps of pleasure fill the room with a heady music that fogs my thoughts.

Emil backs off, pulling a protest from my lips. He tugs his sweater off, then rolls out of his pants with liquid ease, and my eyes fix on the creamy length of his hard cock. A blush of blood fills the head, and pre-cum forms an icy pearl on his tip. I want to taste him, to know how that flush of blood feels sliding down my throat.

My mouth opens, jaw aching with the need to have him, but hot hands pull my head back, black eyes claiming mine.

"No biting," Tobias commands, the order rolling over me. His thumb pushes into my mouth, and my teeth immediately clamp down, the reward of copper a bright pop on my tongue.

Then Kellen slaps me hard on the ass, his cock slamming into me, and my mouth pops open in surprise.

Tobias shakes his head at Emil. "Don't risk it. She's not in control of her hunger."

I hiss my anger, snapping my teeth at him for denying me, and another sharp slap burns across my ass.

"You need to focus, honey, or I'm going to be offended." Kellen grinds into me, his hips swiveling, and my hiss cuts off into a moan.

I've never consciously had all three of them, and all the power and sex overwhelm my senses. I tug on my captured hands, wanting to be free, to take, to gorge myself on this buffet, but Tobias holds my wrists pinned to the bed, only allowing me to lay beneath Kellen and take what he offers.

And offers he does, his thrusts building until they surge like waves through my body, crashing like thunder determined to capsize me. His skin shimmers with lightning, and storm clouds spread from his back, blocking out the light cast by the fire. When his gaze meets mine, a god of storms stares back, mercilessly sweeping forward with the most tender of destruction.

I shake beneath him, pleasure wracking through me, unable to hold back my pleas for his destruction.

His fiery hair glows like a halo around him as he throws back his head, surging inside me, and a cyclone of power rushes through him and into me.

My back arches, my mind short-circuiting and vision turning white before the storm swallows me whole.

THE BEAST WITHIN

Snowflakes dance across my cheeks and melt to trickle down my face as I blink the room back into focus.

White eyes meet mine as Emil covers my body, freezing the sweat on my skin. My gasps turn to frost on the air, my nipples pebbling to hard peaks from the cold. Only my hands stay warm, trapped still within Tobias's hold. I'm not sure where Kellen went, and as Emil dips to catch my nipple within his frozen lips, I don't care. My ice demon will give me more power and soothe the sting left by the storm.

I part my legs as Emil lavishes attention on my breasts until my nipples turn blue and frost covers my chest. I shiver and gasp, my legs restless on the bed, but he keeps his body from mine, dragging out the tease as his hard cock dances between us, just out of the warmth of my sheath.

When he rises above me, my lips part, eager for

the taste of winter, but he denies me once more to reach past me. My head tips back to find Tobias kneeling just above my head, his knees on either side of my trapped hands. His hard cock strains against his pants, and my heart beats faster as Emil deftly finds his zipper and pulls it down.

Tobias's massive cock springs free, ruddy and hot, dripping with cum from watching me with Kellen.

I lick my lips, wanting that heat after the freezing path Emil left on my body, but then Emil leans down over me, his lips painting chill kisses across my forehead, his tongue leaving a trail of frost. He kisses the corner of my eye, and my lashes instinctively flutter shut, then stay closed as the frost spreads, locking me in the chilly darkness of winter.

His lips drift down farther, skimming across my lower lip, and my tongue flicks out, melting away the snowflakes as I try to catch his mouth with mine. But he continues downward, painting frost along my jaw, freezing me inch by inch with his kisses.

Cold hands cup my rib cage, fingers spread wide over my back, lifting me to meet him as his mouth closes once more around my breast.

I shiver from the cold, my lips turning numb and my blood turning to slush in my veins. Without my vision, I can't see what Emil's doing, can't guess at his next move, and the hungry beast inside me prowls back and forth, waiting for the darkness to fade so it can strike.

Tobias's hold on me shifts, transferring my wrists to one hand to free his other. He cups my jaw, tipping my head back with a crackle of ice, and fire brushes my lips, melting away the snow. The scent of ozone and lava fills my nose, and my mouth opens on the first nudge of a thumb on my chin.

"Don't you dare bite," Tobias growls, his cock resting against my parted lips.

My tongue darts out, sweeping across his hot length, and I tip my head back farther, mouth open wide in invitation.

"Careful, it could be a trap," Emil breathes, frost rolling down my stomach and dancing between my thighs.

I smile for my clever demon, ever the cautious one. I may be blinded, but that doesn't mean I'm tamed.

"Such wickedness," Tobias purrs, tracing the curve of my lips. "You want to feast that badly?"

My mouth opens wider, tongue out in invitation.

Emil's breath drifts over my mons, then lower to

settle between my legs. He lifts my hips, slipping a prickly pillow beneath my ass to raise me. Then his skillful fingers trace my outer folds as he laps at my center, and pleasure shivers through me.

While I'm distracted by Emil's slow build of winter at my core, Tobias pinches my jaw between his strong fingers, keeping my mouth open as his cock slides into me. His girth stretches me, my teeth scraping against him as he rubs against my tongue before pushing into my throat.

For a moment, I can't breathe, but I don't care as I groan around his fullness, drool pooling in my mouth and dribbling out of the corners of my lips.

If Tobias finds release inside my mouth, he could break me, but even that I don't care about. Not with the taste of landslides rolling down my throat, with the tipping of scales ringing in my bones. The ice on my face melts away, leaving me able to see once more, to watch the flex of Tobias's thighs and the way his hold on me loosens.

As he drags his heavy weight from my throat, Emil pushes his long fingers into me, his tongue licking a cold line up to my clit. My hips jerk beneath him, my inner muscles clutching at his fingers as they press and rub inside me, heightening my pleasure. Then they withdraw and Tobias's cock surges back into me, filling me once more with heat.

My body becomes a battlefield of ice and fire clashing for dominance, and the beast inside me growls louder with hunger.

The part of me that loves these men loves the way they pleasure me. But something darker grows inside of me, something starved and demanding to be fed.

My jaw aches, my teeth tingling with the need to bite, to devour.

As if he senses it, Tobias pulls free of my mouth. My neck arches, lips straining to capture him, but he slips free, leaving me yearning for the taste of his blood.

Growling at being denied once more, I twist sharply, breaking his loose hold as I roll to my stomach, my knees under me. My eyes lock on Tobias, at the delicious power that rolls through him, and I spring.

Cold arms loop around my waist, catching me before I reach my prey, and ice rolls over me, trying to freeze the beast inside me that demands flesh and the breaking of bones.

I struggle against Emil's strong embrace, his naked body slides against mine.

"It's okay," Tobias says as he crawls closer. "You can let her go."

Emil stiffens behind me. "What?"

Blacked-out eyes meet mine, an abyss ready to consume me. "If this is what she needs, she can take me."

The beast inside me howls with victory, and I snap free of Emil's arms, launching across the short distance to crash against Tobias. We fall off the bed in a tangle of limbs and snapping teeth. The sound of ripped fabric fills the air, followed by the sweet, heady scent of copper.

I rip more of his clothes off, exposing strong shoulders to sink my teeth into, and I groan as finally, *finally*, the power I wanted surges through me just as Tobias pins me against the side of the bed and thrusts into me.

Our bodies move together frantically, each taking what we want from the other, and power rages through me, life and death, pleasure and pain becoming one.

My claws dig into Tobias's back, sinking into his flesh, and he only thrusts harder, growls louder, a defiant roar that rings through me with a power all of its own, a power I want.

No, a power I *need*.

I abandon his shoulder, my claws leaving his back, and I grip his face, pulling his mouth to mine. He licks his blood from my lips before sealing our mouths together, and power pours down my throat, fire filling my lungs and landslides choking me.

It's too much, I realize. I reached too high. But Tobias doesn't relent as he feeds earthquakes and forest fires into me.

I tremble and shake, the onslaught too much to handle. He thrusts hard into me, his cock swelling to stretch my inner walls. His cum floods my channel, and pleasure slams through me.

Too much, everything is too much. Unrelenting, Tobias feeds me the death of starlight, and my world cracks and falls apart.

(UN)SATED

Once more, snow brings me back to awareness, and I stir, my body heavy with the fatigue of long sleep.

A cool hand brushes over my forehead, and cold lips press against my temple.

In contrast, a warm cloth swipes down my chest, leaving behind the light nip of static.

I blink my eyes open, dazed and confused as Kellen swims into focus.

He smiles at me and lifts the warm cloth to rub over my mouth. "Feeling better?"

Brows pinching in confusion, I blink a few more times, trying to remember what happened.

"You went into a feeding frenzy," Tobias rumbles as Kellen cleans my cheek.

I look past my storm demon to Tobias, who stands off to the side of the bed, running another washcloth over his bare torso. It's pink, as is the water that trickles over his hard muscles, and I lick my lips, tasting copper and feel the memory of his flesh giving beneath my teeth.

I lift a shaky hand and almost stab myself in the eye before Kellen catches it, my talon tickling my eyelashes before he pulls it away. I stare as he carefully slips pink mittens over my hands before he returns to washing me. Not that he needs to. Any fluids left should have absorbed by now, turning into more energy to fuel me.

Shaking my head, I look at my catalyst demon once more. "I don't understand."

Tobias tosses the washcloth out into the hall and scrubs himself dry with a fresh towel. "It happens to young succubi. Usually right before they gather enough power to take corporeal form."

How does he know that? Have they experienced this before? With another succubus?

Rage turns my vision red, and my talons shoot through my new mittens.

As tension fills my body, ready to pounce and remind Tobias who he belongs to, Emil's arms tighten around me.

He presses another cold kiss to my temple. "Shh," he soothes. "Landon warned us it might happen. We just thought we had more time before we had to deal with it."

"Landon told *you* but not *me*?" I wiggle, not at all soothed, but his hold stays firm.

Tobias arches one thick brow. "And what would you have done with the warning?"

The comment only spikes my anger, and I strain toward him. "I'm going to rip you to—"

The warm washcloth covers my face, cutting off my threat and blocking my view of Tobias.

"There, there. It's all good," Kellen sing-songs as he scrubs my face. "We're just rainbows and happiness here. One big, loving family."

I sputter and kick out, my heel landing against something soft, and Kellen's grunt rewards my effort. The washcloth drops away to reveal Kellen hunched over, one hand on his crotch.

Unsympathetic, I poke my toes at his face. "There, there."

He glares at me. "Next time, *I'm* going to be the one ripping into *you*."

I lift my mitten covered hands. "Grr."

Emil's hold on me loosens, and one cold hand spreads over my stomach. "Are you feeling better? No longer sick?"

The worry in his tone melts away the last of my

anger at the other two, and I take stock of my body. Energy hums through me, still raw and powerful. I must not have lost consciousness long enough for my body to digest it and convert it to my own energy, but that's only a matter of time.

For now, I finally feel satiated and healthy. Even the burn around my nose and mouth from the chloroform is gone.

I snuggle back into Emil's cold embrace. "I feel good."

"I'm glad." His hand drifts lower. "Though, if you're a little peckish, still..."

Dipping my head back, I nibble the underside of his jaw. "Oh, yeah?"

"Maybe without an audience?" he says pointedly.

Kellen straightens with a wince to scowl at him. "We agreed on a sleepover."

"Agreed. We're staying here, tonight." Tobias strides to the bed. "Adie, show us your wings."

My lips part in surprise. "Excuse me?"

His lips tighten. "Why are you always so hesitant?"

Kellen snorts into his hand. "You really *do* have a feather fetish, don't you?"

"What?" Tobias's gaze snaps to the back of Kellen's head. "I have a *what*?"

"You poor, poor succubus," Kellen coos as he inches closer. "Always having to guard your wings against this pervert."

"Hey, now!" Tobias catches Kellen's ankle and yanks him backward off the bed. "I'm *not* a pervert."

Kellen lands with a thud and breaks out in laughter. "Oh, my god. Even the *imps* know!"

Tobias whips toward the open door and thunders, "None of you better be out there right now!"

Chitters and the patter of running feet sound from the stairwell.

Kellen's laughter increases, and even Emil snickers, while Tobias's cheeks slowly flush red.

As Kellen and Tobias devolve into argument, I pat Emil's arm. "Let me up. I want to run to the bathroom to really rinse off. Then we can resume the discussion of more snacking."

His arms tighten around me, unwilling to let me escape. "You're already clean."

"But I could be *cleaner.*" I nibble on his jaw. "Imagine me all squeaky clean, without anyone else's scent on my skin, ready for you to lick all over."

His hand flexes against my stomach. "I could help wash you. Make sure you get all the spots you can't reach."

As a succubus, there are no spots I can't reach, but I purr my agreement, regardless. "Give me a head start so I can get the shower nice and warm."

"I'll give you one minute. Our water heater is excellent." With a final squeeze, he releases me, and I spring off the bed, the minute already counting down in my head.

"Hey, where do you think you're going?" Kellen demands as I jump over his sprawled body.

When Tobias reaches out to catch me, I dodge and call back, "If the bed's made when I get back, I'll show you my wings."

Tobias freezes, one foot in the air, ready to give chase, before he turns back toward the bed with red-faced determination. That sets Kellen off in another round of laughter that follows me out into the hall.

Spirits high, I skirt around a sleeping Tac who still guards the entrance to Emil's room, and give his ear a quick rub when it twitches toward me.

In the bathroom, I throw the shower curtain back and bend to turn on the hot water.

A wave of dizziness washes over me, and I clutch the edge of the cast iron tub to stop myself from falling headfirst into it.

Another wave weakens my knees and blurs my vision as the mass of power in my body rolls uneasily. Drool floods my mouth before my gut twists and heaves.

I clutch the tub tighter, the iron bending under my fingers as I lean over the basin, my mouth opening wide. Thunder and lightning bubble up my throat, chased by landslides and the burn of fire.

My stomach spasms, muscles clenching tight, and black slime pours like acid from my mouth.

Slime Baby

With the handle of a broom, Reese pokes at the black slime and nudges an inquisitive tendril back into the basin of the bathtub. "Well, I think this clears up some of our confusion over what the marks are supposed to do."

I shiver and huddle on Tobias's lap, swaddled once more in Emil's pink bathrobe.

When Emil had found me bent over the bathtub, puking my brains out, his shout of alarm had drawn everyone out of the bedroom. Tobias took one look and demanded Kellen call his witches here before he wrapped me up and refused to let me go again.

I don't mind, though, as shivers wrack my body. He's a walking heat blanket, and I need both the warmth and comfort. I feel even more empty now than before I fed, and I don't like the sensation one bit.

Emil, wedged against the back wall, glares at the witch. "Elaborate."

Reese pokes the slime again, and it curls around his makeshift stick. For some reason, it refuses to go down the drain, which has disturbing connotations all of its own. He releases the handle, watching as the slime waves it back and forth, knocking loudly against the sides of the cast-iron tub.

"Reese," Kellen prods.

"Hm?" Reese looks up and blinks, as if only just remembering he's not alone. "Oh, right." He reaches into the satchel slung over his shoulder and pulls out a sketchbook, opening it to a page and holding it up. "These are what mainly reside in Adie, in one form or another." He points to the three sloppily drawn symbols. "We believe they're meant to be consume, convert, and separate. Normally, they wouldn't be put together like this, as they conflict. And they're incomplete, so we weren't sure that's what they were supposed to be."

He pulls out a black sharpie, then turns the sketchbook back toward himself, drawing quickly. When he turns the sketchbook back to us, my eyes immediately shift to the side.

He points again. "See? This is what they *should* look like."

"No," Emil growls. "We *don't* see."

"Oh, right. Hold on." He flips to a new page and draws again before turning the book back to us. "Like this?"

Now, the paper holds three symbols, neatly drawn with confident lines. A gap of blank paper bisects the center of the symbols, allowing us to see them. But, to me at least, they look like the ones on the other page, just nicer.

Reese points to the center of the top one. "This line here is only partially formed in the ones in Adie's body. They shouldn't work the way they're drawn, but somehow they do."

As if annoyed at the lack of attention, the broom handle baps Reese in the side, and he reaches out to absently shift it back and forth.

"Based on the effect, we can assume that the other symbols all work together to recreate what Domnall could do to witches, only this one works on other demons." Then Reese's brows sweep together. "Unless Domnall did this to demons, too?"

Emil and Tobias both shake their heads, as Kellen explains. "Domnall could drain witches because he was part witch, and the high-ups messed with him. Adie's not part witch."

Reese's brows shoot up. "Demons and humans can procreate?"

"No, demons and *witches* can procreate, and even that is rare," Emil bites out. "It's even rarer for the offspring to survive. With the separation of our people, it hasn't happened in hundreds of years."

Reese's fae-touched eyes jump to me. "But succubi and incubi have sex with humans all the time. Surely some of them were witches, too. Why aren't there a ton of half-demons running around?"

"One." I hold up a finger. "We mostly feed on people in Dreamland, where there's no real exchange of fluids. And two"—I hold up a second finger—"we consume energy in all forms."

"Ahh." His frown clears. "So, you'd absorb any life force before it could grow."

"Yeah," I say, my voice glum, and Tobias's arms tighten around me.

Reese nods, and I can practically see him filing the information away for later. "So, Adie's not a witch, but she channels witch power, so obviously it's not completely incompatible." He glances down at the tub. "Maybe because it's just another form of energy?"

"I'm sorry, but Adie does what?" Kellen asks calmly from the doorway. "Adie gave up the ley line magic when she returned the last time."

"Yes, I know. I'm talking about the glowing thing." Reese tries to reclaim the broom, but the slime yanks it away, then smacks him with it. "It's ley line magic."

"No, it's not." Emil crosses his arms over his chest. "We've all been in contact with it. It doesn't burn."

Reese shrugs. "Conversion."

"This was before Victor Hesse got his hands on her," he snaps.

"Succubi convert energy." Reese points at the tub. "Is this Tobias's energy? It's kind of cranky."

Beneath me, Tobias vibrates with suppressed indignation, and the towel bar falls off the wall, crashing onto the tiles with a loud *twang*.

Kellen lifts a hand. "It's mine, too."

"I guess that explains the playfulness." Reese glances at me. "You want to keep it?"

My lip curls in disgust. "Hell, no."

"Thank god," Emil mutters under his breath, and I shoot him a glare. He glares right back. "What? You keep strays."

I point at the tub. “That isn’t a stray. That’s vomit.”

“Technically, it’s a combination of your, Tobias’s, and Kellen’s energy.” Reese kneels in the narrow space between the tub and the sink, setting his sketchbook down. “It’s practically your baby. Except that it will never grow past this point.”

I straighten in alarm. “Wait, what?”

“No!” Emil points his finger in my face. “You’re not keeping it.”

“I don’t want to keep it.” My eyes cross as I focus on his finger, then glance at the tub. “Unless…”

“Get rid of it, right now,” Emil commands.

With a nod, Reese uses his sharpie to begin drawing symbols on the rim of the tub.

“What are you *doing*?” Emil squawks in alarm.

Reese glances up at him in confusion. “Getting rid of it?”

“But…” Emil gestures at the tub. “You’re ruining my bathtub. Do you have *any* idea how old that is?”

“Older than I am?” Reese guesses.

“Yes,” Emil snaps. “It’s an antique.”

I snort and mutter, “You’re an antique.”

Emil whips toward me, his frost brows arching. “Excuse me, Ms. Pond? I didn’t hear that.”

Expression innocent, I nod with sympathetic

understanding. "Must be the age catching up to you."

Kellen snickers from the doorway, the sound masking the quiet squeak of the sharpie on the bathtub.

To distract him from the destruction of his precious bathtub, I keep my attention on Emil. "Were you alive the last time the Earth froze over?"

"Who do you think froze it?" Kellen says, still laughing. "Someone needed his afternoon nappy time."

My eyes widen. "Wait, seriously? You're so *old*."

Emil shoots a glare at Kellen. "I did *not* do that. That was just mother nature."

"Sure it was." I cough into my hand. "Granddaddy Emil."

Emil bends, his breath cold on my face. "How about I freeze you over?"

As I lick the frost from my lips, hunger growls through me. "How about you *try*, old man?"

Snowflakes swirl in his pupils. "You think I can't, baby succubus?"

"If this turns into a granddaddy kink, neither of you are living it down," Kellen warns, but it comes from a distance as my world narrows in on Emil and the power that rolls through him.

I shift, leaning toward him as my lips part, eager to drink him down.

"I wouldn't do that, if I were you," Reese breaks in.

"Shut up, witch," Emil growls as he leans forward to close the distance between us. "Adie is hungry."

"And what you're about to do could make it worse." Iridescent light floods the bathroom, and Emil flinches upright, his back slamming against the wall.

We all turn toward Reese, who still sits on the floor with his arms spread out on either side, his fingertips on the rim of the tub. Ley line magic glows from him, painting the bathroom in rainbows, and circles the tub, which shimmers in and out of focus with witch magic.

The black slime within the tub roils and slaps against the sides, but shrinks away from the light. It thrashes, a living thing fighting for existence, before the light rolls down over it, smothering the darkness.

When the light fades, the slime lays motionless as it slowly oozes down the bathtub drain.

I blink the rainbows from my eyes, suddenly no longer hungry. "A little warning next time."

Reese drops his hands to his lap as he blinks up

at me. "Sorry, I thought I was supposed to complete this while you were needling Emil."

"Well, yes, while you finished drawing the symbols." I scrub the soft sleeves of the bathrobe over my eyes to wipe away the black dots left from staring at the ley line magic. "But ley line magic can hurt demons."

"I was well aware of what he was doing," Emil sniffs as he relaxes his stance against the wall. "I've been wanting to remodel this bathroom, anyway."

A collective groan goes up around the room, which earns us all a frosty glare in return.

"What did you mean feeding Adie could hurt her more?" Tobias rumbles, speaking for the first time since scooping me onto his lap.

Reese squints at me, but not like he's looking at my body, more like he's looking *inside* me, which is all sorts of creepy. "I think the feeding deepened the marks, but I need a closer look."

Unease rolls through me, and I pluck at the belt on my robe. "Sure, no problem."

Another rumble comes from Tobias, and his arms tighten around me, locking the puffy bathrobe in place. "No."

"Oh, come on." I flop against his broad chest. "Reese doesn't have any sexual interest in me, and even if he did, I could snap his scrawny neck like a toothpick."

"Now, that's a visual I didn't need." Reese uses the edge of the bathtub to hoist himself back to his feet. "There's a mark over her heart. Is that acceptable? It doesn't require full nudity."

Beneath me, Tobias's body temperature increases, and I snuggle closer to him, enjoying the heat of his jealousy.

After a long minute, while the bathroom grows steadily warmer, Tobias relents. "Fine."

I straighten with reluctance and reach up to push the robe off my left shoulder, exposing my chest and the upper swell of my breast, where I remember the scalpel carving a crescent mark into me. "Here, right?"

"Yeah." Reese swallows as he shuffles forward, one wary eye on Tobias, before he leans over me, his eyes unfocusing.

Slowly, he reaches out to nudge the bathrobe a little lower, his body swaying as his eyes track something only he can see. He shifts, stepping around me and almost bumping into Emil in the process.

Emil lets out a growl of warning, which Reese

doesn't seem to hear as he tugs my robe lower in the back.

Tobias catches the front before my boob pops free, his knuckle hot against my nipple. It perks up with interest, the hunger from earlier reawakening. I look up at him, dragging in a deep breath to pull the scent of ozone and fire into my lungs. It feels good, having him rolling around inside me, and I breathe in deeper, wanting more.

"Feed," Reese murmurs. "But just a little."

I don't need to be told that twice.

Reaching up, I grab the back of Tobias's head and yank his lips down on mine.

Starlight

Searing heat, like boiling water, fills my mouth, and I swallow it down to fill the aching, cold emptiness in my core. Tobias holds himself still, his mouth open as he lets me take what I want. It's a far cry from the demon I fought earlier for dominance. I lick at the back of his tongue, searching for volcanoes, but he gave me almost everything he had when we embraced before.

When I pull back, my lips sting from the burn of his mouth. My lashes flutter up, my eyes rising to meet his, but he looks past me, his focus elsewhere.

"Was that enough?" he demands as his hand fists in the front of my robe.

"Yeah." Reese steps back and bends to grab his sketchpad from where he left it on the floor. "Feeding is definitely strengthening the marks. You should avoid doing that again."

Tobias's lips thin into an unhappy line, and the

temperature drops behind me with Emil's displeasure. Kellen, at the door, crosses his arms, his eyes narrowed in thought.

"But I need to feed." I shrug my robe back into place. "And they need me to feed."

Reese shakes his head. "You'll have to find an alternative. We don't know what will happen if you fully empower these symbols."

At the suggestion, my lips peel back from my teeth. *No, no one else touches my men.*

Then, a prickle of heat fills my body, and my stomach rolls. I lurch free of Tobias's hold to bend over the tub, puking up more black sludge. The thin stream of slime curls into the basin of the tub before it begins to inchworm back up the side toward me.

Reese reaches out to touch the rim, and the spell flares back to life, iridescent magic skating around the tub. It hits my fingers and floods through my body, flickering in and out before it solidifies and completes the circuit.

Rainbow light rises from my skin, easing the ache in my bones made from expelling the slime. I grip the tub tighter, wanting to hang on to this feeling.

But the spell quickly wipes out the life that

clings to the slime, and Reese's hand falls away, ending the spell.

I slump onto the floor, my forehead pressed to the side of the tube. "This is not okay."

"No, it's not." A cool hand cups the back of my neck, cooling the heat that burns my skin. "How do you plan to fix this?"

Silence fills the bathroom, and I lift my head to peek over the rim of the tub to stare at Reese.

His fae-touched eyes shift between us before they settle on Kellen, his owner, who blocks the only exit. I watch as Reese's Adam's apple bobs with a heavy swallow. "I can't."

The air in the room grows heavy, and frost creeps across the floor.

Reese lifts his hands, the sketchpad back in his hands like a shield. "Okay, we can, but not in the time we have."

"Explain," Emil snaps, and I turn to crawl back onto Tobias's warm lap to escape the ice that spreads toward Reese.

Seeing the danger, Reese climbs into the bathtub, which offers only a temporary escape. "All of our studies have been directed toward gathering power and how to harness it."

His eyes flick to Kellen, and he swallows

whatever else he may have said before continuing. “This spell is fixed to Adie’s...soul? The energy that creates her.” He shrugs helplessly. “We don’t know enough about demons to strip it away without permanently hurting Adie. If it was just a matter of shedding this corporeal form, it would be easy, but the symbols go all the way in. They’re tethered to her very essence, and every time she feeds, those tethers are strengthening. I’m not even sure she can go into Dreamland right now to feed that way.”

“How long do we have?” Kellen demands.

“How long before we can figure out how to reverse what was done?” Reese shrugs again. “The more important question is how long Adie can last without replenishing her core.”

Tobias hugs me closer to his chest. “So, we’re just supposed to sit here and watch while she withers away?”

“I didn’t say that.” Reese spreads a hand over his chest. “*We* don’t have the knowledge, but Flint might. Souls are all he works with.”

Emil’s brows sweep together. “Who?”

“He’s part of the cleanup crew we used to scrub the mortuary,” Kellen supplies as he nods slowly. “I’ll contact him.”

“We already did.” Reese dips his hand into his

satchel and pulls out a piece of paper. He hesitates before extending it to Emil. "This is where they're located."

Emil takes the paper and unfolds it, skimming the contents. "This is in the historic district."

"He's expecting you at eight o'clock in the morning." Reese shuffles in the tub. "We won't stop researching, but bringing in someone with more knowledge will help."

"He better." Emil stuffs the paper into his pocket before he extends a hand to me. "Come, Ms. Pond."

I eye the snowflakes that glitter on his hand, then lift my gaze to meet his. "I don't think I should touch you right now."

His hand curls into a fist, and a tinge of red blooms in his cheeks.

My chest tightens, but I stay where I am on Tobias's lap. "You're too tempting right now, Frosty Pants, and I'm too empty to resist you."

His eyes shift from me to Tobias, and he gives a stiff nod. "I understand."

My heart aches as I watch him leave the room, taking his ice with him. I want to chase after him, to snuggle into his frozen embrace, but I can't. Not if I can't put my mouth on him and ease the chill of winter from his body. Unhappy with our current situation, my eyes drop to the cart I shoved into the bathroom to hold my stuff, and the nozzle of the blow dryer catches my attention.

Instantly, my mood lifts. I jump from Tobias's lap and snatch the blow dryer out of its bin. "Wait for me, Emil!"

"What am I?" Tobias grumbles. "Just a space heater?"

"Yes, exactly," I agree as I chase after my ice demon.

Kellen wisely steps out of my way, and I dart down the hall, waving the blow dryer in the air.

Emil, who paused next to the stairs, stares from me to the blow dryer and the stain in his cheeks spreads. "I don't think so, Ms. Pond."

"Oh, yes, you do." I shoo him back toward his room. "I am going to blow you so hard."

From behind me, Kellen coughs to hide a laugh.

Emil casts a glare his way before he turns stiffly and continues on into his bedroom.

I follow, my eyes sweeping over the room where I'd just spent a pleasure filled night with my men.

The fire still burns in the fireplace, and heavy quilts and fur blankets now cover the bed once more, the pillows neatly stacked at the top. Tobias had really wanted to see my wings, if the way he positioned my purple, sequined pillow at the front of the mound is any indication.

My chest tightens once more, but I push away the disappointment, refusing to believe we can't fix what Victor Hesse did to me before it's too late.

"Sit on the poof," I command as I search out the power strip next to Emil's bed.

"That's Tac's," he protests even as he circles around the bed to the giant white bean bag on the other side.

As if called, Tac bounds into the room and over the bed, landing with a heavy thud on the other side. As soon as Emil settles onto the poof, Tac plops his head down on the ice demon's lap, and a loud, chainsaw purr fills the room.

Grinning, I step up behind Emil and flick on the dryer. "Prepare for the best blow job of your life."

I spend the next hour alternating between warming Emil with the blow dryer and wafting it in Tac's face, earning the same contented purr from both creatures.

When the tiny motor begins to smell like it might catch fire, I have to quit.

After that, I leave the sleepy pair to return to my room and dress for the day. I'm surprised Kellen and Tobias didn't come back to the bedroom for their promised sleepover. But, maybe, they knew there would be no sleeping in Emil's room and retreated to their personal spaces. I don't blame them, though I selfishly want them with me. The knowledge I can't be with them the way I want makes me ache for their absences.

When I reach my room, I find I'm not alone. A large lump forms under my quilt, and by the rainbow sparkle anklet on one foot that pokes out the side, I guess my imps refused to be confined to the basement for the night.

Do they feel the tension and worry that permeates the house? It makes the air hard to breathe, like a guillotine ready to slam down.

On tiptoes, I walk to the window and push it up, then open the shutters. The sky outside looks velvety black, without a star in sight. The breeze that ruffles my hair holds the metallic tang of snow, which only adds to my worry. While I drained Tobias and Kellen of their power, I didn't do the same for Emil, and the coming winter storms will build his power higher.

If I can't drain his destructive energies, what will

that mean for my place in this house? It breaks our contract for me not to feed, but there's no way the guys will let me put my mouth on them, let alone other parts, if it means endangering me. If Flint can't fix me, I'll have to accept another succubus stepping in to fill my obligations.

The idea brings with it an immediate rush of possessive denial, and I drag in a deep, cold breath of air to cool the anger that boils in my blood.

As much as I want to tear apart anyone who comes near my demons of destruction, I need to put their safety above my selfish desires.

"That's some deep sighing you're doing, honey," Kellen whispers from the dark, and I choke back a shriek.

Heart pounding, I stare across the empty roof to his open window but don't spot him there.

A hand pokes up into view, waving for my attention, and I lean over the windowsill to find Kellen lying on the roof right under me. "What are you doing out there?"

He folds his arms under his head, his eyes on the night sky. "Watching the stars die."

I tip my head back once more to search the black canvas of night. "There aren't any stars."

"There are. You're just not looking hard enough."

He pats the roof next to him. "Put on something warm and join me."

I shiver as another cold breeze sweeps past me and tiptoe across the room to my dresser. It tilts to the side on its spindly legs, and I grab the top to keep it upright as I dig out a pair of fleece pajama bottoms and a sweater. I quickly trade out the bathrobe for the warmer clothes and tug on a pair of fluffy socks before returning to the window and climbing out.

My sock-covered feet slip on the roof tiles, and Kellen reaches out to help me balance as I slide down beside him.

He keeps hold of my hand as we lie down and stare up at the sky. "So, what were you thinking about so heavily?"

"About my contract," I admit.

He hums quietly under his breath but doesn't prod further.

I search the sky, seeing only darkness. "Where are the stars?"

"There." He lifts our joined hands to point off to the left, across the pointed roof of the turret opposite mine. "Keep watching."

I stare, eyes wide, until the clouds move, and stars shine through. It's only a brief glimpse before the clouds shift to once more block them from view, but my heart lifts at the break in darkness. "They're beautiful."

"Yeah." When I turn to look at him, I find his eyes on me instead of the sky, and my eyes sting with unexpected tears. Then, my lower lip trembles, and I catch it between my teeth to stop the sob that pushes up my throat from escaping.

Silently, he pulls me against his side, tucking my face into the curve of his throat. The usual static spark is missing, reminding me of how well he fed me earlier, and a sob breaks free. What if that was the last time I got to touch him? I should have spent more time making sure I pleased him instead of taking all the pleasure for myself.

Kellen strokes my hair, his lips a soft press against the top of my head. "Don't worry, honey, it's dark now, but we'll find a way through this."

I nod, desperate to grasp onto his hope when I can't find any of my own. After everything we've faced together, this can't be the way we end.

ZOMBIE MAN

Early the next morning, Tobias drives me out to meet with Flint. He had to wrest the information from Emil and force the other man to go into the office. Emil had wanted to come with us, but with the way he ignites the hunger inside me every time he nears, we all agreed it was better we maintain our distance until we find out how bad things are with me.

Boutique stores and low, brick buildings fill the historic district of town. Tobias pulls up to the curb in front of a squat, single-story building and cuts the engine. I press my nose to the window and stare at the glowing crystal ball in the window and the neon sign above that announces accurate fortune-telling.

This can't possibly be the right place.

I twist to stare back at Tobias. "Are you sure Emil didn't give you the wrong address?"

"There's no reason he would have this address

otherwise. Stay there." He pushes open his door and climbs out of the low seat, slamming the door behind him. I watch through the windshield as he strides around the nose of the sports car and stops next to my door to open it and offer me a hand out.

The care he's been showing me in the last twenty-four hours worries me more than the vomiting does. My blunt, domineering demon doesn't show his softer side easily, but he's now treating me with the same gentle touch he does when he's repairing something his catalyst energy broke.

I'd found the towel bar attached back to the wall when I showered this morning, hurrying through my usual routine. I tried not to touch the bottom of the tub as much as possible, because I couldn't stop thinking about the black slime that had filled it hours earlier.

I'm actually looking forward to Emil demolishing the small space. We've put that bathroom through a lot of hardships over the last few months. Replacing it with something new will help wipe away all the bad memories that linger there.

Tobias keeps hold of my hand as we walk to the front door of the fortune-teller, and he pulls me back a step to use his body as a barrier before he opens the door. The sound of some new-age music full of flutes and Celtic singing drifts out, along with a cloud of incense.

I sneeze, my eyes already watering from the potent smell, and hold a hand over my nose before we step inside.

"Welcome, welcome," a breathy voice calls in a fake Russian accent, and I search the dimly-lit front room for the source.

A woman with a red, silk headscarf stands behind a counter. She wears a lacy, black shawl around her shoulders and a peasant blouse that reveals a deep valley of cleavage that puts my own to shame.

Smoke drifts from the copper bowl at her elbow, filling the room with musk and something deeper that tickles my nose. I sneeze again, then again, and even Tobias coughs.

She watches us with bright, alert eyes, her hands suspiciously out of view under the counter as she smiles at us, revealing a bright flash of white teeth. "Are you here to have your fortune told? We promise one-hundred-percent accuracy, and you get the tenth one free."

“No.” Tobias waves a hand in front of his face. “We have an appointment with Flint.”

“Oh, crap.” Her fake accent vanishes, and she quickly slaps a copper, cone lid over the incense bowl. “He didn’t say you were demons. Sorry about that.”

She flips a switch on the wall, and fans buzz to life overhead, sucking up the nasty smoke.

“He was probably expecting Reese.” I sneeze again and wipe my drippy nose on the sleeve of Tobias’s jacket.

“We can’t be too safe.” She hurries around the counter and past us to lock the door and turn off the neon sign. “With the business we’re in, we’ve had more than one demon come here looking for retaliation.”

“Aren’t you guys cleaners?” I wipe my eyes again, trying to dig the smoke out from under my eyelids.

“Yeah. But not just for your kind.” She hurries back past us, her heels a quick *tap, tap, tap* over the laminate floor. “You would *not* believe how many séances actually weaken the barrier and allow big nasties through. Have you ever seen a sorority party after a boogeyman decimated it?”

“Nope.” I shudder. “And I never want to.”

Boogeymen are the generic catchall for some

nasty demons who feed on fear. They range from the slow, creepy stalkers of old horror movies to demons who harvest the organs of their victims, like Jack the Ripper. While easy to kill, they first have to be caught. Since so many different demons fall under the generic category, it's hard to know which one you're up against until you come face to face with it. By then, it's too late.

"Follow me." The woman waves her hand and disappears behind the beaded curtain, leaving Tobias and me to trail after.

The beads click and clack together, creating enough racket that I assume it's a safety measure and not just there for aesthetics. If something got past the woman at the front, the clatter of the beads would warn the people on the other side of intruders.

A long, narrow hallway without doors leads to the back, another safety measure, I'm sure. This kind of tunnel would be easy to defend, so long as the monster who came knocking didn't just punch through the walls on either side. Curious, I reach out and poke a talon against the drywall. It indents a quarter-inch before coming up against reinforced metal.

I glance up at the ceiling, noticing the line of

sprinklers that fill the hall. Way more sprinkler heads than the local fire code requires.

Shivering, I prod Tobias to walk faster. No way do I want to be mistaken for an intruder and get caught in this death tunnel.

At the end of the hall, the woman presses a button on the wall, and a moment later, the thick steel door that blocks our way swings inward to reveal a brightly-lit office space beyond.

Now, *this* is what I expected the Cleaner's office to look like. Low pile, beige carpet with a slightly darker-brown swirl pattern. Beige walls with open office doors that lead into smaller rooms set up with desks. Bright lighting, but not too harsh, and the clean smell of lemon cleaner.

Another desk sits in the middle of the room with chairs in front of it, but it's empty. Our host leads us past it to an office at the back.

She stops in the doorway and knocks on the frame. "Flint, your clients are here."

"Thank you, Meredith," Flint murmurs from within, and a moment later, he appears in the doorway. He spots us and grins. "Come on in."

My pulse quickens as we walk past Meredith and into the office. It's a normal enough space with a desk, low filing cabinet against the wall, and two cushioned chairs. No obvious signs of dead people.

The click of the door shutting makes me jump, and Tobias places a steadying hand on my shoulder, reminding me I'm not alone with the zombie man.

Flint stands from behind his desk, an easy smile on his too-pretty face. His beauty catches me off guard, even though I expected it, and my pulse leaps for a different reason before I remind myself it's just a glamour he wears.

Tobias nudges me toward one of the chairs as Flint perches on the edge of his desk and clasps his hands together.

His blue eyes bounce between us as we sit. "So, I hear you're in a bit of a pickle again. How can I help?"

It feels all sorts of wrong to be coming to a witch for help, even one who only deals in one type of magic. While I'm totally comfortable with Kellen's witches, there's always the knowledge that they belong to my storm demon and are therefore leashed. I'm sure they would chafe at that label, but it is what it is. So long as they're locked into Kellen's contract, they can't act against us.

Flint has no such restrictions, and for all I know, he

can rip our energy cores right out of our bodies and stuff them into one of his handy magic bottles. Is that where the legend of genies comes from? Witches stealing demon cores and leashing them to do their bidding?

My pulse pounds harder, and I clutch the armrests as my talons lengthen.

Flint's smile drops and he eyes me warily. "Don't worry, I don't have any zombies active right now."

I grit my teeth. "I'm not afraid of you."

"Okay." From his expression, he doesn't buy my protest, which is fine since I'm not at all convincing with my death grip on the chair.

Tobias's hot hand lands on my knee, warmth seeping into me, as he faces the other man. "How much did Reese tell you?"

"He said something about more of that nasty, black slime and blood magic?" His voice lifts at the end, turning the statement into a question. "But didn't you guys take care of that nastiness?"

"This is the sequel," I grit out, willing my racing heart to calm down.

We're here because Flint might be able to help us, I remind myself. *He's not going to strip my core from my body.*

"Okay," Flint says slowly as he leaves his perch and circles around his desk to take his seat, putting some distance between us in the process. "Tell me what's going on."

He jots down notes as Tobias and I take turns talking, explaining about Victor Hesse's escape, his ability to elude the high council's guards, and what happened when he captured me.

Flint interrupts occasionally to ask for clarification, what the scalpel looked like, how many jars there were, how long I held onto the energy before I threw it up.

He pulls out a calendar from his desk drawer and makes more notes, the scratch of his pen on paper continuing long after we fall silent.

At last, he sets his pen aside and looks up. "Well, you're screwed."

Taken off guard by his response, I blink rapidly. "Excuse me?"

He folds his hands over his desk. "The way I see it, you have limited options, and none of them are great. One"—he holds up a finger—"you find and destroy him. But, as you said, he's been eluding your council's guards for weeks now, so I'm sure he can hide until his spell completes. Two"—up pops a second finger—"You correct the spells he carved into your body and hope to god it doesn't kill you."

My stomach sinks. “Is there a way to at least slow it while we try to find a third solution?”

He nods slowly, reaches into his desk, then thunks a green clay bottle into the center of the desk. “I rip out your core and stuff it in here.”

The Price of a Life

"Fuck!" I'm out of the chair and halfway to the door before Tobias catches me, and I slap at the strong arms he wraps around my waist. "No! I don't want to go into the bottle! I don't want to become a genie!"

"What the hell are you talking about?" Tobias demands as he swings me around and tries to cram me back into my chair. "That's not happening today, and genies are a myth."

Hands clutching the sides of the chair in a death grip, I stiffen my arms and kick at him, my ass nowhere near that cushion of doom. "Don't think I didn't hear you say *today*! That means it's an option for the future!"

"For the love of—" Tobias dodges my next kick, shakes me free from the chair, and plops down in my place with me firmly on his lap. "Will you calm down? You're not going into the bottle."

I wiggle and bounce hard, aiming for his sensitive bits, but he retaliates by kneeing me hard in the thighs.

"You're making demons look bad, right now," he growls, his body heating under mine.

"I don't care!" I wail up at the ceiling. "You can't make me go into the bottle! I want to go home and make cupcakes!"

"We'll do that in a few minutes." With one arm banded around me to trap both of mine, he none-too-gently strokes my hair, messing up my braid. "Just calm down so we can hear what else Flint has to say."

"I don't like you right now," I grumble as he smooths my hair backward, and I feel the bumps of hair rise on top of my head. "Stop petting me. You're a horrible petter."

"I'm an excellent petter," he counters, then strokes my hair backward some more to prove it until my long bangs pull free to cover my face. "There, there."

Disgruntled, I blow the hair away from my mouth. "I'm so glad we flushed our slime baby down the drain."

He ignores that and drops his hand to my thigh.

"Are you ready to be an adult and listen to what else Flint can tell us?"

"There's not a lot more to say, actually," Flint says, and I blow more hair from my face to find him watching us in bemusement. "Spells are tricky things, and poorly crafted ones even worse. It could be that laying another spell on top of the current one could counteract it, but it's just as dangerous as correcting the current spell." His brows pinch together for a moment as he thinks. "If there was a way to change it though..."

I straighten with interest. "Change it how?"

"I'd need to see the full working to say for sure. The biggest issue is that it's powered by energy, and you said that the new energy you take in strengthens it?" He waits for my nod before he continues. "So, we need to somehow cut off that energy before attempting to change the spell."

"Okay, here, you can look." I reach for the hem of my shirt, only to have Tobias clamp his hand around my wrist to stop me. I twist to glare at him. "What is up with your issues in me getting naked?"

His thick eyebrows dive into a frown. "What is up with how eager you are to strip in front of people?"

I glare at him. "I've got a nice body. I'm not ashamed of it."

"Yes, you have a *very* nice body, designed to tempt people." He pushes my hand back into my lap. "You don't need to be tempting people. This body belongs to us."

"Oh, you want to talk about belonging?" I begin, but Flint clears his throat loudly.

We both turn to look at him, and he raises his hand. "You don't need to strip. I can't see the spells anyway. Not unless I pull your energy core out of your body."

"Hell, no!" I try to leap off Tobias's lap, but his firm hold keeps me in place.

"Reese and Xander have plenty of sketches of the marks," Tobias informs him. "They are at your disposal until this is fixed. If you need a big power boost, Jax and Slater are also available."

"That will be helpful." Flint makes a couple more notes, then spins in his chair to open one of the filing cabinet drawers. He spins back around and slaps a thick contract onto the desk. "I'll just need some blood signatures that you won't seek vengeance should things not go well. I will, in turn, agree to make every effort possible to free Adie of this spell. I'll also need half of my fee upfront, nonrefundable."

Tobias leans forward to grab the contract, and we settle back to read through it together. I'm impressed by the tidiness of it and can't find a single loophole. Tobias must feel the same if the rumble of approval that comes from him is any indication.

Then he flips to the last page and the cost of Flint's help makes my jaw drop in shock before my eyes jerk up to his. "You can't be serious."

His brows lift. "I'm agreeing to put every resource I hold into this job, up to and including my life if need be. It's a small sum by that measure."

I look back at the price and reluctantly agree.

Tobias leaves the contract open to the last page and sets it back on the desk. "Do you take wire transfers?"

"I do." Flint, fully prepared, snaps a card onto the desk with a string of numbers on it.

Tobias pulls out his phone and types them in, transferring the small fortune with the same calm acceptance he'd use to tip his barista. Or even calmer, since he's never once tipped me when he's come to the bakery.

"What?" he demands when he catches me glaring at him.

"You should tip me."

He gives me a wicked smile. "I'll tip you as much as you want once this is over."

I poke him in the chest. "I mean with money. At the bakery."

"No. You already charge too much for a coffee." He tucks his phone away and looks back at Flint. "Do you have something to sign with? Or should we just open a vein ourselves?"

"Best to use the pen. Meredith's always complaining about bloodstains." Flint slides a slender wooden box across the desk and Tobias and I use the needle-sharp fountain pen to draw blood and sign our names at the bottom.

Flint follows suit, scrawling his name under ours in a shining streak of red. "I'll have a copy filed with the Demon Clerk's Office within the hour."

My brows lift at that, but I hold back my curiosity. I don't need to know how a mutilated soul witch has access to the Demon Clerk's Office. I'm just glad to know the contract will be enforced properly.

Flint checks his phone and nods. "We're all set. I'll contact your witches to make arrangements." Then, he looks up to meet my eyes. "You should take the bottle with you. Get used to how it feels, just in case."

I eye the thing with apprehension. "No, I'm good."

"You sure?" When he nudges it across the desk, I shove back against Tobias to keep as much distance between me and it as possible. Flint shrugs. "Okay, just a thought. I've been told it's not a bad existence."

"Yeah, by spirits who don't have real bodies, I'm sure." I turn my nose up. "No, thank you."

"You might not have a real body for long, either," he points out with little sympathy, his pretty face not softening the blow at all. "If it's a choice between a bottle and extinction, you may change your mind."

A shiver runs through me, and I wiggle again, antsy to be gone from here and the creepy-ass zombie man who so casually talks about my imminent demise. "Can we go now?"

"Yeah." Tobias releases me, and I bolt for the door, only pausing long enough to look back and make sure he's following. Instead, I see him tucking the bottle into his pocket as he stands in front of Flint's desk. "You have Reese's contact information?"

Flint nods. "I do."

"Whatever you need, you will have." Tobias glances back at me. "Just fix her."

My chest tightens at the vulnerable expression on his face.

"I'll do what I can." Flint rises and walks around his desk, motioning Tobias ahead of him. "If there's a solution, we'll find it."

The knowledge there might not be a solution hangs in the air unspoken, and I dart out of the room, eager to escape this nightmarish place.

Courtship

Hunger pulls at my belly as we drive back to the house, neither of us speaking. There's really nothing to be said for now. We'll either fix me or we won't, and there's nothing we can do but wait for word from the witches.

When we arrive home, Tobias walks me inside, then leaves once more at my urging. He has a business to run, and him hanging around, tempting me even with his low energy levels, won't help.

As soon as he leaves, I kick the imps out of my bed. We need to head into the bakery soon, and the five of them take a while to run through their showers, even when we utilize both bathrooms. If I didn't plan to send them back to their own house this weekend, I'd have a serious talk with Emil about remodeling the basement.

With Victor Hesse still on the loose, the idea of them leaving makes me uneasy, but I don't think he's interested in my imps. No, he wants to torment me for whatever grand scheme he has yet to reveal.

While they get ready for work, I wander into the kitchen, pulling ingredients from the fridge to fill a muffin basket for Fuyumi. The familiar process helps to calm my nerves and ease the hungry beast that claws at my spine. This isn't the first time I've been starved for energy, and I now pat myself on the back for all that training I did in how to go hungry. Feeding frenzy or no feeding frenzy, this succubus knows how to practice self-denial.

By the time everyone's ready, and Jesse drops the muffin basket off at Fuyumi's door, I feel as peaceful as I can with everything that's going on.

Returning to my normal life comes with a sense of surrealness as we all tromp into the bakery, and I breathe in the scent of sugar and butter that permeates the air. Yesterday, life had been looking good, my relationships and business were on a path to success, and I'd been happy.

Today, that all feels like the distant past. Funny how being tortured and cursed can make everything change.

Tally arrives at ten o'clock on the dot, even

though she wasn't scheduled to come in until the late afternoon to cover closing.

She swoops over to my side, pulling me into her arms. "Adie, I feared the worst when you vanished. Xander refused to tell me anything except that you were sick."

Guilt spikes through me that I hadn't called and talked to my friend myself. But with everything else going on, there hadn't seemed to be *time*. I pat her as best I can with my feet dangling off the ground and my arms trapped at my sides. "I'm okay."

Tally sets me back on my feet only to press a palm to my forehead. "How do you feel? Still sick?"

"No," I say, a little surprised to realize it's true. In all the feeding and vomiting, I had forgotten about my fever. "No, whatever caused that passed."

Or the spell finished settling into my core, though I don't say that part out loud. No reason to worry Tally even more.

"If you start to feel unwell, again, let me know." She pulls me into another hug. "I will cover as many shifts as you need me to."

Warmth spreads through me, and I return her hug. "I appreciate that. You do so much for the bakery and me already."

"That's what friends are for." With a last squeeze,

she releases me and claps her hands together. "Okay, enough doom and gloom. What's on our menu for today?"

I smile at her enthusiasm, and a bit more of my worry eases away. It's hard to focus on a nebulous threat of extinction when there are cupcakes to discuss.

Over the next few hours, we prep for the bakery to open and welcome our first lunchtime flood of clients, every step forward puts more and more distance between me and the horrors of the last twenty-four hours.

Late in the day, I retreat to my office to go over lists of inventory and make plans for the holiday rush.

Through my open door, movement catches my eye, and I glance up to watch Sophia strut into the employee breakroom for her evening shift. I can't help but smile at her glittery stockings and the jaunty chef's hat perched askew on her head. My smile widens when Jesse chases after her into the breakroom to smack her with a spoon.

But when they devolve into arguing, it pulls me from my office.

"Stop it, you tiny monster!" Sophia lunges at

Jesse, grabbing for her spoon, which earns her a smack on the knuckles for her effort. Sophia jerks her hand up to her mouth, and her large green eyes seek me out. "This is employee abuse."

"I have to agree." I point at Jesse. "No more, or I'll take your spoons away."

Jesse turns her nose up. "You won't find them all."

"Get back to the decorating station before I move you to mixing," I threaten, and the tiny imp scurries back down the stairs.

Sophia sucks on her abused knuckles. "Why does she have it out for me?"

I arch my brow at my cousin. "Because you were rude to her when you first started?"

"But that was *forever* ago," Sophia whines and pats herself on her ample breasts. "I'm a changed succubus!"

"You are, which is probably why Jesse still smacks you." At her confused look, I shake my head. "Jesse *likes* you."

"What?" Her perfect cupid's bow mouth pops open in shock. "You mean capital *Like*?"

"More like how grade-schoolers like people by chasing them around and picking on them." I motion for her to come into my office and sit back behind my desk.

Still looking flustered, Sophia sits across from me. “I don’t know... No one has ever *Liked* me before. We haven’t even had *sex*.”

I glare at her. “No sucking Jesse’s energy.”

“I just don’t know what to do with this information.” She reaches up to pat her small chef’s hat, and pink tints her cheeks. “Should I take her out to the movies or something?”

“I think you might get hit for suggesting it,” I say drily. “I think this is a first for both of you, and Jesse’s not handling it well.”

“Well.” Sophia blinks rapidly, clearly unsure how to process this information, then her gaze fixes on me. “Have you heard from Landon lately?”

I reel from the subject change and shake my head. “No, he’s M.I.A. I tried going to the Library, but it’s locked. Why?”

“No reason.” Sophia bites her plump lower lip, then releases it with a pop. “There’s word Cousin Cassandra is sniffing at his border again. I think his absence has been noticed.”

We share a troubled moment of silence before footsteps in the outer room draw my attention to the door.

A moment later, Tally appears carrying a large bouquet of red roses. Excitement sparkles in her mahogany-colored eyes as she sets them on my desk. "Someone has an admirer!"

"Oh, pretty." Sophia stands to come closer and strokes one of the deep violet blooms. "Which one do you think it's from?"

I smile as I stare at the beautiful arrangement. The guys aren't usually the type to send me flowers. They don't really waste effort on human gestures of courtship. But with everything going on, maybe this is their way of trying to brighten my mood.

"Oh, there's a card." Sophia plucks a small, white envelope from within the stems.

I snatch it from her before she can open it. "Mine!"

Wiggling with excitement, I stroke the edges, drawing out the reveal. What words will I find inside? Pretty words from Emil? Something teasing with loads of innuendoes from Kellen? A blunt command to be safe from Tobias?

Tally claps with impatience. "Just open it!"

Sophia joins in. "Open, open, open!"

"Geez, you guys have zero patience." Just as eager to see what waits inside, I tear open the flap, and my blood runs cold.

Something must show on my face, because Tally and Sophia still, before Tally demands, "What is it?"

Slowly, I tip the envelope out over my open hand, and the crushed remains of a blue butterfly tumbles out.

Under Pressure

Sophia gasps, while Tally wrinkles her nose. "Why would someone send you a dead butterfly?"

My fingers slowly close around the crumpled body. "It's a threat." My throat tightens. "Or possibly gloating."

Tally frowns in confusion. "About what, though?"

"Landregath," Sophia whispers, her eyes wide with shock. "But… he's with the Librarian, right? No one could get to him there."

"Unless he's not." I carefully slip the butterfly back into the envelope. "When I went there, the Library was locked. And the hag hasn't responded to my calls."

Sophia shakes her head. "He's too powerful. Even Cousin Cassandra couldn't—"

"We don't know that," I cut her off, my tone

sharp. "Victor Hesse is using magic we have no clue about. I need to go to his house and check."

But I stay planted where I stand, the memory of what happened the last time I went off on my own like a sharp knife against my throat, warning me to stay put.

"I can go," Sophia offers. "No one cares about me. I'll be fine."

"That's not true," I protest. "I care. Jesse cares."

She gives me a rueful smile. "You're kind, but I know where I stand in the line of what's important."

My lips part, but I can't bring myself to speak the lie. She's right. If it was a choice between her and any number of other people, she would lose. But that doesn't mean I don't care what happens to her.

Tally shakes her head. "No one should go alone, no matter who they are." She shrugs out of her chef's coat. "I'll go, too. No one can hurt me. Not on this plane, anyway."

My heart swells at how ready they are to do this for me, and I shrug out of my own chef's coat, draping it over the back of my chair. "I'll call Emil on the way. You can drop me off at the high school portal so I can check the Library, in case he's still there. Emil, or one of the others, will meet me there so I'm not alone."

"Martha can handle the bakery. I'll tell her what's going on and have one of them call to find out where these flowers came from." With a decisive nod, Tally strides from the room.

I meet Sophia's concerned green eyes. "Thank you."

She pulls the small hat from her hair and sets it on my desk. "I'm not doing it for you. If Landregath falls, there's no one to stand between us and Cassandra. You weren't alive when she came into her power, but she destroyed many of us in her path to be the strongest. Landregath could only stop her from continuing her warpath in his territory, he couldn't destroy her completely. It's why so many of our kind live here. We hide in his shadow and hope it never fades."

My stomach turns. "I didn't know."

"You weren't supposed to know." She shrugs. "He wanted to raise you without the fear we've all felt. It was his gift to you."

I look away, ashamed for all the times I thought of him as a bad mentor. He tried his best to give me the life I wanted, and while he didn't always go about it in the best way, he meant well. If something happened to him because of me, I'll never forgive myself.

"We'll stay here until you go inside," Sophia says as I climb out of the back of her car. "Are you sure we shouldn't stay until Emil arrives?"

I had called him on our way to the high school, and he promised to meet me in front of the Library. I shake my head. "It's safer for me inside. Victor Hesse won't dare set foot within the demon plane. The council would know right away."

"Okay." Sophia bites her lip as if she wants to say more but stays quiet.

Tally leans past her, her gaze solemn. "We will call as soon as we reach his house."

"Thank you." I back away from the car, turn, then run across the short swath of grass that separates the parking lot from the small ticket booth that sits beside the football field.

Yanking open the door to the booth, I step inside. Sparklers prick my skin as the portal recognizes me as a demon and allows me to pass through.

Asphalt transforms into hard marble, the quiet of a school in session giving way to the low rumble of many voices speaking at once.

I bypass the ever-busy Demon Clerk's Office, my eyes on the hallway that leads to the Library.

Like every time I've visited before, the tall double-doors stand closed against casual visitors. I pull my library card from my wallet, stuffing it under the card reader attached to the wall.

When the light stays red, anger spikes through me. This is *not* the time for the Librarian to ignore my presence.

Stuffing my card back into my pocket, I march up to the double-doors and slam a fist against it. "Hag! Open up!"

My shout goes unanswered, the doors standing firm against me, and my anger grows. I slam my fist against the door again, then again, my anger growing with every passing minute that the doors remain barred against me.

"What is this ruckus?" a masculine voice demands, and power slams down on me. "What brings you here, again, little succubus, to abuse the sacred doors of the Library?"

My knees tremble with the effort not to fold, and I turn to glare at Lord Marius. "I've had enough of the hag ignoring her duty."

His brows lift. "And what duty is that?"

"To provide knowledge to those who seek it." I turn back and slam my foot against the door.

"Perhaps this means there is no knowledge for you to find here?" He suggests as he walks closer, every footfall pushing his power down on my shoulders, demanding that I bend.

"There is *always* knowledge to be had," I growl as my fingernails lengthen into talons. "And my current knowledge is that the hag is a fucking bitch!"

As I slam my hand forward, hard fingers lock around my wrist. I twist to meet Lord Marius's angry gaze. "You would defile the Library?"

"The hag is defiling it right now," I hiss. "What's a little more?"

"It is not for you to judge the Library's chosen avatar." His power pushes down on me harder. "You need a lesson in your place."

"Lesson?" My knees pop as I force myself straight once more. "All you old demons, constantly throwing your power around. Do you get off on scaring the younger and weaker demons? Does it make you happy to see others cower before you?"

Lord Marius's eyes widen in shock. "Excuse me?"

"You think, because you're the big bad of the demon plane, that you get to walk all over everyone else?" I snarl, all of my hurt, anger, and confusion finding a focus on the man in front of me. "You think, because I'm new, that you can just push me around?" I take a painful step forward, my eyes narrowed on him. "You think you can put me in my place? On the floor, at your feet?"

His gaze hardens. "Adeline Boo Pond, you will show respect—"

"Why? What have you done to earn it?" His power shoves at my skin, demanding I submit. But Lord Marius seems to have forgotten one little thing. "You shouldn't shove so much power at a succubus, Lord Marius." My lips peel away from my teeth. "You're just begging to be consumed."

"You wouldn't dare." His words roll through me like fire, but I'm not scared of fire. "This is a neutral zone."

"And you are *attacking* me." I let go of the part of myself that locks out unwanted energy, and my pores open, the power around me flooding my system, bringing with it a sense of elation.

He rears back in shock. "You'll destroy yourself to make a point?"

"I've destroyed myself hundreds of times before," I hiss as my bones break apart into cinders and reform in the same heartbeat. My blood boils and my flesh chars, only for new cells to take their place. "What makes you think I can't survive you when I have survived far more than you can ever hold?"

"Adie, stop!" Emil's voice comes from behind Lord Marius, and my ice demon steps around him, his arms spread wide. "You can't attack a high council member."

"I'm only defending." I lift a hand, watching Lord Marius's energy roll through my skin before I look at the demon once more. "You call this power?"

Turning, I slam my hand against the doors to the Library, releasing the full weight of what I hold. The shock wave ruptures my eardrums and blows my hair back from my face, but the doors stay firmly closed.

I sag against them, exhaustion taking hold. "This isn't real power. This can't even open a door."

Icy hands cup my shoulders to pull me back, and Emil's voice sounds muffled as my eardrums knit themselves back together. "We need to leave. You've drawn too much attention."

"Why is the Librarian ignoring me?" I whimper, my eyes focused on the door. "I need to know he's okay."

"We'll figure out a different way," Emil soothes as he turns us around, one arm slipping around my shoulders to hold me close to his side. “Come on, I’ll take you home.”

I nod wearily before my eyes land on Lord Marius. He still stands in the hall, his attention shifting between me and the doors to the Library. He looks worried now, and a little afraid, but not of me.

When his gaze shifts to me, I hiss, but not with the same level of anger I felt before. Now, I just feel tired and worried again. And helpless. So much helplessness.

Without another word to either of us, Lord Marius spins on his heel and storms away, off to do important council business, I’m sure.

Emil keeps us walking, and when we enter the main hall, he places his body between me and the demons gathered outside the Demon Clerk’s Office. Low murmurs fill the hall, and I catch a few whispers filled with reverence about a demon of destruction being here. I ignore them, more focused on the nausea building in my stomach. I let all of Lord Marius’s power go, but some of it must have lingered, my body using it to repair itself. The need to vomit it back up tickles at my throat, but I fight it down, unwilling to spew black slime where everyone can see.

We make it out to the football field, and shadows now lay over the parking lot, the expanse of asphalt empty except for the beat-up sports car I bought for Tobias. That feels like a lifetime ago. Emil opens the passenger side door, and I practically fall into the seat as a wave of heat sweeps through me.

My hand lifts to cover my mouth. "I think I'm going to puke."

Emil curses and pulls a plastic bag from the back seat, shoving it at me.

As my stomach heaves, I hold it to my mouth, and the sound of thick, wet splatters fill the car.

When I lower the bag, Emil wipes my face with a wet cloth. "Feel better?"

"No," I groan as I twist the bag to hold the slithering slime inside. "But I don't feel like I'm going to puke anymore."

"That was a stupid thing to do," he admonishes. "Lord Marius isn't a demon you want to cross."

"I know." And I do, though I can't find it within myself to care at the moment. "But he was trying to push me around, and I just couldn't handle it."

Emil refolds the wet wipe and dabs at my chin, then throws the wipe into another plastic bag. "Let's get home and dispose of that."

The bag wiggles in my lap, and I nod. "Yeah, definitely not keeping *this* slime baby."

He eyes the rolling mass. "If you can power the spell, we should keep the bathtub. It can prove useful in the future."

My brows pinch together. "I thought you wanted to remodel the bathroom?"

"Yes." He straightens. "We can move the tub to the basement. I'd never throw away an antique."

"Hoarder!" I yell as he closes the door, but I secretly agree.

A magic-destroying bathtub is a good weapon to keep around.

The Beast

The next two days pass without word from the witches or Flint.

Sophia and Tally had arrived at Landon's house to find his butterfly garden decimated, but no sign that Landon had returned. The destruction of the garden he'd spent so much time cultivating makes me sad, but I'm glad he wasn't there when Victor Hesse tried to track him down.

No one had been able to track down where the flowers came from, either. The company on the delivery box doesn't exist, and no one around here sells purple roses this long after Halloween.

While I wait, I grow more and more anxious about my future, which only increases my restlessness. Since I can't touch the guys, and being too close makes me hungry, I throw myself into baking instead, both at the bakery and at home.

Even Fuyumi can't keep up with all the treats I drop at her door.

On Friday, I pull the plug on the party I planned. It just feels like a bad time to gather people together. I can promote Tally and Martha without a party, and we can celebrate later, once everything settles.

If it settles.

Five minutes after I hit the cancel button, my phone rings. I pick it up. "Boo's Boutique Bakery, where one bite is never enough. How may I treat you today?"

"I didn't give you back your evite password so you could go around getting people's hopes up about parties only to cancel them," Julian drawls from the other end.

Warmth fills me at his familiar voice, and I lean back in my chair. "Now's not a good time. I'll reschedule soon."

"When is it not a good time to party, darling?" The chitters in the background cut off with the sound of a door closing. "What has you down?"

"Who said I'm down?" I force cheer into my voice. "No downness over here."

"That might fool one of your delicious demons of destruction, but I'm an incubus, so don't even try it with me." Rustles fill the line, and I picture him flipping through paperwork. "Tell me what's going on."

Uncertain, I bite my lip. My first urge is to unload the whole sad tale on Julian, but after everything he's been dragged through lately, I don't want to pull him into yet another of my messes.

A long sigh fills the line. "Is this about what has the goons stacking up outside?"

"Stacking up?" Alarmed, I rise and walk to the window to peek through the blinds.

Sure enough, in addition to my usual hulking guard, I spy two more. One stands farther down the street while another stands just outside the bakery.

Ugh, why can't they at least *try* to blend in? I'm surprised no one has called the cops on them yet.

Julian's voice turns sharp. "Has Victor Hesse made a move?" When my silence grows, he curses loudly. "I'm on my way over."

"No, don't come!" I yell before he can hang up. "There's nothing going on at the bakery for you to dash over for."

"Tell me what's going on," he commands.

"I can't reach Landon," I offer by way of explanation. It's one of the many issues on my plate, and the only one I feel okay divulging right now.

Some of the tension drains from his voice. "Did you try going to the Library?"

"It's locked, and the hag's ignoring me." My stomach tightens as I remember the crushed butterfly. "Is everything okay where you are? You haven't seen any signs of Victor Hesse?"

"No, but these damn guards stalk my every step," he growls. "One tried to station himself inside the office, but I drove him out."

Worry for him grows. I'm not the only one who thwarted Victor Hesse's plans. "Don't go anywhere alone, okay?"

"I never do, darling." He sighs again. "I'm going to stop by next week, okay? I expect free cupcakes."

"I'll give you a fifty percent discount," I hedge.

"Deal." Silence fills the line, before he ventures, "So, how's Kellen doing? Need some help offloading that storm?"

"Goodbye, Julian!" I yell and hang up the phone. My hand lingers on it, though, and after a moment, I dial the main line for HelloHell Delivery.

A familiar voice picks up the line. "HelloHell Delivery, Philip speaking."

"Phillip," I whisper. "It's Adie."

"And how is the most delicious su—"

"Stop," I command, still not ready to banter

with him after his betrayal when he told Julian to sell me out.

His playful tone turns businesslike. “How may I service you today?”

“Don’t let Julian go out alone. No making deliveries alone, no driving home alone, no taking a shit alone. Do you understand?”

“I hear you, though I’m not sure I get the reasoning.”

“I don’t trust those guards outside to protect him.” I glare at the guards who failed to protect me. “If something happens to him and it’s because you weren’t there to step in the way, I will personally make it my mission to ensure you regret it.”

Amusement fills his voice. “Oh, yeah?”

“Yeah,” I answer, completely serious. “I won’t behead you, Phillip. I will take you apart in pieces. I will eat you by inches until your corporeal form is on the verge of disintegration, then I will lock up what’s left of you for eternity. Do you understand?”

Hurt fills his voice. “I thought we were friends.”

“We’re not.” I let the blinds close. “Keep Julian safe.”

Pulse pounding, I hang up. I can still feel the guards just outside my small slice of territory, and their presence pricks against my skin, building my anger. They've been stalking my every step for weeks, but when it mattered, they were nowhere to be found. What good are they, if Victor Hesse can get to us right under their noses?

The beast inside me blinks its eyes open, hunger rumbling through my bones. It wants to consume, to destroy. It wants to rip and tear and devour. It reminds me of the ouroboros I melded with to kill the Dreamer, but harder and more blood-thirsty. It doesn't want to create from consuming, it just wants to destroy.

Red bleeds into my vision, and my nails lengthen into talons that cut through the wooden windowsill. This doesn't *feel* like a feeding frenzy, no matter what the guys think. I'm not filled with the mind fuzzing need to find pleasure and glut on the power it can give. This feels darker, a visceral desire to split flesh and spill blood. It sinks hooks into me, trying to drag me into a dark abyss.

Taking in Lord Marius's power had given me a heady feeling of rightness. Not because I wanted to become more powerful myself, but because it weakened him, proving he was prey and I was hunter.

"Master?" A quiet rap on the doorframe accompanies Iris's voice. "You have visitors."

I dig my talons into the wooden sill. "I'll come down."

"It's better to speak up here, Adie," Xander says, and I turn my head just far enough to see the slender, dark-haired witch from the corner of my eye.

Iris steps away, a blur of rainbow and glitter in my periphery before she vanishes completely.

I turn back to the window, staring at the closed blinds. "I'm not sure you should be alone with me right now. I'm not fully here."

"I'm not alone." Two pairs of footsteps enter the office, followed by the sound of the door closing.

I turn to find Flint a step behind Xander, his overwhelming beauty making my mouth water. Knowing it's a glamour just makes it worse, because it means there's power there for me to take.

Xander stops in front of my desk. "We've been working non-stop on this, and I think we might be able to buy some more time while we fix this."

My eyes narrow on Flint. "I'm not going into one of his bottles."

In response, he winks at me.

Xander glares at the soul witch, too. "We're not suggesting that."

"Not yet," Flint revises, then shrugs when we

both scowl at him. "It's a last resort, but still a resort."

Xander shakes his head and shifts everything on my desk to the side to make room for him to lay out the sketches Reese made of my curse. Because that's what Victor Hesse did. He cursed me, stealing my ability to feed from my men, to sleep next to them, or even be around them for too long without hunger taking control

My gaze skims over the images. "These look the same."

"They are." He sets a final piece of paper in the upper left corner, and I recognize the curve of my shoulder.

Eyes shifting to the mark, I study the uneven black lines over my heart and feel an echo of pain in my flesh. That one had been done during one of my lucid moments before Victor Hesse chloroformed me again.

Xander pulls one of the chairs right up to the edge of my desk, sits, then looks up at me expectantly.

Reluctantly, I take the seat across from him and tuck my talons under my thighs. "Go on."

Flint drags the remaining chair forward and sits

beside Xander, his body turned toward the other witch to signal for him to take the lead.

Xander leans over the sketches. "There are a lot of symbols here, but the instruction seems to be the same, repeated over and over again." He points to a smattering of drawings that all look similar. "Consume." He points to another series of images. "Convert." His finger moves over the papers, touching on the others. "Separate."

My brows pinch together. "I thought you already knew this. Reese showed us the symbols when he came to the house."

"We weren't sure, then, because some of the markings differ. A few of the symbols could go one of two ways, but after Reese told us about the slime, and with Flint's knowledge of how this could affect your core energy, we're more confident. The biggest issue was with the symbol for separate, since it would usually directly conflict with consume. Like trying to shove two sides of north pole magnets together. They naturally repel each other. But the convert symbol acts as a link for the two, which is a good thing," he hastens to add. "It means we're dealing with one specific intent instead of a bunch of cobbled-together intents."

I study the images. "Why aren't they all the same, then?"

"He's working from a manual that was likely assembled through studying various broken spells and, probably, torturing witches for more information." Xander looks queasy for a moment before he shakes his head to dispel whatever images his words pulled forth. "Everyone has their own style, like an artist, but the demons recording the information wouldn't have known what parts mattered, so they wrote down everything. And Victor Hesse took that and applied all of those markings to you."

My stomach rolls, and I force myself to nod in understanding.

Flint leans forward eagerly. "This makes correcting what was done easier, since we're not working with multiple spells."

The sense of uneasiness grows. "What happens if this spell is allowed to complete itself?"

"You'll turn into an energy devouring machine," Flint says excitedly. "Bottomless hunger, creating an endless supply of the slime he needs to continue to work magic."

Bile rises in my throat, and I lean away from the

images on my desk. "You really shouldn't sound so enthusiastic."

"No, you shouldn't." Xander glares at him. "And he's *not*."

"But I *am*," Flint objects. "This is big magic here. Horrible, yes, but still amazing. With the knowledge to do this correctly, you can turn any succubus or incubus into a walking source of magic. The spellcrafter would become peerless in their power." His bright, blue eyes meet mine. "You absolutely must destroy this demon before he can share this information. Nothing can be left of his experiment for it to be repeated."

Pale, Xander nods.

I study the two men. "You know about this spell. Reese knows. I'm assuming Jax and Slater know. Tally and Aren. All of the baku..."

"We haven't shown this to the others," Xander says quietly. "And Aren wasn't around when we recorded it. Reese has come up with more amulets based on the one he gave you. By reversing the intent, they block the baku from peeking in on us. He got the idea from the magnet theory. Yours pulls you closer to Dreamland, while ours push Dreamland further away." He pulls a wooden disk from under his shirt to show me. "Only the three of us are aware of what Victor Hesse's spell is capable of."

I lift my hand to the amulet around my neck, and I grip it. The world around me fades to gray, and I look around the room, surprised to find us alone. The baku are always present, snooping in on our lives for their own entertainment. I release the amulet, and color fades back in.

My eyes land on Reese, first, who belongs to Kellen, before shifting to Flint, who has no reason to keep this secret.

Flint lifts his hands. "I have no desire to make superpower demons, but you have no reason to trust that, which is why I'm willing to swear a soul oath."

My brows lift. "What's a soul oath?"

"Similar to a contract, only no one owns it." Flint crosses his legs and leans back. "It would basically mean any attempt to reveal this information would kill me."

"We don't deal in basically," I tell him.

"It will kill me," he states bluntly. "Even if I'm tortured, I won't be able to write it down before I'm dead. Intent to reveal is enough to trigger the oath."

I stare at him, a little shocked and mildly impressed. "And you'd do this willingly?"

"If I'm ever in a position where I want to create a

super demon, then I should be put down." He holds my gaze steadily. "Limitations exist for a reason. They're nature's way of maintaining balance. When that balance is tipped, bad things happen."

Having had bad things happen to me, I fully agree. "I accept this soul oath." Then, my gaze drops back to the drawings. "But I don't accept being turned into a ravenous monster."

"That's where I come in." Flint drops his leg back to the floor and scoots forward to sit on the edge of my desk. "Since you're so against the bottle, we're going to apply the same method but with another succubus or incubus."

My lips part in disbelief before I stutter, "You're going to stuff my core into another succubus or incubus?"

"No, that would be silly." He laughs before a thoughtful look crosses his face. "Though interesting. When this is over, if you want to experiment with co-inhabiting the same corporeal form as another—"

I shake my head. "No, thank you."

"Fair enough." He nods like it's no big deal. And maybe, for him, it is. "No, what we need to do is link your core to another succubus or incubus so they can temper your hunger while we work. Once the spell is completed correctly, we can then undo it, detaching the spell from your core. The succubus or incubus you link to will act as a kind of siphon for you, but they're going to need a massive amount of power to sate you. And there's a catch."

"Of course, there is." I already feel a little dizzy at the idea of what he's suggesting, so why not add further complications to it. "What's the catch?"

"It has to be someone you've exchanged energy with before. Multiple times." He takes a deep breath. "And someone you love, who loves you in return."

Survive for Now

Tension hums through my body as I stare at Flint. "Love?"

"Yeah, you know." He rolls his hand in the air. "Someone you hold above others."

"I'm a demon, not stupid." My talons dig into the cushion of my seat. "I know what love is. Why is it necessary?"

"Because your kind consumes energy," he states flatly. "It's your nature, and whoever you're linked to will not only have to resist the desire to consume you, but they will have to willingly give up what energy they have to feed you. They will make themselves weak to keep you strong."

And that is something no demon would willingly do.

"I was thinking maybe Landon?" Xander says quietly.

My eyes jump to him. "Landon isn't available."

"Ah." Worry creases his brows.

Flint looks back and forth between us. "Who's Landon?"

"My mentor." I dig my talons deeper into the cushion, enjoying the feel of memory foam parting around my fingertips.

Flint nods. "Fatherly love would definitely do it."

My spine snaps straight. "Landon is *not* my father."

"Maybe more like a mother role?" Curiosity lights his eyes. "He nurtured you, taught you how to feed, had all the awkward sex talks..."

I look at Xander. "Is that what mothers do?"

He shrugs. "Not mine. Mine put Reese in a mental hospital and kicked me out when I turned fifteen."

Flint looks at him. "Sounds like a horrible option for an anchor if you ever need one."

"Not even on my top ten list," Xander agrees.

I nibble on my bottom lip as I consider my options. "It's this or the bottle?"

Flint leans back in his chair and roots around in his pockets, then pulls out another of those dreaded green bottles.

Just how many does he have?

He leans forward and sets it on the desk, right on top of the mark over my heart.

Reluctant, I pick it up. I don't know what Tobias did with the one he took. I didn't *want* to know. But burying my head in the sand might not be an option anymore. I roll the bottle between my palms, testing its weight. It's still warm from Flint's body, and the clay tingles invitingly against my skin. I still hate the idea of going into the bottle, but I've had a few days to consider it as a possibility. Being a genie might not be horrible, if the right person holds the bottle.

I pop the cork off and stare into the dark hole. "It's small."

"Size doesn't matter in this specific case," Flint assures me.

I flip the bottle over to tap my fingers against the base the way I'd watched him do, but no magic springs forth to yank me inside. Does that mean it's not actively spelled? Or is it something only Flint can do?

"What about Julian?" Xander breaks in, and I glance up in surprise. "He's been right there with you over the last few months. There's a bond there that you don't have with the other succubi and incubi around you."

"Yes." I return the cork to its place and set the bottle back on my desk. "Will linking me to someone else hurt them?"

Flint hesitates for a moment, and it's all the confirmation I need.

When he opens his mouth, I lift a hand to stop him. "The bottle will have to suffice. I won't hurt Julian. He's already been through too much, expended too much power, and he has others he needs to protect."

Sadness fills Xander's eyes, and my chest tightens to know he cares so much about me. I give myself a firm shake and straighten in my seat. "When do we need to do this?"

"The sooner the better," Flint says after a moment. "Every day that passes just allows the spell to work itself deeper into you. It will be easier to do it now, before that happens."

It's the answer I expected, and I nod, my eyes dropping back to the drawings on my desk. "Are you *sure* you've interpreted all of these correctly?"

"To the best of our ability." Xander reaches across the desk to catch my hand, talons and all. "We'll make this right."

Careful of his human frailty, I squeeze his hand back, but worry still slithers through me with the dark voice of doubt. It feels like a lot of work to be undone this easily.

Is it a testament to how new Victor Hesse is with working this twisted magic? Or is this another layer to his plan? He laid his first plot out well, and we exposed the weapons we hold in our arsenal during our last battle. He's aware of the witches on our side, and equally aware of how they can undo his magic.

My eyes shift once more to the green bottle, and the wavering curve of the symbol beneath it.

Releasing Xander, I move the bottle off to the side and squint at the mark. It tickles at the back of my brain in a way the others don't, and I look at the rest of the marks that Xander said represented *separate*. It does look the same, or similar enough to see how it could be meant to mean the same thing. The other markings hold similar familiarity with each other. Like spells learned through a game of telephone, parts of the design getting lost along the way, but all resembling the original idea.

"We can do it tonight, if you like," Flint says, his voice disrupting my thoughts.

I glance up, the beautiful glamour swimming across his face before my brain stops fighting it, and I see his beauty once more. "We'll do it on Sunday. I have things to settle tonight."

"It won't be forever." Flint reclaims his bottle, tucking it back into his pocket. "Hopefully, it won't even be for twenty-four hours."

I applaud his optimism, but if my time on the human plane has taught me anything, it's to not get my hopes up. Until this is done, anything can go wrong, and with the way my luck runs, that's exactly what will happen.

We arrange a time and the two men take their drawings and leave me alone once more in my office.

I stand and walk back to the window, using one talon to peek through the blinds. Across the street, the three council guards still hunker on the sidewalk, rain pelting their bare arms. But the elements don't seem to affect them as they stare fixedly at my bakery.

Do they really expect Victor Hesse to just waltz up to my front door so they can capture him? He's obviously not coming here, so why do the guards continue to hover, invading my territory and disrupting my life?

Annoyed, I reach for my cell phone and punch in a number, then lift it to my ear.

An operator picks up on the first ring. "9-1-1, what is your emergency?"

I let the blinds snap shut and turn away once

more. "I'd like to report some suspicious men who have been following me for the last few weeks."

"That was ill-advised." The rumbling voice that fills my office doesn't even make me flinch. The tingles of a portal opening in the break room already alerted me to their presence.

The police had just left after taking my statement and telling the so-called bodybuilders to go back to the gym. While the guards have a look-the-other-way power that makes the casual passerby not notice them, if a human is actively aware of their presence, they're easy enough to spot. In the face of human authority, the guards had little choice but to leave, though they'll likely be back with better disguises and stronger camouflage.

Without standing, I glance up to take in the large demon who fills my doorway. "Lord Marius, what a surprise."

"I'll just replace the guards with new ones." He strides into my office uninvited and takes a seat in front of my desk. "Your tantrum wins you nothing."

I lift my brows. "It won me your presence, did it not?"

"You could have made an appointment if you had something to discuss." He crosses his legs and leans back in the chair. "My time is precious."

"But not limited, as mine is at the moment." I watch his expression, but his face remains stony, giving nothing away. "Are you aware of the current situation?"

He waves a hand. "Do you think I have time to watch the Adeline Boo Pond channel?"

I give him a toothy smile. "But you are *aware* there's something to watch."

"I wouldn't be wasting council resources on you if there wasn't." He uncrosses his legs. "Get to the point. I have other meetings today."

The smile drops from my face. "Have you been able to access the Library?"

His lips tighten a fraction. "What makes you think I tried?"

"Because you would want to know if your power, when wielded by you, would be enough to breach the doors." He remains silent, and I nod. "You couldn't."

"One should not mess with the powers of the Library," he demurs, neither confirming nor denying.

I stand to pace. "When was the last time the Library shut down like this?"

"After the Great War." His eyes track my path back and forth behind my desk. "Long before your existence."

"Do you know why?" Not many demons talk about the aftermath of the war between witches and demons. It wasn't a loss on our side, but it wasn't a win, either, and the fallout ruined our world.

Lord Marius studies me for a moment, as if weighing the value of telling me. "It was a pivot point in history. A divergence where our path could go one of two ways."

My brows pinch together. "For all of demonkind?"

He bows his head in a slight nod.

I think about that for a moment, before I stop and look down at him. Lord Marius is too powerful of a demon. Whatever pranks I play on the council guards wouldn't warrant his direct interference if he didn't also have something to discuss. "Why did you come?"

"To tell you to stop messing with our guards." Unlike most demons, he has no problem maintaining his seat while I hold the advantageous position of towering over him.

Whatever he thinks of me, he feels no need to assert his dominance. Not that it worked well for him at our last encounter. Maybe he just doesn't want me to slap him in the face with his own power.

When I stay silent, playing the waiting game, he releases a sigh. "You're right, we've been watching you. Many feel that you are too reckless. That you put our people in danger. There is a vote to take you out of existence."

My wings rustle against my spine, but I don't sense danger from this demon, however powerful he may be. "Why are you warning me?"

"There are those who think you are a pivot, that there is a chance to right a wrong." He looks around my small office, still so new that I haven't had a chance to personalize it yet. "This is an interesting business you've set up for yourself. An interesting choice for a succubus."

A laugh escapes me. "Are you saying that I should have opened a brothel, instead?"

"It would have been expected." His dark eyes swing back to me. "And if you had, I would have put you down myself."

Far from instilling fear in me, the words make me feel even more secure. "So what, exactly, are you expecting of me, Lord Marius?"

"I expect the unexpected." He stands and straightens his suit jacket. "You should link to Julian Poe, as your pet witches proposed. You'll have a higher chance of survival that way."

"Survival is not always worth the cost," I murmur as he heads for the door.

A rush of portal magic tingles on my skin, lifting the fine hairs, and the beast inside me stirs once more. I know, if I let it, I can take that magic, pull it into myself. But feeding the hunger will hurt me, so I ruthlessly leash the desire.

Lord Marius glances back over his broad shoulder. "I'll send more guards."

"I'll send them back to you," I promise, done with being stalked by useless protectors.

He pauses, one step through the door, and the edges of his body begin to dissolve. "Then I will send more. I have a vested interest in your survival, for the moment."

With another step, he vanishes from view, his final words hanging as a threat in the space he left behind.

I don't know what I did to earn Lord Marius's protection, or what he expects from me going forward. But the warning is clear. If I step in a direction he disagrees with, his interest in my existence will change, and my life will be on the chopping block.

BAKING FRENZY

The scent of cinnamon and apples fills the air as I zip around the kitchen, mixing up another batch of muffins. Tobias and Emil sit quietly at the kitchen table, mugs of tea and hot chocolate sitting at their elbows while Tac warms their feet from under the table.

They'd come home to find me already baking up a storm and left me to it. By this point, they've come to recognize a baking frenzy when they see one. It warms me that they abandoned their comfortable seats in the living room to be in here with me, but out of the way of my madness.

And madness it is.

Dozens of cakes fill every available surface, while boxes at the back of the kitchen table hold more, already cooled and ready for distribution. I think Kellen takes what I don't force on Fuyumi to the homeless shelter, but I'm not sure. All I know is that my ingredients never run out, which means there's no reason to stop.

As I crouch in front of the oven to check on my current batch of muffins, the tiles hum under my feet, the house's way of trying to calm me.

Absentmindedly, I pat the floor next to me, trying to send soothing thoughts back. I don't have enough energy right now to spare some for the house, but it doesn't seem to mind. Mission *Adie Steals the House* is still fully underway.

"Mmm, is that apple I smell?" Kellen asks, and I pop up from under the counter to see him striding into the kitchen.

His lightning-kissed eyes sweep over the abundance of desserts before settling on me, and his expression softens.

He circles the large island and stops at my side, dropping a static-filled kiss on top of my head. "Hard day, honey?"

When he cups my cheek, sparks dance across my skin, and the beast inside me stirs with hunger. I reach out and grab one of the muffins, stuffing it into my mouth in lieu of an answer.

He takes the hint and moves to join the others, out of my way, and out of my reach.

"How long?" he murmurs as I zip back to the fridge to search for buttermilk.

Blueberry, buttermilk, streusel muffins. I need blueberry, buttermilk, streusel muffins *now*.

"Since before we got home," Emil murmurs back.

Worry fills Kellen's voice. "Did something new happen?"

"She hasn't slowed down enough to say," Tobias rumbles. "I'm giving her another hour before I tie her down."

I spin at that, throwing a muffin at his head. He catches it easily and drops it into Tac's waiting mouth.

That's one way to dispose of my excess cakes.

When I glare at Tobias, he glares right back, then lifts his hand and holds up one finger in threat.

Chin lifted, I turn back to my next batch of muffins. As if he could tie me down. We've played that game, and I clearly came out the winner.

The sound of the front door opening pulls my attention to the arched entryway into the kitchen, and a moment later, the soft tap of feet fills the house. Martha comes into view first, her round cheeks flush from the cold and a brown, knit cap covering her hair. Jesse and Iris follow, also bundled up for the cold. Kelly and Sophia enter last, my cousin's presence no longer a surprise.

She's been spending more and more nights with the imps, and I turn a blind eye because I have a feeling she doesn't like to go home. I haven't asked, but I think the other succubi she lives with give her a hard time for working at the bakery.

They take in the scene and tromp over to join the guys at the table, wedging themselves in at the back.

"Did something happen today?" Kellen demands as soon as they settle.

Iris immediately tattles on me. "Witches came to the bakery."

Kelly joins in, too, the traitor. "Police came to the bakery."

"A council member came to the bakery." Fear fills Sophia's voice as she makes this revelation.

"Adie canceled the party," Jesse adds for good measure.

Only Martha remains quiet, probably because the others already laid everything out.

A beat of silence follows while the guys digest that before Emil says, "Why did the police come?"

As the imps break down my not-very-fantastic-day, I start creaming egg yolks and sugar together. The guys stay silent through most of it, with a question thrown in here or there, before silence once more fills the kitchen.

The ding of the oven timer breaks the silence, and I crouch once more in front of the oven, opening the french doors. Hot air blows back the fine strands of hair around my face, and I reach in to gently test for doneness.

Satisfied, I use a hot mitt to pull the tray out and stand, using my foot to kick the doors shut once more to retain the heat. I'll have more muffins to go in soon enough.

I turn to place the hot pan on the waiting rack and find Tobias there, his expression firm.

My eyes narrow on him. "It hasn't been an hour."

"It's past two in the morning," he counters. "It's time to stop."

"No one is keeping you up." I dump the tray over the cooling rack, uncaring if the tops crush and break. I need the pan for more muffins.

As one of the muffins rolls toward the edge of the island, Tobias catches it and tosses it back on the rack. "We need to discuss this."

My spine snaps straight. "There's nothing to discuss. You were at the meeting with Flint. The bottle's the only choice."

I turn back toward my next batch of muffins, but Tobias's hand on my stiff shoulder pulls me back around.

Angry black eyes meet mine. "That is *not* the only option. That's the option you hated the most."

I jut my chin out stubbornly. "It's the only option I'm willing to take. And it will only be for twenty-four hours. Max."

"You know that's a best-case scenario." His hold on me tightens. "I agree with Lord Marius. Link to Julian."

"I'm not risking him just so I can avoid a little bottle time!" Angry, I jerk out of his grasp. "Why are you guys always so fast to use him to protect me?"

Tobias's face flushes, black bleeding out from his pupils to mask the whites of his eyes. "Because he means less than you do!"

"No, he doesn't!" Red floods my vision, and I throw the hot pan at Tobias's head.

He easily knocks it aside, but can't stop me as I launch myself at him.

We hit the floor with a crash, Tobias taking the brunt of the fall, and I tangle my talons in his collar, lift him up, and slam him back down. "Julian is not expendable! He is not a doormat for us to walk all over!"

A blur of green streaks in from the side, and a force greater than me lifts me from Tobias, hyperspeeding us across the room.

I screech in Sophia's hold, struggling to break free, but she holds my arms at my sides, wrapping her body around mine. A comforting scent permeates the air, shimmering up from her body and surrounding me in a second layer of binding. It clouds my thoughts and makes my eyes heavy, like a soft blanket of exhaustion wrapping around me.

I shake my head, trying to stave off the effects, and she strokes my hair soothingly. "Shh, it's okay, don't fight. Julian would not be pleased if you hurt someone you love because of him."

The words break through the haze of red, and I stare at Tobias, still sprawled out on the floor. The collar of his shirt lays open, the tears from my talons visible even from across the room, and regret shoots through me.

No, I don't want to hurt Tobias. I don't want to hurt any of the people I love.

The scent grows stronger around me, and I

breathe it in deeply, letting it push back my anger, push back my fear and worry, push back my constant hunger, until nothing is left inside me, and I fall into unconsciousness.

Endless Hunger

I wake in my own bed, pillows mounded around me, and my purple, sequined one tucked tight to my stomach. It takes a moment for memory to return, and when it does, I groan and roll to my back, dislodging the makeshift nest and sending pillows tumbling around me.

God, what is wrong with me? Tobias didn't say anything I hadn't already heard, so why did I attack him like that? Is it the hunger? Is it making me lose my reason?

I lift my hands, fingers spread wide, and stare at the sharp points of my talons. I will them to retract, but they stay stubbornly out, ready to rip and rend, to draw blood and pain. My fingers curl in toward my palms, slicing through my own flesh, and blood seeps down my arms.

This isn't who I am, *what* I am. I'm not a monster.

My hands open once more, the tips of my fingers red with blood. The last time I saw my hands like this, I had killed hundreds of akuzal on the demon plane. But they'd been attacking me, mindless creatures who climbed over the bodies of their slaughtered brethren in the endless drive for food.

Am I no better than an akuzal, now? Driven by the beast that prowls inside me? Maybe I should call Flint and have him do the transfer today, before I really do hurt someone.

"Sophia said you were awake. You've been asleep for almost fifteen hours," Emil murmurs from my doorway.

I tuck my hands close to my chest before he sees the blood and twist to look out my window. Gray fills the sky, on its way to full night. I should feel guilty for wasting the day away, but better the oblivion of sleep than endangering those around me.

Emil walks into my room, his hand out in invitation. "Come downstairs."

"No, I'm good here." I turn onto my side and curl around my purple, sequined pillow. "You guys relax without me."

His thighs butt up against the edge of the bed, and he pulls the pillow away from me. "Come downstairs. Be with us."

"I might hurt you," I whisper as tears burn in my eyes.

He reaches out and lifts one of my hands, kissing my bloody knuckles. "Then, we will heal. Come."

Sniffling, I sit up and wait for the blood to sink beneath my skin before I scoot to the edge of the bed and let Emil help me stand. "Are you hungry? I can make spaghetti."

Heedless of my sharp talons, he holds my hand tighter. "Just come downstairs."

Frost burns against my palm, the lure of power tugging at me. My bones vibrate with the beast's hunger, but I ruthlessly shove it down. Soon, the beast will be destroyed, one way or another.

Emil pulls me from the room, and we walk down the stairs hand in hand, then step out into the living room.

"Surprise!" Lights flash and cheers fill the room.

I rear back, my teeth bared on an instinctive hiss before I register Julian and my imps, Tally and her witches, and Sophia with Fuyumi hovering off to the side. Tac bounds over the couch, both whelps attached to his back, and headbutts me hard in the stomach.

The tears I'd held back spill over, and I bend to wrap my arms around Tac's large, wedge-shaped head, taking a moment to bury my face against his soft fur while I collect myself.

At last, I straighten. "What are you doing here? I canceled the party."

"And I uncancelled it." Julian shakes his head. "I also revoked your access to evites again."

I choke back a laugh. "Asshole."

"You clearly can't be left to your own devices, darling." He steps forward and presses a cup into my hand. "Enjoy yourself tonight. Tomorrow, I'm going to be there linking us up, you hear?"

I blink rapidly to chase away my tears and step into his embrace. "Who tattled?"

"Don't you mean, who tattled *first*?" He hugs me close. "Stop being stupid. I'm here for you the same as you're here for me, understand?"

I bury my nose in the curve of his neck, snuffling in the familiar scent of coconut and warm bed sheets. "What if it hurts you? You don't understand what will be asked of you."

"If I can't handle it, then we'll go into the bottle together, okay?" He nuzzles the side of my face. "We'll be bottle buddies."

I hiccup out a laugh. "Have you seen the bottle? It's so small."

"Tobias showed me." He pats my back. "I've been in tighter quarters. We'll be *fine*."

I nod, wiping my face dry on his shirt, before I straighten and glance around the room. Someone made an attempt at decorating, probably Sophia and Iris based on the amount of green, glittery streamers and balloons spotting the room. It goes well with the stupid, green bottle I might soon be inhabiting with Julian. While I balk at dragging him into this, it still brings comfort to know I won't be alone if it comes to that.

I search the faces around me. "Where's Philip."

"Trussed up in the closet back at the office." Julina shakes his head as he releases me. "The damn imp is so afraid something will happen to me that he followed me into the bathroom. I'm giving him the night to rethink his actions."

I cringe at the revelation, feeling bad for putting Philip in his current predicament, and some of my hurt toward the imp vanishes. He had been putting Julian and the imps at HelloHell Delivery before me. I can't fault him for that forever.

Sharp claws dig into my shoulders, and then tiny wings smack the side of my head as Prem makes the short flight from Tac's head to my body.

Wincing, I hold still while the small monster

drapes himself around my neck like a warm, furry boa. I reach up to scratch at one delicate wing joint, earning a mini chainsaw-purr in response.

Julian steps to the side as Sophia shuffles forward, a green, plastic cup clutched in front of her. She holds it out in offering, and I accept it before pulling her into a hug, silently thanking her for interfering when I needed her to. Prem squeaks and drives needle claws into me for balance, but refuses to give up his position. Sophia stays stiff in my arms for only a second before sagging against me, offering her own silent apology in return for putting me to sleep.

When she pulls away, Tobias takes her place.

I tip my head back to stare up at him, my solid catalyst demon who I've treated so poorly.

He doesn't wait for an invitation, just yanks me against his hard chest with all the delicateness of a bull in a china shop. I crash against him, one arm coming up to brace against his chest to protect Prem, and breathe in ozone and landslides, frozen earth and fire, the dizzying pinnacle of choice. His power tempts the beast less than Emil had, but it's still there, the stirring of hunger. Tobias's power is already refilling, and he'll need me to offload it soon.

Flint better have been right about that twenty-four-hour thing. I want to be ready and able when my men need me.

The party is a quiet affair, filled with many hugs and booze that the imps liberate from Kellen's secret stash. We toast Martha and Tally's new positions at the bakery and binge on muffins and pizza that Kellen orders for delivery.

It's a quiet, somber affair, but I'm glad for the company. Being surrounded by my loved ones helps to push back some of the impending doom that seems to always hover on my periphery. I hug Julian more than once, thankful the decision to include him was taken out of my hands.

When the conversation lags, Kellen turns on quiet music, and the imps practice their dancing for when we have the next party. Which I'm sure Julian will be happy to plan.

Tally and the witches leave around eight with promises to return the following day.

With them gone, more booze comes out, everyone feeling the need to relax but unable to do it without liquid assistance.

The alcohol goes to Jesse's head, and her body melts into a cat form. She chases Prem and Merp around the house under Tac's and Fuyumi's watchful eyes before she exhausts herself and crawls onto Sophia's lap to pass out.

Fuyumi collects the whelps shortly after that and departs with her arms full of boxes of desserts, which she grumbles about before adding another box to the top of her pile.

I send Kelly along with her to make sure she doesn't trip during the short trek between our houses. Her frosty robe is long, and between the whelps hiding under it and the boxes she can't see over, there's a high chance the frost demon is going down. I kind of want to watch, but don't want to risk her wrath if it really happens and I witness it.

Sophia takes that as her cue and lifts Jesse in her arms, then herds Martha and Iris, who sway drunkenly together in front of the fireplace, toward the kitchen and their beds in the basement.

This leaves me alone with Tobias, Kellen, Emil, and Julian.

Emil and I sit on the couch facing each other, Kellen lays sprawled on my floral couch with a tumbler of whiskey balanced on his stomach, and Tobias looks cozy, ensconced in his chair.

Julian glances between us and stands. "Looks like it's time for me to head out, too."

"You can stay," I offer, and Tobias rumbles a protest that earns him a glare from me.

"We'll be together soon enough. darling." Julian bends over the couch and presses a kiss to my cheek. "I'm going to stock up on all the energy so I'm ready for you tomorrow."

"I'll walk you out." I pull my legs off Emil's lap and get to my feet, hurrying after Julian as he heads for the door. As he slips on his shoes in the entryway, I stop next to him and drop my voice. "Are you really okay with this?"

His expression softens, and he pulls me into a hug. "You've shared energy with me before. It's time I reciprocate."

"This is different," I protest as I pull away. "This is dangerous."

"It can't be worse than Cousin Cassandra." His lips thin into a tight line. "At least I *like* you."

I shiver and clutch my elbows close, following him as he opens the door and steps out onto the porch. "Sophia said there are rumors she's been spotted near the borders of Landon's territory. Have you seen her?"

He shakes his head and pulls a cap over his white curls to stave off the chill of the night. "Nope, and I hope not to for a *long* time."

I nod in silent agreement. Nothing good ever comes of Cousin Cassandra being around. I walk with Julian to the steps. "You'll let me know if you do, though, right?"

He jogs down the stairs, then turns to walk backward. "Don't worry so much. One crisis at a time, okay?"

I force a smile for his sake. "Yeah, okay. See you tomorrow."

Still walking backward, he waves. "See you tomorrow."

"Adie, come back inside," Emil calls, and I glance back to see him hovering in the open door. "You're letting out all the heat."

"In a minute." I turn back toward Julian, who jolts to a stop.

A brisk breeze carries the scent of decaying meat to me, and my lips part in warning.

Too late, the smile on Julian's face freezes as he looks down.

A bloody fist punches through his chest, holding his still beating heart. Then, the fist yanks backward, and Julian crumples to the cold stones of the walkway.

Victor Hesse stands in his place, his skeletal face stretched in a smile. "I'm enjoying this game, Ms.

Pond, but there's no need to bring in more players. Don't you agree?"

Frozen in horror, I watch as he lifts Julian's heart to his mouth and takes a large bite of the still steaming meat.

I jolt forward a step before Emil's icy hand closes on my bicep, pulling me back toward the house.

"Tick tock, Ms. Pond," Victor Hesse calls, blood glistening on his cracked lips.

Emil pulls me into the house while, off in the distance, police sirens sound, coming nearer.

The sound shakes me out of my stupor, and my heart pounds in denial.

I fight free of Emil's hold and rush back to the porch, ready to kill Victor Hesse.

But only Julian's body remains, abandoned on the walkway as a pool of blood spreads out beneath him.

Under Investigation

"So, what you're saying is you didn't see anything and have no idea how someone's heart was seemingly ripped out of their chest on your front walk?" the detective asks, doubt clear in his voice.

"That's what I've been saying for the last hour," Emil growls, the air around him a good ten degrees lower than anywhere else.

"And that's what everyone else keeps saying." The detective taps his pen against his notebook. "And yet we had an anonymous call that shouts were coming from your house."

"I don't know what that would be about," Emil says tightly. "You're welcome to ask our neighbors. There was no shouting."

The detective turns to look at the sheet-draped body on our walkway. Bright lights now fill our yard, and strangers move back and forth over the scene, collecting evidence.

I stand at the railing, keeping one eye on Julian's body and one on the detective.

Julian's corporeal form should have disintegrated before the police arrived, and my pulse races with panic that he's still lying there, just like a human would after being murdered.

Did Victor Hesse *do* something to him? Did he have enough time to cast a spell? Is Julian *trapped* inside that husk, feeling what's going on around him and unable to alert anyone to his presence?

My hands tighten on the railing, making the wood creak. We can't let him go to the human morgue. We can't let them cut him open and root around his insides in search of more evidence.

"Ma'am, are you okay?" another detective asks, stopping next to me.

I turn my head far enough to catch his eye and thread power through my voice. "*Go away.*"

The detective's eyes glaze over, and after a moment, he wanders away.

Too bad I can't make the other detective do the same. I tried when they first arrived. Tried to whammy their minds so they'd just leave, and I could care for Julian the way he *should* be cared for.

But the other detective is less malleable, his control over his mind too firm to give way to my suggestions.

It's not even an issue of power. Sophia had come out at the noise and tried her own skills at sending them away without success. There's something hinky about that one detective, maybe even something witchy, though his eyes look normal enough, so at least he's not fae-touched like Reese.

"I'd like to talk to the others in the house, one more time," the hinky detective announces.

"You've already talked to them." Emil stands firm in the doorway. "Any more questions will have to wait until morning, when we come down to the police station. With our lawyer."

"Yes, your lawyer." He taps his pen against his notepad in an offbeat rhythm that grates on my nerves. "You are a co-owner of K&B Financial, are you not?"

Emil's eyes narrow, but he gives a tight nod.

"Where a car bomb was set off in your parking lot?" Tap, tap, tap goes the pen. "I remember you had no idea who would be targeting you back then, either."

Great. Not only do we get a hinky detective, but we also get the same guy who was on the scene the last time Victor Hesse tried to kill people I love. Only, this time, he succeeded.

As Emil responds to the question, my eyes drift back to the sheet. Julian wouldn't like that sheet. It's too white, too obviously cotton. He's strictly a silk and satin kind of man. He likes quality, and that sheet is most definitely *not* quality.

"Ma'am?" a voice asks from beside me.

I whip around, my lips peeled back in a snarl. "*Go away.*"

"That's not happening, Ms. Pond," Detective Hinky responds calmly. "How are you related to the deceased?"

"We're friends," I grit out through clenched teeth.

The detective's eyes lift to my white hair, a distinctive shade of pure white that can't be obtained through bleach, then drift to Julian's body, where the sheet covers his equally distinctive white hair. "You're not related?"

"You can take a blood test if you doubt it," I seethe. It takes everything in me not to smash this too inquisitive detective to a bloody pulp.

"You own Boo's Boutique Bakery, correct?" He waits for my nod before he continues. "And you reported you were being stalked yesterday?"

I stiffen and briefly meet Emil's eyes over the detective's shoulders before refocusing on the man in front of me. "Yes, that's right."

"Is this the first time you've been followed?" he asks. "Do you know why you're being stalked?"

"The police who came to investigate said I was probably being paranoid." I clench my teeth before adding, "The men left as soon as they were asked to."

He makes a couple notes, then looks back at me. "You were at the mortuary across town last month, were you not?" He references his notebook. "Owned by one Kellen Cassius, who also lives here? Where we had a report of a homicide?"

"An unfounded report." I clench my fists. "We are obviously being targeted. I don't know why you're wasting so much time here when you could be tracking down the person harassing us."

"Mr. Poe was there with you that night, was he not?" He doesn't even check his notebook before he asks his next question. "Are you aware the house next door burned down a few nights later?"

"I heard." There's no way I can deny it. It shut down the mortuary for a few days and even made the news, briefly, before more sensational events moved it out of the public's awareness.

He stares at me steadily. "Were you at the bank, too, when the car bomb went off?"

The way he asks the question makes me think he already knows the answer. My car was there, and any number of security cameras could have seen me going into and out of the bank. "I have no idea who caused the explosion."

His gaze hardens. "Don't you?"

Emil steps between us, forcing the detective back a pace. "She's answered enough of your questions. If you want to talk further, contact our lawyer."

Emil motions for me to go back into the house, but my focus returns to Julian. It doesn't feel right to leave him out here, surrounded by the humans.

"Adie, come inside," Tobias calls from the doorway, breaking through my thoughts.

I drag my eyes away from Julian and force myself to walk stiffly back into the house. Emil follows a pace behind, with the detective right behind him.

"I'll be contacting you in the morning," the detective promises. "You know something you're not telling me. Bad luck doesn't follow someone without reason."

I flinch and look back at him before Tobias catches my hand, tugging me past the entryway and out of view.

The door closes with a bang, blocking out the detective, but the lights from the investigation team still shine through the window, bright as daylight. They'll probably still be out there when the sun rises.

Tobias cups the back of my neck. He doesn't ask if I'm okay. It's obvious that I'm not. It was obvious from the moment Victor Hesse ripped out Julian's heart and his body failed to disintegrate.

Shrugging out of Tobias's touch, I march for the stairs.

When footsteps follow me, I stop, my back stiff. "I want to be alone."

"That's not a good idea," Tobias rumbles. "Not after what just happened. We're under attack."

I turn my head far enough to see Tobias from the corner of my eye. "Are you concerned because my scapegoat just got murdered?"

The scent of his anger fills the air, but he reels it back in. "I'm concerned because someone you care about just died."

"We don't know that he's dead. I'm going to Dreamland."

He catches my arm, pulling me around. "Reese said it's not a good idea."

"No." I yank myself free and back up the steps.

"Reese said it might not be possible. I'm going to find out."

I turn and hurry up the stairs. When he follows, his steps heavy behind me, I spin to glare down at him. "You're not welcome right now."

The muscles in his jaw jump as he clenches and unclenches his teeth. "I need to know you're safe. *We* need to know you're safe. If something goes wrong when you try to access Dreamland—"

"I don't care if something happens!" I roar, the horror of the night, the past week, the past months, pouring out of me. "You're not welcome!"

The stairwell shudders around us. For a moment, I think it's Tobias's anger, but then the stairs buckle and flatten beneath Tobias, sliding the catalyst demon back into the living room. The walls ripple, the railing pulling away from the wall and weaving across the stairwell in a latticework of separation between me and the demons below.

Through the gaps of wood, Tobias stares at me in shock and anger, while Emil's hurt expression appears through another gap. Kellen is nowhere in sight and hasn't been since before the police arrived. I think he went after Victor Hesse, but I'm not sure. All I know is that he's not *here*.

Rage at my helplessness rolls through me, and I

turn away from Tobias and Emil to sprint up the stairs to my room. My door slams shut on its own, and a ripple of power rises around me as the house throws energy into my barriers, locking out anyone who wants to enter.

I fall onto my bed, pulling pillows around me until I can't see anything else. Reaching up, I tug the Dreamland amulet from beneath my shirt, wrap my hand around it tightly, close my eyes, and cast myself from my body.

Dreamland takes shape around me, the gray city sharper than usual, more defined. The house I live in feels more solid now, more tangible, and I reach out a hand to push on the wall. It resists, my hand unable to shove through it like usual.

My feet make noise on the gray floor as I walk down the steps and out through the front door. I need to find Julian, to verify that his core came back here like it should have. That his corporeal form remaining on the human plane was a fluke, and he's not still trapped inside of it.

The street outside my house looks normal, with soft drifts of fog forming the hazy shape of other houses. Lights flicker here and there, the sign that a human sleeps within, ready to be stalked for food. But that's not what I'm here for.

I search the street as I walk toward the center of town, keeping my senses on high alert for any sign of a baku or another of my kind. Searching the entire city alone will take time. There's no radar for succubi and incubi to locate each other in Dreamland. But the baku have resources I don't possess.

I barely make it to the end of the block before the baku find me.

They arrive in a tiny herd of four, with Janet at their lead. I recognize her by the desiccated eyeball she still wears in the small tuft of fur on top of her head.

They come to a stop, and Janet lifts her small trunk in salute. "Adie! What is your mission here?"

Mission. As if there's any other reason I would visit Dreamland. Though, with my demons of destruction to feed on, and my preference to avoid feeding on humans, there really is no other reason for me to come here.

I take a knee in front of them to put us on the same level. "Julian. Is he here?"

The baku exchange worried glances. I don't usually ask them to seek out one of my kind. It's something of a sport for succubi and incubi to hunt baku for fun. They're little energy packs that don't require wooing to give up the good stuff. I've never participated in the sport, but now, I wonder if Julian is one of those who have fed on the little nightmare eaters.

"He won't harm you, if he's here," I promise and plan to make sure it's so.

No one I call family is allowed to munch on each other without consent.

As soon as this thing with Victor Hesse is over, I'm making a new rule board. The Code of Conduct, as dictated by me.

A small baku at the back prances forward. "Timjim of the BBBB, at your service, Protector of the Baku!"

I give him a solemn nod while internally groaning. Will I ever have a cool name? Everyone else gets Destroyer and Devourer and I get Protector of the Baku. Not even a *little* threatening as a demon. "It's a pleasure to have you in service, Timjim."

He prances in place for a second, kicking up little tufts of fog. "There have been no recent arrivals in this sector, Adie Sir!"

Sector? I take another look at the small herd and

notice they each wear a badge attached to the furred ruffs around their necks with the number four on them. Have they divided Dreamland into territories much like the powerful demons on the human plane do?

"What about in another sector," I ask.

"We will check-in and report back!" Janet trumpets loudly, and the other three baku peel away, galloping in different directions. Once they're gone, Janet turns back to me. "I will take you to Headmaster Aren for a report."

Headmaster Aren? I mouth as I stand. What in the everloving hell has been going on since the last time I visited Dreamland?

THE HEADMASTER

We find Aren in the park at the center of town, but now, it looks more like a headquarters of sorts, with pieces of Dreamland ripped up and repositioned to form what looks like one of those briefing rooms I've seen in police dramas on TV.

Aren stands at the center of the room, larger than the other baku around him, though not nearly as big as the first time I met him. He had given up a large portion of himself in the fight against the Dreamer, and now, only stands at head height to me instead of towering over me as he had before.

As soon as I step through the fog trees, he flaps his ears in greeting. "Adie, girl, where have you *been*?"

I brace myself as he stampedes forward to wrap his trunk around me and pull me in for a hug that manages to put my boobs right at his mouth level.

"I have missed you *so* much," he motorboats into my cleavage.

"I've missed you, too." I hug him back, giving him two more seconds of boob time. Then, I yank on one floppy ear to signal he needs to release me or face the consequences.

He steps back and turns his head to stare at me from one large, liquid black eye. "What's the doing, girl? Or should I say lack of doing? No steam on the Adie channel, huh? Your ratings are going to plummet if this keeps up."

"Oh, no. Whatever will I do?" I say drily.

"It's a serious issue." He pats me on the shoulder in sympathy. "Is that why you're here? Want to try a little dream time fun? There's a frat party that should be winding down soon. Lots of passed out man meat."

"No... Wait, maybe?" Julian loves university parties for an easy feed, and after being ripped out of his corporeal form, he'd need some energy. "Yes, let's go there."

Aren takes a step back in surprise and turns his head to stare at me from his other eye. "Seriously? I mean, I'm game to see you get down, but that's not usually your style."

I shake my head. "I'm looking for Julian."

Aren folds his back legs and sits on his haunches. "Oh. Yeah, that's more his style, but he's not here."

"What?" Worry shoots through me. "How do you know? Janet *just* sent out the search call."

Aren looks down at the smaller baku. "Go check the perimeter. We don't want any eavesdroppers, okay?"

"Yes, Headmaster!" Janet salutes and trots back through the trees, trotting straight through their foggy trunks.

Aren watches until she vanishes, then turns back to me, his nightmarish face serious for once. "I know because I can feel it every time someone enters and leaves Dreamland. It started after the fight with the Dreamer, and it keeps getting stronger. I can even kick people out, now, like you did that one time."

I look around once more at the meeting room he built here. It's not something that should be possible in Dreamland. This place mirrors the human plane, though not always the most current version of it. Any changes made should dissipate quickly as the place returns itself to the static structure it always holds. But I've seen Aren, and some of the other baku, do things in Dreamland that I didn't think were possible. It gives way to the baku the way it doesn't to the succubi and incubi who merely visit here.

"Do the other baku know?" I ask at last, focusing on this new development over his revelation about Julian.

"Hard to hide that kind of stuff from them." He sticks his trunk into the foggy grass at his feet and pulls up a chair. "Here, have a seat."

A tremor runs through me, so I take the offered chair, barely surprised it holds my weight. "That's amazing, Aren. Congratulations?"

"It's scary as hell." He drapes his trunk over my lap, and I pet it absently. "If the higher-ups hear about this..."

"Then, you'll bar them from Dreamland." I stroke his scales gently. "If Dreamland obeys you now, then they can't do a damn thing about it."

"No one is supposed to own Dreamland," he whispers.

"Nonsense." I shake my head again. "Dreamland didn't create itself any more than the cities on our side of existence created themselves. Someone put Dreamland here, and in their absence, it's chosen you to be its master." I pinch his trunk. "Or should I say *Headmaster*?"

He lets out a happy trumpet. "I'm going to make

the BBBB little uniforms, too. I wanted capes, but they don't stay in place."

I smile at that. "The badges are nice."

His ears perk up. "You think?"

"I do."

When I fall silent, his ears droop. "What happened to Julian?"

I remain quiet for a minute while I collect my thoughts. I had hoped the peeping Tom had been watching, so I wouldn't have to explain. I don't want to remember the moment Julian stilled, the moment his smile froze, or the confusion in his eyes as he looked down at his own bloody heart.

"Victor Hesse," I say at last, and Aren's trunk stiffens beneath my hand.

"Got it," he says, not asking for further information. "When you cut ties with your body, you went to the wasteland. Maybe that's where Julian is?"

At the suggestion, I straighten in surprise. "You're right. He'd only come here if he was still attached to his corporeal form."

"You can't go to the wasteland like you are now, though," Aren points out.

I look down at my body. I feel solid enough, but I'm not actually here. This is a construct designed to interact with human dreams. If I want to go outside of Dreamland, I need a *real* body, which means either abandoning the one that lies sleeping in my bed at home, or returning to the human plane and going through the portal that links to the Demon Clerk's Office.

"Okay, I'll check there." I pat Aren's trunk one last time and stand. "Thank you, Aren."

He smacks me on the ass. "Anything for you, Adie." Then, he straightens to alertness and turns, staring through the trees at something only he can see. "You should get going."

I step up to his side. "What's wrong?"

"Trouble." As he speaks, the sky in the distance turns red.

I shiver and huddle closer to him. Dreamland doesn't have color, so what could cause such a disturbance. "What's going on?"

"Someone I've blocked is trying to enter." He turns and nudges me in the opposite direction. "Time for you to vamoose. The Headmaster needs to lay the smackdown on a persistent succubus."

"Are you sure you can handle it?" I ask as he shoves me through the trees, their foggy leaves brushing against my cheeks. "I can help."

"You have problems of your own. I got this." He

shoves me out onto the street, then looks around for Janet. She trots back into view, and he turns to face her. "Gather the BBBB."

"Yes, Headmaster." She rises onto her back legs, lifts her trunk into the air, and lets out three loud trumpets.

From around the city, answering trumpets fill the air, and baku begin to appear through the buildings, pouring out to fill the street.

I stare at them in amazement. I've never seen so many baku. Didn't even know this many existed. The ground trembles beneath my feet as they gallop closer, converging on the park.

Aren pushes me again. "Go, Adie. This is baku business."

Trusting that Aren knows what he's doing, I reach up to touch the amulet around my neck, and Dreamland fades around me.

I come to in my bedroom, the ceiling over my head still covered in shadows. The rafters crisscross, forming the shape of a star, and I stare at it as I try not to give in to the surges of panic inside me.

Not finding Julian in Dreamland doesn't mean

he's dead, dead. Aren was right. He's probably in the wasteland or the demon city by now. If I go look for him, our paths could cross. Time is weird there. I could arrive before him or years after he already left. And I don't know if I can risk it while the curse rides me. What if I go to the demon plane and go completely feral, with no way for Flint to capture me?

But I need to know that he's okay.

My eyes sting, and I close them tight, fighting back the tears. I can't give in to grief. Mourning now makes it too real, and I'm not ready for that.

Something thumps outside my window, and I sit up, then twist around to stare at the closed shutters. I'm on the third floor. Nothing should be thumping outside my window, unless Kellen crossed the roof to try to get to me.

Slowly, I push my pillows aside, crawl off the bed, then tiptoe to my window. I strain my ears, listening for another sound, but outside remains silent. My hands shake as I push open the window, then reach out to unlatch the shutters before hesitating. The last time something came to my window, it had been a creepy ass, floating eyeball. I don't know if I have the courage to face something like that again.

I nudge the latch up, shove the shutters, then yank my hands back inside to the safety of my barrier. It hums with power, tickling my skin with the reassurance that nothing can cross into my room.

The empty expanse of the roof greets me, and when I check Kellen's room across the way, his window lays dark, his shutters closed tight.

Frowning, I step to the side to get a view of the street. Bright lights still fill our yard, making it look like daylight even though it's still the middle of the night. Not even an hour has passed since I came upstairs.

Stepping to the other side, I squint at the shadows that fill our backyard. Something moves in the darkness, and I step closer to the window, trying to get a better view.

Is that another one of the council guards out there? Invading our property? My hands clench into fists, my talons biting into my palms with the need to tear apart any invaders on our property.

A quiet thump comes from closer to my window, and my heart lurches into my throat. That sounded like it came from directly under my window.

Not for the first time, the helplessness of my situation gets to me. I don't have enough power for hyperspeed or super strength. My core feels scraped bare, and hunger gnaws at my spine. I need to feed, but feeding won't help. Nothing will help except stripping this curse out of my body.

The thump comes again, and I crouch to pull one of the toy knights I bought for Merp and Prem from under my bed. It has a little sword that I tug from its sheath. It won't do much in a battle, but it's better than nothing.

Weapon in hand, I creep back to the window and step up onto the sill, brandishing my sword.

Kellen leaps back, his hands in the air, then loses his footing and pinwheels his arms for balance.

Startled, I reach out to grab his arm as I hiss, "What are you *doing*?"

He finds his balance, then lifts a finger to his lips before he points to the backyard.

I nod and jump the short distance to the rooftop to land beside him.

Together, we slip down the steep slope of the roof, close to the edge, and peer into the darkness below.

The movement comes again, close to the tree line that runs the length of the wall separating our yard from Fuyumi's. It's not big enough to be Tac, sneaking out to visit his whelps, though.

I pass Kellen my sword and shrug out of my

sweatshirt. Beneath, I wear a low cut tank-top that allows plenty of room for my wings to slip free from their hiding place along my spine. With a quiet groan, I flex my wings, ruffling the feathers. It's been too long since I let them out, and they feel cramped and sore.

Next to me, clouds unfurl from Kellen's back, draping me in a light, chilly mist. He passes back my sword, and by silent agreement, we slide over the edge of the roof and circle in opposite directions, coming at the intruder from both sides.

Whoever it is sees Kellen first, lets out a surprised shout, and turns to run straight toward me as I land.

When I hold out my sword, point first, they fling their hands into the air. "Adie, it's me! Philip! Please don't kill me!"

If anything, that just makes me want to murder him more. He was supposed to protect Julian, and he failed.

With a snarl, I shove the point of the sword toward his chest.

One Day

Philip squeals as the point of the sword stabs against his chest. Of course, the rest of the blade then folds under the pressure. Which absolutely does *not* stop me from stabbing Philip again.

Stab, stab, stab. It gives me a vicious sort of pleasure, and Philip's wails just add spice to the whole experience.

"Shut up, man." Kellen slaps a hand down hard on the imp's shoulder. "You're going to draw attention."

Philip's cries of pain cut off, and he unclenches his eyes to stare down at the sword that is most definitely *not* plunged into his ribcage.

His eyes widen in disbelief. "Is that a *toy* sword?"

I poke him again. "If you hang on a second, I'll gladly go grab a real one."

"Emil keeps his daggers in his nightstand," Kellen offers. "I can hold him here."

"No, that's okay." Philip waves his arms in surrender. "I'm sorry for trespassing. But when I got here, I saw the police out front and thought I'd come through the back door."

"*When* you got here." I prod him again with the broken sword. "You should have been here to begin with."

"I *know*." His arms drop to his sides, and his shoulders slump in defeat. "But Julian's *really* good at tying knots, and even imps have limitations." Then, he peers toward the house. "Is he inside? I saw his car still at the curb. He's going to be pissed that I went against his wishes, but I am totally prepared to guard his body."

At the reminder, grief washes through me. "Too little, too late."

"What?" Philip looks back toward the house. "Did he go home with someone?"

The sword trembles in my hand. "No. He didn't."

"You should go," Kellen advises.

"But..." Philip's gaze shifts to the walkway, where the crime scene lights illuminate the path. "No... He would have popped back into existence at

HelloHell…" He turns to stare at me. "Why are there human police in the front yard?"

His obvious distress only adds to my hurt and worry. If Philip hasn't seen Julian, then he's definitely not back on the human plane already and just selfishly neglecting to call and let me know he's okay.

Philip reaches out and grabs my shoulders. "Adie, where's Julian?"

Snarling, I shrug out of his hold. "He's in the front yard."

"But… How?" Confusion and disbelief twist his baby face, his features rippling as he loses control of his form.

Julian was more than Philip's boss. Julian contracted with him over and over through the centuries, paying a steep price to get him out of the demon plane whenever misfortune sent Philip back.

"You should come inside," I say tiredly. "I'll hold off killing you for another day."

Footsteps heavy, I trudge toward the deck at the back of the house, but lighter footsteps draw my attention to the path that leads to the front. Kellen curses, and I snap my wings back into hiding, tuck the sword behind my back, then step in front of Philip to give the imp time to fix his face back into place.

The sweep of a flashlight fills the backyard, followed a moment later by Detective Hinky. His light finds us on the first sweep, as does the nose of his gun.

We all freeze, and Philip slowly raises his hands into the air before I elbow him to lower them.

"You're intruding on private property, detective," Kellen calls as he moves to block me from potential harm.

The detective lowers his gun but keeps his flashlight trained on us as his gaze sweeps the backyard. "I heard screaming. With what happened tonight, I thought it was prudent to check it out."

"Yeah, Philip was having a moment," I say tightly. "He just found out about Julian."

"Philip Davis?" The detective steps to the side, his light shining on Philip's face, which I'm glad to see is back to its baby-faced appearance. "Co-owner of HelloHell Delivery?"

"Ye— Wait, what?" Philip looks from the detective back to me and shakes his head. "*What?*"

"Yes," I answer for him.

"You weren't here earlier." The detective finally holsters his gun and fishes out his notebook. "Care to explain your whereabouts?"

"Not tonight." I shove Philip toward the

backdoor. "It's cold, and we'd like the chance to grieve in peace."

"I expect to see all of you in the station tomorrow," he calls as I yank open the backdoor, and a blast of heat sweeps out. "This is a murder investigation. You can either come in voluntarily, or we can force you to come in."

"You'll see us with our lawyer," Kellen snaps, herding us the rest of the way inside and slamming the door shut.

For good measure, he also draws the curtain over the glass door, just in case the detective gets the urge to peek inside.

The kitchen lights flare to life, blinding all of us, and Philip lets out another small shriek.

"Shut up!" I growl, stabbing him in the back with my bent sword.

"What are you all doing down here?" Tobias rumbles as he stares at us. "Adie, weren't you upstairs? And what's Philip doing here?"

"We caught him skulking." Kellen reaches out and grabs the imp by the shoulder, marching him toward the living room.

"I'll make tea," I offer as I set my useless weapon on the table before I glance up to meet Tobias's dark eyes. "Do you want chamomile?"

He walks farther into the kitchen, his sleep pants hanging low on his hips and his t-shirt tight across his chest. "Are you willing to accommodate me?"

"It's just as easy to make four cups as it is to make three," I grumble as I fill the teapot and set it on the burner. "Is Emil up, too? Do I need to make hot chocolate?"

"He hasn't come down if he is." Tobias walks around the kitchen island. "Are you still angry at me?"

I hunch my shoulders. Blunt asshole. Can't he just accept the offer of tea as my olive branch?

His warm fingers slip down my chilled arm, leaving a path of fire in their wake. "You know I didn't want Julian's death."

"I know." Shivering, I step away from him to gather the mugs and tea. "I shouldn't have said that."

He follows after me, caging me against the counter. His warmth seeps into my back and chases away the chill from the outside. He bends, his lips close to my ear so each word vibrates through me. "I value your existence. I value your place in this house. I do not wish to lose you."

A gasp catches in my throat, bordering on a sob. He's not a demon who easily voices his feelings. Usually, he allows his actions to speak for him. That he feels the need to express himself now speaks to the depth of his worry.

"You locked yourself away from me when you were hurting," he continues with the rumble of earthquakes, and my hand freezes, the tea bag I hold hovering over the cup. "You hid from us and turned our very home against us. You went into Dreamland, despite the damage it could have caused you. You will atone for these actions."

I turn my head far enough to see him from the corner of my eye. His face looks hard with the expression of a judge dealing out a heavy sentence.

I wronged Tobias, wronged the men I love, and no matter the reason, payment must be made. Turning back to the tea, I nod in understanding.

He eases away from me. "Come to my room when you're done with Philip."

I nod again, my throat too tight to voice the words.

On the stove, the kettle releases a quiet whistle that slowly grows in volume. I grab two of the mugs and turn, only to find Tobias gone from the kitchen.

Philip takes the mug of tea with shaky hands and holds it on his lap without drinking. He stares numbly down at the golden liquid, his expression filled with loss and bewilderment.

Kellen accepts the mug I hand him, laced with whiskey from the stash he keeps in the kitchen. Instead of his usual chair, he moved my floral couch aside to build a fire, and he now sits close to the crackling flames, as if he needs it to warm himself after being out in the cold. Which shouldn't be the case. Demons don't feel the elements the same way humans do. Not unless they're low on energy or there's something wrong with them.

I brush my hand over Kellen's brow, checking for a temperature, and he smiles before pulling me down to sit beside him, closest to the fire. "Warm yourself up."

My chest tightens in realization. He built the fire for me, not for himself. When he pulls the blanket off the back of the couch and swaddles me in it, it makes me want to cry all over again.

What is wrong with me that I'm a giant crybaby now?

"I don't understand what's happened," Philip says numbly, his head lifting. "How can Julian's body still be here? Why hasn't he come back? He always comes back."

Grief rolls over me once more, and I pull my legs up under the blanket. "I went to Dreamland. He's not there. He could be in the wasteland…"

Kellen shakes his head. "His body wouldn't still be here if that was the case."

Acknowledging the truth of that hurts. I didn't even need to go into Dreamland, but I was desperate to be proven wrong and Julian was still out there, trapped in a corpse and unable to alert us.

I take a shaky breath. "Victor Hesse must have done something. Locked him in his body or something like what happened with Domnall. We need to get it away from the humans so we can free him."

Kellen's hand settles on my knee, the thick blanket buffering the sparks that crackle on his skin. "That won't be easy. We can't just walk into a human morgue and take him. There are cameras and paperwork."

"We can blow the place up," Philip's face twists with desperation. "Take the body in the confusion."

I stare at him in surprise. "There would be casualties. The human morgue is in the hospital."

"Who cares?" His fingers turn white on the mug

he holds. "This is *Julian* we're talking about. Or don't you care?"

A growl vibrates in my chest, my lips peeling back from my teeth in anger. "I wasn't the one passing time in a supply closet while they were supposed to be protecting him."

"No, you're the one who was *here* and did nothing." Slamming his tea onto the coffee table, he thrusts to his feet, his entire body rippling. "How could you let this happen? After everything he's done for you?"

Hurt and anger rush through me in a hot tide, but I reign it in, knowing Philip is lashing out from a place of pain himself. It's an emotion I know well.

Kellen, though, passes me his tea and stands, lightning flickering through his hair. "That's enough."

"If you're not going to reclaim Julian's body, I will!" Philip turns toward the front door as if he can just march out to the front yard and scoop Julian up right now.

"And what will you do once you have him?" I demand as I struggle to reign in my anger and guilt.

Philip spins back to me. "I'll destroy the corporeal form myself."

"And you'll destroy Julian with it, if he's locked

inside." I hug my legs to my chest to stop myself from springing into action. Philip's not the only one who feels the urgency to free Julian, but his method will only hurt Julian while causing harm to humans, as well as risking exposing us all. "Give me time. I'll figure something out."

"One day." Philip holds up a finger. "I'll give you one day to reclaim his body. And then, I'm blowing the entire place up."

Without waiting for our response, he storms out of the house.

Kellen turns to me, his brows raised. "Do you want me to take care of him?"

Not sure what, exactly, he's offering, I shake my head. "Leave him be. He's confused and hurting right now."

Kellen glances back toward the door. "He's dangerous."

"So am I." I stand and set Kellen's untouched tea aside. "If I can't figure this out before tomorrow at midnight, I'll take care of Philip myself. I owe him my revenge, anyway."

"Are you sure about that?" Kellen comes to stand in front of me and grips my arms, sending static cascading over me. "Whatever else, Philip is important to Julian. He won't appreciate you permanently damaging the imp."

"Then, I better find a way to get to Julian before it comes to that." Hunger growls through me, the beast inside awoken by the power Kellen throws off. Gently, I push his hands away. "Stop tempting me, Sparky Pants, or I'm going to eat you."

"That was so much sexier a few days ago." His hand lifts toward my face, then drops. "I don't like not being able to touch you."

"I don't like it, either." I reach back, grab the blanket, then use it as a buffer to hug him. "We'll figure this out."

"What about the plan for tomorrow?" he asks as he leans his weight against me. "Without Julian..."

Without Julian here to act as my anchor, I'll have to go into the bottle. There's no other choice if I want to keep everyone safe from my growing hunger.

Silent, I hug Kellen tighter, refusing to acknowledge that, tomorrow, I'll be leaving them.

Absolution

I jolt back to awareness, my heart pounding with panic as my talons dig into the couch cushions. Kellen and I had stayed downstairs to watch the fire burn out, and from the chill in the room, it had done so a while ago.

The storm demon shifts on the cushions beside me and lets out a quiet snore. We'd fallen asleep, with the barrier of the blanket to keep us separate, and he now shifts restlessly, which must be what woke me. I smile at his sleeping face, his fiery hair rumpled and his mouth hanging ajar.

Then, memory shoves away my quiet happiness as I remember once more what happened tonight. Julian's murder at the hands of Victor Hesse replays in my memory, growing more and more grotesque with each rewind. Julian's chest exploding open. Blood everywhere. And the look on Victor Hesse's face as he ate Julian's heart.

My stomach twists, bile burning up my throat.

He'd looked so gleeful as he destroyed someone I love.

I scrub my hands over my face, trying to wipe away the memory, but Julian's death keeps looping through my mind, and I choke back tears. It feels like so much of my life now revolves around death, something I fought so hard to avoid when I first arrived on the human plane. I starved myself by refusing to feed on humans, believing their lives held greater worth than mine, and now, I starve myself again to stop from hurting those around me.

For every step I take toward a normal life, I take two steps back to being a monster. Logic tells me to lay all this death at Victor Hasse's feet, but he wouldn't be here if I hadn't killed Donnell. If I'd just listened to Landon and stayed in Dreamland where I belonged for another twenty years. Julian never would have crossed paths with the mortifer demon, and he wouldn't now be dead.

Beside me, Kellen shifts restlessly, his elbow finding my ribs and shoving against me, unable to tolerate sharing the couch any longer.

Before he takes the choice from me, I climb to my feet and drape the blanket over him before heading for the stairs to the right of the fireplace. My legs shake, and tears blur my vision as I drag myself up toward Tobias's room, craving the punishment he promised.

If given the option to do things over, would I change my actions? I don't know that I would, and the guilt of that knowledge eats at me.

With one hand on the railing, I stumble up the stairs, not seeing where I'm going until I find myself at Tobias's door.

I need Tobias's judgment, need his blunt truths, even if they're cruel. Tobias never lies to spare my feelings.

Without hesitation, I twist the knob and step inside his room.

The light from the hall briefly illuminates the black satin sheets of his bed before I shut myself inside.

My heart races as I take a step toward his bed. My feet make a quiet *shushing* noise as I shuffle across the hardwood floor. Tobias isn't one for extravagance and keeps his room minimally furnished. Like the man himself, he doesn't decorate his surroundings with plush carpets and chairs or a fireplace.

He's not soft, nor does he pretend to be.

In the quiet of the room, the sheets rustle,

followed by a low growl. "I thought you would hide, little succubus."

My knees bump up against his bed, and unable to pull words from my tight throat, I stare blindly into the dark.

Hot hands slip against my bare arms, and I shiver at the reminder I'm cold. He pulls me unresisting into his bed, peeling the clothes from my body.

Fiery lips graze the racing pulse in my neck before lifting to my ear. "Do you want me to hurt you?"

I choke in a breath that burns my lungs and nod.

Blunt nails scrape down the curve of my breast. "Because you deserve punishment?"

Shivering in his hold, I nod again. I need to be punished, to give payment for the death I couldn't stop, to somehow offer compensation for my inability to save Julian.

Tobias's nails scrape over my neck, one hard thumb pushing my chin up to leave my throat exposed. My breath grows harsher, the only sound in the darkness.

"Are you sure you want this?" Tobias asks, demanding my consent. When I go to nod, he presses against my chin harder, arresting the motion. "Say the word, little succubus."

"Yes," I whimper.

His touch vanishes, emptiness filling the space above me. His voice comes from off the bed, somewhere to my left. "Turn your back and grasp the headboard."

I swallow down the lump in my throat as I roll onto my belly and feel my way up his bed. My fingers bump against the cold, iron rungs of his headboard, and I feel my way up until I grasp the curved top, my arms above my head. The position leaves me stretched out and vulnerable, and the skin between my shoulder blades ripples, my wings pushing for release.

"Keep your wings sheathed." The command comes from right in front of me, and I flinch back in surprise.

I hadn't heard Tobias move, and the darkness and silence press in on every side. I stare into the blackness, trying to catch any hint of movement, but it's complete, without even a hint of light from the door to help me. Head turning, I listen for movement but hear nothing. When a supple, leather strap slips over my wrist, binding my hand to the bed, I jump.

Instinctively, I try to pull free, and the strap tightens, biting into my skin.

"If you fight, it only gets worse," Tobias murmurs as he catches my other hand and slips a second strap into place. "The faster you give in, the easier this will be."

My heart races in sudden fear, and despite his warning, I pull against the bindings. I came here for punishment, but deep inside, I didn't really think Tobias would hurt me. Foolishly, I thought he would use words to rip me open, lay bare all my shame, then hold me the way Kellen did.

Shame washes through me for the realization. That kind of punishment is only self-serving, more reward than restitution.

I sag against the headboard, my hands tingling with blood loss. My wrists hurt, the straps cutting into my flesh, but Tobias doesn't ease them for me. I was warned and fought anyway. This is part of the punishment.

Something long and soft trails over my bare calves, like a heavy tassel. "Do you know what this is?"

I've built enough BDSM fantasies to guess, and my voice wavers. "A flogger."

"Good," he purrs. "And do you know what I'm going to do with it?"

I swallow down my fear. "Whip me."

The whip drags up the crease of my ass and over my bare back. "Do you want to escape?"

Biting my lip, I shake my head.

"Speak!" he commands sharply.

"No," I choke out. "I deserve this."

"Why?" The word drifts around me, disembodied as if he inhabits the darkness itself.

"Julian died because of me."

"You feel responsible for his death." The flogger withdraws. "For drawing the mortifer demon's attention."

"Yes." I twist to pinpoint him, and the bindings grow tighter.

"Julian challenged the mortifer the same as you did. Why do you get to claim the blame for that?"

I force my numb fingers around the iron headboard to ease the bindings. "I killed Domnall, and Victor Hesse killed Julian to get back at me."

"Julian helped in that killing. You are not responsible for what happened to him."

"But he wouldn't have done that if I hadn't drawn Domnall's attention," I protest.

Air whistles, and the leather snaps against the back of my thighs.

I yelp, more from surprise than pain.

"Julian was already linked to Domnall and wanted him dead. His path would have crossed Victor Hesse's regardless of your actions." The leather straps trail over my calves. "Did you know what he would do?"

My toes curl at the ticklish sensation. "I knew he was threatening those close to me."

"Julian knew of the risk, and he chose to face it anyway." Quick as a snake, the snap of leather comes again against my thighs, leaving behind fiery pain this time. "Claiming responsibility for Victor Hesse's actions fixes nothing."

"But Julian died," I choke out. "I should have protected him better."

"He was more powerful than you and couldn't protect himself." The snap comes again, this time across my ass. "What makes you think you could have stopped what happened?"

"If I'd never come to the human plane—"

The sharp crack against my lower back cuts me off, and my spine arches, my stomach and breasts pressing against the cold iron in front of me to escape the pain. Quick snaps to my thighs and ass follow, and I clutch the headboard tighter.

Every muscle in my body tenses, the air freezing in my lungs as I wait for another blow

"What would staying in Dreamland have accomplished?"

My breath hitches, my brain scrambling for the answer. "The Hunters wouldn't have come—"

Snap. "Domnall would have come regardless. He's been circling our territory for years. And without you here, Julian's imps would have died under the Hunters' attack. Next!"

My head spins. "Domnall..." I flinch, waiting for the strike that never comes.

"What about Domnall?"

I rest my forehead against the bars. "I killed him. I knew he took the spell that locked him to his corporeal form, and I destroyed it anyway." Tears leak down my face. "I killed him, and because of that, Victor Hesse was able to harvest his magic."

The flogger caresses my stinging flesh. "Did you kill Domnall out of spite?"

"No." I shake my head, the bars painful against my forehead.

The hard handle of the whip nudges under my chin, lifting my head. "For vengeance?"

That had been part of it, but not what drove my hand into his chest, not what curled my fingers around his heart. I shake my head again. "No."

Tobias's voice fills my ear. "Then, why?"

He had hurt Julian and planned to continue. He had threatened Tally and her witches.

The flogger trails down my throat. "Why, Adie?"

More tears roll down my cheeks. "He was going to hurt the people I care about."

Tobias pulls away, leaving me alone in the darkness once more. "And if you could do it again?"

Guilt and anger war within me. Domnall needed to be stopped. He had hurt so many people, including Julian, and he would have continued his path of destruction. "I would rip his heart out without hesitation."

"Even knowing it would bring Victor Hesse here? Even knowing what he would do?"

My hands clench the headboard hard enough to bend it. "Yes."

The darkness presses in around me. "Why?"

"Because I can't stand aside while those I love are hurt!"

The mattress dips behind me. "And if someone threatens them again?"

The headboard creaks within my hold. "I'll destroy the threat!"

"Good," Tobias purrs. He grips my hips, his hard body pressing against my back. "Don't let anyone make you weak, Adie. Embrace what you feel, acknowledge its source, and accept the decisions you've made." His hands slip up my waist, brushing the sides of my breasts, before they travel down my arms to curl around my wrists. "If you let guilt shackle you, you'll hesitate when it matters, and if that happens, I won't hold back on punishing you." His fingers curl around my bindings hard enough to make my bones ache. "Do you understand?"

"Yes." I flex my fingers, trying to work feeling back into them.

Tobias plucks at the straps, and they loosen enough to allow blood to flow back to my hands in a tingling rush of pinpricks, but he doesn't free me. Instead, he pats my bare ass, then settles on the bed. The sheets rustle as he pulls them back into place.

I stare down in confusion, unable to make him out in the dark. "Tobias?"

"Shh." He pats my leg. "Be good and let me sleep, now. We have a lot to do tomorrow."

"But..." I tug at the bindings. "You didn't—"

"This is your punishment for turning the house

against us and locking yourself out of reach." His hand curls around my calf. "And before you decide to escape, if you're not here until morning, I'll make you wear that flogger as a tail and prance you around the house like a pony. Now, not another word."

My mouth drops open in shock before I snap my teeth close, wisely staying silent.

Body Snatchers

The exterior of the fortune-telling place looks the same as the last time I visited, and the bell above the door jingles happily as I enter. The incense is just as strong today as the last time, too, and I breathe shallowly through my mouth, trying to inhale as little of the fumes as possible.

Just how often do demons come knocking, that they have that stuff on a constant burn?

When I'd woken, I found myself freed of Tobias's binds and my body wrapped in a thick blanket that smelled like ozone and fire. I didn't want to leave his room but forced myself out while Tobias still slept. I'd gotten ready quickly and left a note for the guys before I headed out. With my time limited, I need all the hours I have left. And my first mission of the morning is to speak to Flint.

The woman behind the counter recognizes me

and snuffs out the incense even as she frowns. "I don't have you on the books until later today."

I stop in front of the counter. "I'd like a consult for a different issue."

Still frowning, she reaches for the phone that hangs on the back wall. She speaks into it too quietly for me to hear, and I don't waste the minimal energy I have to try to heighten my senses.

After a moment, she hangs up and pulls the beaded curtain aside to expose the hall that leads to the back offices. "He can see you now."

Nodding, I step through and hurry down the creepy hallway with its too many sprinklers. The thick, metal door at the end swings open before I reach it, and I step into the company's main office.

A woman I haven't met before offers me a smile in greeting, waits for me to walk past, then bolts the door behind me. She even swings down a thick, metal crossbar I didn't notice on our last visit.

I shiver at the level of fortification this place has. "You need that a lot?"

"You can never be too safe." She gives me another smile, like this is all perfectly normal. And maybe, for her, it is. "I'm the office manager around here. Would you like some coffee? Or tea?"

"No, thank you." I glance toward Flint's office,

the clock in my head ticking with every second we waste on niceties.

She must sense my impatience because she motions for me to follow her. "This way."

We walk the path to Flint's office, passing the same empty offices we did before. Does no one else come in to work this early?

Flint waits for me behind his desk, a curious look on his way too pretty face. "Adie, you need something else?"

I stop in the doorway, much to the office manager's consternation. "Your presence. Grab whatever bag of tricks you need and come with me."

His brows lift, and his eyes shift past me. "It's fine, Hilda. I'll take it from here." He waits for her to leave before returning his attention to me. "I need more information. I don't have a one-trick bag."

My brows pinch together. "You don't?"

Reese always has exactly what they need in his giant duffle bag, and Xander always has his laptop at the ready.

"No, I don't." He motions for me to come inside, and I reluctantly perch on the edge of one of his chairs. "Where are we going, and what are we doing when we get there?"

"Julian, the incubus I planned to link my core

to, was killed last night," I state with as little emotion as possible. Grieving more for Julian won't change what happened, so I need to focus on moving forward. "His corporeal body didn't disintegrate, and unfortunately, it's been claimed by the human police."

Flint blinks a couple times as he takes in the information before nodding. "That...certainly changes things. Go on."

My hands clench into fists in my lap. "I need you to come with me to the morgue to see if his essence is still trapped within his body, and if it is, I need you to free it."

He purses his lips for a moment. "That's high-level magic you're asking for."

"I also need for his body to not disintegrate once you free his essence." I hold his gaze steady. "The humans can't be made suspicious by a vanishing corpse."

Flint leans back and folds his hands over his stomach as he thinks. "I can check if his essence is still in his body, that's no problem. Freeing it is a little more complicated and takes time during which the humans will grow suspicious, but I can certainly do it. Having the body not disintegrate though... Without magic powering the corporeal form, I can't stop it from going through its natural process. I'm not that kind of witch." When my lips part, he holds up a hand. "What I *can* do is swap it with a doppelganger. But I'll need another body to act as a stand-in."

Unease rolls through me, but I refuse to let my fear of zombies sway me. "We'll be in a morgue full of bodies."

"And full of cameras and witnesses," he points out. "I'm going to need help. Which means a steeper price."

I frown at him. "You bound yourself to help see me through this curse. Julian is part of that. You will do this, or you will forfeit your contract."

He sighs heavily. "Demons aren't the only ones capable of creating contracts. I know what's in mine, and Julian is *not* required. This is a job separate from the one I agreed to perform and comes at a different price with a new contract, which will include compensation if I'm thrown in jail for stealing bodies."

My eyes narrow on him. "If you do your job right, you won't be caught."

"Well, yes, that's the goal." He reaches across the desk, his hand out. "Do we have a deal?"

"Fine." I gasp his hand in mine. "Deal. Show me this contract."

After some haggling and surrendering all of the funds I saved from selling my feathers to Tobias, we come to a deal. Once he has my signature, Flint makes a series of phone calls. When he finishes, he puts on a disguise, fills his pockets with more of those terrifying little bottles, and announces himself ready to go.

We arrive at the morgue before I'm emotionally ready and follow the signs down to the basement. This part of the hospital lacks the pretense of the more public spaces. A white plastic covering protects the walls from denting, and the white floor, while clean, holds scuff marks from years of heavy traffic.

It makes me miss Kellen's mortuary, where everything is done in wood and earth tones to help soothe the nerves of the people who come to view their dead. I could use a bit of soothing right now.

We stop at a check-in desk, and the guard behind the counter checks his list, then waves us through.

One of Flint's many phone calls was to a hacker,

who put our name on the list of approved people to visit Julian's body.

Farther down the hall, another guard greets us. He takes one look at the black shirt and white-collar Flint wears and dips his head. "Father."

"Be at peace, my child." Flint waves his hand through the air to draw a cross. "We are here to give last rights to Julian Poe, before his body is desecrated."

"Of course, Father." The guard lifts a walkie talkie from his belt and talks into it, then clips it back in place. "They're readying his body now. You may go as far as the viewing room."

"Of course." Flint lifts the Bible he carries. "We seek only to deliver his troubled soul to his next destination. We will not interfere with the police investigation."

"Thank you, Father." The walkie-talkie crackles, and the guard lifts it once more, then looks at us. "You may go in now."

He presses a button on the wall beside him, and the double doors swing inward.

We walk into a utilitarian room with plastic seats and a long wall filled with a window. Through the window, the room stands empty, the metal lockers that fill the back wall all shut tight. Only a single gurney sits at its center, a white sheet covering Julian's body, except for his head.

Someone cleaned the blood from his face and closed his eyes, hiding the surprise he had in death. I drift closer to the window, my gaze locked on him. He looks peaceful, the pallor of his skin the only sign he won't just sit up and demand to get out of here.

Flint joins me and stares silently into the room, waiting for some signal.

After a few minutes, he nods and heads for the door into the room. "Come on. We only have a few minutes while the cameras are on loop."

We'd talked out the plan in the car. Flint would draw out Julian's essence while I grab a body to use as a doppelganger in his place. Whatever spell Flint had cooked up would transfer Julian's appearance to the new body, complete with the hole through his chest.

I feel bad we'll be robbing someone else of the chance to bury their loved one, but desperate times call for desperate measures.

As Flint pushes through the conveniently unlocked door into the morgue—another courtesy of his hacker friend—the acrid smell of disinfectant fills my nose. The scent burns my nostrils, and I know I won't soon forget it.

I stride straight for the wall of lockers, while Flint veers over to Julian's body, pulling a blue clay bottle from his pocket as he moves.

Even before he reaches Julian, he taps the bottom of the bottle in a rhythmic *thump, thump, thump* that fills the quiet room with the sound of a heartbeat. I feel the tug to answer at my core, the desire to follow the beat into the bottle. But then, the beast inside me roars to life, sinking claws into my essence and locking me within the shell of my body, the curse Victor Hesse laid claiming my core.

Pain slices through me, and I stumble a step before I continue on, my hand finding the lock on the first refrigerator. The tray I pull out holds a woman. I shove it back into place and move on to the next. Flint had said a male body would make the spell stick better.

The next locker holds a child, and I force myself not to focus on the young features as I shut it away, too. Even if the spell would work on a child, I wouldn't be able to bring myself to use one. Some griefs deserve closure, no matter what.

The thumping grows louder, filling my ears, and the pain I pushed down surges forth, even stronger.

It hadn't felt like this when Flint pulled

Domnall's essence from his body. Is it the curse? Or does he need more mojo for Julian?

When the sound abruptly cuts off, it leaves a vacuum of silence in its wake, and I freeze, one hand on the handle to the next freezer. "Is it done?"

"No," comes the quiet response. "Leave the body. We need to get out of here."

I spin to face him. "Finish it."

"I can't." He strides toward the door. "Julian's not in there."

Panic races through me, and I chase after Flint. "What do you mean he's not in there?"

"Just what I said." He pushes through the door and walks back to the viewing window, gesturing for me to hurry. "Get into position. We need to be in place when the loop ends."

I step up to his side and bow my head as if in prayer while my heart breaks.

If Julian's not in his body, does that mean he's really, truly gone?

Interrogation

Numbness fills me on the drive back to the fortune-telling shop, where I drop Flint off at the curb with the promise to meet later for my scheduled trip into the bottle, though I now wonder if that's still an option. The beast inside me seems to think otherwise and might tear itself free before Flint can safely contain me.

The drive back home passes in a blur. The shock of Julian not being in his body crushed my last hope that he survived Victor Hesse's attack. The only recourse left is to file a blood debt against the mortifer demon, but that does nothing to assuage what he took from me. Revenge and money won't bring Julian back.

He's gone. Snuffed out of existence.

When I stumble into the house, the guys are there waiting, Tobias with his anger that I left alone,

Kellen with his carefully blank face, and Emil with his frozen composure.

I walk straight toward my ice demon, needing the numbness that his arms can offer, but freeze a foot away from touching him. The smell of snow hangs heavy in the air around him and tickles at my skin, asking to be let in, and hunger rolls through me. The beast awoken by Flint's call refuses to lay back down to sleep. It wants the buffet in front of me, wants to tear into Emil's stomach and feast on all of the power he holds.

A shudder rolls through me, shaking my entire body, before I force myself away. No, I won't see another person I love hurt.

I wrap my arms around my stomach as if that will hold the beast back and stumble to the couch. Falling face-first onto it, I burrow my head between the cushions and scream. Scream for the loss of Julian. Scream for the loss of being able to touch my men. Scream out all the grief bottled inside me and the anger at my inability to fix what's wrong.

The others gather around me, their presence pushing at my senses, and I scream again for the loss of their touch. I *need* them with an ache that rips at my insides, and I know I can't have them because I'll tear them apart.

I scream until my pain blocks out the beast's hunger, drowning it in grief. Only when my throat burns and the taste of copper fills my mouth do I stop.

Tobias, Kellen, and Emil remain silent, giving me the time I need to collect myself, waiting with the patience grown over centuries of existence.

At last, I push myself upright. My throat feels scraped raw, and a hollow ache fills me, an emptiness that can't be filled.

Blurry eyed, I stare at the concerned faces around me. "Julian's gone."

Understanding passes between them, and Kellen walks away, his phone in his hand. Quiet conversation drifts from the kitchen as he calls Philip to inform the imp there is no need to blow up the hospital.

I look at Tobias. "How long before we need to go to the police station?"

He shakes his head, his chestnut-brown locks falling over his forehead. "We can skip it."

"No. I need to go make my statement before tonight." I swallow, my throat aching with the motion. "If something goes wrong, we don't want the police to become suspicious about my disappearance."

"I'll get you some honey tea for your throat." Emil strides for the kitchen, his steps stiff with purpose.

I watch him go, watch the icy footprints he leaves behind melt. My ice demon is losing the ability to contain the power he holds. "What's going to happen?"

"You're going to go into the bottle, and in twenty-four hours, you're going to come out healed," Tobias says fiercely, as if sheer determination will make it so. "Then, we're going to go on that beach vacation, all of us, and we're going to relax in the sun and spend every night together. Your imps will take care of Tac while we're gone, and when we return, we'll throw a party and celebrate the life Julian lived."

I smile at the images he paints, wanting that future. "You know the imps will take over the house if we leave them here alone. All of your stuff will become theirs."

He frowns at that. "Maybe we'll have Tac go stay with them at *their* house."

I laugh softly. "You can't take Tac away from his whelps."

His frown deepens. "Fuyumi will just have to go with Tac, then."

"Okay, I'll let you inform her of that." I look around, missing my giant cat monster. "Where is Tac?"

"Crooning at his babies in the backyard, I think." He shrugs. "Either that, or he crawled over the wall again."

I shake my head. "He has a death wish."

Tobias smiles. "He took another oil lamp from the basement."

"What's with that, anyway?"

"It's the fish oil in the lamp," Emil says as he returns with a steaming mug of tea in hand. He passes it to me. "Nekomata are especially fond of fish oil."

"Eww." I wrinkle my nose. "I didn't realize you kept the lamps in the basement filled."

"Oh, I don't." Emil shudders. "Imagine the mess Tac would have made."

"Then why...?"

"No one ever said Tac was smart." Emil looks me dead in the eye. "He tried to woo an ostrich, remember?"

I snort with amusement. "But imagine what those babies would have looked like."

We all take a moment to picture that and break out in laughter.

Kellen returns and stares at us in bemusement. "What's so funny?"

"Ostrich monsters," I say, and Tobias and Emil laugh harder.

Not getting the joke, Kellen just shakes his head. "Okay crazy people." He checks his watch. "If you're determined to go to the station, you'd better do it soon."

The reminder sobers us, and I lift the mug Emil gave me, chugging the sweet contents. The tea burns going down, but the thick honey helps to soothe my throat.

I pass it back, then push to my feet. "I'm going to go change, then I'll be ready."

Despite all the other scents in the house, I can still smell the morgue. If we had more time, I'd take a shower, but I doubt any amount of scrubbing could wash away the scent of death.

When we arrive at the police station, a uniformed police officer directs us to an ill-lit room with a metal table at the center. We take the seats facing the one-way mirror, and I fiddle with the metal rung welded to the table where they handcuff dangerous suspects.

Detective Hinky leaves us waiting for a while, but that's okay, since I can feel his stare from the other side of the mirror. If he wants to make us sweat, he'll have to try harder.

At last, he joins us in the interrogation room and pulls out the seat across from us. "Thank you for coming today."

"We didn't have a choice." I flip the metal rung back and forth, liking the way it clangs. "You have a shitty way of treating victims, you know?"

He frowns at that. "We need to know what happened before the memory of the event fades."

I lift my gaze to him. "That memory will never fade."

He ignores that and pulls a recorder from his pocket, sets it in the middle of the table, then presses the button on the side. "This is Detective Sharpe. Please, state your names."

Tobias looks at the recorder. "Tobias Braxton."

When Detective Sharpe's eyes move to me, I say, "Adeline Boo Pond."

"We are here today to go over the events of Julian Poe's death. Now—"

Tobias lifts a hand to stop him. "Are we being charged with anything?"

Detective Sharpe glances between us. "Not at this time."

"So, we are free to leave whenever we want?" he presses.

"Yes," Detective Sharpe agrees. "Though it's in your best interest to just answer the questions."

I look at Tobias. While I want to leave, we need to get this over with.

He glares at the detective for a moment before saying, "If this turns accusatory in any way, or makes Ms. Pond uncomfortable in any way, we will be leaving, and you will have to go through me for any further contact."

Detective Sharpe pulls out a notebook. "So, you're here today as Ms. Pond's lawyer?"

"Yes," Tobias states. "I am also here to represent myself. And I will be present when you interview Mr. Cassius and Mr. König."

Detective Sharpe makes more notes, his handwriting illegible from the opposite side of the table. It all looks like shorthand and chicken scratches from where I sit.

When he looks up once more, his face is serious. "Tell me about last night."

Tobias nods at me, and I clasp my hands in my lap. "We were having a small get together. Julian was heading home when he was attacked. He was walking to his car, then he was dead."

It's the same thing we told the detectives last night, and the same thing we'll continue to tell them.

Detective Sharpe looks at Tobias. "And where were you at the time of the attack?"

Beside me, Tobias stiffens. He doesn't like the fact he wasn't there at the time of the attack. "I was inside. I didn't know what happened until after it was over."

I want to reach for his hand, to reassure him it's not his fault, but I keep my fingers woven tightly together.

"There was a hole punched through Mr. Poe's chest, and his heart is missing." Detective Sharpe looks between us. "Any idea what could have caused that?"

Once more, I see Victor Hesse's bloody fist with Julian's still-beating heart held in its grasp. "No idea. I've never heard of a weapon that could do something like that."

The detective nods. "Tell me about Mr. Poe's

business. Did he have any enemies you are aware of?"

"He owned a catering service," I tell him. "As far as I'm aware, caterers don't have enemies."

"Yes, a catering business that only employs attractive young strippers." Condescension fills his voice. "Not your normal catering service. Was Mr. Poe a pimp?"

The question catches me off guard. "Excuse me?"

"Was Mr. Poe a pimp?" Detective Sharpe asks again.

"It's not unusual for companies to hire attractive young *people*," Tobias rumbles. "HelloHell Delivery is legit. You can ask any of his clients."

"Oh, I will," Detective Sharpe assures. "What was his co-owner doing sneaking around your house last night?"

My spine straightens. "Philip wasn't sneaking. He was supposed to meet Julian there and was running late."

Detective Sharpe lifts one brow. "So, he came in through the back door?"

"Was he supposed to tromp through the crime scene?" I demand.

"You will have to ask Mr. Davis about last

night," Tobias cuts in. "We are not here to speak for his actions."

Detective Sharpe makes a note. "He left rather quickly."

Of course, he would know that. They were still going over the scene when Philip stormed out. He hadn't used the backdoor in his rush to leave.

"He was upset," I snap. "He had just found out his friend was dead."

"Tell me about the car bomb."

The segue gives me whiplash, but Tobias takes it in stride. "Shouldn't I be the one asking *you* about that? You're the lead investigator, and we have yet to hear that you solved the case."

A flush creeps up the detective's cheeks. "You weren't helpful to that investigation, either."

"I had no information to impart." Tobias leans back in his seat, perfectly relaxed. "I don't know why anyone would blow up my car."

"Was Mr. Poe a client of yours?" he asks.

"He was," Tobias concedes. "We handled his business finances, as well as his personal account."

"Yes, his business finances." He flips through his notebook. "In addition to owning HelloHell Delivery, Mr. Poe also acted as a landlord for quite a few properties around town."

Seeing where this is going, my stomach tightens.

"Properties owned by Mr. Cassius, whom you both live with, correct?" At our nods, he looks at his notebook again. "He also owns the mortuary, where we had reports of a possible homicide. Where the neighbor's house caught fire shortly after we received a tip about suspicious activity going on next door."

My pulse jumps, and I clench my hands tighter together until my fingers go numb.

Detective Sharpe leans forward like a bloodhound on a scent. "Mr. Poe worked for Mr. Cassius and is now dead, as are the mortician he employed and his funeral director. As are the neighbors who may have witnessed what goes on in that funeral home." He looks at me. "And based on your report of stalkers, it sounds like you are being targeted as well. You are Mr. Cassius's *woman*, are you not? That's how he refers to you with his employees."

"Are you getting to a point?" Tobias grinds out.

A slow smile creeps across his face. "How long has Mr. Cassius been running the local mafia?"

FIREPOWER

My mouth drops open, and I instantly snap it shut.

That's the conclusion he came to? Okay, yeah, Kellen sometimes makes bodies disappear, and he's a bit of a slumlord, but...

Wait, does Kellen actually run the mafia?

I carefully avoid looking at Tobias for answers.

Detective Sharpe's gaze shifts to me. "You didn't know who you were dating."

"I still don't know." I lift my chin. "You need some proof to back up an accusation like that."

"I have a line of bodies that all point back to him and, by association, all of you." He leans across the table, his eyes intent. "Someone is obviously trying for a coup by taking out Mr. Cassius's people. If you confess now, we can work out a deal. We're not after small fish, and by our records, you only came into contact with these men last summer. You can't be in too deep. We'll protect you from whatever actions they'll take against you for turning on them."

At that, I laugh in his face. "You can't be serious." More laughter bubbles up, sounding hysterical. "*You*, protect *me*? From *them*?" I hook a thumb at Tobias. "No, I really don't think so."

Tobias stands, grabbing my arm in the process and hoisting me to my feet. "Unless we're being charged with something, we're leaving. Any further contact with me or my roommates will have to come with a court order."

The laughter keeps bubbling out, and Tobias practically drags me to the door.

"We can help you, Ms. Pond." Detective Sharpe follows us out into the hall. "Whatever they have on you, we can protect you."

My laughter cuts off, and I look back over my shoulder, my teeth bared. "You don't have the firepower to protect me from shit, Detective. Have a good day."

Tobias shushes me and marches us out of the police station and back to his car, where he stuffs me inside.

"Well, that was pointless," I say as soon as Tobias joins me in the car.

"Not pointless." He jams his key into the

ignition. "At least, now, we know the angle they're taking on this investigation."

"Is Kellen running the mafia?" I demand as Tobias pulls away from the curb and traffic moves out of his way. "I thought he just... helped dispose of bad people."

"He doesn't run the mafia." Tobias changes lanes without looking, and the cars around us magically change lanes to make space. "He played that game back in the fifties but didn't have a taste for it."

"He did?" I ask in surprise.

Tobias's dark eyes cut to me. "We've all done bad things over the centuries, for one reason or another."

"They're going to figure out a way to pin all this on him, aren't they?" I ask, my amusement from earlier dying in the face of Tobias's grim expression.

"They'll try." He rolls his head, his vertebrae popping. "We'll deal with it when it happens."

"What's the exit plan?" I ask, because of course they'll have one. They're too crafty not to.

"We'll still take that vacation. We just won't come back." Tobias speeds through a yellow light. "We have accounts all over the world, different identities, different businesses."

My heart lurches. "Oh, yeah."

He looks at me. "We'll get you a new bakery. Moving isn't the end. It's just a new start."

But it would mean leaving behind the friends I've made here. And my imps. I couldn't uproot them. Not when they've begun to find places for themselves in the human world.

As a demon, I always knew living on the human plane would mean uprooting every thirty years or so. I just thought I'd have more time.

I drop my eyes to my lap. "Why can't you permanently contract with me?"

The question has been burning in the back of my mind since Emil refused the idea, and with everything else that's happening right now, I want to know the answer to this specific issue. I love them, and they love me. Those emotions aren't changing, so what's stopping us from making this relationship permanent?

Silence fills the car, and when I look up once more, I find Tobias focused on the road, his hands clenched tight around the steering wheel.

A tremor fills my voice. "Tobias?"

"It's complicated." He peels one hand off the wheel to reach out and grasp mine. "We're trying to uncomplicate it. We just need some time."

Time is something I'm not sure I have, though.

It took a lot for me to ask for a permanent contract to begin with. It's not something demons go into lightly. Not with how long we live. But Julian's death drove home how abruptly our existence can be cut off.

I want to bind myself to these men and bind them to me in return. It will make going into the bottle so much easier. Whatever happens while I'm trapped won't matter if I hold their lives in my hands.

"We have time," Tobias repeats with another squeeze to my hand.

"Sure, we do." I pull my hand from his. "We just have to get through this new obstacle first, right?"

"Right," he agrees, and silence once more surrounds us.

At five o'clock, Tally and her witches arrive. We had discussed the best place to try to fix me and decided the house where I feel the safest would be our best bet.

Reese and Xander begin to set up as we move the furniture out of the living room to clear the space for the coming spell. Reese had said we were closest to the ley line in here, and any bit of extra oomph will help. Emil doesn't even protest when Jax gets out his tool bag and kneels on the floor to dig out a circle. No chalk for us today. There can be no room left for error tonight.

I had offered to do this at Tally's house, where there's already a gold circle we could use, but the guys hadn't wanted to risk it. If something goes horribly wrong, and I have to be locked in the circle, they at least want me to be home, surrounded by the people I love.

Tally walks over to stand at my side and slips an arm around me. Out of everyone here, I pose no risk to her. Though her body is made of magic, it's not the kind the beast inside me craves. Unlike Domnall, I don't want witch magic, which means his curse was laid specifically to force me to hurt my demons of destruction. Forcing me to rip them apart would be the ultimate revenge and destroy the last thread of what holds me together, turning me into a mindless monster.

The smell of hot metal fills the air, and I look over to find Tobias standing with a bowl in his hands. The witches had brought a torch with them to melt the gold, but they don't need it with Tobias around.

Hunger grumbles inside me, and I force my eyes away from temptation.

"It will be okay," Tally says, and I try not to let the words get to me.

Everyone keeps saying that. Like they're some kind of magical blessing that will make the spell go off without a hitch. But in reality, no one is sure what Victor Hesse did to me, and messing with the markings cut into my body could explode with catastrophic consequences for everyone involved.

"If this goes wrong, I will take you to Dreamland," Tally adds. "I will not let you harm those here."

I look at her in surprise. "You know this has the risk of turning me into a ravenous monster. You'd set me loose on the baku?"

"We are good at hiding." Her mahogany eyes hold mine. "You will not harm us. And you will not fall into Victor Hesse's clutches. I promise you."

Some of the tension eases from me. Demons don't make promises lightly. If Tally says she will drag my crazy ass to Dreamland to protect everyone here, then I believe her.

"I'm still hoping that this Flint man will succeed, though," she adds with a troubled look toward Reese and Xander. "They have been studying hard, but this soul magic is difficult."

"I trust them to do what they can." Wrapping my arm around her, I give her a side hug. "They're powerful. And clever. They would make good demons."

"They would, wouldn't they?" She smiles softly. "I will mourn them when they pass."

"Then, get them working on immortality, once this is done," I advise. "If they can master soul magic, surely they can figure out how to pause time."

"Such things would have consequences." She looks at them again. "But I would pay the price to keep them longer."

I feel the same about my demons of destruction. My eyes find Tobias once more, then shift to Emil, who stands as far from me as possible while still being in the same room. Frost coats his cheeks and glistens in his hair. It makes my mouth water, filling me with the desire to lick away all that ice. He needs me every bit as much as I need him.

As if he senses my thoughts, his eyes meet mine, and snowflakes drift across his pupils. Winter rides him hard right now, but he's keeping it together, waiting patiently for me to be able to embrace him once more.

Tac nudges up against his side, one feathered wing lifting to drape around Emil like a living blanket. The cat monster looks at me, his saucer-sized, green eyes blinking slowly, and images of fire and heated blankets fill my mind, without a single knight in sight. Tac wants to keep Emil warm, too, and expects me to be here to help.

I nod at the giant cat, agreeing to do my best.

When Jax stands, Tobias walks forward with the bowl, tilting it until a thin, liquid stream of gold flows out to fill the new circle. Tobias walks slowly around, the gold flowing in a steady stream until he completes the circuit. Then, Emil steps forward, the chill from his body as he walks the circle cooling the gold into place.

It's not as pretty as the one at Tally's house, but it hums with a purpose even I can feel. Protect. Guard. Heal.

At a quarter to seven, a knock sounds at the door, and I slip free of Tally's hold to go let Flint in. He's cutting it close to the appointed time, but I'm grateful for the time to be alone with my family before he shoves me into a bottle.

Heart heavy, I pull open the door, then stumble back a pace.

It's not Flint who stands on the porch.

Blood-red eyes meet mine, and Cousin Cassandra smirks as she pushes past me into the house.

Anger instantly floods through me at her invasion, and I reach out to catch her arm. "What are you doing here? You're not allowed in Landon's territory."

"But Landon's not here, is he?" She pouts her ruby red lips at me. "Poor baby Adie, abandoned just like every other toy Landregath gets bored with."

I growl low in my throat in warning, but she ignores me as she shakes free to strut farther inside. "I'm glad I didn't miss the big event. I can't wait to watch you being locked up."

How does she know about that?

I dart in front of her to stand in her way. "You're not welcome here. You're trespassing."

"Am I, though?" She cocks her head to the side as she studies me like a bug under a microscope. "Poor, naive little thing. Haven't they told you?"

Cold pushes back my anger. "Told me?"

She leans in closer. "Who do you think steps in when there's no other succubus in this house? Who do you think is called on to drain these delicious creatures of all that energy?"

Nausea bubbles in my stomach. "What?" I shake my head. "No, you only just met…"

But then, I remember the last time she was in this house and how she'd laid her hands on Emil, and he let her. I hadn't thought of it at the time, because I hadn't known them well. But I know better now, and these men aren't given to casual touches.

The realization must show on my face, because she throws back her head and laughs.

I look at Emil, and for the first time, his eyes don't meet mine.

"I'm their council-appointed succubus, stupid girl. And as soon as you go into that bottle, I'll be taking over again." As my eyes widen in shock, she grins to reveal sharp, pointy teeth. "What, you didn't think you were *special,* did you?" She *tsks* quietly. "They really led you on, huh? But, don't worry. Soon, none of that will matter, because you're going bye-bye, baby Adie."

Time to Choose

The floor seems to tilt, leaving me unbalanced as Cousin Cassandra steps around me, her predatory gaze fixed on Emil.

No. The word pounds through me. *No, not* her. *Not my men.*

My hands curl into fists, my sharp claws biting into my palms.

"You need to leave, Cassandra," I say, my voice low and shaky with the restraint it takes not to fling myself at her. "You're not welcome here."

She tosses a derisive look over her shoulder. "Like you can make me? Landregath's not here this time to fight your battles."

"You need to leave," Tobias says as the air fills with the scent of burning. "When our current contractee is present, you have no right to be here."

She tosses her head. "It's a matter of minutes. Are you seriously going to make me wait on the porch?"

"Yes," Emil snaps. "Better yet, wait outside our territory, where you belong."

"I belong *here*." She spreads her arms wide to encompass the room. "I don't know why you three keep fighting it. At the end of the world, there will only be us, so you should just get used to it."

I hold my breath, waiting for them to force her out, but they don't move. She won't leave on her own, and they're bound not to hurt her.

Anger boils through me, and I stomp over to stand in front of her once more. She'll have to go through me to reach them, and I'm prepared to fight tooth and claw to stop her.

The beast in me rumbles with interest, seeing prey I actively despise. It whispers for me to grab her, to tear her apart and dig out her insides. It tells me how good it will feel to feast on her power and eat her whole.

A low rumble starts in my throat as my claws lengthen, turning into daggers made to rent flesh from bone.

Cassandra's brows shoot up. "Are you seriously

threatening me, baby Adie? Don't you remember what happened last time?"

"This isn't like last time," I growl, flexing my fingers. "You won't find me such an easy target anymore."

Her nostrils flare, scenting the air, before she throws her head back and laughs. "Please. I can barely smell you. You're wasted away to nothing and just haven't accepted it yet."

Not true. I feel it in my bones and in my blood. The more I lose my succubus self, the greater the space becomes for the beast that grows inside me.

I step forward, ready to attack.

Before I can reach her, though, someone yanks me back, spinning me across the brand-new circle of gold engraved in the hardwood floor. Tobias, Emil, and Kellen join me, and a moment later, a wall of magic rises around us, locking us on one side and Cassandra on the other.

Snarling, I launch myself at my prey only to bounce off the wall and tumble to the floor. I hiss and whip around to focus on Xander and Reese, the ones keeping me from tearing Cassandra apart.

They stare at me with wide eyes before Tally steps in front of them, gossamer wings lifting from her body to shield her men. "I will not allow you to harm those you care for, my friend."

I don't want to harm them, though. I just want them to let me out so I can devour Cassandra the same way she's taken so many of our kind. It would be a fitting end for her to be consumed.

But when I try to tell them that, to reason, all that comes out is another growl.

"What are you protecting her for?" Cassandra calls from right next to me, only a shimmering wall of iridescent magic between us. "Let her out. I'm more than happy to put her down like the bitch she is."

"Leave, Cassandra," Kellen commands, none of his usual playfulness in his tone. "As Adie said, you're not welcome here."

"Welcome or not, it's my place to stay." She paces a step away from me, her eyes fixing on Emil. "Look at you, my ice god. Look at how she's neglected you. Do your frozen bones ache? Does the slush in your blood make you tired? I can warm you."

Snarling, I launch myself at her again, and the barrier around us shivers.

She ignores me, her voice a sweet siren song of invitation. "Does the call of extinction tempt you with every day that passes? The need to release those ice ages and finally free yourself? I can ease that for you, remind you of summer."

No. Not my Emil. She will not feed on my ice demon. The word throbs through me, and I slam against the barrier again. When my shoulder pops at the impact, I barely register the pain.

Her focus shifts to Kellen. "And what about you, my storm god?"

I snarl at her claiming and slam my body against the barrier over and over.

"We can fly through the lightning-heavy clouds and drink from the rain," she croons. "When was the last time you allowed yourself such freedom, locked in this house with an incompetent child?"

Kellen glares at her, lightning snapping from his skin like sparklers. "Leave."

Instead, her focus shifts to Tobias, and she purrs with anticipation. "I have new toys for us to play with. And brand-new skin for you to break. I've missed being bound to your bed. Missed your wrath."

Red clouds my vision as I picture her in the place I knelt, subjected to Tobias's punishment and left yearning for more. *Never. She will never feel that sweet torment again. That relief of acceptance brought through pain.*

Pulling back my arm, I slam my fist forward. My knuckles pop and break before sweet air kisses my split skin and I feel freedom.

Then, rough hands pull me back, and the hole I made snaps shut.

The smell of burning lava surrounds me, and Tobias stares down at me as his pupils slowly expand to block out the whites. "You will not lose what's left by feeding on that trash can. Do you understand? She's not worth it."

Cassandra hisses with anger. "What did you just call me?"

"A trash can." Tobias turns his head to stare at her. "You're the waste bucket we're forced to toss our power into. Nothing more. And we replace you at every opportunity because your filth disgusts us."

She sucks in a sharp, angry breath. "You will regret that when you're on your knees, begging me to take you."

"I have never begged for anything from you." Tobias turns back to me, starlight in his eyes. "But I am begging you, my sweet Adeline, to stay with us. Don't give in to this curse. We need you."

My heart breaks at the desperation in his face,

and I reach up one broken, claw-filled hand. The bones pop back into place, the skin over my knuckles knitting back together as my fingers straighten. With a loud pop, the shoulder on my opposite arm snaps back into place.

It costs energy I don't have to spare, but it's worth it when Tobias takes my hand and presses it to his cheek before turning his mouth against my palm to kiss me in the only way he can right now.

The warmth of his lips promise love and hope, emotions that confuse the beast and force it back.

My thoughts begin to clear, and I stare from him to the others. No matter what secrets they hide, their feelings for me are real. They chose *me*, a broken and incompetent succubus, over Cassandra. She's just the interloper forced on them by others.

"I love you, too, Grumpy Pants," I whisper, the words cracking from my raw throat. "I'm not leaving."

Cassandra's bitter laugh cuts through the moment. "You don't have a choice, you stupid child. Or don't you remember your date with your prison?"

No, I haven't forgotten, but I won't be in the bottle for long. Reese and Xander will help Flint fix me. Then, I'll be out again, ready to feed and grow strong enough to kick her ass if she ever looks at my men again.

Thumping comes from the kitchen, and I look past Tobias to see Tac entering the living room, his giant, green eyes wide with curiosity. Merp and Prem peek out from around his wing joints, chirping out questions.

When Tac spots Cassandra, his ears flatten against the top of his head, and he lets out a rumbling growl of warning. His wings rustle and tuck tighter around his whelps as he backpedals toward the kitchen.

An evil smile spreads over Cassandra's lips as she stalks toward him. "Tac, what do you have there? Are those babies? Let Auntie Cassandra see."

Tac's lips peel back to reveal dagger long canines and his eyes narrow.

Seeing my babies in danger, the beast slams back into possession of my body. I launch myself forward, only for Tobias to catch me and hold me tight. I snarl, claws reaching for my prey, and Tobias struggles to contain me.

Emil lurches toward the edge of the barrier. "Stay away from them!"

Cassandra looks back over her shoulder with a

pretty pout. "If you refuse to play with me, then I'll have to find my fun some other way."

"Touch them and I'll destroy you, contract or not," Emil snarls, then whips around to glare at Xander. "Let me out."

"I can't without dropping the whole barrier." His focus jumps to where Tobias contains me. "Can you hold her?"

"Shouldn't the question be if you can stop me from ripping her apart before you can get your barrier back up," Cassandra purrs.

At the possibility of freedom, I lift my feet from the ground and shove them against Tobias's thighs, my body straining toward Cassandra.

She lets out an evil cackle. "Time to choose, boys. Your pet, or your bitch."

I snarl and rip at Tobias's hands. *Not my babies.*

Emil looks between Tac and me, and his expression ices over before he steps back, away from the barrier.

I scream a denial, ripping at Tobias's arms to no avail.

Tac lets out a loud whine before hissing at Cassandra, his claws digging up the tiles from the kitchen as he prepares to defend his whelps.

Then, a loud blast echoes through the house, ringing my eardrums, and everyone freezes.

The blast comes again, and Cassandra's body jerks as she stumbles. Blood drips to the floor around her, and she looks down in confusion at the hole in her stomach.

The sound of a shotgun reloading comes from the entryway, followed by the steady tread of boots on hardwood. Marc strides into view, with Pen and Flint a step behind.

Cassandra rears back as she stares at Marc in shock. "You. How are you still ali—"

The next blast takes off half her face, and she flies backward before slamming to the floor.

Marc calmly continues forward until he stands over her still-moving body and blasts another hole into her stomach. Then he reloads and blasts two more into her head.

Finally, her body stills.

The smell of blood fills the air with the taste of copper, and I lick my lips in hunger. The beast wants to spring forward and feast, but the power it craves in Cassandra's body already fled this plane. A moment later, so does her body as it disintegrates into dust, leaving not even a drop of blood behind.

Everyone remains frozen in shock. Where magic

couldn't have forced Cassandra out, a human weapon did with frightening ease.

Marc nods in satisfaction and lifts the shotgun to his shoulder, the muzzle pointed at the ceiling. "It won't take her long to come back, so do what you need to do. I'll keep a watch on the perimeter."

And he turns and stomps back out of the house.

"Right." Flint steps forward and eyes the barrier surrounding us. "Looks like we're all ready, so let's get this show on the road."

CORKED

Tobias's hold on me slackens, and I finally free myself to launch across the room and slam into the barrier.

Flint lifts his brows. "Are we too late? Is the curse in full effect?"

"No, she's still in there." Tobias peels me away and tries to stroke my hair.

When I snap my teeth at his fingers, he settles for just holding me with both arms banding mine to my sides and my back pressed to his chest.

His voice sends vibrations through mine as he speaks firmly. "She's still in there."

"If you say so." Flint looks around at everyone else in the circle. "But we can't work like this. Unless everyone wants to go into the bottle?"

"Drop the barrier so everyone else can get out," Tobias instructs.

At the knowledge freedom will soon be within

reach, I renew my determination to escape, and Tobias struggles to contain me.

"Are you sure?" Xander asks, worry clear in his voice. "If you let her go—"

"I won't." Tobias leans in to press his cheek against mine. "I'm not leaving you. You're not going alone."

In answer, I headbutt him hard enough to fill the air with the scent of blood once more.

Around us, the barrier drops, and everyone else springs to the other side of the golden line before it rises once more, locking only me and Tobias inside.

I hiss and snarl, thrashing within Tobias's hold. In the back of my mind, I know what it means that he's on this side with me, that he's risking his existence to help control me. And I don't want that, but I can't make my body stop fighting. The beast has full control now, and given freedom, it will hunt. It's taking the last of my control to stop it from tearing apart the people I love, and I can feel those threads fraying.

Looking at Flint, I snarl, trying to convey everything I feel in the wordless sound.

Whether he understands or not, he steps forward, a squat green bottle in his hand. He already has the cork pulled, and the small, dark opening points toward us.

He looks past me to Tobias. "Are you sure?"

I feel him nod. "Do it."

Without giving him a chance to change his mind, Flint begins to tap the bottom of the jar, out of rhythm at first, then slowly falling into the pattern of a heartbeat.

As the sound tugs at my core, pulling it forward, the beast who controls me turns inward. It hooks claws and teeth into my being, trying to hold me in place, to stop me from escaping. It needs my consciousness to control my body, and it refuses to let me go.

I fight against it, focusing on the feel of my heartbeat, matched to Flint's rhythmic tapping, and stare at the small, dark opening that waits. I will myself to go, to leave this body and enter the bottle.

The beast continues to fight, but I pull its claws out of me one by one, unhook its fangs, and shove hard.

For a moment, I float outside my body, free of the constant pain, free of the hunger and aching emptiness. I see the tethers that still hold me to my corporeal form like shining threads that lead from my core to my body, and other strings that shoot outward, connecting me to Tobias, Kellen, and Emil. Then, narrower threads that connect me to my imps. And buried among them is a thin, almost invisible thread of pink that shoots away across the city to a place I can't see.

Elation shoots through me, and I reach for it, eager to follow. But then the thread of red that binds me to Tobias strengthens, and his core leaves his body, rolling down our connection like an avalanche and catching me in the process.

I try to fight, to tell him *Not yet*, but I have no voice, and he drags me forward, through the barrier of magic, and into the bottle.

For a brief moment, I see all the threads leading out of that small opening, then they vanish, and only darkness remains.

As Flint said, the inside of the bottle is much roomier than I thought it would be. It feels like it goes on forever, the darkness unending. I can't feel the walls, as I thought I'd be able to. This isn't a vessel like my corporeal form, or like the body I build in Dreamland. There's no floor, and no matter how high I stretch, there's no ceiling, either.

It's simply emptiness.

Then, something brushes against me, and a sense of burning determination wraps around my core of energy.

Tobias.

I feel him all around me, fire, earth, ice, and storm. The scales of choice and the possibilities of those unmade. Paths fill me with the options of what could have beens. I see death, so much death. Humans and demons alike consumed. But next to it is life, and both species living in harmony. I see war, and I see peace. Worlds filled with life and those left scorched and barren. Hundreds, thousands of choices spinning outward, more than my mind could handle if I were still corporeal.

Is this what Tobias lives with every day? Tipping the scales here and there to achieve the outcome he desires?

Of all my demons, I had thought his power the least threatening. He doesn't embody an ice age that can wipe out humanity or storms that can destroy everything in their path.

No, his power is more than that. He is the tipping point, the dice unrolled, and while he may not be able to cover the world in ice, he can trigger that to happen. Or he can choose not to. As he has chosen to do again and again over the centuries.

When I went to the Library and opened his book, I saw him at the center of destruction, yes, but what stories did the book hold of all the times he chose life instead? His path weaves in and out of Kellen's and Emil's, both chaos and order going hand in hand.

Without Tobias, the other two would lose their battles against their natures. There would be no tipping them back toward restraint, no cautioning toward mercy.

His energy swirls around me, reminding me of his most recent choice, to come into the bottle with me. For a moment, I see the shadowed path of another choice, one paved with the bodies of those I love, before his power pushes me away from it, telling me not to dwell on what never happened.

Instead, he swirls around me like a cyclone, spinning me out until I'm stretched thin as a thread, before he spirals inward, twisting us together like a candy cane.

We take turns making shapes and rolling together, the freedom of being without bodies removing the tension that usually exists between us. Here, there are no questions of dominance or reservation, no expectations. There's only us, and Tobias lets his playful side take control.

Time passes, though I don't know how much, and it doesn't really matter. With our bodies went the sense of urgency, the need to take action. In the bottle, we simply exist with—and sometimes within—each other.

And, for the first time in a while, I find myself at peace.

(UN)BOTTLED

Light floods the darkness.

Tobias and I weave tighter around each other in the dark, knowing the light means separation.

The world around us turns into a vacuum, trying to pull us from the darkness that's come to feel like home, and we cling tighter. But the vacuum won't be denied, and with nothing to grab onto, it yanks us out of the bottle.

For a moment, we hang suspended in air, the room registering from every angle at once.

The house hums and pulses with life, its joists and walls filled with magic, though not yet sentient. It feels lonely, like it missed me.

Tally stands with Tac in the archway by the kitchen, holding Prem while Merp crouches between Tac's large, tufted ears. They give off worried vibes, some focused on me and some on others in the room.

My imps and Sophia, huddled near the stairs to my room, clump together for comfort. They radiate distress, and I regret all the worry I continue to put them through.

Jax and Slater sit on the floor outside the circle, powering the barrier. They give off a sense of resolve, the feeling of doing a task that needs to be seen to completion.

Kellen and Emil hover in front of the roaring fireplace, as close to the shimmering wall of magic as they dare.

And inside, Flint, Xander, and Reese crouch over my and Tobias's bodies, which lay on the floor between them. Tobias clutches my hand, while a sheet covers my still form.

For one heart-lurching moment, I think I've died like Julian did, that the sheet is a shroud, and the witches kneel in mourning. Then Flint looks up to where we hover, his gaze fixing unerringly on us.

In energy form, I see through the glamor that he wears. See the scars that cover his face and the missing eye that he hides. I see, too, the power that rages through him, and the dozens of souls that hover at his shoulders, offering up their energy freely. He shines brighter than Reese and Xander, so bright that it hurts to witness him.

That powerful light flexes, ghostly hands reaching out to scoop Tobias and me from the air.

We cling together, unwilling to be parted now that we know what it means to be together, but Flint's pull is too strong to resist. With infinite patience, he separates us until we become two separate beings once more. With the division, the feeling of a vacuum returns, and the threads that bind me to my corporeal form yank me down.

I slam back into my body, my energy splashing outward to fill my extremities, flooding life back into me before rolling inward to my core.

Eyes snapping open, I lurch upright. The room spins around me, narrow and unfocused except for the demon beside me.

I reach for Tobias at the same time he reaches for me, and we cling together once more, our legs weaving together as we try to become one.

But corporeal forms aren't designed for that, no matter how tightly we hold each other. A sense of loss opens a cavern inside me that only Tobias's energy can fill, and my head lifts, my lips parted.

Tobias, knowing what I need, bends toward me.

"No, don't!"

The shout hurts my ears, then insistent hands pull us apart.

The second separation hurts more than the first, and I fight, reaching for Tobias as the barrier drops. But Flint drags him outside the circle to where Emil and Kellen wait to take him and hold him prisoner.

"No!" I strain toward Tobias, but the energy that fills me is only enough to animate my body, and not enough to give me inhuman strength. I thrash, but Xander and Reese hold me firm. "Give him back!"

Flint returns to this side of the circle, and the barrier rises once more, locking Tobias and me on opposite sides.

The witch turns to me and lifts his hand, then presses it toward the floor. Weight settles over me, as if lead fills the surrounding air, and my thrashing slows.

Flint steps closer, his hand still out near his waist. "I have control of your core for a little longer, Adie. Do you understand what I'm saying?"

My eyes jump from him to Tobias, who snarls at his friends as he tries to escape them.

"Adie, are you with me?" Flint demands, pulling my attention back to him.

No, I don't want to be with him. I want to be with Tobias. But something inside knows I need to answer, that if I don't, I'll go back into the bottle, this time without Tobias, and I can't stand that thought.

My head jerks up and down in the semblance of a nod.

Flint kneels in front of me. "Try to speak."

My throat clicks with dryness, and I swallow convulsively before I try again. "Yes, I'm here."

"Good." He sits cross-legged on the floor. "What you're feeling right now will fade in a few minutes as you readjust to your body. But until then, we need to keep you and Tobias separated, or you risk trying to inhabit the same form."

That doesn't sound bad to me, and my eyes return to Tobias, finding the same longing mirrored there.

Flint shifts to block my view of my catalyst demon. "I need you to focus on me right now. Can you do that?"

It hurts, but I do. If I focus on him, maybe he'll let me go to Tobias.

"Do you remember why you were in the bottle?" Flint asks.

I lick my lips, wishing for water. I feel brittle,

like papier mâché in the process of drying. "To remove the curse Victor Hesse put on me."

"Yes." He nods and glances at the other witches. "That was the plan."

"Was?" Nervous now, I look around for a sign of what could have gone wrong.

But everyone appears safe and whole, and the house looks the same as when I left. I search inside myself and discover I no longer feel the beast inside that pushed me to hurt those I love. Instead, a hole exists, an abandoned cavern that echoes without life. I don't have enough energy in my core to fill that hole, and even if I did, I'm not sure I could. I feel scooped out, a piece of me gone forever to the beast's hunger.

Unnerved, I focus back on Flint. "What happened? How long were we gone?"

"Less than six hours." Slowly, he drops his hands to rest on his thighs, and the sensation of weight dissipates.

Reese and Xander slowly release their grips on my arms, and everyone holds their breath, waiting to see what I'll do.

I stay where I am, the urgency to reconnect with Tobias still strong, but not compulsory. Lifting my bare arms, I look down and realize I lost my sheet in the struggle. My naked skin bears black marks now where I remember Victor Hesse cutting his curse into me.

Lifting my forearm to my nose, I sniff and catch the distinct odor of Sharpie. I touch the other marks, prodding at my body, but my skin feels firm, if a little too tight. And it's way too easy to feel my bones beneath. Starving myself of energy has left me in bad shape.

My attention shifts to Emil. Frost glitters on his cheeks and turns his lips blue. My mouth waters as hunger roars to life. With the beast gone, that means I can take winter from him. I can make him warm while replenishing what I've lost.

Flint waves a hand in front of my face, breaking my fixation, and I turn back to find his expression serious. "We weren't able to remove the curse, Adie. If you feed, it *will* continue to strengthen the spell."

I frown at him. "But I don't feel the beast anymore."

"That's because we were able to extract it in a similar way as I extracted your core." He reaches into his pocket and withdraws a red bottle. Holding it at eye level, he waggles it. "I chose red for *Danger* because, if you break it, this thing is going right back inside you."

When he holds the bottle out to me, like some kind of twisted gift, I lean away as far as Reese and Xander's bodies allow. "I don't want *near* that thing."

Flint stretches forward, insistent. "You have to take it."

"No!" Desperate, I shove a foot against his chest to hold him back. "I don't want it!"

"Adie, you have to keep it close," Flint insists as he thrusts it toward me. "If you get too far away, you'll stop feeding it, and it will escape."

"What?" I look down at myself, searching for a link that connects me to the bottle, but all I see is bare skin and sigils. I shake my head in denial. "No, I'm not still connected to it."

"You are." Expression hardening, Flint tosses the bottle at me.

Frantic, I scramble to catch it before it breaks on the floor.

As the disgusting thing pulses in a disturbing mirror of my heartbeat, I glare at Flint. "Why did you do that? It could have broken!"

"Just don't let it out of your reach, and you'll be fine." He pushes to his feet, then bends and grabs the abandoned sheet, tossing it over my naked body. "We bought you time, but it's not a fix. And unfortunately, we *can't* fix what was done to you."

"Then, why did you let me out of the bottle?" I demand as I pull the sheet up over my breasts.

"Because you can't feed the beast from inside the bottle," Xander squeezes my shoulder. "And if the beast isn't fed..."

"It breaks out of the bottle." I nod in understanding. "So, how do I feed the beast if *I* can't feed?"

Silence fills the room, and I look up to find faces filled with uncertainty.

My lip trembles. "You don't know?"

"We have some theories," Flint hedges. "But we won't know until you try."

"Okay?" Confused, I twist to look at Reese and Xander for more explanation.

Reese glances at the barrier around us. "Ley line magic."

I frown. "I can't feed on witch magic."

His brows shoot up. "Have you ever tried?"

I stare at him for a long moment before admitting, "No..."

He tilts his head to the side. "It's just more

energy, right? And not one the beast craves, or you would have tried to eat the barrier earlier, so it's not what powers the curse. So you should be okay using it as a power source."

My eyes narrow. "I'm not sure it works like that."

"But you're not sure it *doesn't* work like that, either," he points out.

Suspicion trickles through me. "Is this more of that *belief matters more than reality* business?"

"We don't think *any* succubus could do it," Xander cuts in with an exasperated look at his brother. "But you've already shown a certain level of compatibility for ley line magic, so it *might* be possible."

"It's not compatibility," I argue. "It's a refusal to let it destroy me."

He shrugs. "If pure stubbornness is what it takes, then continue to be stubborn and try. You need this, because there's one more thing we have to tell you."

"It gets worse?" I ask, my voice barely a whisper. I don't know if I can take another blow. Not after our big solution failed so epically.

When he reaches out to tap the spot over my heart, and I cross my eyes to stare down. I remember a mark being carved into me there, but I don't see a matching Sharpie mark correcting its purpose.

Xander's hand falls away. "We were wrong that this one was another *separate* mark. It's a *recall.* It tethers you to Victor Hesse, and once his monster is complete, it will pull you to him. You will become his slave, and through you, he will have limitless magic."

Assigning Purpose

From the silence that hangs heavy in the room, everyone else already knew about this, and it doesn't come as a surprise to me, either. Flint and Xander had warned me this was Victor Hesse's intention when they came to me in the bakery. We had chosen to keep quiet about it then, but I guess the cat's now out of the bag.

I trust everyone in the room to stay silent about it, though, and know any one of them would take the same oath Flint did to make sure this secret was never revealed.

The tether, though… Well, that's a new level of psycho that I should have seen coming. Of course Victor Hesse would have a way to pull me to him once the curse was complete. He wouldn't want a magic-puking monster falling into just anyone's hands.

Staring down at the trapped beast in my hand, I

nod in grim acknowledgment. The bottle pulses back at me. Even trapped, it knows what I'm doing. It feels hungry, but its hunger no longer drives my actions.

Carefully, I set it aside and gather the sheet, tying it toga style at my shoulder, then tuck the bottle into the folds across my chest. I don't like it there, so close to Victor Hesse's intended leash over my heart, but I'll have to get used to it.

With it secure for now, I gather the rest of the sheet into my lap and shift around to face the inner rim of the circle.

I study the shimmering barrier before I turn to peer over my shoulder at Flint. "Okay, so, just dive right in? Get to feeding?"

"You should go in with a little more intention than that." Reese settles on the floor beside me, with Xander on the other side. "If you just grab it, it will fight you. You have to give it a purpose."

"Right now, Jax and Slater are giving the ley line purpose, so they'll have to drop their spell before you can try accessing it through the circle. Once they do, call the magic to you and give it direction," Xander explains with confidence.

"Right." I don't feel any of the same confidence,

but I nudge my fingers toward the gold circle engraved into the floor, anyway.

Every time I come in contact with ley line magic, it tries to unmake me to create something new. Simply giving it direction sounds way too easy, and at the same time, not something I'm equipped to do. How can a succubus of less than a hundred years of existence direct the very force of life?

Then, I glance at Reese and Xander. They have even less time to understand magic and power, but handle it with ease. Of course, they're wired differently than I am. They were born with the ability to harness this vast power, while I was born of the smallest storm to ever create a succubus.

Tobias settles onto the floor directly in front of me, a shimmering barrier all that separates us. The yearning to be with him surges forth once more before quieting. If I can do this, I can touch him again, but I can't be with him the way we're meant to be, and I see the same loss echoed on his face.

He lifts a hand to hover just beyond the wall of magic that could destroy him. "I know what you're capable of, Adeline Boo Pond. You can do this."

Releasing a slow breath, I nod. "I can do this."

Slowly, Jax and Slater lift their fingers from the circle, and the barrier falls.

Tobias draws in a sharp breath but stays seated, and his hand drops to grip his thigh. His black eyes fix on me with determination. "Feed, Adie."

I bite my lip and slowly press my fingers to the edge of the circle. Ley line magic, already close to the surface, snaps up to meet me, and iridescent light explodes from my skin. It resembles my glow, but brighter and uncontrolled as it tries to unmake me and remake me at the same time. I shiver, my bones trembling as they threaten to come undone, but I hold onto my form through sheer determination.

Reese crouches beside me, his hand fearlessly touching my shoulder. "Spindle it. Make it yours."

Fissures form along my bones, and I grit my teeth. "How?"

"Give it purpose." He squeezes my shoulder, helping me to focus. "You need energy to sustain you, and the magic wants to give you what you desire. Just let it."

It's hard to imagine this wild power allowing itself to be converted to food. It rushes through me like a conduit, replacing the blood in my veins and turning them into pathways that bring it back into itself. I try to catch the edge of it and divert it into my core, but it resists being contained.

"Come on, Adie," Kellen encourages as he

crouches behind Tobias. "This isn't magic that's already been tamed. This is like my lightning. You've wielded that before."

I lift my head to glare at him. "This is *nothing* like your lightning."

Reese nods in agreement. "She's right. It's what births the lightning. It's more than elemental. It's what creates the elements."

"It's choice." Tobias leans forward. "You just have to choose."

He reaches for me, heedless of the ley line magic that coats my skin. The magic that can unmake demons. Panic shoots through me, and I yank the magic inside, drawing it beneath the surface where it can't hurt Tobias.

His hands settle on my knees, trusting me to keep him safe. "Remember what it feels like to choose. There are paths in front of you. Find the one that holds the outcome you want and *take* it."

My breath catches, and I focus on his eyes, seeing the void and starlight married together. Extinction and life, darkness and light. Just like the ley line magic.

Instead of trying to grab the magic inside me, I focus on the endless opportunities it offers and ask it for life, for sustenance, for existence. The magic surges to make it happen, eager now that I gave it direction. Life floods through me, filling out the sunken hollows created by starvation and plumping my flesh once more with health. The ache of hunger fades, the cavern left by the beast filling, and strength surges through me once more.

I gasp as the constant pain vanishes to leave me with the satiated feeling of a good feeding.

But the magic pushes for more, offering to fix things that aren't broken, to turn me into *more* than I am.

Hands grasp mine, pulling them from the circle of gold, and the magic cuts off.

I blink my eyes open to meet Reese's fae-touched gaze, and he offers me a smile of understanding. "When it starts tempting you, it's time to stop."

"Right." I nod, my body feeling floaty with too much magic.

But it doesn't make me sleepy the way I usually get when I've taken power and need to hibernate to convert it into my own. The ley line magic already did that step for me, leaving me fully powered and ready to go.

I lift my arms above my head, enjoying the stretch of healthy muscles before I lean forward and loop my arms around Tobias's neck and pull him forward.

I stop when our noses touch, and whisper, "Hey."

"Hey." He grins, the expression both foreign and familiar on his face.

I've never seen that specific look of softness and yearning before, but in the bottle, I felt it on a level that engraved itself into my being.

Then, Kellen launches over Tobias's shoulders and joins the hug. His touch sparks against my skin, but full of power, it doesn't tempt me.

Relieved, I free one arm from around Tobias to wrap it around Kellen and pull him closer.

Tobias, smashed between us, grumbles his displeasure, and I laugh, the relief at being able to touch them so strong that it leaves me light-headed.

Then, the imps join us in a cloud of baby powder and chitters that sound like scolding and happiness combined.

Tobias's rumbles turn into full growls, and the imps instantly back off with quiet chitters of reproach.

I straighten and look around for my ice demon only to find him still huddled by the fire, Tac pressed close to his side. Snow fills his eyes, and frost coats his skin despite the heat generated by the flames.

Seeing it, my happiness plummets in an instant.

While we found a workaround for me, I still can't perform the necessary task of draining off my demons-of-destructions' power. Without being drained, they run the risk of not only destroying the human plane, but also exposing the existence of demons to humans.

Tobias's hot hands cup my cheeks, drawing my attention back to him. "How do you feel? Do you need the bucket?"

"No, I think I'm fine." I focus on the magic inside me, trying to find any sign my body will reject it, but the power hums with contentment. "It's....happy where it is."

Kellen's fiery brows shoot up. "It's happy?"

"Yeah, happy." I mentally stroke the ball of power, and it pulses, much as Torch does when I give him treats.

Tobias pulls me to my feet. "Try to hyper-speed."

I tell the magic to fill my limbs, to give me speed, but it bubbles at me in confusion. I frown, trying to prod it to do my bidding, and it just spins in a circle. "I don't think I can."

Kellen frowns. "What about lifting something?"

I grab his waist and heave, but he barely rises onto his toes before I drop him. "No."

Confusion fills both their faces, and Tobias says, "But you're not hungry anymore, right?"

I nod and glance at Reese.

The witch shrugs. "What purpose did you give the magic?"

Now, it's my turn to frown. "To feed me?"

He shrugs again. "Then, that's all it will do."

My hands move to my hips. "But, when I consume power the normal way, I can make it do multiple things."

"That's because you don't assign it a specific purpose. Or maybe you assign it multiple purposes at once?" He shrugs a third time, making me want to smack him.

As if she senses my growing annoyance with her witch's lack of information, Tally pulls Reese a few feet away from me. "This is a new type of energy consumption. You'll have to experiment with how you direct it." She smiles brightly. "Think of it as starting over as a new succubus."

"You can do things right this time," Tobias teases.

Glaring, I shove out of his hold. "I don't like you anymore."

He swoops in and wraps me in his hot embrace. "Yes, you do. I felt how much you like me while in the bottle. There's no changing that."

I wiggle in his hold. "I've already forgotten our time together!"

He nuzzles my face with his scratchy cheek. "There are no take-backs in this. You're stuck with me."

At his words, memory spikes through me, bringing with it disappointment and pain, and I stop fighting.

Sensing the fun is over, he releases me slowly. "Adie?"

I focus on fixing my toga. "You should have told me about Cassandra. I had a right to know."

"We had a deal with Landon—" Tobias begins, then cuts off as Emil glares at him.

But the damage is already done, and I turn to stare at Tobias. "The deal to take me in?"

He glances at Kellen and Emil, looking helpless for the first time in my memory.

"Honey, you have to understand." Kellen reaches for me. "We didn't *know* you when we made the deal—"

I snap up a hand to stop him. "I get it. I really do. But you could have told me since then." I look at

Emil. "I *asked*, and you chose not to tell me. You never planned to tell me."

"We bargained to keep her *away*. She doesn't matter to us," Emil says, ice cracking in his voice. "You do. And as soon as we can get out of that contract..."

But when will that be? The knowledge burns through me that they may *never* escape that contract. The High Council doesn't just rip up their mandates. If they did, every demon under their rule would be looking for loopholes to wiggle out of their bindings.

Once demons hold the advantage, they don't let it go.

I look back at Tobias. "There's no end to it?"

He shakes his head. "So long as we're on the human plane and she exists, no. And we're bound not to harm her, the same as we're bound not to harm any succubi under contract with us."

I flex my fingers, suddenly missing the weight of claws. "I'm not restricted from harming her. She's owed retribution."

Alarm shoots across his expression. "Not even Landregath can destroy her. He could only keep her from his territory. She has centuries of power, Adie, and even after you live that long, too, she will always be that much more powerful."

He's not wrong to be cautious, but I remember the ease with which Marc shot her down, and I remember the red light that tried to enter Dreamland. Aren had been keeping someone out, and now I wonder if that malevolence was Cassandra.

If he somehow blocked her from Dreamland, then she's left to feed in her corporeal form, which could account for her sudden desire to reclaim my demons. It takes more time and care to feed on the human plane. If she's not making the extra effort and simply hunting humans, then she's putting demons at risk. And we all know how the High Council feels about that.

I just need to keep her from my men and bide my time until I find my opening.

Wannabe Destruction Demon

The next morning, I wake up snuggled beneath Tac's wing with his fur in my nose.

I don't remember falling asleep last night after Tally, her witches, and Flint and his team left the house. Tobias, Kellen, Emil, and I had stayed up, putting the living room back together, then finding reasons to linger downstairs. No one had been willing to be the first to leave, and at some point, exhaustion must have claimed me.

I stretch, then freeze when sharp, needle claws dig into my side and twin tails bap me in the face. Patting my hand around, I find small wings, tiny tufted ears, and a muzzle filled with sharp baby teeth that clamp onto my finger for daring to disrupt Prem's sleep. Gently, I disentangle myself and lift him to rest beside his sister on Tac's side before I crawl out from under his wing.

The beast's bottle swings from a strap around my neck, clacking quietly against the Dreamland talisman. I don't know if the talisman will work in my current state, or if Dreamland is once again off the table. I was too overwhelmed last night to try, and today, it scares me to find out if I've lost yet another part of myself to this curse.

As I stand, I tuck both necklaces inside my tank top. My usual yoga pants and sleep shirt had sounded like a good idea last night when I was curled up with the fire roaring. But now, despite the dancing flames, it feels like winter inside the house. The chill raises goose bumps on my bare skin and my breath fogs in the air.

Shivering, I wrap my arms around my stomach and glance around.

Kellen lays sprawled out on the leather couch, while Tobias leans back in his chair, his mouth slightly agape as he snores softly. Tac had wedged himself into the space in front of my floral couch near the fireplace, and I have no idea how I ended up on the floor, tucked beneath his wing like one of his whelps.

My eyes sweep over the room once more, searching for Emil, but I don't see him. Did he go upstairs to his heated blankets?

The quiet click of glass sounds from the kitchen, and I tiptoe to the archway to peek inside. In the shadows of early morning, Emil stands at the stovetop, holding his hands out to the lit burner the kettle heats on. The special mug I gave Emil for Halloween sits on the counter, and I spot open cocoa packets beside it.

When I step into the room, his head jerks up, his eyes wide with alarm for a moment before he spots me and relaxes once more.

"Morning," I whisper as I join him at the island.

"Good morning." He looks back down at the kettle as if willing it to boil faster. "Did you sleep well?"

"I did." I glance around the shadowed room before counting the number of empty cocoa packets, and my gut tightens. "Did you sleep at all?"

He shakes his head, his white locks disheveled and making him look younger than his years. "Someone needed to stay awake to guard the house."

In case Cassandra returned to try to claim her spot once more. But I'm still free, and my contract with the demons of destruction is very much active. She has no place in this house.

Angry it's even a factor, my hands curl into fists

beneath the counter, out of his view. "Did you think I was her when I came into the kitchen?"

His shoulders tense, and he refuses to look up to meet my eyes. "It wasn't that we never planned to tell you about the contract. It's just...." He takes a shaky breath and releases a white cloud of frost into the air. "If you knew, you would also know we are weak. And that is a difficult thing to reveal to the one we want to protect above all others."

My lips part in surprise, and the urge to go to him shivers through me. But Emil holds up his hand, asking me to maintain my distance, so I settle onto one of the stools. If he needs the separation to say what needs to be said, then I'll give him that. I need to hear this story, to understand the reason for their secrets.

The kettle releases a quiet whistle, and Emil pulls it from the burner before turning to the cabinet behind him to bring out a regular mug. He then opens his drawer of fancy cocoas and selects two packets before adding them to the waiting cups. The smell of white chocolate and strawberries fills the air, and he slides one across the counter to me.

I curl my fingers around the warmth and wish I had a sweatshirt, but it's not worth leaving to get one if it means interrupting this moment of trust and vulnerability.

Emil remains on his side of the island, sipping his cocoa from the mug I asked the witches to spell to withstand even his chill. For a moment, the blue in his lips fades, a blush of pink showing through the ice before he lowers the mug and the frostbite returns. "When the mandate demanding that demons who could not pass as human return to the demon plane first came, we didn't know that our world was dying. The spread of the wasteland took time, but when the summer storms stopped coming, and frost never chilled the air, we knew that we would not survive in our homeland much longer."

He takes another sip of cocoa and sighs, snowflakes dancing in the air before melting on the countertop. "We could pass for human, so we returned to the human plane, but the temptation to destroy was too strong. It was a dark time for us, and the High Council demanded a solution. Our existence for a cessation to our destruction. A solution was found that allowed us to remain on this plane without destroying humans."

"The Succubus Contract," I guessed.

He nods stiffly. "Volunteers were requested, but

our powers were feared, even with the compensation we offered. Only one stepped forward."

"Cassandra," I whispered.

A shudder wracks through him. "Cassandra very much wants to be a demon of destruction, and she made no attempt to disguise her reason for volunteering. She had been devouring other demons for some time, and she did not fear our destructive powers. The deal was made, but with the caveat that, if another succubus stepped forward, they could temporarily supersede her claim."

His white lashes flutter. "She fed voraciously, and because of the contract, there was no way to stop her. Eventually, she grew discontent with the speed with which we recharged, and she left to hunt for other sources of power. But the time she spent with us proved to the other succubi that our powers would not destroy them, and with a large cash incentive, others stepped forward to fill Cassandra's place. It worked to keep her away, for a while."

My gut clenches, and I hug my mug close to stop from going to him. The pain in his voice belies the frozen mask of indifference he wears, and it makes me want to destroy Cassandra all the more.

When the silence stretches, I prod, "What changed?"

"Landregath put the word out that if the succubi and incubi living in his territory wished to continue to receive his protection, they would not sign further contracts with us." He glances at me. "Then, he contacted us about you, his new apprentice who was struggling to find her place on the human plane. There were *many* conditions on how you would be handled, and in return, he agreed to keep Cassandra away."

I hunch my shoulders. "So that's why you guys were so lenient with me. You had no other option."

"We could have moved," he points out. "We've been in this city longer than is prudent, and we have other businesses that we've left alone long enough that returning to them wouldn't raise suspicion."

My brows pinch together. If they had so many options, then why let Landon shoehorn them into taking me in? No demon likes to lose in a test of wills. Was the risk of leaving Landon's territory and running into Cassandra again that horrible?

"Why didn't you go that route?" I ask because I need to know, even if it will hurt.

"You may have noticed I'm resistant to change." He offers me a humorless smile. "I was stuck in how we currently lived, and I really didn't care who filled the spot in our house so long as it meant I didn't have to put effort into it. I very much desired life without effort. I was growing…tired of this existence, but lacked the will to change that." He sips his hot chocolate and sighs with appreciation. "But then I actually met you, and you were unlike any succubi I'd encountered before. You didn't want our power or wealth, you wanted nothing to do with us." His smile grows. "You were very troublesome."

I lean forward across the island. "I interested you."

"You irritated me," he counters. "I don't know the last time I felt so irritated. And then you showed up with your *own* contract, which demanded nothing of us beyond skimming the bare minimum of our energies. It was quite…irritating."

Warmth fills me at the way he says the word, like it's a placeholder for an endearment. "You were pretty irritating yourself, Frosty Pants."

"I'm glad we found each other equally abrasive," he murmurs before the humor flees his voice. "But you're right to be upset. No matter what light it shone on us, we should have told you about Cassandra when it became apparent we would want more from you than the year our contract allows."

"Yeah, you should have." I slip off my stool and circle the island to press up against his frozen body.

"We could have been working on this problem together instead of leaving me in the dark about it."

"I didn't want you to go after her." Slowly, he slips an arm around me. "You are precious and filled with possessive jealousy. I would not see you crushed by her."

"I'll sign another year-long contract." Unhappiness fills me at the idea, but if it's all we can do for now, so be it. "And another year after that, and another year—"

Emil bends, his frozen lips claiming mine. They burn with ice and freeze me in an instant, but the pain is worth it to touch my ice demon again. But he keeps the kiss chaste and pulls away before he tempts me to take the winter from him, no matter how much damage it will do to me.

My numb lips make forming words difficult. "Want to take a shower? We can drain all the hot water."

He shakes his head with regret. "I'll freeze the spray."

Dread pools in my gut, and I force myself to ask the next question. "How long do you have?"

He cups my cheek, and ice crystals creep across my skin. "As long as necessary to fix this curse."

But how long will that be? No matter what Emil

says, he can't contain the power growing inside him forever.

"We have other methods to stave off the winter," Tobias says from the archway.

I jump at his appearance. How long has he been standing there? Are my senses so dull that I don't even register when another demon enters the room?

Tobias strides over to join us and wraps an arm around Emil's shoulders. Steam hisses between them, and Emil shudders but doesn't pull away.

"Come, my friend," Tobias says as he presses Emil's hot chocolate into his hands and turns him toward the back door. "Let's go outside and create ice sculptures, then let me hold you for a while."

Emil grumbles with discontent but nods, allowing the other man to lead him toward the rising sun.

New & Shiny

Safe beneath the heater on the deck, I watch Emil and Tobias.

An hour later, Sophia comes out with a cup of coffee. Alerted to the waking of the imps, I rush back inside to claim my shower before they take up the bathroom for hours.

When I come back down, I find Emil and Tobias casually cuddling under a blanket on my floral sofa while the flames in the fireplace rage full force.

The sight fills me with longing. I want to crawl in there with them and share in the bonding. But Emil needs Tobias more than he needs me right now.

Kellen is nowhere in sight, but I hear the pipes groaning from the stairwell that leads to his and Tobias's rooms, alerting me to my storm demon's location. I lean over and press a kiss to Tobias's hot cheek and Emil's cold one, then leave them to whatever coping methods they can use while I join my imps and Sophia in the kitchen.

Only, the imps are gone when I enter, with only Sophia remaining, hunched over a plate of scrambled eggs and bacon. Another plate sits on the counter beside her, covered by a metal dome.

I have no idea where the dome came from. It looks ancient, and possibly made of real silver, so likely one of the imps excavated it from Emil's hoard in the basement. When I lift it, I find more eggs and bacon, as well as toast and hash browns.

"Fuel up," Sophia instructs around a mouthful.

My stomach rumbles, and I settle on the stool beside her. "Where are the imps?"

"They went home to do some laundry and do imp things." She scoops a pile of eggs onto her fork, then glances at her cell phone on the counter at her elbow. "Hurry up. Tally will be here soon."

My brows pinch together in confusion. "Why is Tally coming here?"

Sophia lifts a piece of bacon and eyes it the same way she would a randy, frat boy ready to give up all his energy for a night of fun. "We're going shopping."

My frown deepens. "I'm not in the mood to look at dresses. Besides, with everything going on—"

"We're not going dress shopping," she cuts in before snapping off the top of her bacon with her teeth. She groans and wiggles on her stool before her green eyes flash over to me. "You need to relax. There's so much tension right now that you need something normal to focus on, even if it's only for a couple hours."

I don't want to leave the guys, but there's nothing to be done sitting here, watching Emil slowly freeze over. Maybe getting out of the house will help distract my mind enough to come up with a solution. "What are we shopping for, if it's not for clothes?"

Sophia winks. "That's a surprise. Now, hurry up and eat."

Resigned to leaving the house, I grab my fork.

When Tally directs me to the back end of the shopping mall, a smile forms on my lips. There's only one store open at this time that they could be taking me to.

Without needing further direction, I park in front of Baker's Paradise and leap out of the driver's seat before the others get their seatbelts off. I've been wanting to come here for weeks, but with how busy everything else has been, I kept putting it off, relying on online ordering to stock our shelves. But nothing beats being able to browse the new, shiny, seasonal items in person.

The little bell over the door jingles as we enter, lifting my spirits in an instant. Who can focus on negativity when there are bells ringing?

The air in the store smells like spices and sugar, and I pause in front of a Christmas display to drag in a deep breath. This is *exactly* what I needed to clear the funk from my soul and realign my mojo. It's been way too long since I lost myself in baking.

Grabbing a cart, I start at the first aisle, which turns out to be pans. I have more than enough of the standard kind, but the fun shapes draw me in. I spend time cooing over the present-shaped pans versus the enticing spirals that would look beautiful with colored powder sugar sprinkled over the top. Then the cookie molds catch my eye, and I wave them at Sophia, whose eyes light up with interest.

She hurries over, lifting a cookie press that comes with dozens of disks for different shapes. She points out a couple on the back of the box. "Look, there are snowflakes and trees!"

"You'll give Jesse new shapes to decorate." I nudge her in the side. "I bet she'd like that."

"Oh, more shapes!" She grabs another, smaller box off the shelf to compare the designs.

I add a few new cupcake pans to my cart and leave her to venture on to the toppings aisle. There, I throw edible gold and colored sheets of frosting into my basket. It's easy to imagine Jesse's excitement at being able to work with edible paints to create designs that she can apply to cookies and cupcakes. With that in mind, I also add edible paints in every color, along with the edible glitter, because Iris deserves to sparkle as much as she wants to.

In another aisle, I grab chocolate-covered espresso beans for Martha, and new cleaning supplies for Kelly, because his favorite broom is starting to look a little worn.

In the next section, I find Tally studying holiday-themed tablecloths, and we choose some lovely white ones with bright holy berries around the edges.

"Should we get centerpieces?" Tally asks as she lifts a small, fake wreath.

While tempted, I shake my head. "We'd just have to move it if customers come in wanting the cupcake and tea service."

"True." She sets it back down and lifts a package of jeweled poinsettia with twist ties on them. "Maybe something to decorate the serving trays to make them festive?"

Nodding in agreement, I toss a couple into my cart, then add a couple packs of snowflakes, too.

When I reach the next aisle, I have to rein in my impulse to buy every sparkly toy and spinner I see. It's been a while since I've needed to hide treats around the shop for the imps, but a couple here and there can't hurt, right? And a holiday plate and cup for Vova to change up his usual offering. And a new fire-resistant dish for Torch's food.

Before I know it, hours have passed and my shopping cart overflows with all my selections. My greedy self wanted to fill another cart, but I restrain the urge as I wheel it to the front, where the clerk's eyes widen in surprise before she begins to ring me up.

I bite my lip and look at Sophia and Tally. "It will all fit in the car, right?"

Tally smiles. "What doesn't fit in the trunk, we can hold on our laps. But it's a good thing Jax finished the upstairs space, because this wouldn't have fit in the supply room with the break area still in there."

Sophia holds a small shopping basket of her own, and in addition to the cookie press, I spot a couple wooden spoons. When she catches me peeking, she flushes a pretty pink before lifting her chin as if to dare me to comment.

Smiling, I turn back to the cashier and my eyes bug out at the growing total. I really overdid it, and I don't have the surplus of cash I possessed a couple days ago. I signed almost everything over to Flint for the failed attempt to reclaim Julian's core. Some of my happiness dims at the reminder, and an answering pain twinges in my chest.

Tally pokes me in the cheek. "Hey, turn that frown upside down. This is supposed to be making you happy."

"It is," I rush to reassure her. "I have so many plans for new decorations to try when we get to the bakery."

Seeing through me, she gives me a sad smile. "You must keep up hope."

I nod jerkily, trying to reclaim the sense of peace I held a moment ago.

The bell over the door jingles, and I look over to see another early morning shopper entering the store. At the sight of red hair, my gut clenches before I realize the woman looks nothing like Cassandra.

Unease rolls through me, though. Without Landon around, there's nothing to stop her from returning and taking out her wrath on the succubi and incubi who have hidden from her under his protection. There's no one else strong enough to stand against her. Not unless we all band together to take her down.

Considering the idea, I glance at Sophia. "How many of us live here?"

Her full lips purse in consideration. "I'm not sure. A lot. Why?"

"We should have another gathering." I pull my wallet from my pocket and surrender the last of my funds to the baking gods. "We need to talk."

As soon as we pull into the parking lot at the bakery, I know something's wrong. And it's not because my imps huddle in front of their van, staring toward the shop as they chitter nervously.

No, it's a tingling in the back of my brain, a broken warning that someone trespassed here who meant me harm.

As soon as I park the car, I jump out, calling back to Tally, "Guard the imps."

I make it three steps across the parking lot before Sophia hyper-speeds past me in a blur of shimmering green. She reaches the bakery ahead of me, and not for the first time, I mourn the loss of my succubus powers. I'm not even sure how long it will take for me to process the large dose of ley line magic I took in so I can experiment with assigning the next influx a better *purpose*.

Ugh, I really am like a baby succubus trying to figure out power conversion.

By the time I reach the door, Sophia blocks it with her body, her arms braced on either side.

The sympathy on her face drives panic through me. "Let me pass."

Her lip trembles before she squares her shoulders. "Adie..."

"Let me pass!" I dart under her arm and elbow her hard in the side to make her move.

She flinches, which gives me enough room to wiggle through.

My foot slips in the hallway, and I fling an arm out to catch myself against the wall. Flour, sugar, and cocoa powder litter the floor, Sophia's passage through the bakery a clear line down the middle.

A hand curls around my bicep. "Adie, you don't have to look. Let us clean it up."

"No." Heart in my throat, I shrug out of her hold and make my way carefully toward the kitchen.

The center island lays toppled on its side, the utensils stored there scattered everywhere. Empty frosting tubes rest in a mess of colored frosting, and broken decoration dishes glitter on the floor. Pieces of the large mixer litter the kitchen, the metal twisted as if ripped apart by an angry force.

My pulse pounds as I spy a little door among the pieces, and the twisted remains of a food tray with small pellets of wood still inside.

"Torch?" My voice shakes, and I fall to my knees beside the ovens.

The door on the far left hangs by one hinge, while the others are missing completely, but my eyes focus on the dark opening on the side.

I crawl forward to peer inside. "Torch? Come on, baby, where are you?"

Holding my breath, I wait for a flicker of an answer that doesn't come.

Glass breaks under my knees, cutting through my slacks, but I don't even register the pain as I crawl across the floor to the crack between the ovens and wall.

"Vova?" Fear tight in my throat, I poke my

fingers into the shadows. "Vova, are you there? Did you see what happened to Torch?"

The shadows remain just shadows, and I look around frantically for an offering to draw Vova out.

When all I see is destruction, I twist to shout, "I need a cupcake!"

Footsteps shuffle behind me, and a plate with a cupcake appears.

I take it without looking back and press it as close to the crack as it will go. "Vova, we have an offering. Please com—" My voice cracks, and I take a shaky breath to try again. "Please come out and take your offering."

"Adie, give him time," Tally whispers. "The domain he protects was destroyed. He's scared."

"Or he's not here anymore," I choke out before I twist to stare up at my friend. "What if he's not here? Where's Torch?"

Tears shimmer in her mahogany eyes, and she blinks quickly to banish them. "Come on. Let's assess the rest of the damage." Firmly, she pulls me to my feet and toward the two-way door that leads into the front of the shop.

There, we find overturned tables and broken chairs, but the glass display case somehow survived the rampage. Most of the destruction seems centered on the kitchen and, from the mess in the hall, on the pantry.

Had my ward on the display case prevented more damage out here, or did the threat of the windows detour the vandal?

"This isn't too bad," Tally says with forced brightness as she sets one of the tables upright. "A little rearranging to open the floor space up, and no one will know the difference."

I stare at her in confusion before her words sink in. "You want to open? Without ovens? And while Torch and Vova are missing?"

"I have Kelly on the way to the baking shop for a new mixer, and Iris and Martha are taking supplies back to their house to get a couple batches of cupcakes going." She pauses beside me. "This is meant to destroy you. Don't let that happen."

"We'll run out of product," I point out as I slowly move to help pick up the pieces from one of the broken chairs. "The imps only have one oven at their house."

"We can have a limited menu for the day, discount espresso, and hand out coupons to bring them back," she says with determination. "I'll take some ingredients back to our house, too. We can create a relay system."

"I can make cookies back at our house," Sophia calls, and when we both turn to look at her, she flushes. "I mean Adie's house. I'll make cookies at Adie's house. There's plenty of ingredients there for sugar cookies, and Jesse can decorate them."

Jesse pops up behind her and gives a firm nod, her narrow shoulders set with determination.

"Okay, but..." I look around at the tossed floor space. "What about tomorrow? And the next day? We don't have ovens, even if we find Torch—" My throat tightens, cutting me off.

"I called a repairman," Sophia says as she kneels in front of Jesse. "Come on, tiny tormentor, we're running back to the house."

"Tell Kelly to get little bags." Jesse hops up on her back, her arms and legs wrapping around Sophia with more elasticity than a human could. "We can give small cookies away with the coupons. Give order forms, too."

"Good idea." Tally nods in approval. "We'll turn today into a win for the bakery."

Confusion sweeps through me. "Who did you call—"

But Sophia hyper-speeds out of the room before I can finish the question.

I turn a frown on Tally, who shrugs in answer.

The bakery had sat on the market for a long time because the previous owners were also demons and the ovens were set up to be powered by an ignis demon. Kellen had been too cheap to retrofit it with regular ovens. The last person to do repairs on the bakery was—

Out front, a sports car in need of a paint job pulls up to the curb, and Tobias climbs out, a tool bag in hand. When Jax exits from the passenger seat, I burst into tears.

A Mask for the Broken

As soon as they walk inside, Tobias drops his tool bag and gathers me into his arms, which only makes me cry harder.

"Shh." He strokes my hair and rocks me in place. "We'll fix this."

"Torch," I choke out.

He rubs his cheek against mine. "We'll find him."

"What if we can't?" I tip my head back. "This was Cassandra, wasn't it? Revenge for kicking her out of the house." Clutching him, the fear I've been trying to suppress pours out, "What if she ate him?"

He wipes the tears from my face. "Torch is resilient. He's probably out blazing up the town, again."

We both carefully avoid looking down, where little footsteps would be scorched into the flooring if Torch had escaped.

Instead, I force a wobbly smile. "Yeah. He's out lighting dumpsters on fire."

"Exactly." He scrubs his hand over my face. "Now, stop crying so much, or I'll start gathering all these tears and make a fortune."

Sputtering, I swat at him, but he ignores me as he meticulously wipes away every tear. When every trace is gone, his fingers trail down my cheek, then skim along my jaw.

His caress pauses at my chin, his thumb swiping over my bottom lip. My breath catches as heat simmers in my veins. Heat simmers under his skin, his power rebuilding steadily. Instinct tells me to take it, and the bottle that hangs between my breasts pulses with encouragement.

Slowly, I step back before I give into temptation.

When his eyes lift to mine, I catch his hand and squeeze it. "We need to find Victor Hesse and take him out."

"We will," he promises fiercely as he returns my squeeze. "We put a bounty on his head. It won't be long."

My eyes widen. "Please don't say you promised favors."

"Conditionally." He bends to press his forehead against mine. "You're worth a dozen favors."

Warmth fills me, and I reach up to cup his cheeks. "I'll give you favors in return."

His gaze heats and a low rumble comes from him. "Conditionally?"

I rise onto my toes. "I'm open for negotiations."

He growls softly. "Stop tempting me, little succubus. I have a kitchen to fix."

The reminder crashes me back to reality, and I drop to my heels. "But how will you do that without—"

His fingers press over my lips. "Let me worry about that. You help pick up the front room so you're ready to open on time."

I shake my head. "You're all crazy."

"Then be crazy with us." Booping me on the nose, he heads into the kitchen. "And no more crying. I still have the bottle I took from Flint, and I'm not afraid to use it."

Gentle, playful Tobias throws me for a loop. I want to explore this new, more open side of him, but following him to the kitchen will just remind me of everything I lost today. So, instead, I turn to help Tally and Jax pick up tables and chairs.

Jax fixes what can be salvaged and hauls what can't to the dumpster out back. As Tally leaves to bring in the table clothes we bought, Kellen arrives with Slater in tow. When I spot the extra chairs they bring with them from Club Fulcrum, I want to cry all over again. Tobias's threat holds me back, though. I have full faith he'll follow through, and he already owns a bunch of my feathers.

As Kellen sets down a stack of four chairs, he looks around the shop, none of his usual playfulness present. "If she shows her face here again, she won't be getting another easy trip back to the demon plane."

Slater grunts in agreement. "Though, it was nice to watch her be blown to pieces."

"Yeah, it had a certain visceral appeal." Kellen shakes his fiery hair back from his face. "Too temporary, though, obviously."

"You can't hurt her. You're under contract," I remind him.

Lightning sparks across his pupils. "Don't worry, honey, I won't be the one doing the hurting."

I frown at him. "You can't order people to do it, either."

His lashes drop to veil his eyes. "I won't be ordering, either. The actions others take are their own."

Slater and Jax carefully keep their attention focused on dispersing the new chairs around the room, pretending they can't hear Kellen, but that kind of loophole won't fly with the higher-ups.

Grabbing my storm demon by the collar, I haul him down to my level. "If you get Tally's witches hurt—"

"*My* witches," he reminds me with a humorless grin. "Their lives are *mine* to do with as I please until they fulfill their contracts."

"Don't make me defend my friends, Kellen," I growl.

"Then don't make friends with my possessions," he growls, a rumble of thunder in his voice. "I'll use any tool at my disposal to protect you."

Eyes narrowing, I rise onto my toes, puffing out my chest.

Expression grim, he reaches out to grip my shoulders and push me back to my heels. "This is *not* like using Julian as a scapegoat, Adie. What Cassandra will do to you is not a matter of imprisonment. You will not exist somewhere removed from us where I have the hope to reclaim you. I *will not* stand aside and let her remove you from existence because of some mandate handed down by the High Council. The witches knew their lives could be forfeit when they signed my contract."

"What other choice did they have?" I demand.

"They could have stayed where I found them." Gently, he detaches my hands from his collar and presses a spark-filled kiss to my forehead. "They had a price, and I met it. What happens to them is not up to you."

My hands tremble in his hold, and I pull them away to tuck behind me. "I don't like this side of you."

He nods in acceptance and steps back from me. "I don't either, but it exists."

"We need to go, boss," Slater says, his face void of emotion. "You have a meeting in an hour."

I frown at that. "It's a bit early in the day for that, isn't it?"

"Vendors like to meet early." Kellen runs a hand through his hair in frustration. "I'm sorry I can't stay to help more."

"You've helped enough." I look at Slater. "Thank you."

He nods, his gaze intent. "It's the least I could do for you."

My frown deepens. Is he referring to the time he couldn't protect me from Domnall's attack and I hid it from Kellen? He's more than paid me back since then. All the witches have. And I'll do my damnedest to make sure Kellen doesn't use them as cannon fodder to distract Cassandra.

Cassandra's not just my problem, and I plan to make the other succubi and incubi who've grown lazy under Landon's protection aware of their responsibility.

A sense of disquiet fills me as they leave, and Jax stops pretending he's deaf to face me. "He's right, you know. We didn't go into this agreement blind. So, don't worry about it."

I cross my arms under my breasts. "And what happens to Tally if you all die? Does she just get sucked back into Dreamland? You're her anchors, right?"

I've never asked for the details of how my friend became the first and only baku to escape Dreamland, but Jax's gaze dropping from mine tells me I'm not wrong in my guess. Whatever they did, her presence here is tied to them, and if they disappear, so will she.

Ducking down, I snare his gaze once more. "You took on a responsibility when you gave her form. So, don't be so fast to run to your deaths when it's not your place, no matter what Kellen may think."

"What does Kellen think?" Tally asks as she walks back into the room, her arms laden with tablecloths. She glances around the room and brightens. "Did he bring in reinforcements? Is Slater still here?"

"They had to head back right away." I rush over to take some of her burden. "I'm sure he'll come back by when he has a break."

She smiles softly. "Club management keeps him so busy. Kellen should give him more days off."

My chest tightens, but I force a smile. "I'll mention that to him."

Her smile grows. "You're a good friend."

The constriction in my chest grows. She wouldn't look so happy if she knew we'd been discussing the death of her men moments ago. No, she'd pack them up and take them far away from here. And I would help her do it, if I didn't know Kellen would just track them down.

For the first time in a long while, I'm ashamed to be a demon. People's lives shouldn't be ruled by contracts that bind them to promises made when their worlds were different. Our people don't allow leniency for change or growth. They lock us into moments of time and expect everything to simply stop. But that's not what life is, nor should we want it to be.

"Don't frown so much," Tally chides as she

drapes the first table in white cloth. She steps back to admire the effect. "Look how bright the place will look once we're done."

"Beautiful," I agree with a heavy heart.

By the time we finish, it will look like we're being festive instead of trying to hide the vandalism.

But inside, I know it's just a temporary mask to hide what's been broken.

VANISHED

Somehow, Tobias rips out the broken ovens and new, regular ovens arrive thirty minutes before we open. I mourn the loss of Torch's home, but vow to find the tiny ignis demon a more secure place to live, once we locate him again.

The first delivery of cupcakes and cookies arrive right as Tally unlocks the front door and flips the sign to open.

I fill the display case with the small assortment of vanilla and chocolate cupcakes, along with trays of beautifully painted sugar cookies listed as a featured item. I don't know how Jessie and Sophia managed to make so many cookies in such a short amount of time, let alone use the new frosting paint I bought. The holiday-themed designs make it look as if we'd been planning it for months, and I'm eternally grateful.

I sprinkle the jeweled poinsettia and snowflakes

in the empty spaces trays would usually fill to make the lack of offering intentional.

When Kelly returns with the new, stand mixer, Tobias hooks it up, then helps the delivery man bring in the new ingredients to replace what had been destroyed.

When the bell over the door tinkles the first welcome for the day, we're ready with coffee brewing and treats for sale.

As I watch the customer happily leave with a box of four cakes and a coupon with a cookie sample, Tobias rubs the tension from my shoulder. "You did well. Cassandra tried to make a statement by destroying your bakery, and by opening, you're letting her know her actions mean nothing."

I reach up to squeeze his hand. "I didn't do it alone. You will be compensated."

"Good," he purrs, sending a shiver down my spine. "How about we start this compensation with some tea? I haven't had my first cup for the day."

"I'll make it personally." I nod to the empty seats. "Go rest your feet. I'll bring it to you."

With a hot kiss against my temple, he walks out to the main floor and takes a seat in front of the picture window, which perfectly frames him for every passerby to see.

I both love him for that and hate it. Whenever one of the guys sits there, we always have a large influx of horny women in the store, and while I appreciate the boost in sales, we're not exactly flush with products right now. But the quiet hum of the mixer tells me we will be soon, and it's still early for the lunch rush, so we might be safe.

Or not. As I pop a bag of mint tea into a mug, the bell over the door jingles to announce another customer, then jingles again as three more follow her in.

They eye each other then the single empty seat across from Tobias with enough competitiveness that I half expect them to bypass the counter altogether in their rush to gain his attention. But they show some semblance of reason as they make their way to the counter and Kelly takes the first order.

While he does that, I carry the mug over to Tobias's table and set it in front of him.

When his thick brows shoot up at the tea bag still floating on the surface, I set a small plate and spoon next to him before dragging the extra chair at his table away.

His soft chuckle follows me back to the counter, where I stand behind Kelly and glare at the women, daring them to misread my silent message.

They take the hint and get their orders to go.

But that doesn't stop the next wave who enters a moment later, rubbernecking as they pass Tobias's table.

Is he doing this on purpose? Tipping the scales to draw them into the store?

When he casts me an amused glance, I mouth, *Stop it.*

He shakes his head and fake frowns, as if he doesn't know exactly what I said.

Annoyed, I pull a cookie from the display case and march it over to him. Thunking it down hard enough to draw attention, I mold myself against his side and say loudly, "Don't you need to get to the office, darling?"

His arm slips around my waist, his hand dangerously close to the swell of my ass. "The president has things under control, for now, sugar dumpling."

I'm surprised Emil went into the bank in his current condition, but I guess most of his clients are demons, so it doesn't really matter.

Reaching out, I pinch Tobias's cheek. "But surely your time isn't so free, snookums."

He smiles up at me. "I always have time for you, kumquat."

Kumquat? I mouth, and he shrugs as he lifts his teacup.

It freezes halfway to his lips as something catches his attention out on the street. I follow his line of sight in time to catch Detective Sharpe stepping into the bakery, and my stomach sinks.

We really don't need this right now.

The detective barely glances around the bakery before he zeroes in on us and marches over.

"Detective," I say stiffly. "To what do we owe the pleasure?"

He grabs one of the chairs from the nearest table and sets it down across from Tobias, then sits and looks up at me. "I had a call from the mortuary earlier."

My grip on Tobias's shoulder tightens. "Are they releasing Julian's body for burial?"

"No." He looks between us, his gaze assessing. "It would seem it went missing last night, sometime around midnight. Care to cast a guess as to where it went?"

Damn Phillip and his inability to follow basic instructions.

"We're not in charge of keeping track of corpses, Detective Sharpe," Tobias says smoothly when I don't answer. "Did you ask the guard on duty? Or view the security recordings?"

"The guard didn't see anything." His eyes flick up to me. "But when I viewed the recordings over the last few days, I did see some interesting visitors."

I release my grip on Tobias to move my hands to my hips. "You have a problem with me bringing a priest to read my friend his last rites?"

Detective Sharpe reaches out and hooks a finger onto the edge of the small plate with Tobias's cookie and pulls it over to his side of the table as he stares at me. "Yes, Father Hendricks, was it?"

I have no idea what name Flint signed in under and search the Detective's eyes for any sign of a trap. But he remains frustratingly unreadable, and I know from experience his mind would be impossible to manipulate, even if I had the power to do so. Which I don't at the moment.

At last, I give a grudging nod.

Detective Sharpe takes a bite from the cookie, and his eyes widen in surprise. "These are pretty good."

My eyes narrow on him. "I'll let the baker know."

"There are three Father Hendricks in town." He nibbles some more and groans with appreciation before setting the half-eaten cookie down and brushing the crumbs from his fingers. "Do you know what they all have in common?"

"Why don't you just tell us," Tobias says as he eyes his stolen treat with annoyance.

Not that he wanted it. He doesn't like sweets very much. But it was still something I gave *him*, and only the detective's humanity stops Tobias from demanding payment of equal value. Which I'm sure he'd price well above the cost of the sugar and butter that went into it.

Detective Sharpe doesn't look at him as his gaze remains locked on me. "None of them are the person who visited the morgue with you, Ms. Pond. And a close study of the video footage shows a gap in time that's unaccounted for."

So much for Flint's hacker. I want a refund.

I offer the detective my most sympathetic expression. "It must be so hard to find good equipment on your department's budget."

He leans forward. "I want the real name and contact information for the man who went with you to the morgue, Ms. Pond."

"Why?" I tilt my head to the side. "When we left, Julian's body was still there. What happened to it after that is your issue."

"Will I find him on the list of Mr. Cassius's known employees?" he presses.

That depends entirely on how much they've linked to Kellen. Do recordings exist somewhere of us with the cleaners? If so, I'm sure they'll turn up. That's the kind of luck I have.

"We've answered enough of your questions, Detective. I did tell you to bring a warrant next time you wished to speak to any of us. And since I don't see one…?" Tobias stands. "It's time for you to leave."

Instead of standing, Detective Sharpe glances around the shop. "You've rearranged in here."

I stiffen at the implication he's been here without my knowledge to know what it used to look like. "Tis the season. Now get out."

His eyes pause on the floor behind me. "Did you have an incident recently, Ms. Pond? Something you'd like to report?"

Twisting, I follow his line of sight to a piece of chair leg that we somehow missed under one of the booths, and my pulse lurches. "Just an accident. Nothing to worry about."

The phone rings at the counter, the sound sharp against my eardrums before Kelly picks it up. After a moment, he glances at me and wiggles the receiver.

I turn back to the detective. "I have a business to see to. Please escort yourself out."

Turning, I stride to the counter and grab the phone. "Adie speaking. How may I sweeten your day?"

"I didn't think you'd be this resilient, Ms. Pond," a familiar voice crackles from the other end. "Did you enjoy my flowers?"

My hand tightens around the receiver. "Victor Hesse."

Across the room, Tobias's head snaps toward me.

"A pity your mentor wasn't there when I dropped by to pay my respects." He lets out a bone-cracking laugh. "I was sad we couldn't visit longer the last time I came to your house. But that's okay. I have another present for you. One that you'll find rather...freeing."

The blood drains from my face, my numb hand releasing the phone to let it clatter to the counter. Panic rushes through me as I spin toward Tobias and stumble forward a step as the ground rolls beneath me.

For a moment, I think I'm light-headed with fear. Then, the tables and chairs dance across the floor as a loud boom rattles the windows. Customers scream in panic as a second boom sounds, and I struggle to stay on my feet and reach Tobias.

Detective Sharpe leaps to his feet and stands to the side of the window, his eyes locked on the street outside. "Nobody panic. There was an explosion, but it's not in this immediate area. Police will take care of it. Please, nobody panic."

His words have the opposite effect as panic pulls me across the room. Club Fulcrum lays in the direction he looks, and Kellen went in early today for a meeting.

I reach Tobias and grip his arm. "Kellen."

He already has his phone in his hand, and he hits speed dial before lifting it to his ear.

Blood crashes through my veins as I push past him to peer out the window. A large, black cloud of smoke rises into the air from the next block over, right where the club should be.

"Tobias," I whisper as I turn back to him.

A loud crack of breaking glass ruptures behind me, and Tobias jerks, the phone falling from his hand. Warm droplets of blood splatter my face a moment before a heavy weight knocks me to the ground.

I go down fighting, desperate to reach Tobias as he stumbles a step forward, blood dripping from his chest. Fire sparks at his fingertips as he looks around for an enemy to fight.

"Shooter!" Detective Sharpe yells. "Everyone, get down!"

The sharp crack comes again, and Tobias's head flies back, thick blood and viscera spraying across the shop as he falls.

"No!" I scream as I try to untangle myself from the detective to reach Tobias.

"Stay down!" Detective Sharpe yells, trying to wrestle me into submission.

Another crack comes, and the display case ruptures, my sigil of protection shattering.

No, this isn't how demons end. Not by human weapons. This isn't how we fight, and it's not what we guard against. We use magic and wield elements. We don't use *guns*.

Twisting an arm free, I strain toward Tobias.

My fingertips brush his hand a moment before his body crumples and dissolves, vanishing even as I try to reach him.

The Monster

For a heartbeat, I stare at where Tobias existed only moments before. Not even his suit remains. Only the lingering heat of where our fingers brushed. Pain knifes through me, followed by relief that at least he disintegrated, unlike Julian. It means he'll be able to return from the demon plane.

My fingers curl against my palm, trying to hold onto that small warmth for a second longer before self-preservation kicks in. I twist back, elbow flying up to crack against Detective Sharpe's head.

With a grunt of pain, his hold on me falters.

It's all I need to wiggle free and crawl toward the counter, screaming, "Jax! Barrier!"

There's only one reason Victor Hesse would take out Tobias before destroying my sigil. He's coming, and he will kill everyone here.

The witch appears from the kitchen, holding one

of the old oven doors as a shield as he darts behind the counter. "I don't have a connection!"

"What do you *mean* you don't have a connection?" I shout back. "What about all those bombs you've dropped?"

"The ley lines follow Xander or Reese around." He peeks out from behind the counter, then ducks back into hiding. "I'm trying, but it takes me longer to establish a link."

"Then just use me!" I scramble across the floor, the skin between my shoulder blades itching at being exposed.

Relief fills Jax's voice. "That should work!"

As I near the counter, a bullet digs up the floor in front of me, and a customer hiding beneath the booth nearby screams.

Undeterred, I continue forward. Victor Hesse just proved he's a crack shot. He doesn't want me dead. He just wants to strip away everyone around me and remove my reason to continue fighting.

I reach the counter and duck behind it next to Jax. Martha and Kelly huddle together behind him, closer to the espresso machine, their eyes wide, but their expressions determined.

Giving them a nod of encouragement, I reach for Jax's hands. "Put up a barrier."

He releases the oven door to link his fingers with mine, but uncertainty fills his eyes. "I power things and purify them through an overflow of magic, Adie. I don't do this fine-tuned stuff."

"And I don't feed on ley line magic." My lips pull back from my teeth in a bitter snarl. "Time to add a new skill to your repertoire."

Nodding, he grips my hands tighter.

Something brushes against the magic spindled inside me, and a ring of acknowledgment vibrates in my bones. With a gentle tug, Jax pulls the ley line magic I hold to the surface.

Sparks crackle between our palms, then zigzag across our fingers, growing faster and faster until a ball of energy hums between us. I can feel the purpose it still holds to heal me, to help me live, and I can feel Jax's natural instinct to turn it toward purification. Somewhere in the middle lies what we need.

"Protect those in the bakery," I whisper, eyes on the ball of magic. "Guard them against harm."

"Ward against evil," Jax says. "Ward against death."

I latch onto the word death, remembering the last time I saw Victor Hesse, how the mortifer demon had felt, his scent, the sound of his voice.

Stop Victor Hesse. The command rings through me as Jax releases my hands.

The crackling ball of magic falls to the floor between us and shatters into thousands of sparks that roll outward. They crawl along the floor and up the wall, then across the ceiling, dragging a part of my consciousness with them.

I can *feel* the bakery in the same way I've sometimes felt the house where we live, and it awakens with a similar, alien sentience. I know where Tally and Iris are upstairs, hiding in the break room, where Sophia and Jesse crouch in the kitchen, where each of my customers huddle in fear.

Eyes wide with wonder, Jax looks around at the gently glowing structure. "Do you feel that?"

I smile at Jax. "You did good."

He shakes his head. "No, this wasn't me. This was *you*."

From the hollow left by the beast comes a gentle flutter of awareness and acceptance.

Is that the ley line? Or something new I'll have to dig out from inside of me?

The flutter stills, as if aware of my thoughts, and guilt shoots through me. Whatever this is, it doesn't feel demonic, but it doesn't feel bad or necessarily separate from me, either. It just feels *new*.

Reaching inside, I find the place the sensation came from and gently stroke it until the flutter returns.

The two-way door slowly pushes open, and Sophia and Tally peek around the edge of the door, their eyes wide.

"Did it stop?" Sophia asks, apprehension darkening her green eyes.

"We put up a barrier, but it's not over." I feel that in my gut, and in the way the bottle hanging between my breasts pulses. Victor Hesse is almost here. I catch Sophia's gaze. "Take care of the customers."

She bites her plump, lower lip before nodding and stepping all the way out of the kitchen. Shoulders tense, she creeps past the safety of the counter and over to the first human hidden beneath a table. She murmurs to them in a soothing voice, and soon, the human lays down, eyes closing and body relaxing.

I rise from my hiding place and stride back to the broken window.

Detective Sharpe stares at me from his hiding space on the floor below the picture window. Then, his sharp eyes move to the empty place where Tobias had fallen before his attention shifts to Sophia as she quietly puts all the humans to sleep.

Finally, he looks back at me. "You're not human."

Studying his eyes, I once again search for that splash of magic that would mark him as fae-touched like Reese. But whatever's going on with Detective Sharpe isn't so obvious.

I look back out at the empty sidewalk. "I'd say you aren't entirely human, either. You probably see strange things all the time and make up justifications to explain to yourself why what you saw is completely normal. But people like you don't get to have normal lives, Detective Sharpe. People like you usually just disappear for the betterment of everyone else." I glance over my shoulder at the room of sleeping humans. "They won't remember what happened here today. I suggest you pretend not to remember, either."

"It's not that easy," he growls as he pushes to his feet. "My duty is to uphold the law, no matter what."

"Whose law?" I lift an eyebrow. "Certainly not one that controls me."

Movement draws my attention down the street, to a tall, skeleton-thin figure striding toward us, a black trench coat billowing behind him like a cape. Victor Hesse isn't pretending to be human anymore. He's committed fully to the war he chose to wage. Gone is his top hat and suit. Now he wears the skull of an akuzal, and the feathers lining the collar of his coat look suspiciously like those from a succubus.

Detective Sharpe follows my line of sight. "Who is he?"

"Victor Hesse." Anger rushes through me, and my hands curl into fists. "He's the monster behind everything you accused Kellen of being."

The detective reaches into his jacket and pulls out a handgun. "*What* is he?"

"I don't know," I answer truthfully. "He used to be a mortifer. They're demons who eat corpses. But he's evolved into something else."

He takes that in stride, cataloging the information away for later. "What does he want?"

"Me." The bottle that contains the beast vibrates as if it wants to fly to its master, and I press a hand over it. "I helped take out his mass-murdering partner, so he wants a replacement."

"What's so special about you?" he asks without judgment. "Are you some big, bad demon, too?"

I shake my head. "Just a succubus who wants to sell cupcakes and be left alone."

"Oh, come now, Ms. Pond," Victor Hesse calls, his voice crackling like breaking bones. "Don't sell yourself so short. Not just *any* succubus could have survived being part of my creation." He stops in front of the broken window, his milky-blue eyes fixing on me. "Believe me, I've tried with others. You're unique, as I knew you would be."

My stomach drops, and I lurch forward a step, only to come up short. "I'm going to make you pay for every person you've killed."

He grins wide, his dry, blackened lips cracking to reveal rotting meat beneath. "I'm going to enjoy you coming to heel at my side."

His gaze shifts over the window before he lifts a finger toward the bullet hole in front of me.

His finger stops an inch from contact, and his smile broadens to display gray teeth caked with decaying flesh. "You do continue to surprise me, Ms. Pond. I'm enjoying this game far more than I expected. It will make the final outcome all the sweeter."

He glances toward the billows of black smoke that rise into the sky from a block over and sighs. "I just wish you could have seen Mr. Cassius's demise as clearly as you watched Mr. Braxton's." His eyes jump back to me. "Did it cause you pain? Watching him disappear? Did it hurt more than when I killed Julian?"

My lips peel back from my teeth. "Stay here longer and Emil will rip you apart himself."

Victor Hesse cocks his head to the side. "It's odd, don't you think? That someone as powerful as a demon of destruction hasn't *already* regained his corporeal form?"

Trepidation shoots through me. "What did you do?"

"Oh, I wish I could take credit, but I was simply a means of delivery in this." He looks the opposite way down the street from Club Fulcrum. "I wonder how Mr. König is doing?" He fakes a shiver, rubbing at his skeletal arms. "Winter must be hard right now, without you feeding from him. How will he take the loss of his companions?" He gives me a sly look. "I imagine it will be quite explosive, unless someone steps in to stop it."

My heart lurches with panic, and I stride for the door, Victor Hesse following me pace for pace.

A strong hand wraps around my bicep, stopping me from rushing to Emil's side, and I whip around to hiss at Detective Sharpe.

His hold on me doesn't budge. "You're playing right into his hands." He nods to the door, where

Victor Hesse waits. "Whatever is keeping him out, I'm guessing it doesn't extend past this building."

"Should I head to the next event without you, Ms. Pond?" Victor Hesse calls through the glass door. "I don't want to miss the show."

I strain against the detective's hold. "What are you planning?"

"It's not *my* plan." He runs long, stick-like fingers over the barrier. "Well, not *all* my plan. I simply got the cogs moving faster."

He reaches into his jacket to pull out a familiar black jar and unscrews the top as he continues, "The great and powerful elders are so *afraid*, they just keep pulling back farther and farther, hiding in the shadows while this world barrels forward."

He dips a finger into the jar and pulls out a wiggling black tendril of slime. "Every demon who threatens to expose us must be locked away, Ms. Pond. They will keep us hiding until there is nothing left." He traces an oozing black symbol over the door. "But we shouldn't have to hide. You and I are going to change that."

Worried, I back away from the door, dragging the detective with me. "Jax, what's he doing?"

"I don't know." Jax appears next to us, studying

the symbol, before he shakes his head. "It's not something I recognize. If Xander were here..."

"Everyone, go hide in the pantry." I yank my arm free of the detective's hold and turn to find Sophia. "Take the humans. Lock yourselves inside."

She nods and blurs into a green streak of motion, the humans vanishing one-by-one from the front room.

Detective Sharpe takes a wide-legged stance and raises his weapon, pointing it at Victor Hesse.

I stare at him in surprise. "You should hide, too, Detective."

"My name's Gavin," he grunts. "And I don't run from murderers, human or not."

"Nice to meet you, Gavin." I take up a stance beside him. "My friends call me Adie."

"I'm Jax," the witch says as he steps up on my other side.

"Tally." My friend waves from beside Jax as gossamer wings lift from her shoulders.

"Sophia." My cousin appears on Gavin's other side.

I stare at them in surprise. "I told you all to hide."

"We're family," Martha says from behind me. "We stand together."

I glance over my shoulder to see the imps at our backs, Jesse holding a wooden spoon like a sword, while Martha and Iris lift sheet pans like shields and Kelly wields a broom.

My heart swells with pride, and I face forward, my wings slipping free from hiding.

Victor Hesse stares at us, a malicious glee shining from his dead eyes as he completes his drawing, and the door explodes inward.

Third Time's the Charm

"Isn't this just heartwarming?" Victor Hesse sneers as he steps through the shattered opening.

His movements slow as the weakened barrier tries to repel him, but the spell was attached to the building, and it can't bridge a gap as wide as the blown out doorway.

"Jax." I reach for the witch's hand only to find him already reaching for mine.

As our fingers link together, the magic inside me jumps down our connection, and Jax lifts his free hand. Raw magic jumps from his fingers. Not the organized ball of crackling energy he usually throws around, though. No, there's no time for that. Instead, the magic splatters outward in a net of power that shoots toward mortifer demon.

Victor Hesse turns to the side, lifting his arm, and the magic rolls around him like water crashing around an immovable rock before it fizzles out altogether.

Dry cackles come from him as he straightens and pulls the akuzal's skull down over his face, his milky-blue glow coming from the shadows of its eye sockets. "I expected more from your famous witches. Is that the best they can offer?"

Jax tugs harder on the magic inside me, and the next net he casts out crackles and pops with power.

This time, Victor Hesse doesn't even flinch as he holds up a hand, fingers spread wide. Something red pulses and glows at the center of his hand, a mark carved into his rotting flesh. The net halts in mid-air for a heartbeat, then flings back toward us.

Panic shoots through me, and I release Jax to dart into the net's path, spreading my wings wide to protect those who stand behind me. The threads of magic slam into me, hissing and sizzling against my skin, and I drop to one knee as pain eats through me.

Jax falls to his knees at my side, trying to stop the spell he created, but as he said before, he's no good at the fine-tuned stuff, and it slips free of his grasp to wrap tighter around me.

A sharp crack fills the air, followed by another, and Victor Hesse stumbles a step back toward the entrance. Detective Sharpe keeps shooting, the bullets pelting against the mortifer demon without harming him. But they offer the distraction Tally and Sofia need as they dart forward from opposite sides.

In a blur of motion, Victor Hesse's fist swings, knocking Tally from the air. She flies across the room, her body crashing into one of the booths and toppling over the table.

Before she even lands, Victor Hesse catches Sophia, plucking her out of hyper-speed. His hand wraps around her throat, lifting her high off the ground. Her legs kick for purchase as she clutches at his skeletal arm, and choked noises come from her gaping mouth as her eyes bug out.

Jax flinches, half rising to go to Tally, before he shakes his head and returns to pulling at the net that contains me.

A screech of anger comes from behind me before Jesse darts past. The tiny imp flings herself at the larger demon, the spoon in her hand slamming into his chest handle first.

Victor Hesse grunts, then reaches down to grab Jesse by the hair and tosses her aside. She slams against the wall, her small body losing shape.

Terrified, I pull at the strings of magic that cut

into my flesh as I struggle to rise, to protect my friends.

The other imps charge forward, swinging their makeshift weapons, but he swats them aside with frightening ease before he gives Sophia a hard shake. Something snaps, and Sophia's body falls limp within his hold before slowly disintegrating in a shower of green glitter.

Victor Hesse smacks his palms together, brushing away the dust as he steps forward, his voice conversational. "Witch, won't you drain more of that nasty magic out of my creation? Or have you already expended your usefulness?"

Jax freezes, his hands hovering over me, unable to help and unwilling to run. I whimper with pain as the net sinks beneath my skin and meat to find my bones.

Desperate, I open myself to the agony, flinging my senses wide. This was my magic originally, it just needs to return to its original form. But it struggles against me. I let it go, let its purpose be changed, and it doesn't want to be tamed again.

The click of a gun being reloaded sounds, and Victor Hesse turns to Gavin. "I'm going to enjoy eating you, piece-by-piece. I've gotten very good at keeping my meals alive during the process. If I'm patient, we could be together for years to come. If I'm *very* patient, I'll even leave you your eyes so you can watch the world burn."

In answer, Gavin unloads his gun once more, straight into the center of Victor Hesse's chest.

The mortifer demon stumbles back a pace, the impact stalling him while the bullets bounce off and ping to the floor like metal rain. He sweeps his hand forward, and something red flashes from his palm.

A string of black slime whips out to wrap around Gavin's throat. The detective crashes to the floor, his weapon falling from his hands as he scrambles to stop the slime from choking him.

"Adie, what do we do," Jax whispers, desperation in his voice.

"Run," I plead, my voice thick with pain. "Just run."

Jax doesn't run, though. He wraps his arms around my pain-filled body and drags me toward the kitchen.

Victor Hesse cocks his head to the side, the skull that covers his face giving him the appearance of a grotesquely curious bird. "Where are you going with my prize, witch?"

Not answering, Jax continues backward, Victor Hesse following us at a slow pace like some sort of movie monster. I kick my feet weakly, trying to help as we slide past the two-way door.

Jax releases me to lock the door in place before he frantically pulls his cell phone from his pocket, his fingers fumbling on the screen.

The door rattles, and I hold my breath, waiting for another explosion.

Instead, clattering comes from the other room, and Victor Hesse pokes his head through the pass-through over the decorating station. "This is getting tiresome, witch."

I push back across the floor, pain shooting through me with every inch, until my back comes up against the newly installed ovens. My heart pounds, flooding my body with adrenaline as Victor Hesse slithers through the opening in the wall, his heels coming down hard on the plates waiting to be filled with desserts. They shatter beneath his weight, pieces falling to smash against the floor. He hops down, then lifts an arm to block the sheet pan Jax swings at him.

With a deft snap of his wrist, the mortifer demon catches the edge of the pan and shoves it at Jax's face. It slams into his forehead, and the witch crumples to the ground, unconscious.

The net around me vanishes, leaving pain and

weakness behind. I scramble for power, any shred of energy left to me, but find only the ley line magic I don't know how to use.

Victor Hesse brushes imaginary lint off the outside of his duster as he steps toward me. "It was a good effort, but it's time to admit defeat. You're mine, now, and we will do such magnificent things together."

Growling, I lift my trembling arms, my blunt fingers hooked like claws.

He chuckles as he bends over me, his arms spread wide as if to welcome me home.

Behind him, a small, hairy figure steps out of the shadows between the mixing station and the wall, his hands cupped around something that flickers like fire. Relief sweeps through me to see that Vova and Torch are okay, even as the rest of the world crashes down.

Victor Hesse pauses, his hands inches from my skin. "Why are you suddenly happy?"

I lift my gaze to stare into his horrifying mask. "You could never understand."

Vova runs forward and flings his hands outward, launching Torch through the air. As he flies, his fire changes from red, to orange, to dazzling white.

He lands on Victor Hesse's shoulder, and the

feathers around his collar ignite as if fueled by acetone. He shrieks and jerks upright, slapping at the fire as Torch races across his shoulders, spreading the flames into his mask.

Victor Hesse shrieks, grabbing at the skull as fire shoots from the eyes and nose holes. He catches Torch, throwing the small ignis demon toward the sink before he rips the skull from his head and throws it aside to display skin blackened to charcoal, his hair melted to his skull. Flinging off his trench coat, he slaps out the few flames that made it to his shirt beneath.

He draws in ragged breaths through clenched teeth as he turns back to face me. "Now *that* was exciting."

A loud crack vibrates through the kitchen, and Victor Hesse's head snaps to the side, surprise registering in his eyes before he falls to the ground and disintegrates.

Looks like the third time's the charm when it comes to killing the mortifer demon.

Shocked, I stare at where Detective Sharpe who leans through the pass-through, his gun once more in his hand.

Black slime coats his throat and the collar of his shirt, and his dark hair sticks up in every direction.

But his eyes remain calm as he keeps his weapon trained on the spot where Victor Hesse had stood. "Is he gone? Or is this like a horror movie where I have to kill him five more times?"

"He's back on the demon plane, for now." I drop my head back to rest against the oven behind me. "How long he remains there is questionable, though."

Gavin curses and holsters his gun before climbing through the narrow opening with far less grace than Victor Hesse had displayed. His foot slips on the broken serving trays, and he holds onto the sill for balance as he steps down to the floor.

He strides over to Jax first, checking the witch for a pulse, before he comes to kneel in front of me.

His brows pinch together. "How are you doing?"

"I feel like shit," I groan.

"You look like shit." He frowns as his gaze sweeps over me. "Well, not like shit, actually. But that's probably due to you being a…succubus?" He waits for my nod. "Objectively speaking, you're somewhere between sexy orphan and mud-wrestling nympho."

My brows shoot up. "Know a lot of mud-wrestling nymphos?"

His serious gaze meets mine. "Arrested one a couple of times."

"Nymphos rarely learn their lesson," I say drily.

His lips twist with annoyance. "I think being arrested is part of the appeal."

"Must be Vicki."

Surprise widens his eyes. "You know Vicki?"

"Everyone knows Vicki." I shift and groan. "She's a bit of a legend among my kind."

"Huh." His eyes move once more to where Victor Hesse had stood. "Not that I'm looking a gift horse in the mouth, but why did shooting him work *this* time?"

I lift one shoulder, then grunt as the motion sends pain shooting through me. Note to self: no more stepping in front of magical nets. "The outfit must have been what was shielding him." I nudge the skull with my foot. "Probably cast some twisted barrier spells on it. Once it was off, it left him vulnerable."

Gavin stares at the skull and the smoking remains of the trench coat. "He probably won't make that mistake again."

"Probably not." I lift a hand. "Help me up. I need to check on the others."

"No one's body disappeared." He grasps my

wrists and lifts me to my feet. When my legs threaten to collapse, he slips an arm around my waist. "Not disappearing is good?"

"Usually, yeah." I hobble with him toward the door, then freeze when the sink catches my eye. I lean my weight toward it, and he changes direction, half carrying me to the counter.

My pulse quickens once more as I peer into the basin.

Torch, back to a steady red glow, hovers against the side, as far from any drops of water as he can get. When he sees me peering down, he flickers and waves stubby little arms.

"Oh, buddy, I'm so, so sorry," I breathe as I reach into the sink to scoop him to safety. "You and Vova were so brave."

He flickers and hugs my thumb, his body hot against my skin, but not burning.

"What is that?" Gavin whispers as he stares at Torch.

"This is the best cupcake baker in town," I coo at Torch.

The little guy flickers blue for a second, and I wince. But the pain quickly fades as my body repairs itself instantly, the ley line magic that remains inside me following its original purpose to keep me healthy.

The pain of the net fades, too, but the weakness in my body remains. I need to return to the house, to restock my energy. But, first, I need to make sure everyone survived and that they get somewhere safe.

Leaning heavily on the detective, I hold Torch away from my clothes. I should find his box and not expend the power needed to hold him with bare hands, but I'm reluctant to let him go just yet.

Shuffling to the door, Gavin unlocks it, and we step out into the shattered remains of my bakery.

My chest tightens, this pain deeper, but relief quickly follows as I see bodies moving, and groans fill the air.

As Kelly helps Martha and Iris up, the collapsed table that had caught Tally scrapes backward, my friend's pink hair appearing. Kelly stumbles over to pull the table farther back, then helps Tally up.

She looks around. "Jax?"

"Knocked out in the kitchen," Gavin informs her, and the baku demon rushes past us to find her witch.

Jesse crawls out from behind one of the booths, her body rippling and reshaping as she looks around with wide brown eyes. "Sophia?" She chitters, the sound filled with panic as she wobbles to her feet, looking around. "Lazy succubus?"

Heart breaking, I release Gavin to hobble over to my smallest imp, pulling her soft body against mine. "She'll be okay. She'll be back."

The other imps swarm around me, filling the air with their unique smell of baby powder, underscored by fear. I hold Torch above my head as they glom onto me and Jesse, chittering out comfort while seeking it for themselves.

Over Iris's rainbow colored hair, I see Tally helping Jax from the kitchen, and the witch's eyes jump to find me. Finding me safe, some of his tension melts away.

He leans heavily against the baku demon as she practically carries him to one of the chairs that remains upright. She settles him there before she darts back into the kitchen. She returns a moment later with a glass of water, then hovers over him as he drinks.

When the kitchen door bangs open, everyone flinches, and Detective Sharpe reaches for his weapon.

Slater stumbles out, and Tally releases a cry of relief, rushing across the room as Slater stops next to the counter for support. Soot covers him, and he winces as Tally's arms wrap around his waist.

Hope surges through me as I fight my way free of the imps. "Kellen?"

Slater shakes his head. "I was helping unload crates in the parking lot when the building blew. I tried to go back in, but…" He coughs into his hand. "No one walked out of there."

My throat tightens for the loss of my storm god, stolen without even the chance to say goodbye, before I nod in acceptance. Like Tobias, I have to assume he safely returned to the demon plane. Anything less is too painful to bear.

Detective Sharpe's eyes shift toward the front of the shop, and he stiffens. My gut tightens, and I spin to face the new threat.

But instead of Victor Hesse swooping back in for round two, I see a white van pulled up to the curb, with a simple sign on the side that reads: *The Cleaners. No mess is too big.*

"I called them," Jax volunteers as he stands to join Slater and Tally. "I figured they'd either save us like last time, or be here to clean up the mess after we were slaughtered."

Tally hushes him, her hands flitting between her two men, checking for more wounds.

I frown at the van with suspicion. Even if they came directly from their offices hidden behind the psychic's shop, it should have taken them at least ten more minutes, if not longer with the commotion from the explosion closing down nearby streets.

"How did they get here so fast?" I demand. "You only just called them."

"They probably hopped into their van as soon as they heard news about the explosion." When I turn to look at the detective in surprise, I find his narrowed eyes focused on the van. "They have police scanners."

"Do you know—"

"What in the ever-loving hell happened here?" Flint's voice cuts me off as the beautiful man sweeps through the busted front door.

Then, he freezes as his eyes land on Gavin.

Pen, right behind him, huffs with annoyance. "Clear the way. We have a shit ton of work to do, and not a lot of time."

"Um, Pen, we should probably—"

Marc, bringing up the rear, stops just outside the shop with a concise, "Fuck."

"Move out of the way!" Pen yells.

Flint, obviously shoved from behind, stumbles farther into the bakery to leave Pen exposed. Her golden-brown eyes sweep over the wreckage before landing on the detective.

"Well, fuck." She whips around to pin her glare on Marc. "You're supposed to be keeping track of him!"

"I'm not your freaking clairvoyant!" Marc snaps back. "He's not even on duty today!"

"Hey, Detective Hot Stuff." Flint flutters his lashes at the other man. "Any chance you can forget you saw us here?"

The detective folds his arms over his chest, a hard look settling on his face. "You want to tell me again how crazy I am for thinking the paranormal exists? Or does someone finally want to tell me what the hell is going on?"

Playtime is Over

I abandon the cleaners while they explain things to Detective Sharpe and return to the kitchen. There, I find Torch's fire-safe box, tuck him inside, then bolt out the side door into the alley.

Yeah, it's not the best idea to go out alone right now, and it's *definitely* not the brightest idea to be driving, but without hyper-speed, the car is my fastest option for reaching Emil.

It's possible Victor Hesse was just taunting me to lure me out into the open, but my gut says I need to find my ice demon, even if it's just to be there when he learns of Tobias's and Kellen's corporeal deaths.

Uneasiness rolls through me, my mind shying away from what else Victor Hesse had implied. They're demons of destruction, and they wield forces few demons could stand against. There's no way they'll be trapped on the demon plane so long as there's still access to the human world.

They're just being a little slow to return to me.

I keep repeating that to myself as I speed toward K&B Financial, honking the horn through intersections when the lights don't turn green fast enough.

The tires bump up onto the curb as I wedge my car into a spot that's too small for it directly in front of the entrance. It leaves the back end sticking out, but I don't care. They can tow me.

Grabbing Torch's box, I throw the driver's door open, leap out, and rush into the bank. I bypass the tellers at the front and stride down the hall that leads to the conference rooms and the personal offices. An employee spots me and leaps from his desk, but I zoom past before he can try to hold me up.

He follows me down the hall. "Miss, do you have an appointment? Is there someone I can call for you?"

"No, thank you," I call back without slowing as I pass a series of offices with frosted-glass doors.

When I turn down another short hallway that leads to Emil and Tobias's offices, worry enters his voice. "Miss, if you'll return to the check-in desk, I will let Mr. König know you're here."

I tuck Torch's box closer against my side. "I don't need an appointment."

The hall ends at a set of double-doors made from rich mahogany, and I grasp the handle, flinging one door open.

"Miss, you can't go in there!" the employee yells in panic.

Emil looks up from the large desk that dominates the space, his brows lifting, before his pale-blue eyes move past me. "It's fine, Mr. Garcia. Ms. Pond is on the permanent guest list."

"My apologies, Mr. König," the man murmurs, followed by the almost silent snick of the door closing.

Emil rises from his padded chair and circles around his desk. "Adie, what are you doing here?" His gaze moves past me once more, and his white brows pinch together. "Where's Tobias? He's supposed to be with you."

My heart wobbles, setting off a ripple of reactions inside me that must show on my face because Emil goes still as an ice sculpture. My bottom lip trembles, and I catch it between my teeth, biting hard to push back the sting of tears.

Emil's icy gaze drops to my mouth, and he shakes himself back into motion. His hand lifts toward my cheek before he freezes once more, his fingers slowly curling against his palm to stop himself from comforting me.

The reminder we can't touch rips the sob from my throat, and I shove my hand over my mouth to stop it. Now isn't the time to break down. Not when I need to be strong and make sure Emil stays safe until the others return.

Another sob escapes, muffled against my palm.

"Adie?" he breathes, frost filling the air between us. "What's happened?"

Knowing I shouldn't, but unable to stop myself, I surge forward to close the distance between us. I press against his frozen body, not caring that the chill of his skin burns where we touch. I'd rather freeze to death than spend another second outside of his arms.

He embraces me carefully, his cold lips pressing against my temple as he whispers, "It's okay. Everything will be okay."

"We don't know that," I gasp out, and words roll off my tongue as I tell him everything that happened.

He listens silently, the temperature slowly dropping around us until I shiver in his arms, my teeth chattering as I speak. The power in his touch caresses my skin, demanding I let it in, but that could be the very thing Victor Hesse wants. Maybe one more feeding is all that's needed to complete his spell. There's no way of knowing.

When I slow, then finally stop talking, Emil cups the back of my head, his fingers threading through my hair. Ice crystals bloom across my scalp, but I only press closer, accepting that frostbite is the cost of his comfort.

"They'll return," he says at last. "You said Tobias vanished. He probably met up with Kellen and they're filing a change of location while they're there, since so many humans saw them die."

Straightening, I blink frost from my lashes. "Yeah, that must be it. Tobias said we'd need to move at some point."

Emil cups my cheeks. "Yes. Somewhere warm this time. The Caribbean."

I sniffle, the cold burning my nose. "I've never been to the Caribbean."

"You'll love it." He leans down to rub his nose against mine. "The ocean there is warm, and the beaches have sand so fine it feels like sugar."

"That sounds beautiful," I choke out.

"We'll drink out of coconuts and nap under cabanas." A light kiss flits over my lips, there and gone before he tempts me. Then, his hands drop to the box I hold. "You brought Torch with you?"

"Yeah." With a jerky nod, I step out of Emil's arms and slide back the safety lid to the box.

Torch flickers in welcome, his flames running the gamut between red and white as he waves his little arms and hops up and down.

His adorableness pulls a wet chuckle from me. "I think he's asking for up-sees."

"Well, we can't leave him wanting after how brave he was." Before I can stop him, Emil reaches down and scoops Torch out of the box.

His skin hisses, and steam rises, but Torch only takes that as a challenge and burns blue with heat.

Emil releases a sigh of appreciation. "That feels nice."

"I didn't know you could hold Torch." I reach out to rub his little belly and ignore the flash of pain. "I should have been bringing him home every night so you could play with him."

Torch flickers his agreement while panic fills Emil's eyes.

Quickly, he returns Torch to his metal box. "Now, let's not be hasty. I already have Tac to care for."

"But isn't he *cute*?" I lift the box toward Emil's face. "And *warm*?"

Emil's gaze drops to the open box, and another sigh of appreciation escapes him. "Maybe just a *little* more playing."

Torch flickers with excitement before he stills, his flames banking to a dull-red shine. I frown at the sudden change, and Emil pauses, his hand hovering over the box. Then a rush of tingles dance across my skin, and everything happens in fast forward.

Emil pushes me behind his back as portals open in his office and council guards suddenly appear around us. I fumble Torch's box, almost dropping him, and a streak of red rushes past. For a second, I think Torch escaped again, but then Emil suddenly vanishes from my side.

A crash comes from his desk area, and I whip around to find Cassandra pinning him down, her lips latched over his.

Rage spikes through me, and Torch flares blindingly white in response. But before I can rush to Emil's aid, strong arms grab me from all sides, holding me back.

"No!" I shout, my anger making the ley line magic inside me bubble and stir. "Let him go!"

A tall figure steps in front of me, blocking my

view, and I look up into Lord Marius's hard eyes. "This is what must be done, Adeline Boo Pond."

"You're wrong!" I fight against the guards, and Torch's box falls from my hands.

The small ignis demon leaps free and runs to the guard on my left, trying to light the slag demon on fire, but stone won't burn. The guard kicks his foot, and Torch tumbles away, leaving a trail of burnt carpet in his wake.

"Calm yourself," Lord Marius commands. "You can do nothing to stop this."

"You're wrong," I seethe, the anger in me growing stronger, and my skin begins to glow with iridescent light as my wings slip free from hiding.

The guards who hold me disintegrate, and I feel their power sink through the foundation to the earth beneath, then farther down to the thin stream of a ley line.

Lord Marius's eyes widen, and he gestures for more guards to come forward. They hesitate, their eyes on my glowing skin, before they stomp finto action.

A growl rips from my throat, and I grab onto the stream of magic deep beneath the ground, yanking it to me. Power floods my body, and rainbows splash through the office. There's no time to fix on a single purpose, or try to finesse this power into something I'm used to wielding. All I can think is *Die* as I dart away from the guard. Their bodies puff to dust, and I yank their energy to me, fueling the magic to grow stronger as more guards rush forward.

These, too, turn to dust, and through their ashes, I see Emil's limp body being carried toward a waiting portal. Cassandra strides beside them, a victorious smile curving her lips, and my anger rushes out of me in a tide of magic that unmakes the space between us. Carpet disintegrates and chairs unravel. The floorboards buckle, foundation crumbling, until a cavern of darkness rushes toward her.

Cassandra's smile falters and fear widens her eyes a moment before she vanishes in a streak of red, taking Emil with her.

"No!" I shout.

As I lurch forward, the portal snaps shut.

It's too late.

Around the room, the rest of the portals close, leaving me alone.

I fall to my knees, screaming out my denial that the last of my loves, my ice demon, my stuffy Emil, has been ripped away.

Not Laughing

The bank security arrives only after the fight is over, but I can't dredge up the effort to punish them for their failure to protect Emil.

How can I blame them when I stood in the room and could do nothing?

The head of security kneels in front of me, his neon-green eyes filled with a respect that didn't exist the last time we met. "Ms. Pond."

"Leonard," I acknowledge. "Your timing sucks, as usual."

"We cannot stand against the high council." His eyes sweep the room, taking in the destruction. "Though, it appears you did okay."

"I did *nothing*." Smoke tickles my nose, and I glance over at Emil's desk, where fire flickers around the base. "You might want to get a fire extinguisher. My ignis demon is setting the office on fire."

As one of the guards hyper-speeds out of the room, I grab Torch's box and crawl over to the desk. "Come on, buddy, time to go."

He waddles out from under the desk to belly flop into the open box.

"Yeah, I bet you're tired. You've been setting all sorts of things on fire today, haven't you?" I hug the box against my chest. "You're such a good ignis demon."

He flickers and rolls onto his back, stubby arms patting his stomach.

I glance around, and my eyes settle on a pile of sawdust where one of Emil's fancy chairs used to be. Reaching out, I scoop up a handful and sprinkle it over Torch, who flickers happily as he burns it away.

The security guard returns with the fire extinguisher and sprays down the desk, covering the entire front with white foam.

Leonard's voice rises over the noise. "What will you do now?"

I twist to peer over my shoulder at him. "I'm going to the demon plane. I need to find where they took Emil." My heart lurches, and I swallow the sudden lump in my throat. "And why Tobias and Kellen haven't returned."

Because, no matter what Emil said, they wouldn't have left us wondering this long.

Leonard stares down at me. "Sophia said you wanted a gathering. That you would take down Cassandra."

Clutching Torch's box tighter, I stand so Leonard no longer has the advantage of looming over me quite so much. "Yes."

"We had a good laugh about that. A baby like you, taking on that monster." He looks around the office once more. "No one is laughing now."

My pulse quickens. "Then you'll come?"

His neon-green gaze returns to me. "Landregath used to boast that you would become the best of us. We laughed about that, too, behind his back. Laughed about how he had become doting in his retirement. We thought he meant you'd become *human*, with your bakery and your refusal to feed properly."

My heart beats faster to hear that Landon thought so highly of me, even when I continued to fail.

"Today, seeing what you did here..." He straightens his spine. "Bring back the demons of destruction, and we'll stand with you against

Cassandra. We will follow you, Adeline Boo Pond, to whatever end you lead us."

My wings shiver against my spine, and my lips part, tongue flicking out to taste the promise in the air. This has the feel of a contract, of a binding, not just with Leonard, but with every incubi and succubi within the city.

I pull my shoulders back and lift my chin. "I'd bring them back regardless. They are mine."

He nods approvingly and tilts his head toward the doorway. "There's an access point in the security control room."

"Won't work," a familiar voice calls, and a moment later, Sophia appears in the office. "They're locking down the borders. I barely made it back."

Happiness fills me at her fast return, followed by panic as her words register.

When her eyes find me, sorrow fills them. "Adie, they're gathering up all the powerful demons and locking them in the Between. Your demons of destruction were the first to go."

"That's not..." My mind struggles to accept her words. "They can't..."

She walks farther into the room. "With everything that's been going on lately, the higher ups are worried about humans finding out about us. The way station is shut down, too. If we go to Dreamland, we won't be able to return here."

The security guards in the room still. As incubi, Dreamland is their primary hunting ground unless they're willing to risk feeding on humans here, where the temptation to take everything is so strong. If humans start dying from feedings, succubi and incubi will be pulled back to the demon plane, too.

It's exactly what Victor Hesse warned would happen. The higher-ups are afraid of another war with the humans, and they're pulling back when they should be moving forward to figure out safer ways for us to openly cohabitate. Because hiding is no longer working. We need a different solution, a better way.

"We need the witches," I whisper, my mind latching onto the idea and running with it.

Everyone in the room stares at me in confusion, but I shake my head, unable to explain the thoughts forming.

Instead, I stride toward the door. "We need to go back home." I reach into my pocket and toss my cell phone at Sophia. "Make the call. Tell everyone to meet us there."

Eyes wide, she starts dialing as I walk from Emil's destroyed office and out into the hall. Demons stand silently in the open doorways to the smaller offices, their gazes following as I stride past. Word is already spreading, and the scent of fear burns against my nose.

Out on the street, cold wind whips my hair into my face, and I hold Torch's container closer until we reach the car, where I carefully buckle the box into the backseat.

Still talking into the phone, Sophia climbs into the passenger seat.

When I glance back at the bank, demons hover in every window, staring out at us. My stomach squeezes tight, seeing them on one side of the glass and us on the other. It's like they're already locked up, unable to escape their cage.

Unwilling to accept that future, I turn away and slide behind the wheel.

When we pull up in front of the house, cars fill the driveway and line the street, alerting us that the others have already arrived.

I grab Torch from the back seat, and we head inside. The imps huddle together on my floral couch, and Sophia immediately goes to them, lifts

Jesse, and settles in among them, with my smallest imp sitting on her lap.

Jesse snuggles in with a relieved, "Lazy succubus."

Around them, the others huddle closer, welcoming Sophia as if she's one of their own.

My heart lifts for a moment as I remember how much they started out hating each other. They're proof demons can change, that the way we are is not how we must remain.

Tac squats in the stairwell to my and Emil's rooms, with Fuyumi perched in front of him, Prem cradled in her arms while Merp sits on her folded knees. Ice coats Fuyumi's skin and forms icicles on her chin. She's never once tried to pass for human, and Tac can't. Tac's not even considered a demon, though his whelps would be half-breeds. What happens to them under these new restrictions?

Tally stand with her witches near the archway, further proof of how we can change and evolve. Proof that our differences don't have to keep us apart.

Next to them, Flint, Pen, and Marc stand at an uneasy distance from Gavin, who leans against the wall, his arms folded over his chest as he takes in the rest of the room.

The only people missing are my demons of destruction, and I intend to change that, *right now.*

Setting Torch's box down, I turn to face Xander. "It's time."

His brows sweep together, and he exchanges a look with his brother before facing me once more. "Time for what, Adie?"

"Time for Kellen's contingency plan." Stepping into the center of the room, I drag the coffee table out of the way as I continue to speak. "You were gathered together and given a singular task. To study the ley lines."

"Yes," Xander says slowly, his confusion still clear.

"Kellen assumed he would be here to launch this grand scheme of his, but he was wrong, so we need to move forward without him." I leave the table against the wall and go back for Tobias's chair, shoving it out of the way, too.

"But, he never told us what the plan was," Xander protested. "He just threw books at us and told us to learn as much as possible."

"He thought you'd be able to break me out of jail, if it came to that." I push Kellen's chair against the wall, too. "That means he thought you'd be able to access the demon plane. And if you could access that, then you can access the Between, where they're now locking people up."

"We don't have enough power for that, though." Reese shakes his head. "We barely opened a way to the Between with the help of Landon, Kellen, and the Librarian. With just us, it's impossible."

"Yeah, I know." I stride across the room and grab the leather couch on one end and drag it out of the way to leave the gold circle engraved into the floor fully exposed. "Which means he didn't want you to open a way to the Between specifically. But what he wanted from you would allow him to access any part of the demon plane, including the Between."

"You're not making sense," Jax says. "He didn't want into the Between but he wanted into the Between?"

"Yes, exactly." Straightening, I return to the circle. "The Between didn't always exist. The same way Dreamland didn't always exist. It was created, which means it requires power to continue to exist." I turn to stare at the witches. "There's only one reason he would have you studying ley lines."

Realization sweeps over Xander's face. "Because these pockets of reality are powered by ley lines."

"Which means we need to pull the ley lines away from where they're holding the demons of destruction." Reese glances at Tally. "But what will happen to Dreamland if we do this. And I'm not saying we *can*, but if we take away the power…"

"Dreamland exists from the minds of thousands of demons and millions of humans. It doesn't need to be powered by the ley lines anymore," she says.

He nods and looks at his brother, then at Jax and Slater. "But... There's no way we can do that with just the four of us. Not at our current level. I don't know if we could even do it with a dozen more years of study. We're talking about pulling on the magic of creation and asking it to move."

"We're not *asking* it." I slash a hand through the air. "You're always going on about intention. So we're going to give it a very precise intent to *move*. I've been in the ley line before; I'll go back into it. All you have to do is be my anchors on this side, help ground me and remind me of my purpose."

"But you'd need direct access to a ley line." Reese's brows sweep together. "We don't have that here."

"No, but we have it on the demon plan. They sit on the surface in the wastelands. That's how I got into it the first time, and it's how I'll get back into it."

"The portals are closed, though." Sophia points

out as she hugs Jesse closer. "Even if you go to Dreamland, you won't be able to get to the way station, let alone out to the wastelands."

I turn to face Flint. "Which is where *you* come in."

He lifts a brow. "It is?"

With a decisive nod, I pull my shirt over my head, leaving me covered by only my bra, and point to the spot above my heart. "You're going to complete this symbol. Victor Hesse is on the demon plane right now, and he's too smart to leave things to chance. If this is the leash that binds me to him, then all we have to do is complete it, and it will pull me through the veil, shut down or no shut down."

LIFE AFTER BURNING

"This seems like a foolhardy mission," Marc points out as Flint and the other witches join me in the circle, and Flint pulls a sharpie from his pocket.

Flint twirls the pen between his fingers as he studies my cleavage. "Are you offering an easier way across the border?"

Surprised, I glance over at Marc. "Is that an option?"

Pen looks up at him, too. "Yeah, *Marc*, is that an option?"

Something dark flickers through his eyes before he looks down at his partner. "What are you offering in payment? I don't need the succubus's money."

Pen folds her arms under her breasts. "You're a real asshole, you know that?"

"Wait." I turn to face Marc fully. "*Is* that an

option? Can you make portals like the Librarian and Lord Marius?"

Pen's lips twist with distaste as Marc's focus shifts to me. The creature who stares back is very much *not* human, or the person I've been dealing with up to now, and my wings razorblade against my spine in warning. I've gotten glimpses of the demon who lives inside Marc before, but never to this extent, and it sets off all my alarm bells.

I move to put myself between him and the others in the room. "Who are you, exactly?"

"He's a useless, selfish asshole who should just go back to sleep while the adults work," Flint announces cheerfully.

The demon's attention shifts to Flint. "Lord Marius will not be pleased that you are assisting in this foolishness."

"Lord Marius can go fuck himself." The amusement slips from Flint's face as he turns toward the other man. "And if you'd like to get the fuck out of my friend and run home to tell him that in person, that would be just *great*."

"He can't make portals," Pen breaks in, refusing to look at not-Marc. "But he can tear through the veil if there's already a weak spot."

That would be safer than my original plan, but...

I lift a hand to my chest, to where I know the mark is, but feel nothing.

I dive inward, ferreting out all the links I share with other demons. Here are the threads for the imps, shining strong and bright. Here are the ones that connect me to the demons of destruction, less vibrant and stretched thin, vanishing into a space I can't follow. And mixed deep within them, a fraying pink strand that grows dimmer by the day.

This link to Julian could mean anything. It's possible that whatever Victor Hesse did, Julian's energy remains somewhere, trapped like we trapped the beast. Or it could be his memory, locked in the Library, my last connection to him. Either way, he's out of my reach. So, after a moment, I let his thread go and continue to search for an unknown link that ties me to Victor Hesse.

But I find nothing.

I shake my head. "I need the link to find Victor Hesse, regardless. He needs to be stopped if we're ever to be safe. There's no reason to pay for something when this will suffice."

"How do we know he's still on the demon plane?" Tally asks from where she hovers just on the other side of the circle. "He could have returned before the lock down."

My hand shifts to the bottle that hangs around my neck, and it practically leaps into my palm. It pulses with hunger, and there's a sense of yearning, too, a desire to be somewhere else. But it can't pinpoint the location. It's just not *here*.

"The beast can't sense Victor Hesse here, so he must be on the demon plane." I drop the bottle. "The only other place he could be is Dreamland."

Tally shakes her head. "Aren would know."

"How's complete sovereignty treating him?" I ask.

"He's insufferable." Tally rolls her eyes. "It was bad enough when he became the first baku to break into the Between and to shrink without sundering. I think he's making himself a crown."

"You won't succeed," not-Marc cuts in. "Do you really think you're the first demon to try to affect the ley lines? If it were possible, they would have already been moved and our world wouldn't be on the brink of death."

"No, I assume it's been attempted many times," I say slowly as I fight down my irritation. "This has been going on for hundreds of years. Of course, an attempt would have been made to reverse what was done at the end of the great war."

His eyes narrow on me. "Then what makes you think you're so special?"

"I don't think that." I hook a thumb over my shoulder at the witches. "I think *they're* special. Humans are the ones who pushed the ley lines out of whack. It stands to reason they'll be the ones who can change it again. And we're not on a mission to move *all* the ley lines, just the one powering the Between."

"Just shut up and let them try," Pen snaps at Marc. "It's no skin off your teeth if they all die in the attempt."

He stares back down at her. "And if they mess things up even more?"

She shrugs. "Then they've proven the ley lines *can* be changed."

"You say that because it's not your home that could be destroyed by their foolishness," he hisses.

"You're right." Her face hardens. "For all I care, the demon realm can burn."

"Such a *positive* atmosphere we have here, huh?" Flint pulls off the sharpie's cap and focuses on my chest once more. "Now, I believe the mark was somewhere around..."

Xander snatches the pen from his hand. "You can't even see it."

Flint scowls at him. "You're ruining my dream of drawing on her boobs."

"You can draw on my boobs all you want if I make it back," I offer, and he brightens.

"Flint," Pen warns. "I'm not pulling your ass out of the fire if her demons of destruction decide to crush you."

"They're very nice boobs," Flint sighs heavily. "It might be worth it."

"Thank you." I turn said boobs toward Xander. "Let's do this."

"Wait." Reese grabs the cap from Flint and shoves it back on the marker Xander holds. "We need more preparation than simply completing the leash."

His brother nods. "If we're going to act as anchors to pull you back once you're in the ley line, then we need links, and a spell big enough to reach you across the planes of existence."

Impatience pushes me to insist we move forward right away, but I restrain the emotion. They're right, and we need to do this as accurately as possible if we're going to succeed. "What do you need?"

"Give us..." Xander looks around the room, his shoulders tight with strain. "Just give us a few minutes to set this up. This has all been theory up until now, so..."

He trails off as he strides back across the circle to grab his satchel.

"You should power up while we get things ready," Reese advises. "We have no idea how this leash thing works. For all we know, you could pop in right next to Victor Hesse as soon as it's complete."

"Good idea." I flex my fingers. "Just need to think how to give it the right purpose."

Reese pats my arm before he joins the others, and Xander begins to give him, Jax, and Slater directions. Reese kneels next to his large duffel bag, pulling out items and passing them to Jax and Slater, who disperse them around the circle.

Teeth worrying at my bottom lip, I step onto the ring of gold set into the floor. Ley line magic floods up through my feet and legs, then streams into that empty space inside me, pooling inside of it. Magic spills down my arms to my fingertips, rises into my chest, and fills my mind with temptation.

Give me the strength to stop Victor Hesse. Give me the will to save my men. I repeat the request over and over, letting the ley line interpret the request. I don't know enough about what Victor Hesse can do, or which part of the network of magic powers the Between.

But the ley line is everywhere and knows everything. In one hand, I hold the images of Emil, Tobias, and Kellen in my mind and wrap them in my need to protect. In the other, I hold the need to cleanse Victor Hesse's poison from existence, to stop him from doing more harm.

The magic surges through me, making my bones ring, before it sweeps back into the circle, leaving behind a fragment of its power.

When I open my eyes, the world looks brighter. I find Reese crawling around the circle, drawing chalk symbols onto the floor inside the ring of gold. One layer of symbols already loops around the room, and his brow furrows as he works on a second layer.

Careful not to smudge the lines, I step back next to Flint as Pen joins me.

She looks at her partner. "Shouldn't you be helping them?"

His brows lift. "You want me to..." He points at the others, and at her hard stare, he nods. "Yeah, totally getting on that right now, boss."

When he leaves, Pen looks back at me. "So, you've been in the ley lines before?"

"Yeah, hundreds of times." At her surprised look, I shrug. "I needed power fast."

Her lips purse, and she looks away. "He's right that changing the ley lines has been attempted before. Have you heard of Enyo's Prophecy?"

"Enyo as in the Librarian?" I ask. At her nod, I shake my head. "No, never heard of it."

"It was buried as inaccurate after the high council's last attempt to fix the ley lines." Her eyes flicker to me and away. "It said that a being born of human and demon desire would bridge the worlds and set right what was broken."

"Sounds like an incubus or succubus," I note.

"This being must hold both life and death at once." She watches as Reese starts on a second band of symbols inside the first. "The last time they found someone who fit this prophecy, it didn't end well."

I frown at her emotionless profile. "What happened?"

"Nothing," she says simply. "She died, and it changed nothing for the demon plane."

I study her expression. "So you think I'll fail?"

She shakes her head, her blond hair slipping around her shoulders. "What you did just now, you're holding ley line magic, right? Like a witch does?"

I nod, though I'm not sure it's exactly like a witch does.

"And you've held the power of destruction." Her lips twist. "I think you have a chance. If you don't die."

"I'm not trying to fix the ley lines," I remind her gently. "I'm just trying to free my men."

"Your purpose doesn't really matter. It's the result that does." She extends her hand. "I wish you luck, Adeline Boo Pond."

Confused, I reach out to grasp her hand. "I thought you wanted the demon plane to burn."

Her fingers curl around the back of my hand. "New life can come after a fire."

A sizzling fire burns between our palms, unlike anything I've ever felt before. It sings of death and life born from ashes, and I gasp at the power contained within this slender woman who neither registers as demon or witch to my senses.

She smiles, and releases me. "I think you're right. It's time."

Tethered

Xander takes a deep breath and positions the sharpie over my heart. "This is going to work."

"Are you trying to convince me or yourself?" I whisper, then shiver as the tip of the pen touches my skin.

"Kellen never came right out and said what exactly he planned to use us for," he murmurs as he concentrates on drawing the symbol. "If we were discovered, we couldn't implicate him beyond sheltering witches. Everything we're doing today is only theory we've talked about."

I stare down at the mark slowly appearing. "What's the theory?"

"Why there are so few witches, and how to make accessing the ley lines easier." He frowns as he makes a swoop over the crest of my breast. "There are places where the magic is stronger, and other places where it barely exists."

"On the demon plane, there are nodes of magic, just sitting on the surface, with offshoots that burrow beneath the ground." I lick my lips, tasting the mingle of emotions in the air. "Maybe the offshoots that go deep are what you feel the most on this side."

"The Between won't be powered by an offshoot." The pen hesitates near my collarbone. "Something that can power a pocket of existence will be large."

"My connection to the guys will show me the way," I say with more confidence than I feel.

While I believe what I say is true, entering the ley line is so much *more* than simply taking power to fuel my corporeal form. I escaped it before by focusing on my desire to return to Emil, Tobias, and Kellen. But, this time, I'll be commanding it to move. Even if it's just a piece of the greater web, the ley line doesn't think of itself as pieces, it simply exists.

"Okay, that's it for this one." Xander's words break through my thoughts as he kneels to draw a new symbol over my stomach, where my core of power resides.

From what I can see, it resembles Victor Hesse's, but far more complicated.

When Xander pauses with the pen above my belly button, I reach back and unclasp my bra, shrugging it off. I pull the beast's bottle over my head, too, and hold it out from my side to provide an unobstructed canvas for the spell.

Xander stands, drawing a straight line up my center, between my breasts, up my throat, chin, over my lips and nose, before swishing across my forehead. I don't need to wonder what this mark looks like. Most everyone in the room already wears one on their body, most on their foreheads, though Tally stands with her shirt off as well and sports two of the marks, one at the center of her chest and the other on her stomach, where her power resides at its strongest.

Even Gavin wears the mark, his sharp eyes taking in every part of the ritual. When I'd told him he didn't need to take part in the spell, he'd just shaken his head and said he wanted to know.

Only Marc, or not-Marc, stands separate from everyone else, refusing to take part.

Xander caps the pen and steps back. "Ready?"

I swallow the sudden lump in my throat and

nod. Demons don't bind themselves to others lightly, and tonight, I will bind myself to everyone in this room, giving them a part of myself while taking a piece of them. If I fail, they'll lose a part of themselves, and if I prevail, we will forever be connected.

Xander's gaze drops to the marks on my body, double-checking to make sure everything looks right. "You can put your bra back on. It won't affect the symbol, now that it's drawn."

As he steps back to the other side of the circle, I loop the bottle back around my neck before shrugging back into my bra. By no means is it as good as armor, but it makes me feel a little less vulnerable.

Reese, Jax, Slater, and Xander take up positions at equal distances from each other around the circle, and everyone else fills in between them and kneels. Only Flint and Xander remain standing.

Flint lifts one hand, open and pointed toward the ceiling. Slowly, he taps two fingers against his palm, the rhythm reminding me of when he summoned my energy core from my body and into his bottle. The power inside me stirs and rises to his call, suffusing my skin with iridescent light.

He continues to steadily tap his palm as Xander paces around the circle, pausing behind each person to lay his hands on their shoulders. He murmurs something too low for me to hear, but I feel the tug on my energy, and threads pull from my body, arcing through the air to connect me to each person.

An answering ring in my bones sounds as each link establishes itself, and flickers of unfamiliar emotions sift through me, similar to what I feel when I try to read people's desires, but less defined. I shiver as I take them in, accepting them as part of myself.

When Xander finishes, he stops once more at Flint's side, and the other man stops tapping.

Instantly, the power sinks beneath my skin once more, burying these new threads deep, and I sway, suddenly lightheaded from too much sensation.

But the spell isn't done, and I force myself to stay upright as Xander kneels and places his fingertips to the circle. Jax, Slater, and Reese follow suit, and the circle flairs to life in a brilliant ring of gold.

Xander looks up at me. "We'll give you as much time as possible."

I nod in understanding. They won't be able to funnel the ley line magic indefinitely, and if their bodies give out, then the spell will end.

A scrape of sneaker against floor pulls my attention around as Pen inches forward, the skin around her eyes tight. She flexes her fingers, gives herself a shake, then presses her fingers to the circle. A hiss escapes her lips before the circle brightens with added power.

I stare at her in surprise. Even though she doesn't register as a demon to my senses, after that flare of power she displayed, I had assumed she was just very good at hiding her nature. But a demon wouldn't funnel ley line magic. At least, not unless they were crazy succubus like me, which I'm certain she's not.

Ignoring my surprise, Pen glances at the detective. "Come on, Sharpe. In for a penny, in for a pound."

He glances from her to the glowing circle. "You want me to touch that?"

"Call it hands-on experience." She looks across the circle at Flint. "You, too. Get on your knees."

"It's usually sexier when you say that," he grumbles as he finds space next to Xander and adds his support. He winces as he connects to the circle, and it brightens even more. "The things I do for love."

After another moment of hesitation, Detective Sharpe tentatively presses his fingers to the circle. He gasps, the sound filled with wonder, and the glow jumps up another notch.

"Thank you," Xander murmurs as he looks at the new additions before his focus jumps to his small coven. "Pull back a little. Reserve until we need it."

They nod, and the glow dims to a level that doesn't threaten to burn my retinas.

Xander takes a deep breath as his attention shifts to me, and I brace myself for what comes next.

His lips move, shaping words that slip past my ears, and the mark on my chest rips open.

Agony stabs through me. I stumble, blood flowing from the wound as if it was newly cut by Victor Hesse's knife. A powerful tug comes from my center, like a giant force turning me inside out.

The wooden floorboards vanish from beneath my feet, replaced by the cracked and burned earth of the demon plane. Hot wind, laden with ozone, lifts my hair and steals the breath from my lungs.

Eyes wide, I stare at the living room that still exists on the other side of the circle, and the shocked faces of those I hold most dear.

Another sharp tug comes, dragging at my insides, and I stumble forward, falling to one knee. Pain burns across my chest, and I clench my fists, fighting against blacking out, and the beast's bottle pulses with awareness.

A howl sounds in the distance, followed by another, and when I next look up, my home is gone, replaced by the wasteland of the demon plane.

MOUNTAIN GUARD

The burn of ozone and dying earth fills my nose as I force myself to straighten, on high alert for the approach of a hunting akuzal. The power that pulled me here won't have gone unnoticed, and if I don't get moving soon, I'll be swarmed and torn apart by the ravenous monsters who roam the wasteland.

But which way do I go?

I turn in a slow circle, scanning the hazy horizon, and see no sign of Victor Hesse or a node of ley line energy. Just ash and clay, the surface of the world so dry and dead that fissures form along the surface and dust rises into the air, riding the heat waves from the sun that blasts down.

No clouds fill the smoggy orange sky, and no trees live here to offer shelter. Far, far off in a distance I can't make out will be mountains filled with lava, home to ignis demons like Torch, and in the opposite direction, the last of the demon cities, holding on by tooth, nail, and imagination.

But here, everything looks the same, with no clue to give me direction.

I hadn't considered what would happen if I arrived here and Victor Hesse wasn't waiting to claim me. If I can avoid a direct confrontation until I have my demons of destruction with me to ensure he's properly smited, all the better, but I'm suspicious of the sloppiness of his work after all that scheming. It feels more like a trap than an oversight.

I scan the area around me again, but there's nowhere for him to be hiding. However much I expect him to, he doesn't pop out of one of the cracks in the earth like a creepy jack-in-the-box, which leaves me to hunt down the nearest ley line and deal with him at a later date. My demons of destruction are my primary focus, not my battle with Victor Hesse.

Another screech sounds, coming closer, so I move in the opposite direction, keeping my senses open.

Five steps in, the pain in my chest flares to life once more, and fresh blood seeps from the open wound. Shuddering, I back-pace and the pain eases, though the wound doesn't magically seal itself shut.

Fucking Victor Hesse, tormenting me even now that I'm at the end of his game.

I try veering to the left, which will set me off course from the incoming akuzal, and the pain stabs through me once more, the blood flowing freely and staining my bra red.

Scowling, I grab the bottle that hangs around my neck. "Your dad's a real asshole."

The beast pulses against my palm in answer.

I lift it to eye level, studying the innocent looking red clay container. "I'm going to kill him."

The bottle shivers with excitement.

I skim my thumb over the cork. "You want to kill him, too, don't you? He's filled with the type of energy you're craving. Not this stupid witch magic."

The bottle pulses again, like a racing heartbeat.

Does the beast understand what I'm saying? Or can it just sense my attention and the nearness of its master?

With no way to know, I drop the bottle to hang between my breasts once more as I turn around and step toward the incoming akuzal. The pain stays at a steady throb in my chest, and the blood slows to a trickle.

Oh, I see. He wants to make sure I'm properly worn down and consumed by the beast before we face each other. What obstacle course of nasties stand between me and the mortifer demon?

I flex my fingers, wishing for my claws, and stumble in surprise when my nails lengthen into sharp points. I lift my hands to marvel at the razor-sharp edges, perfect for tearing apart flesh, and my lips peel away from my teeth in a vicious smile.

So he wants to see his killing machine in action, does he? I can do that.

When the next shriek sounds, I throw back my head and scream in answer as the akuzal appears on the horizon, a shimmering mirage of liquid black that takes shape as it sprints toward me.

I pick up my pace, arms pumping at my sides. It's not hyper-speed, but it's faster than I've been in a long time, and my hair lifts from my back to flow out behind me in a banner of white and blue.

The akuzal lifts its long nose to the sky, its bell-like ears pinned back against its large skull as its talons rip through the packed clay of the earth straight for me. It moves with liquid grace and predatory intent. A killing machine focused on its target.

But the thing about akuzal is that they're dumb.

At the last moment, I drop into a forward roll, passing beneath the threat of the beast's front talons to its vulnerable underbelly. I thrust my hands into its unprotected stomach and let its own momentum help in its evisceration.

Hot ropes of intestine spill out, and I grab fistfuls as I roll out from under the body, dragging its guts with me. Black ichor coats me, making the dust stick to my body like mud.

Screaming with anger, the akuzal pivots, sharp teeth snapping with rage.

I dance out of range as I yank harder on the entrails, reeling in the stomach with its small heart attached. I crush it beneath my heel, and the akuzal's body stumbles and crashes to the ground, the sharp scream cutting off.

In the distance, another takes up its call, then another, until their screams come from every direction.

Well, shit.

Dropping the guts, I turn and run, letting the pain of Victor Hesse's leash pull me forward.

I kill the next two akuzal, but quickly realize that every pause slows me down and allows for the larger hoard to close in.

With no idea how far Victor Hesse will make me travel, I dodge the next monster and the one after.

The ground beneath my feet shakes as they change course and follow in pursuit.

Without hyper-speed, I have no hope to outrun them, but even handicapped without my normal powers, I'm still faster than average and manage to stay out of reach of their vicious talons.

Dust fills the air and clogs my lungs as I sprint ahead of the growing pack, and my heart pounds, rushing adrenaline through my body. More black streaks fill my periphery, and I push my legs to move faster until I barely register my feet touching the scorched earth.

In the distance, black mountains rise, belching smoke into the air, and worry flits through me. Ignis demons aren't predisposed to cruelty, but they *are* territorial, and they're not above crushing another demon who crosses their path. But there's no turning back now, not with death on my heels.

As I near the base of the mountains, the blackened earth crunches beneath my feet, and rivulets of magma glow from just beneath the surface. The heat in the air intensifies, the ash thickening until it sticks in my throat. I cough and lift a hand to my mouth, trying to block out the worst of it, but I feel my body slowing, the gap between me and my pursuers shrinking.

Scanning the area, I spot a place where two slabs of stone come together with a boulder at the top, forming a cave of sorts, and I focus on that destination. It offers safety from side and overhead attacks and will reduce the number of akuzal that can attack me at once.

Shadows drop over me as I pass beneath the stones, but the temperature only grows hotter as the slabs trap the heat inside. Sweat evaporates from my skin, making it tight against my bones, and every breath burns.

A sharp snap of teeth warns me of danger, and I drop into a side roll. Talons brush over my skin, leaving shallow cuts that sting as the akuzal flies past, not fast enough to change its course.

Rolling to my feet, I spring onto its back, the hard knobs of its spine digging into me. I grab its large, bell-shaped ears and yank backward, sending it into a tumble of dangerously flailing talons.

Before it can regain its balance, I grab its skull and twist hard. A sharp crack sounds, but the legs keep moving as it snaps its teeth at me. I break its front legs next, then flip it onto its back and punch a hole through its stomach, dodging its hind legs as I search out its heart and crush it.

It stills, but more shrieks fill the narrow cave as akuzal fight each other to be the first in.

I clench my fists and scream back with all my might. I will kill all of them, just as I did before. I will create mountains of their skulls and bathe in their black blood.

The ground rumbles beneath me, rocks hopping around, and the walls shift, pulling backward as enormous hands rip from the ground to slam down on either side of me.

I stumble and fall on my ass. Panicked, I stare up at the large slag demon who crouches over me, a cousin to the ignis, but no less terrifying. The stone slabs I mistook for shelter form its arms, and the boulder on top is its head. The ground rumbles harder, and the back of the cave shifts as the demon pulls its body from the mountain.

Oh, fuck. I'm screwed. I can't rip this one apart. I fumble for the magic inside me, for the ability to turn it to dust like I did the council guards in Emil's office, but that happened through instinct, and the magic slips through my fingers now.

Why can I only make this work when I'm protecting others? Doesn't saving my own ass matter enough to trigger it?

The boulder-sized head rolls with a grating of

stone, raining pebbles down on top of me, and molten eyes meet mine. "Go, Life Giver to Torch the Tiny Flame. None shall harm you here."

My mouth drops open in shock before I leap to my feet and run. No one needs to tell me twice. Like Gavin said, don't look a gift horse in the mouth.

Behind me, the ground continues to shake, and akuzal scream their deaths.

The leash that binds me to Victor Hesse drags me around the outer skirt of the mountain then back out into the wasteland on the other side.

Or, what should have been a wasteland.

Where cracks exist everywhere else, here is a small oasis of dead trees, the ashy trunks and brittle branches stabbing toward the sky. The clay earth turns to dark soil that sinks beneath my feet and releases the scent of decay.

The tug in my chest pulls me forward, deeper into the dead forest that shouldn't exist here.

Is this the result of Victor Hesse's will imposed on the demon plane? Such changes usually take the concentrated effort of dozens of creators.

My legs tremble, and I stop to rest against a tree and catch my breath. Somehow, the bare branches block out the heat and dust, and I hack out black phlegm, clearing my airway of ash.

In their hiding place, my wings shiver with trepidation as I look around, the eerie silence pressing in around me. There are no shrubs or foliage to block my view, yet I can see no sign of Victor Hesse.

As I push off from the tree, the bark scrapes away beneath my palm to reveal the skulls of tiny demons trapped beneath. My gut tightens, and I pull more bark aside, revealing more bodies. The entire tree appears to be made of the corpses of other creatures, and I look around, trying to count the number of trees, but I can't see far enough.

How has he done all this and the council guards still not found him? This is like waving a red flag in the council's face and being ignored. Were they even *trying* to stop him?

Anger burns away the queasy feeling in my gut. All the lives lost, all the damage done, and he was *here* this whole time, creating a kingdom of death.

The bottle between my breasts pulses, the beast feeding off my rage. Around me, the branches clack together, sounding like bony hands clapping in welcome.

"Ms. Pond," a gravelly voice calls from deeper within the forest. "You've come home at last."

Forest of Bones

I abandon the skeleton tree and prowl toward the voice of my tormentor. The stench of death grows stronger, filling my nose with the sweetness of rotting meat and the metallic tang of stale blood. I no longer need the pain of the leash to lead me, I could find him with my eyes closed.

The shadows deepen, the trees growing broader, the dead branches thicker, until they form a canopy over a clearing, the tiny hints of sunlight that peek through dotting the clearing like stars.

Victor Hesse stands at its center, reclined on a throne of akuzal bodies, his skeletal frame draped over the protrusion of bent limbs and skulls. He wears a pale, ash suite the same color as his flesh and a bandelier of black vials across his narrow chest. The evidence of Torch's attack still mars his face, blackening his skin and turning his hair into a melted helmet over his skull. With the power he holds to build this sanctuary, he could have healed himself, but he wears his scars like jewelry, enhancing his corpse-like appearance.

His milky-blue eyes watch me approach. "You have not given over to the beast."

My lips peel back from my teeth. "I am beast enough for you."

"Were that true, I would be delighted." He slides off his throne to stand in front of it, his narrow body resembling the trunks of the trees that ring us. "But, somehow, I don't believe that you are suddenly amiable to my proposal."

I study the ground in front of him, searching for a trap before stepping closer. "Why wouldn't I be? You've taken everything from me. What do I have left to cling to?"

His dead eyes sweep over me, and his lips curl with disgust. "Morals."

I tilt my head to the side. "Do demons ever truly have morals?"

"In my new world, they won't." His hand lifts to curl around one of the bottles across his chest. "And neither will you, soon enough."

As he throws the bottle, I dodge to the side, then dart forward, but he vanishes in a blur of motion I can't follow. He moves faster than a succubus, but he already revealed that trick when he killed Julian.

I spin and swipe, my claws raking through the air behind me. My nails graze cloth before he vanishes again.

"I feel my beast still with you, Ms. Pond," he says, his voice seeming to come from the trees around us. "Is it in that bottle around your neck?"

My heart pounds, and I turn in a weary circle, my senses open for movement.

"It was a clever trick, separating it from yourself, and not a loophole I'll leave open next time."

The branches rattle behind me, and I kick back, connecting with a bony leg. Pain shoots up my heel, traveling the length of my shin. It feels like I kicked a freaking rock, not a bone man.

Stick-thin fingers graze my breasts, and the cord cuts into my neck as Victor Hesse yanks the bottle free. "Such a vulnerable place to keep something so precious."

I spin to find him back near his throne, the bottle clasped in his hand, and my heart pounds harder.

He shakes his head as he reaches for the cork. "Really, after all this struggle, I expected more from you, Ms. Pond. Perhaps it's better you'll have no will left when this is done."

"You'll regret this," I promise as my hands clench into fists.

"No, I will relish every moment." He plucks the cork free, and a rolling mass of anger and hunger boils out.

For the first time, I see the beast, a twisted amalgamation of akuzal, wyvern, and boogeyman, designed to be the ultimate, terrifying hunter.

As it lands in the clearing with a physical weight, the soil beneath its clawed feet dissipates, turning once more to clay as the beast consumes the energy used to create this dead forest. More cracked earth appears as the starving beast drags in the power surrounding it, growing in size as its mass continues to solidify.

"Claim your host," Victor Hesse commands, throwing his arm out toward me.

The beast turns as directed, fixing feral eyes on me. The symbols engraved into my body flare to life once more, promising a prison filled with ley line magic it can't consume.

The tether that binds us together strengthens, and I step toward it, our eyes locked. Inside the beast, I see hunger and anger, but beneath those instincts, I see a desire for freedom.

The beast and I aren't so different, both creatures driven to feed on the energy of others and yearning for something better than what life gave us. It's lived inside of me, knows the limits of my body, and knows that it is *more* than what I can offer.

On the human plane, where food was scarcer, it might have been willing to compromise. But here, surrounded by a feast, the beast pauses.

"Claim your host," Victor Hesse commands once more, drawing the beast's attention to him, a far more appealing meal than anything I offer.

Victor Hesse grabs another black vial from his bandolier and holds it out before him. Red energy flares in his fist. "I command you to claim your host!"

"You should have spent more time studying witch magic," I say as the beast turns toward him. "Domnall didn't teach you enough. And why would he, when he liked to keep people powerless?"

For the first time, Victor Hesse's confidence flickers.

Together, the beast and I take a step toward him, and Victor Hesse bolts.

The beast blurs into motion as well, blocking off

his escape. When he turns, I dart into his path. Where I can't keep up with his new speed, the beast can, and we play a game of cat and mouse, working together to narrow the mortifer demon's escape.

Although the beast can reason, it moves more on blind instinct, while Victor Hesse possesses a twisted mind he's spent years sharpening. The pile of akuzal bodies explode into the air, distracting the beast, and Victor Hesse blips out of sight.

A crackle of bones comes from behind me, and I spin, but too slow as a skeletal hand wraps around my throat.

Panic shoots through me, and I drive my elbow back, connecting with stone-hard ribs that make my bones ring and my arm go numb.

The hand around my throat tightens, cutting off my air. "You're too young to be clever, Ms. Pond."

As the beast shakes its way free of the bodies, Victor Hesse drags me back with him toward the edge of the clearing, using my body as a shield.

"You just can't help messing with other people's business, can you?" he seethes.

I dig my claws into his arm, piercing through dead flesh and meat to scrape against bone. I never asked for Victor Hesse's attention to begin with, never asked to become his target in a convoluted game of revenge. The only thing I ever wanted was to live a normal life, baking cupcakes and making people happy.

My mouth gapes, desperate to draw in air that can't make it past the vice-like hold he has on my throat. Frantic, I dig my heels into the ground, trying to slow his retreat.

His other arm wraps around my body, lifting me easily. "You will become my beast, even if I have to cut you open again and shove it inside of you. No baby succubus is going to ruin my plans."

The edges of my vision turn gray, the dead forest fading from view. Instead, I see the waiting faces of my friends back at home, feel their determination as they hold their threads, demanding that I succeed, that I return. Then they fade, too, replaced by shadows and mist, and I see Emil, Tobias, and Kellen, pacing in the Between, angry and frustrated at being trapped.

As if they sense my gaze, they turn toward me, but the mist rolls up to shroud them from view. Pinpricks of light spot my vision, and Landon and the Librarian come into view. Landon throws himself at the doors of the Library, his rage so fierce I can taste it, while the Librarian's head rolls on her shoulders, her sagging eyelids lifting to pin me with sharp, black eyes.

"It's time to let go," she says, but her lips don't move, the words ringing in my mind. "Shine bright, Adeline Boo Pond. As bright as you can."

The command rings through me, and my wings burst from my back, cleaving through Victor Hesse like butter and ripping him in two as iridescent light bursts out of me, bright as a beacon.

His hold on me slackens, then falls away, his body landing in pieces on either side. I fall to my knees, gasping for breath as the ground shivers beneath me.

The beast, bounding forward, freezes in mid-air, and the light rattle of dead branches silences, time stopping between one heartbeat and the next.

Beneath me, the ground splits open, and ley line magic bursts forth, answering my beacon. Victor Hesse had built his forest on top of a power node. No wonder no one found him here. No one goes near the nodes for fear of being consumed.

The thought barely registers before magic wraps around me and through me. I feel my body disintegrating, my consciousness being pulled down.

No, I tell it as I struggle to hold onto the pieces

of me. The threads that bind me to the others hum, reminding me of my purpose.

The ley line pulls harder, demanding death, demanding creation.

I build a picture of the Between in my mind and shove it at the ley line, demanding that it release this pocket of space, that it free those who are trapped there.

A latticework of glowing lines fills my mind in return, showing how the lines spread between the planes of existence, that one cannot be moved without the others. It holds a question and a demand, something I'm familiar with as a demon. There is no give without take, and if the price of this is that I join the ley line, so be it.

With a last gasp, I let myself go, and the ley line consumes me.

SPARK

I return to existence with a gasp, finding myself back in the dead forest just as time resumes.

Confused, I watch as the beast pounces forward, landing on one half of Victor Hesse's body and consuming it. As it does, the dead forest crumbles, bones raining from the trees.

How did either of them survive the eruption of ley line magic? Did it simply pass them by? Or was all of that in my head?

I bend to smooth a hand over the cracked clay earth, devoid of any evidence of the node I know exists beneath the hard surface. I lift my hands in front of my face and turn them back and forth. They look normal, and I *feel* normal for the first time in a while, if a little hungry. Maybe even ravenous.

Bones crunch and break as the beast feasts beside me, and I cringe. Okay, not *that* ravenous.

My attention shifts to the other side of me, to what remains of Victor Hesse. He doesn't look like someone who was living only moments before. Instead, he resembles the remains of mummies, dried and preserved over centuries. Which may be a more accurate description of what he was. One of those evil, cursed mummies, bent on destroying the world.

Yeah, definitely not *that* ravenous.

About to look away, a flicker catches my attention. I almost miss it, hidden in the dried, hollow remains of his stomach. When the brief flash of pink comes again, my heart lurches.

Hand shaky, I reach out and gently scoop up the light. It shivers and pulses in my palm, and I gasp out a sob.

The beast, done with its meal, growls and paces around me, its hungry eyes fixed on the light I hold.

I cup my hands protectively around it. "No, not this one."

It growls, and I growl back, flaring my wings wide. I don't want to fight the beast, but for this small core of energy, I will give my last breath.

The beast flares its own wings as if to show it's not afraid of me, then paces to the remains of Victor

Hesse's body and snaps its jaws around the leg before dragging it into the trees.

Should I try to stop it? What will leaving such a beast alive do?

But the demon plane is full of monsters far worse than it, so I stay where I am, waiting for any sign that the leash still binds me to Victor Hesse or his creation.

When no new pain flares to life, I push to my feet.

With the light cradled against my stomach, I stumble out of the crumbling forest. It needs energy to grow, energy I don't have. If I tried to feed it ley line magic, it would be destroyed.

My eyes fall on the mountain, and my feet turn toward it, retracing my path.

When I reach my destination, the slag demon is gone, but I know I'm in the right place by the crushed bodies of the akuzal.

I kneel next to the first, searching the squashed remains for a spark of life and drinking it down. Then I move on to the next, and the next.

Some of the creatures were too starved for energy and have no life force to give, but there are hundreds here, far more than I expected. They must have come from all over the wasteland, only to be crushed against the mountain.

Slowly, a ball of energy forms in my core, rolling with death, chaos, and hunger. I thread ley line magic through it, stripping away the imprint of the akuzal until only pure energy remains. Then, I lift the flickering energy core to my lips and breathe life into it.

The ball shudders and pulses, growing stronger, though not yet able to take on a corporeal form. But that's okay, we have time. All the time in the world now that Victor Hesse's out of the way.

Tucking the ball close to my stomach once more, I stand and look around. "Hello? Is anyone here?"

My voice echoes off the side of the mountain and fades before the ground rumbles. A shower of pebbles bounce down around me, and a slag demon rises.

It turns with a grating of stone and stares down at me. "Yes, Life Giver to Torch the Tiny Flame. I am here."

I tip my head back to stare up at it. "Which way is the citadel?"

In answer, it lifts one heavy arm and points toward the setting sun.

I dip my head in acknowledgment before

turning and striding back into the wasteland, my ball of energy held close.

When I arrive at the Demon Clerk's Office, I find utter chaos. Demon's jam-pack the hall, and I turn toward the wall, using my body as a buffer of protection for my precious cargo.

"Adeline Boo Pond!" a voice yells, and my head turns to find an imp pushing through the crowd toward me, a familiar box of red licorice sticking out of his pocket.

"John Smith," I say in surprise. "Good to see you again."

He grins, his soft, gray cheeks bunching, before he looks down. "What do you have there?"

Cautiously, I pull my hand away from my stomach to reveal the small energy core.

"Oh, well, isn't that a sight." He reaches out and gently strokes the light. "Can't say I've ever seen one so small."

"He'll grow," I say with conviction, then glance around. "What's going on?"

His soft brown eyes widen in surprise. "You haven't heard?

I huddle closer to the wall. "Heard what?"

He leans in close, his breath smelling of red dye 40 and corn syrup. "The Library's vanished."

"What?" Panic shoots through me, and I half turn, prepared to go see for myself.

"But that's not all."

John's words stop me, and I turn back with trepidation. "What else?"

Excitement shines in his eyes. "The veil's thinning. At the rate it's going, we won't need transfer approval to get to the human plane. The missus and I are packing up our spawn and heading over now, before they figure out how to fix it." He bounces in place. "First stop on our tour is Boo's Boutique Bakery. Do you have licorice flavored cupcakes?"

Shocked, I stare at him as my mind struggles to process his words. "The veil is thinning?"

He nods and reaches out to squeeze my arm with excitement. "See you on the other side!"

With that, he steps back out into the crush of demons and vanishes.

My heart pounds, and anxiety makes my limbs shake. How can the Library be gone? What about Landon and the hag? Did it take them with it? And what does it mean that the veil is thinning? Did that happen because I asked the ley lines to move? But then, what does that mean for the human plane?

It had felt like an all or nothing option, and I had asked for all without even considering the ramifications that choice would bring to the humans whose world hasn't been destroyed by prolonged exposure to so much power.

Slowly, I push forward, moving farther away from the hall that would lead me back to the Library. There's no reason to go looking there if it's gone. Like John Smith, I need to return to the human plane as soon as possible. That's where Emil, Tobias, and Kellen will be waiting if they were able to escape the Between.

"Move aside!" someone shouts, and hard feet pound the floor.

The demons who fill the hall press to either side, nearly flattening me against the wall. Through their bodies, I watch guards from the council stomping past, with the high council at their center.

As Lord Marius's eyes sweep the crowded area, I duck lower, staying out of sight. Somehow, I don't think I want his attention on me right now. If at all possible, I'd like to avoid his attention for the next century. Hell, maybe even the next millennia.

As soon as they pass, demons disperse in all directions.

I wedge myself into a group of imps, walking in a fast crouch. If anyone knows where the nearest crossover to the human plane is, it will be imps. I just hope I fit through whatever cracks they use.

Triumphant Return

Arriving on the human plane turns out to be the easy part. Hailing a cab in my bra while covered in blood and dirt and sporting weird symbols drawn all over my body turns out to be a whole new adventure.

Eventually, one brave, desperate soul pulls over for me. Beyond grateful for the power I was able to take from the akuzal, I use my limited reserves of demonic power to whammy him into driving me three cities over to Clearhelm.

By the time we pass city limits, it's already dark out, and a light flurry of snow fills the air.

I feel bad that I don't have money to pay the driver, but all of that vanishes as my home comes into view. Despite the late time, every window in the house blazes in welcome, and I practically fly out of the cab and up the steps, slamming through the front door.

The house smells of sugar and spice and *home*. Tears prick my eyes as I dart around the short entryway and into the living room.

Everyone is still here, and they leap up at my sudden appearance, swarming over to me with exclamations of surprise and welcome. Warmth fills me at their happiness that I made it out, and tears slip down my face.

Excited, I search the group for my demons of destruction, but I don't see them. Happiness dimming, I push past my imps and into the kitchen to find it empty.

Now, worry sets in, and a tremble rolls through me as I turn to face everyone.

Tally steps forward first. "They haven't come back."

"Okay." I nod jerkily.

She hurries forward. "Maybe they just need more time. We have no idea how long it will take for the Between to dissipate once it lost power."

"Right." I nod again and look around the room. "Thank you, everyone, for what you did today. I owe each of you a debt."

"Not us." Xander slashes a hand through the air. "This ended our contract with Kellen. Helping you freed us."

Reese nods. "We knew the second you succeeded in moving the ley lines." He snaps his fingers. "Just like that."

Jax and Slater nod in agreement, and Tally backs up to grasp their hands, her eyes shining bright.

I bite my lip. "Will you be leaving, now?"

"We'll need to find a new house," Xander says. "I don't see Kellen letting us live there rent free, anymore."

My eyes sting, and I nod again.

"We might know a few places looking for renters," Pen announces. "And if you need some side jobs, we'd be thrilled to hire you on as freelancers."

"We can hook you up with the local coven, too, if you want to learn more magic," Flint adds. "I'm sure Gwyneth would be happy to get some witches who are actually trained."

Reese and Xander both look interested, while Jax and Slater shake their heads and murmur polite refusals.

Flint shrugs. "Offer's open. Take some time and talk it over."

"We should head out." Pen looks at Gavin, who's stayed silent through all of this, taking everything in. "Do you want a ride, Sharpe? We can have another sleep ov—"

"No," he cuts in, his expression inscrutable. "I've had enough of you and your lies for now." He grabs his jacket from the back of the couch. "Stay out of police business, Pen, or I *will* arrest you, paranormal bullshit or not."

"Boo," Flint hisses, giving him a thumbs down. "Way less hot, Detective."

Ignoring him, Gavin gives me a brisk nod and stomps out the door.

The cleaners follow at a slower pace, giving him time to reach his car to avoid another angry confrontation, and the front door closes behind them.

"Sophia." I find her in the middle of the imps. "Can you bring Torch's box over?"

She nods and releases her hold on Jesse. "Sure thing."

She returns a moment later with his heat proof box in hand, and I gently set the pink energy core inside. "Now, don't try to eat each other, you hear?"

Sophia gasps. "Is that Julian?"

"Yeah." I stroke the small ball of energy. "But he's going to need a lot of energy if he wants to be a real boy again."

The energy core pulses with irritation, and Torch waddles over to greet his new house guest.

Tears fill Sophia's eyes, and she clutches the box closer to her chest. "I'll give him some now. And I'll call the others. Everyone can provide. We owe it to him."

My chest tightens as she rushes away, and I resist the urge to chase after her and snatch back the energy core. It's not that I don't trust Sophia, but I only just found him.

Fuyumi steps forward, her robes swishing against the floor. Merp lays around her shoulders, twin tails swishing, while Prem struggles in her arms.

She thrusts the squirming whelp into my arms. "You will pay your debt to me by finding a home for Prem. He is outgrowing his mother's tolerance for her offspring." She reaches up to stroke Merp's head. "At least his sister knows how to stay out of the way. *He* is just clumsy." She casts a frosty glare at Tac. "Like his sire."

She turns back and gives me an icy nod. "It is good you are back and whole. I expect two baskets of offerings in recompense for the trouble you have caused."

With that declaration, she sweeps out of the house, taking Merp with her.

Small wings bap against my arms, and Prem hisses up at me, angry to be separated from his sister.

Jesse immediately leaps forward. "I will take the kitty as payment for your debt."

I narrow my eyes on my smallest imp. "How is your piggy bank doing? You've gotten him used to filet mignon."

She juts out her narrow chin. "The debt—"

"We do not exchange living beings to pay debts without prior negotiation." When her face puckers up, I sigh. "I will assign you as Prem's caretaker. And you will continue to work on your savings while weaning him *off* of filet mignon."

She gives me a begrudging nod and reaches up for the tiny monster.

As soon as I drop his wiggling mass into her arms, she bolts for the kitchen, and a moment later, the door to the basement slams shut.

I'm going to have to check her suitcase when they all move back to their own houses to make sure she doesn't try to sneak him inside.

The other imps come forward to give me hugs and rub their scent all over my dirty body before they follow after her.

"Do you want us to stay?" Tally asks. "We can sleep on the couches."

"No, but thank you." I look around the room. It

feels empty even with people in it. "I'm going to shower and go to bed."

"Okay." She rushes forward to pull me into her strong arms. "Don't worry about the bakery. We'll make sure it's taken care of. Just focus on recovering, okay?"

I nod against her shoulder, my nose filling with the familiar, comforting scent of clay.

Reluctantly, she releases me, and they file out of the room.

After the door shuts, I stand in the abandoned living room, feeling the ache of loneliness from the absence of my demons of destruction.

With a chuff, Tac stands and pads over, circling around me to butt his large head against my back, nudging me toward the stairs like I'm one of his recalcitrant whelps, up past my bedtime.

I let him move me along, my feet finding the first of the steps, then the one after, and the one after that until I arrive at the first landing.

There, I stop to look down the short hallway to Emil's room, where the shut door and dark shadows at the threshold once more remind me of his absence.

A large, black wing lifts to block my view, then gently baps me toward the bathroom.

I look down at the thick layer of disgusting crust that coats my body. "Yeah, a shower's a good idea."

Once Tac herds me to the bathroom, he flops down in the open doorway.

I lift my brows at him. "You're going to watch?"

A quiet whine rises from him, and he nuzzles my foot.

"Yeah, I miss them, too." I rub the soft spot between his tufted ears. "But they'll be back. We just have to wait."

I say the words as much for me as for him. I need to believe that what I did was enough, that my men will return to me, that the high council didn't catch them and lock them up somewhere else.

If that happened, I don't know how, but I'll find a way to free them. They're mine, and we will *not* be separated.

With one last rub I peel myself out of my grimy clothes, leaving them on the floor. Black footprints mark the pristine tiles, and ash and dried gore flakes off my skin, raining down on the bathmat. "Emil's going to kill me when he gets home."

Tac chuffs in agreement.

I pull back the shower curtain and turn on the hot water, dancing from one foot to the other until steam fills the small bathroom.

When I step beneath the hot spray of water, I let out a groan of appreciation and call out, "When Emil gets back, let's talk him into a hot tub. What do you think?"

I lather soap into my hair, scrubbing until the bubbles turn gray. "And I think we should figure out a way to attach a weathervane directly to Kellen's bed frame. Can you imagine his shock when it gets struck by lightning?" I snicker to myself. "Get it? Shock?"

I make a buzzing noise with my lips as I duck under the hot water to rinse before grabbing the squishy puff and loading it up with soap.

"And I think I'll buy a flogger and have it sent to the bakery so it's a surprise," I say as I scrub my body until only clean, pink skin shows. "We'll see who prances who around the house like a pony."

I duck back under the spray, rinsing off the last of the soap. "Hey, be a dear and grab my robe for me, would you? The house is kind of cold."

While I wait, I give my hair another scrub, just to make sure I got all the dirt out. It helps distract me from the silence of the house.

As I turn off the water, the shower curtain rustles, and the edge of my fluffy pink robe pokes around the edge. Surprised that Tac actually went and got it for me, I reach out to take it, only to have him pull it back.

"Hey, no tug of war with my bathrobe." Fisting the soft material, I pull on it again as I sweep back the shower curtain.

Black, star-filled eyes meet mine. "What was that about a flogger, little succubus?"

My heart slams against my ribs, and I drop the robe to fling myself at Tobias.

REUNION

Tobias catches me against his hard chest, his hands slipping over my wet skin as he drags me up to claim my mouth with his.

I open beneath the press of his tongue, welcoming him deep within before I push back, needing to taste him, to assure myself he's whole.

Our tongues tangle together, our hands roaming over each other's bodies, pressing and stroking. I drink the volcanoes from the back of his mouth, and whimper with desire as landslides rush down my throat. This is everything I've been yearning for, everything I've been missing.

Then static-filled hands drag me from Tobias, and Kellen stands before me, my storm god, here to fill me with thunder and lightning. I taste spring rains and frozen sleet on his tongue, feel the crackle of lightning against my skin and the rumble of thunder in my bones.

But before I can delve deeper, the water freezes on my skin, and my ice demon, my Emil, claims me, his lips blue with frostbite and his tongue like vanilla ice cream in my mouth.

We stumble out of the bathroom, and I press him against the wall, drinking the chill of glaciers from him before heat scorches my back, and Tobias once more fills my arms, his hands hard on my ass as he half walks, half drags me down the hall.

Clothes are shed along the way, ripped from his body by my frantic need for bare skin against bare skin. I yank his fly open, and he lifts me fully in his arms, pulling my legs around his waist as he walks out of his pants and into Emil's room.

We crash to the bed in a tangle of limbs, our motions frantic as he thrusts into my slick heat, hitting the end of me.

My back arches, my legs tightening around his waist as he pulls back, then slams forward, demanding I make room to take all of him.

My body ripples around him, my muscles tightening and releasing as orgasm crashes over me, but he doesn't stop, his pelvis slapping hard against my inner thighs as he drives into me with a desperation that matches my own.

Earthquakes shake my body, and my hips lift,

greedy to meet each of his thrusts. It feels like an eternity since I last held him, last felt the power of his body move within, last felt the burn of his touch and broke from his release.

I feel the first pulse of his dick, feel the first power-laden rush of his cum, before he pulls back, holding only the tip of himself within my body, feeding me his power without locking us together as one. I reach between our bodies to wrap my hand around the base of his cock as his knot swells, offering him more pleasure for his show of restraint.

Before I even catch my breath, Kellen pulls me from Tobias and deftly flips me onto my stomach before thrusting into me. I cry out, my hands pushing against the soft mattress for support.

Cold hands lift my head, pushing back my hair and opening my mouth wider. Emil's cold cock pushes past my lips, and I moan as I grab hold of his hips, urging him closer as Kellen takes me from behind.

The snap of lightning in my bones and the burn of frost on my lips fuzzes my senses as storms and blizzards swirl through me.

I moan with pleasure, my body rocking between the two men as Emil thrusts into my mouth in counterpoint to Kellen rocking into my swollen folds. The desire for these men strengthens, and I urge them faster, needing their releases inside of me.

It's been so long, and now that the torment of not touching them is gone, I can't get enough. And their hunger matches mine. Like me, they need to connect, to celebrate our reunion in the most primal way a demon knows how, by laying claim to each other.

Emil pulses first against my tongue, filling my mouth with the sweet burn of glaciers. Kellen shouts, his fingers digging into my hips as a tsunami rushes into me. I shake with my own release, my body fisting around him even as I swallow Emil down.

Then Tobias returns, pulling me on top of himself, his hot body easing the chill from my skin as he cups my cheeks and pulls my mouth down, licking the cum from my lips. My fingers dig into his shoulders in warning, and I growl at the theft. He growls back before opening his mouth wide and offering for me to steal it back.

I do, nipping and sucking at his lips as he thrusts his hard length against my stomach, letting me know more power will come, but not yet, not from him.

Emil covers my back, and I spread my legs wide in offering. He sinks into my heat with a groan, his lips cold against my spine, leaving snowflake kisses that melt against Tobias's heat. Tobias shifts me between them until my clit aligns with his cock, my folds parting until the nub at the height of my sex rubs against his hot length.

Once more, dual sensations rush through me, this time fire and ice clashing together. I clutch at Tobias and thrust back against Emil, writhing between them as pleasure builds between us. It fills the air with a heady scent and presses against my skin, feeding my hunger.

Emil reaches between us, his cold hands finding my breasts and pinching my nipples, shooting pleasure down to where our bodies join. Then he grasps my shoulders, lifting me far enough for Tobias's hot mouth to claim one breast, the temperature change shocking my system.

When lightning-filled lips claim my other breast, my hand tangles in Kellen's fiery hair. I drag his head up, my eager mouth finding his just as Tobias bites down on my nipple. I cry out, the sound muffled by Kellen's lips.

Kellen pulls back, his thumb sweeping over my lower lip, nudging my mouth open, and my eyes drop to his hard cock, standing glorious and ready for the taking.

Pulse racing, I bend, and he rises onto his knees to meet me, his hand fisted around the base of his cock to guide it into my mouth.

Sparks snap against my tongue, and I take him in deeper, needing the feel of thunder in my throat.

Emil stills behind me, the tip of his cock poised at my entrance as he lifts my hips. The blunt head of Tobias's cock nudges up alongside Emil, and I shiver with the sudden desire to feel those two opposites inside me at the same time.

Kellen's hand on the back of my head guides my mouth around his hard length as Emil and Tobias slowly push into me at the same time, taking it slow as my body adjusts to make way for their combined girth. It leaves me stretched and aching with pleasure, and I suck on Kellen harder, hollowing my cheeks around him.

He groans, the hand on the back of my head flexing, and Emil and Tobias move deeper, stretching me wider until they fill me completely. I moan and wiggle my hips, telling them to move, and they find a pace that matches with Kellen's until all three men surge within my body at once, the force of their destructive power rolling through me in waves that crash ever higher.

I don't know where the first shiver of release

comes from, but it creates a ripple in all of us, our releases coming as one, making the lights flicker and the floor beneath us shake. Power rolls through me in ever growing waves, and my wings bust free, my feathers spreading wide as they splash iridescent light around the room, painting it in rainbows.

Gasping, we slump to the bed, limp with release.

I lay sprawled across Tobias and Kellen, while Emil rests with his head on my lower back, his body finally warm to the touch.

Still not completely sure this is real, I grope whatever body parts lay beneath my hands.

Tobias tickles the small feathers near my spine. "What are you doing, little succubus?"

I squeeze again and identify a hard pec by the nipple that pebbles against my palm. "Just making sure you're really here."

Kellen laughs breathlessly. "What we just did wasn't proof enough?"

I pinch his ear. "You weren't here when I got back."

Emil stirs and slides farther up my body to rest his head between my wings, making Tobias grunt with the added weight. "We got dumped back to the human plane four cities over. Do you have any idea how hard it is to catch a cab in the middle of nowhere, without a phone?"

Nodding, I smoosh my face into Kellen's stomach. "I'm so happy you're back."

"Are you talking to my abs or to us?" Kellen teases.

I mouth the hard muscles. "Yes."

He laughs, making my head bounce, and I add teeth to my nibbles to make him stop.

Emil blows out a contented sigh. "We're glad we're back, too. I don't know what you did, but it worked."

I pinch Kellen again. "He knows."

"I didn't think they'd actually be able to move the ley lines," he says, amazement in his voice. "Especially not so soon. Those witches are barely trained."

"They couldn't have." Tobias smooths a hand down my hair. "Not without Adie."

I lift my head to stare up at him. "Did you know what would happen? Did you see it on one of your paths?"

His dark eyes meet mine. "I see hundreds of paths, but there's no way to know what will happen until you're on one, and even then, there are dozens of ways that path can deviate. There's no way to tell the future."

"Speaking of the future." Kellen stretches beneath me in a languid roll of muscles. "When are we moving?"

I turn wide eyes on him. "Huh?"

He reaches up to boop my nose. "We all died, honey. We can't go back to work as if nothing happened."

The reminder sobers my mood, and I drop my chin back to his stomach. "You can just stay home and be house husbands for a while."

"I like that idea," Emil murmurs as he snuggles in. "We haven't taken a break in a long time."

"Break?" Tobias says as if the word is foreign to him.

"I'm bringing the TV down to the living room," Kellen announces. "We can binge so many new shows."

Emil groans. "Never mind. I want to go back to work."

I bump my butt up against his stomach. "Nope, you're officially off duty until further notice."

"I guess I can do some remodeling," he grumbles.

The rest of us groan in unison.

"What?" He rears up, shoving me harder against Tobias. "I haven't remodeled anything in ages."

"We just added a back door and deck," Kellen reminds him.

"That's an addition," he protests. "It's completely different."

As he and Kellen devolve into argument, Tobias's hand on my cheek brings my face back to his.

I smile down at his soft expression, remembering when our essences twined together. "Hey, you."

"Hey." His fingers sweep over my cheek. "Thank you for freeing us."

I turn my head to press a kiss against his palm. "You'd have done the same for me."

"Yes," he says simply as he turns my head back to him, then draws me forward. "I would do anything for the woman I love."

As his lips claim mine, my wings glow once more, my happiness too much to be contained.

There are still things still left undone, Libraries to find, and a loved one to nurture back to health, but for now, I allow myself to embrace and be embraced by the men I love, back in my arms where they belong.

Adie's (mis)adventures continue in:

Succubus Reborn

ABOUT THE AUTHOR

L.L. Frost lives in the Pacific Northwest and graduated from college with a Bachelor's in English. She is an avid reader of all things paranormal and can frequently be caught curled up in her favorite chair with a nice cup of coffee, a blanket, and her Kindle.

When not reading or writing, she can be found trying to lure the affection of her grumpy cat, who is very good at being just out of reach for snuggle time.

To stay up to date on what L.L. Frost is up to, join her newsletter, visit her website, or follow her on social media!

www.llfrost.com

patreon.com/llfrost
amazon.com/author/llfrost
bookbub.com/authors/l-l-frost
goodreads.com/llfrost_author
facebook.com/L.L.Frost.Author
instagram.com/ll.frost

Printed in Great Britain
by Amazon

15927457R00316